About the Authors

TODAY bestselling author **Jules Bennett** has [pen]ned more than fifty novels during her short career. [Sh]e's married to her high school sweetheart, has two [act]ive girls, and is a former salon owner. Jules can be [fou]nd on Twitter, Facebook (Fan Page), and her website [jul]esbennett.com. She holds contests via these three [out]lets with each release and loves to hear from readers!

[S]arah M. Anderson won RT Reviewer's Choice 2012 [De]sire of the Year for *A Man of Privilege*. *The Nanny [Pla]n* was a 2016 *RITA®* winner for Contemporary [Ro]mance: Short. Find out more about Sarah's love of [co]wboys at www.sarahmanderson.com

[Li]ndsay Armstrong was born in South Africa. She [gre]w up with three ambitions: to become a writer, to [trav]el the world, and to be a game ranger. She managed [tw]o out of three! When Lindsay went to work it was in [trav]el and this started her on the road to seeing the [wor]ld. It wasn't until her youngest child started school [tha]t Lindsay sat down at the kitchen table determined [to t]ackle her other ambition — to stop dreaming about [writ]ing and do it! She hasn't stopped since.

Passionate Encounters

Passionate Encounters
Tempted by
the Boss

JULES BENNETT

SARAH M. ANDERSON

LINDSAY ARMSTRONG

MILLS & BOON

First Published in Great Britain 2022
by Mills & Boon, an imprint of HarperCollins*Publishers* Ltd,
1 London Bridge Street, London, SE1 9GF

www.harpercollins.co.uk

HarperCollins*Publishers*
1st Floor, Watermarque Building,
Ringsend Road, Dublin 4, Ireland

PASSIONATE ENCOUNTERS: TEMPTED BY THE BOSS © 2022
Harlequin Books S.A.

Trapped with the Tycoon © 2016 Jules Bennett
Not the Boss's Baby © 2014 Sarah M. Anderson
An Exception to His Rule © 2014 Lindsay Armstrong

ISBN: 978-0-263-30436-7

MIX
Paper from
responsible sources
FSC™ C007454

This book is produced from independently certified FSC™ paper to ensure responsible forest management.

For more information visit: www.harpercollins.co.uk/green

Printed and Bound in Spain using 100% Renewable electricity at CPI Black Print, Barcelona

TRAPPED WITH THE TYCOON

JULES BENNETT

When I proposed a mafia series for Mills and Boon Desire, I had no idea how it would go over with my editor. But when Stacy Boyd's face lit up with excitement, I knew we were on the same page...literally. This book is for you, Stacy!

One

The second her ex's fingers closed around her arm, Zara Perkins jerked from the firm grasp. "I'm not dancing, I'm working."

Having Shane Chapman show up at the biggest job she'd ever taken on for the most prestigious family she'd ever worked for was just her luck. She prided herself on her business, on doing everything in her power to make her clients' parties the event they hired her for. And Shane could ruin it all.

"You're such a tease," he mocked, the whiskey on his breath repugnant. "I saw you looking at me."

Sure, with disdain when she realized he was in attendance. She'd rather walk barefoot over shards of glass than let his arms wrap around her. Zara prayed Shane would go away. This was a new job, a job she desperately needed. The last thing she wanted to do was have to defend a man she had the misfortune of dating a few times.

"Dance with me."

The low, demanding words sent shivers through her body. Zara knew without turning around who would be behind her…her new employer and rumored-to-be corrupt business mogul Braden O'Shea.

With Shane directly in front of her and Braden behind her, Zara was literally stuck in the exact predicament she didn't want to be in on her first big night of working for the O'Sheas. But right now, she was bracketed by two powerful men. One she wanted nothing to do with and the other set her heart racing as only a mysterious, intriguing man could do. The few times she'd been in his office had been a bit difficult to concentrate. Braden O'Shea exuded authority, control and sex appeal.

Humiliation flooded her at the idea that Braden had to intervene. She was here in a professional capacity. Having her ex confront her was not exactly showcasing the reputation she'd worked so hard to build, and coming off as anything less than professional could be career suicide.

Shane glared over her shoulder, silently telling Braden precisely what he thought of the interruption, but before Zara could say a word to either man, Braden took hold of her arm and pulled her to the dance area in the ballroom of his lavish, historical home.

Instantly she was plastered against the oldest of the O'Shea siblings…not a difficult position to find herself in, actually. She had often appreciated the visual of his broad, sexy body wrapped in the finest of black suits with black shirt and no tie. But being up close and personal, breathing in what was undoubtedly expensive, masculine cologne that had her eyes fluttering closed as she inhaled, was another level of torture entirely.

The man exuded sex appeal, but he was her new boss, and she needed this job for the prestige and the insanely large paycheck. This was her first official event with this prominent family after being officially hired a few months ago. Screwups…screwing of *any* kind…was not allowed.

So, no sex thoughts. None. Okay, maybe later when she was alone.

"I really need to be working."

A little protest was in order, wasn't it? Even if sliding against Braden felt like some sort of foreplay in itself, she was the events coordinator for this party. Dancing with the host and boss was a major professional no-no, even if they'd always gotten along well with each other before tonight. There'd always been some ridiculous magnetic energy between them that she'd never experienced before but refused to explore.

Braden's dark gaze studied her, his mouth unsmiling. "With a dress like that, you should be dancing."

The sexual undertone wasn't lost on her. She'd thrown on her go-to black dress with a low V in the back and front, long sleeves, with the hem stopping at her knees. The dress was simple, yet made a statement. Hiding her curves wasn't an option unless she wore a muumuu. Besides, this was the best dress she'd found in her boxes of belongings since she hadn't unpacked from her move…three months ago. Because unpacking meant settling in, making roots.

"You're not paying me to dance," she told him, though she made no motion to step out of his powerful embrace. Her mind told her this wasn't professional, but her stubborn body wasn't getting that memo. "I'm positive this isn't professional to ignore my position here."

"You're on break."

With one large hand at the small of her back and the other gripping hers, Braden led her in a dance to an old classic. Crystal chandeliers suspended from the ceiling, illuminating the polished wood floor in a kaleidoscope of colors. The wall of French doors leading to the patio gave the room an even larger feel. The O'Sheas were known for their lavish parties, and now that she was in the ballroom, she could see why. Who had an actual ballroom in their house?

Other couples swirled around them, but with few words

and those dark, mesmerizing eyes, this man captured her undivided attention. She needed to get back control over this situation because even though Braden insisted she was taking a break, she wasn't paid to socialize. She was given an insane amount of money to make this annual party an even bigger success than the last one, and she'd heard a rumor the last events coordinator for the O'Sheas was fired in the most humiliating of circumstances. She couldn't afford slipups.

Or crazy exes.

"I could've handled him," she told Braden. "Shane was just…"

"I'm not talking about another man when I have a beautiful woman in my arms."

Okay, yeah, that definitely crossed the professional threshold. Each word he spoke dripped with charm, authority… desire. He held his feelings back, remained in control at all times. From what she'd seen, he was calculating, powerful and the aura of mystery surrounding him was even more alluring and sexy.

But, no. She'd just ended things with one powerful, controlling man. She was fine being single and focusing on her year-old business. Her goal was to be the company all major names turned to when needing a party planned or hosting a special event. Having the O'Sheas was a huge leap in the right direction. No matter the rumors surrounding their, well, less-than-legal operations behind the front of their world-renowned auction house, the O'Sheas had connections she could only dream of. She hoped this event led to new clients.

"If you keep scowling, I'm going to think you prefer Shane's company," Braden stated, breaking into her thoughts. "Or maybe I interrupted a lover's quarrel?"

Zara nearly recoiled. "No. Definitely not a lover's quarrel."

Had Braden overheard what Shane had said? Heat flooded her cheeks. She'd dated Shane briefly and had broken things off with him weeks ago, yet the man was relent-less in trying to get her attention again. When they'd gone on only a few dates, he'd started getting a bit too control-ling for her comfort. Thankfully she hadn't slept with him.

Still, he'd made a point to tell her how fast he could ruin her business. Did he honestly think that would make her give him another chance? Threats were *so* not the way to a woman's heart.

She wasn't one to back down without a fight, but she was realistic, and Shane did have money and connections. She shivered at the severity of his words.

"Cold?" Braden asked.

Braden's hand drifted up, his fingertips grazed across her bare skin just above the dip in her material.

With the heat in his eyes, there was no way she could claim a chill. The firmness of his body moved perfectly with hers; that friction alone could cause a woman to go up in flames.

"Mr. O'Shea—"

"Braden."

Zara swallowed. "Fine. Braden," she corrected, forc-ing herself to hold his heavy-lidded stare. "I really should check on the drinks—"

"Taken care of."

"The hors d'oeuvres—"

"Are fine."

He spun her toward the edge of the dance floor, closer to one set of French doors leading out on to the patio. Snow swirled around outside; a storm for later tonight was in the forecast. February in Boston could be treacherous and un-predictable.

"You've done a remarkable job with this evening," he told her. "I'm impressed."

She couldn't suppress the smile. "I'm relieved to hear that. I love my job and want all of my clients happy. Still, dancing when I should be working isn't something I make a habit of."

His thumb continued to lightly stroke the bare skin on her back. The man was potent, sparking arousal without even trying. Or maybe he *was* trying and he was so stellar at being charming, she couldn't tell.

It took her a moment to realize that Braden had maneuvered her into a corner. With his back to the dancers, he shielded her completely with those broad shoulders and pinned her with that dark, mesmerizing gaze. "I heard what he said to you."

Zara froze, took a deep breath and chose her next words carefully. "I assure you I would never let anyone or anything affect my ability to work. Shane is—"

"Not going to bother you again," he assured her with a promising yet menacing tone. Braden's eyes darted over her body, touching her just the same as his talented fingertips had done mere moments ago.

No. No, no, no. Hadn't she already scolded herself for having lustful thoughts? He was her boss, for pity's sake. No matter how intriguing Braden O'Shea was, she had no room for sex in her life right now. No wonder she was grouchy.

"Storm is kicking up." Braden nodded over her shoulder toward the floor-to-ceiling window. "Do you live far?"

"Maybe twenty minutes away."

"If you need to leave—"

"No." Zara shook her head, holding a hand up to stop him. "I've lived in Boston my entire life. Snow doesn't bother me. Besides, I would never leave an event early."

Braden studied her a moment before nodding. "I'm happy to hear that, but I don't want you driving on these roads. My driver will make sure you get home."

"There's no need for that."

Braden leaned in, just enough for her to feel his breath on her cheek. "Let's not waste time arguing when we should be dancing."

Snaking an arm around her waist, he pulled her against his body once again. Apparently her break wasn't over. Good thing, because she wasn't quite ready to leave the luxury of brushing against his taut body.

Her curves were killer from a visual standpoint, but to have them beneath his hands was damn near crippling. Braden knew she was a sexy woman, but he hadn't expected this sizzling attraction. He had a plan and he needed to stay focused. Those damn curves momentarily threw him off his game.

Zara in her elegant black cocktail dress with a plunging neckline showcasing the swell of her breasts was absolutely stunning, eye-catching and causing him to lose focus on the true intent of this party.

Which was why he hadn't missed the encounter when one of his most hated enemies sidled up next to the woman Braden had been gazing at off and on earlier in the evening. A flash of jealousy had speared him. Ridiculous, since Zara was merely the events coordinator…and that job had not come about by chance. Braden had purposely chosen her. He needed to get closer, close enough to gain access into her personal, private life and into her home. His family's heritage could be hidden in her house, and she'd have no clue if she stumbled upon the items.

Nothing could keep him from fulfilling his deathbed promise to his dad.

Braden was all for adding in a little seduction on his way to gaining everything he'd ever wanted. Pillow talk always loosened the tongue, and if Zara could tell him everything he needed to know, then he wouldn't have to break any laws…at least where she was concerned. He'd be a fool to turn that combination down and there was no way he could ignore how her body moved so perfectly against his. He also hadn't missed how her breath had caught the second he'd touched her exposed back. He had to admit, just to himself, the innocent touch had twisted something in him, as well. Arousal was a strong, overwhelming emotion, and one he had to keep control over.

For now, he needed to remember he was the head of the family and as the leader, he had a duty to fulfill. Flirting, seducing and even a little extracurricular activities were fine, so long as he kept his eye on the target.

Tonight O'Shea's Auction House was celebrating not only being a prominent, world-renowned auction house for over eighty years, but also the opening of two more satellite locations in Atlanta and Miami, thanks to his brother, Mac, who had moved down to Miami to oversee the properties.

Boston would always be home to the main store, Braden's store, now that his father was gone. And now that Braden was fully in charge, there were going to be some changes. This family had to move toward being legit. The stress and pressure Braden had seen his father go through wasn't something Braden wanted for his future. The massive heart attack that stole Patrick O'Shea's life wasn't brought on by leading a normal, worry-free life.

Braden had a five-year plan. Surely in that time they could remove themselves from any illegal ties and slowly sever those bonds. The killings had to stop. That was the first order of business, but tonight, after seeing Shane manhandle Zara, Braden was almost ready to go back on his vow.

Death was nothing new to him. He'd witnessed his father give a kill order multiple times for reasons he'd always justified. Braden may not have always agreed with his father's ways, but his father was an effective businessman and well respected.

Zara's deep chocolate eyes shifted around the room before landing back on him. "Your brother is coming this way."

Braden didn't turn, didn't relinquish his hold on Zara.

The music continued, guests around them danced and chatted, but Braden paid them no mind.

"We need to talk," Mac stated.

Braden stopped dancing but didn't let go of Zara as he threw Mac a glance over his shoulder. "I'll meet you in the study in five minutes."

"Now."

Braden resisted the urge to curse. He prided himself on control. "Five minutes," he said, before turning back and focusing solely on Zara.

He picked up right where they'd left off dancing. He could still feel Mac behind him, so Braden maneuvered his partner toward the edge of the dance floor. Zara was his for now, and sharing their time wasn't an option.

"You can go talk to him." Zara smiled, a deep dimple winking back at him. The innocence of the dimple and the sex appeal of that dress were polar opposite. "I should be working anyway, you know."

He *was* paying her to work, but that didn't mean he didn't like the feel of her in his arms, against him. There would be time for more later. He'd make sure of it. Gaining her trust on a personal level would lead him exactly where he needed to be.

Gliding his fingertips over her exposed back one last time, Braden stepped away from Zara and tipped his head. "I'll find you when I'm done with Mac. If you have any more problems with Shane, you come straight to me."

Zara nodded, clasping her hands in front of her and searching the room as if trying to get a location on the man in question. "I'll be fine. Go talk to your brother, and thank you for the dance. I have to get back to work."

Braden closed the space between them, picked up her hand and kissed her delicate knuckles. "I should be thanking you."

Her mouth parted as she let out a slight gasp when his lips grazed her hand. Yes, enticing her would be no problem at all. He'd been waiting on the right opportunity, the moment he could get the greatest impact out of this game of seduction.

First things first, he had to see what the issue was with his younger brother. Braden excused himself and went in search of Mac.

The entire O'Shea family had come for the party despite the bad weather predictions for the Boston area, including cousins from Boston and down the East Coast, his brother, sister and Ryker.

What kind of celebration would this be for the O'Sheas if the whole Irish clan didn't attend? Mac would be overseeing the southern locations, a job he was all too eager to take over and to get out of the cold winters for, especially since his best friend, Jenna, had moved to Miami about a year ago.

Once in the study, Braden closed the door behind him and crossed the polished wood floors. Mac leaned against the old mahogany desk, swirling bourbon around in his tumbler. Braden knew it was bourbon without even asking because the O'Sheas were simple men with simple needs—power, good bourbon and women. The order varied depending on the circumstance.

"You need to calm down," Mac commanded. "That murderous look in your eyes is scaring our guests."

"I'm calm." To prove it, Braden flashed a smile. "See?"

Mac shook his head. "Listen, I know you hate Shane Chapman. We all do. He's a lying prick. But, whatever his personal—"

"He's harassing Zara."

Braden stopped short just before he reached his brother and crossed his arms over his chest. Shane Chapman was the bane of the O'Sheas' existence. A few years ago, he'd attempted to hire the auction house to acquire an heirloom illegally. Braden had made a valiant effort to get it, spending more time and money than he really should've, but to no avail.

Viewing it as a deliberate slight, Shane had attempted to blackmail the O'Sheas. His laughable threats were quickly taken care of by means nobody discussed. Shane was lucky he was still breathing because that had been during the Patrick O'Shea reign.

Shane was only at this party for one reason—the whole "keep your friends close and your enemies closer" wasn't just a clever saying.

"Keep your eye on him," Braden went on. "This can't interfere with the plans. If Shane needs to go…"

Mac nodded. "I'll let Ryker know."

Ryker. The O'Sheas' right-hand man, who may as well have been born into the family. Instead, he'd been unofficially adopted as a rebellious preteen, and he'd been with them since.

But damn it, Braden didn't want blood on his hands. He wanted to concentrate on retrieving the heirlooms and relics their auction house was officially known for. They had an elite list of clients, and word of mouth always brought more on board. The timeless pieces the O'Sheas uncovered all over the world kept their business thriving. Several pieces were "discovered" by less-than-legal means, but they were paid hefty sums to be discreet. Smuggling in items with legal loads for big auctions was easy to do.

"I think your approach to Zara isn't the smartest." Mac sipped his bourbon. "You're coming on too strong and not focusing."

Braden narrowed his gaze. "That's a pretty bold statement coming from the man who has a woman in every major city."

Mac eyed him over the glass. "We're not talking about me. Unless you'd like me to seduce the beautiful party planner."

"Keep your damn hands off her."

Why was he suddenly so territorial? Braden had no claims on Zara.

But he'd held her, felt her against him and seen a thread of vulnerability when Zara had been looking at Shane. He refused to see any woman harassed or mistreated.

His sister, Laney, was currently dating some schmuck, who could be demeaning at times. Yet another issue Braden would deal with now that he was in charge. No way in hell would he allow his baby sister to be belittled by anyone. Ever.

"Leave Zara to me, and you concentrate on your new locations," Braden told his brother. "Is that all you needed?"

Mac finished off his drink, setting his tumbler down on the desk. "For now. I'll keep an eye on Shane. Ryker will be a last resort. I know you want to move in a different direction, but Shane can't interfere. We're too close to finding those scrolls."

Braden nodded and headed back out to the party. Those scrolls, all nine of them, were centuries old and held immense power over Braden's family. He wanted them back, and at one time, during the Great Depression, they'd been in the home Zara currently lived in. Supposedly they'd been stored in a trunk that had been sold decades ago. Unfortunately, the trunk had been recently tracked down but as the scrolls hadn't been inside, they were back to square one with Zara's house as the last known location.

Just as Braden cleared the wide opening leading to the ballroom, he spotted Shane standing over Zara. She shook her head and started to turn when Shane's hand whipped out and gripped her bicep, jerking her back to his chest.

Braden didn't care about moving stealthily through the crowd. He felt Mac right behind him as he charged forward. His brother always had his back.

"Remove your hand from Miss Perkins's arm." Braden didn't try to mask the rage in his tone. He waited a beat, but Shane still held tight and kept his back to Braden. "Remove your hand or I won't need to get my security team. I'll throw your ass out myself."

Over his shoulder, Braden heard Mac telling someone, most likely one of their employees, to have security on standby. Braden knew Mac was only looking out for everyone's best interest, but Braden could only see red right now. Thankfully, Shane had backed Zara into a corner, and the guests were still milling about, oblivious to the action.

Shane threw a glance over his shoulder. "This doesn't concern you. Zara and I have a little unfinished business. Just a lover's spat."

The look on her face told Braden there wasn't anything unfinished here and this sure as hell wasn't a lover's spat—she'd told him as much earlier.

Zara's wide, dark eyes held his. Even though she had her chin tipped up in defiance, her lips thinned in anger, there was a spark of fear in those eyes, and Braden wouldn't tolerate Shane one more second.

Braden grabbed on to Shane's wrist, applying pressure in the exact spot to cause maximum pain. "Take your damn hand off her. Now."

Shane gave Zara's arm a shove. "You can't keep avoiding me," he told her, rubbing his wrist where Braden had squeezed. "Next time I call, you better answer or I'll come by your office. I doubt you want that."

Just as Shane turned, Braden blocked his exit. "If you ever touch her or any woman that way again and I hear of it, you'll wish for death. Feel me?"

Shane hesitated a second before he laughed, slapping Braden on the shoulder. "You're Patrick O'Shea's son, right down to the threats. And here I thought you were too good to get your hands dirty."

Even though the bastard had touched Braden, he wasn't about to take the bait Shane dangled in front of him. Flexing his fists, Braden was more than ready to hit Shane, but he knew deep down he wasn't like his father.

Braden had never ordered anyone to be killed, had always said he wouldn't. Right now, though, he was reconsidering that promise he'd made to himself.

"There's a first time for everything," he promised just as two security men in black suits came to show Shane the door.

They didn't put their hands on him, as that would've caused even more of a scene, but they did flank either side of the nuisance and walk him toward the closest exit. People around him stared for only a moment before going back to their conversations. Nearly everyone knew to mind their business if they wanted to remain in the O'Sheas' tight circle.

As soon as Shane was gone, Braden went back in with Zara.

"You okay here?" Mac whispered behind him.

With a nod, Braden wrapped his arm around Zara's waist. "We're fine. Cover for me." He silently led her to the small sitting room off the ballroom and closed the door behind him before turning to face Zara. She rubbed her arm, and it took all of Braden's willpower not to rush back out and follow through on his need to punch Shane.

Braden gently took Zara's other arm, trying to ignore the brush of his knuckles against the side of her breast, and guided her toward one of the leather club chairs.

Flicking on the light on the accent table by the chair, Braden squatted down in front of her.

"Braden—"

He held up his hand, cutting her off. "Let me see your arm."

"I'm fine. I really need to get back to work. I'm sorry I caused a scene."

"Either pull your sleeve up or pull the shoulder down so I can see."

Zara hesitated a moment, then pulled the material off her shoulder, exposing creamy white skin and a royal blue strap from her bra. She shrugged enough to pull her arm up a bit.

Rage bubbled within Braden at the sight of blue finger-print-shaped bruises already forming on her flawless skin. "I should've knocked him out."

Slowly, Braden eased the material back over her arm and shoulder. Her eyes held his and her body trembled as she placed her hand over his, halting his movement.

"I'm fine," she assured him again. "I really need to get back to work. I appreciate what you did, though."

He hadn't realized how close he'd gotten until he felt her soft breath on his cheek. He glanced up to her, his eyes darting down to her lips.

"My motives aren't always so selfless."

The corner of her mouth quirked. "Whatever your motives are, they were effective."

He leaned in closer, close enough that barely a breath could pass between their lips. "I'm always effective."

Two

Effective. Thorough. Protective. So many adjectives could be used to describe Braden O'Shea. Yet he'd come to her defense without question earlier when Shane had snapped.

Zara nestled deeper into her coat as the heat from Braden's SUV hit her. This dress had been such a good idea when she'd been inside. Now that the snow was near blizzard-like conditions, not so much. She'd had to swap her sexy heels for snow boots, which she'd packed with her once she'd seen the forecast. So now the allure of her favorite LBD was lost thanks to the thick, rubber-soled, sensible shoes.

"When you said you'd have your driver bring me home, I didn't know you were the driver." She glanced over, taking in his profile illuminated from the glowing dash lights. In the dark, Braden seemed even more mysterious, more enigmatic.

"After the incident with Shane, I'm not placing your safety in anyone else's hands." He gripped the wheel as the tires slid, then gained traction again. "I wouldn't want you driving in this mess anyway. I heard a couple at the party say the forecasters mentioned feet instead of inches."

Zara's breath caught in her throat as Braden carefully maneuvered around a slick corner with skill. The back end fishtailed before he righted the vehicle. They'd only passed two other cars since leaving his historic Beacon Hill mansion.

"I'm so sorry about this," she told him, once the car was on a straight path and she could focus on breathing normally. "I should've left when you suggested it earlier because of the bad weather. Then Shane wouldn't have been a problem, and you wouldn't be out in this mess."

"Shane will be a problem until he meets his match." Braden flashed her a wicked grin that looked even more ominous due to the minimal lighting. There was also the veiled implication that Braden was the perfect match for Shane. "As for the weather, don't worry about it. This storm came on faster than I thought, and I have nothing else to do tonight."

"Hopefully the guests all made it home okay," she said, voicing her thoughts. The caterers had left around the same time she did, so hopefully they were safe, too. "They left over an hour ago, so maybe it wasn't too bad then."

She'd stayed behind to clean up and make sure the place was just as it had been before she'd entered—as she did with every event. All part of the party-planning business. Still, there would be a few people left from the cleaning service. She hoped they all got home okay, as well.

"You live alone?"

Braden's question sliced through the quiet. As if she could actually forget she was this close to the world's sexiest man. Then again, she didn't know every man in the world, but she'd still put Braden O'Shea and his sultry eyes and broad frame against anyone.

"Yes. I actually just moved into my grandmother's home three months ago. She'd just passed away, and I'm the only relative she had left."

"Sorry about your loss." In a move that surprised her, Braden reached across the console and squeezed her hand in a gesture of comfort before easing back. She didn't take him for the comforting type, but she knew in her heart his words and his touch were sincere.

"My father has been gone six months," he went on, his tone understanding. "On one hand, it seems like yesterday. On the other, I feel like I'm going to wake up from a nightmare and he'll be fine. None of us had a clue his heart was so bad."

Zara swallowed. She knew that nightmare-versus-reality feeling all too well. In the midst of her fantasizing over Braden, she'd not figured in the fact this man was still vulnerable, still suffering from a loss just as big as her own. Great, she'd not only been unprofessional tonight, she'd also been heartless.

"It's rough." For the first time since her grandmother's passing, Zara felt comfortable opening up to someone. Shane certainly hadn't been consoling in the few times they'd dated...another red flag where he'd been concerned. "Living in her home feels strange. I remember sleeping over there when I was little, but now it just seems so much larger, so empty."

Zara had never been afraid to live alone, but in a house this size, she was a little creeped out at night—the old ghost rumors didn't help, either. Perhaps once she rid the house of some of the antiques and actually unpacked her own things, that would help the place feel more like home. But she wasn't to that point yet. Removing her grandmother's favorite things just didn't seem right yet. And unpacking... Definitely not something Zara was comfortable with. A shrink would have a blast digging inside her mind over the reasons Zara had a fear of commitment even when it came to a house.

Red-and-blue flashing lights lit up behind them. Braden threw a glance in the mirror, his jaw clenched as he maneuvered cautiously to the side of the road.

Zara tensed, gripping her coat even tighter. What was wrong? They certainly hadn't been speeding. The rumors about the O'Sheas having illegal operations going flooded her mind. She didn't know whether the myth was true or false and it wasn't her place to judge, but she couldn't help but wonder. All she knew was they were powerful and they were paying her well. Oh, and Braden was the sexiest man she'd ever laid eyes, or hands, on.

Braden glanced at her. "Don't say anything."

Stunned, Zara nodded. What would she say?

Braden put his window down as the officer approached. "Evening, Officer."

The trooper leaned down and looked into the car. "The roads are at a level two now, and they're getting ready to up that to a three. Are you folks out because of an emergency?"

"No, sir. I'm giving my employee a ride home because I didn't think it was safe for her to be out alone."

The officer's eyes scanned over Zara, and she offered a slight smile.

"How far away is her house?"

"Just right up the street," Braden said, pointing. Zara had given him directions before they'd started out, and they were actually only a few houses away from hers.

"I suggest you plan on staying put once you drop her off. Any drivers caught out once the level three goes into effect will be ticketed," the officer stated. "I'll follow you to make sure you get there all right."

The full impact of the trooper's words hit Zara fast. Braden had to stay put? As in…stay the night? At her house? A ball of nerves quickly formed in her stomach. Her boss was spending the night? Her boss, whom she found utterly sexy and nearly irresistible, and there was already crackling sexual tension charging between them? Sure, this would be no problem at all.

"Thank you, Officer," Braden replied "We appreciate that."

Braden rolled his window up as the officer went back to his car. Silence filled the vehicle, and the weight of what was about to happen settled between them.

Zara risked a glance at Braden, but he didn't seem affected one bit. He kept his eyes forward, occasionally checking his mirrors as he pulled right into her drive. The cop gave a honk as he passed on by. Braden maneuvered the SUV around the slight curve that led to the detached garage around back.

Once he parked and killed the engine, Zara couldn't take the tension another second. She unfastened and turned to face him.

"I'm so sorry," she started. "Had I known you'd have to stay, I wouldn't have let you bring me home."

Braden threw her a lopsided smile. "No reason to be sorry. I don't mind spending the night with a beautiful woman."

Braden was well aware of his power. Hell, everyone who'd ever heard the name O'Shea knew the authority this family possessed. They even had a few of the local cops and federal agents in their back pockets...which had kept them out of the proverbial hot water more than once.

But even Braden couldn't have planned the timing of this snowstorm better, or the condition of the roads. Under different circumstances, he probably would've chanced driving back home regardless of the officer's warning. Wouldn't be the first time he'd gone against the law. But why would he want to leave? A forced stay at Zara's home was the green light he'd been waiting for, and it had come so much sooner than he'd ever intended. No way in hell was he leaving now. Not when this sexual chemistry between them had skyrocketed since he'd held her in his arms.

As he pulled his vehicle up to the garage, the streetlights went out. He cursed under his breath as the entire street was plunged into black. "Looks like the power went."

"Great," Zara muttered. "I don't have a generator. But I do have some heat that isn't electric. I've only used those gas logs once in my bedroom, and I've never tried to light the ones in the living room. Guess I'll have to figure it out in the dark."

Braden didn't know what got his blood pumping more: the fact he'd be able to fulfill his father's dying request and search this house, or the fact he'd be all alone in the dark with his sexy new employee.

He pulled to a stop by her back door. "Stay there. I'll come around to help you in."

He didn't wait for her to agree as he hopped out into the freezing temps to round the hood, using his phone to light a path. Even though he was still wearing his suit from the party, he'd thought ahead and changed from his dress shoes to his boots.

Jerking on the frozen handle, Braden opened the passenger door and took Zara's gloved hand as he settled his arm around her waist. The second she slid down from her seat, her body fell flush against his—well, as flush as it could be with the layers between them. Zara tipped her face up to his. Snow drifted onto her long, dark lashes, framing those rich chocolate eyes. Her unpainted mouth practically begged for affection as flakes melted against pale pink skin.

Damn it. That punch of lust to the gut was going to get him in trouble if he wasn't careful. He had a goal, and Zara was merely a stepping-stone. Harsh as that sounded, he had to remain fixed on the objective his late father had been adamant about—finding the family's lost heirlooms. Braden was near positive they were hidden somewhere inside Zara's house...a house that used to be in his family up until they lost everything in the Great Depression.

"You know, I can walk," she laughed, holding up her heels. "I swapped shoes, so I'm good."

"Maybe I'm holding on to you so *I* don't go down," he

retorted as he closed the door behind her and locked his vehicle. "I'll hold the light so you can get your keys out."

He kept an arm around her as they made fresh tracks to her back door. The snow was already well past their ankles, and the fat flakes continued to fall.

Zara pulled a set of keys from her coat pocket and gestured him into the house ahead of her. Once inside, she turned to the keypad and attempted to reset the alarm. With a shrug, Zara said, "Habit to come in and enter my code. Guess that's out, too."

Braden ran his light over the room, noticing how spacious the kitchen was and the wide, arched doorway leading into the living area. More light would be nice, now that he was actually inside. Somewhere his father was laughing at the irony of Braden finally getting in…and not being able to see a damn thing. But a power outage wasn't going to stop him from making use of this opportunity.

"Do you have flashlights and candles?" he asked, bringing his light back around but careful to keep it from shining in her eyes.

"I know where my candles are, but I'm not sure about the flashlights. I've only been here a few months. I haven't actually unpacked everything, yet." Zara removed her coat and hung it by the back door. "Let me hang your coat up since you're staying."

Braden removed his coat and started to hand it over when Zara reached out, her hand connecting with his cheek. "Oh, sorry. I didn't mean to punch you."

Braden welcomed the impact, as her fist caused no damage but reminded him that he needed to focus. "I'm fine," he stated as he maneuvered out of his coat while holding his light. "It's hard to see, so I'd say we'll be bumping into each other."

Not that he was complaining about the prospect of randomly brushing against her. Braden actually welcomed the friction. So long as he kept his goal in the forefront of his mind, bumping into Zara was definitely not a hardship.

"I know I have a candle in here and one on the coffee table in the living room. The matches are in the drawer beside the sink." She placed his coat on a hook beside hers. "I should try to figure out these gas logs in the living room first with the light of your phone."

She eased past him, her feet shuffling along the floor. Braden held his light over to where she was heading. Pulling open a drawer, Zara grabbed a box of matches before coming back to him.

She started forward but stopped. "You better stay close so you don't bump anything. I have several boxes in each room that are left from the move."

Stay close? No problem at all. Braden slid his hand around the dip in her waist and gave her a light squeeze as he leaned down to whisper in her ear. "How's this?"

Beneath his touch, her body trembled. Just the reaction he'd wanted…except now he was on the verge of trembling, too, because damn, she smelled so amazingly good and her silky hair tickled his lips. Wait, wasn't he the one who was supposed to be seducing? She wasn't even trying, and she nearly had him begging.

"Well, maybe not that close," she murmured as she attempted to put distance between them.

He moved with her, keeping their contact light so as not to freak her out right off the bat. Let her get used to his touch, his nearness. He planned on getting a whole lot closer.

"You realize this isn't a good idea?" she asked.

"Lighting the logs is the best idea. It's going to get colder in here if the electricity doesn't come back on."

Her soft laugh filled the darkness. "You know what I mean. I work for you."

"I'm aware of your position." With his hand on her waist,

Braden held his phone toward the living room. "I know we need to get heat in here, and if it's not with the logs, then we'll have to use a more…primal method."

Zara slowly started forward. "Acting on any desire because of the circumstances is a bad, bad idea for both of us."

"I've forgotten nothing, Zara." He allowed his body to move with hers, making sure to stay close. "Why don't we work on keeping warm and finding more sources of light? Then we can discuss the circumstances and what's going on between us."

Zara threw him a look over her shoulder. "We can settle this right now. I need this job and even if I was attracted to you—"

"Which you are."

"*If* I was," she countered in a louder tone to cut him off. "I wouldn't risk sleeping with you and damaging our working relationship."

He could barely make out her face in the darkness, and his light was facing ahead. But the way her body slightly leaned against his, the way she continued to tremble beneath his touch told him that her little speech was as much for her as it was for him. A slight obstacle but nothing he couldn't handle.

At first he'd been all about searching her home, and he still was, but there was no reason a little seducing couldn't come into play. He was an expert multitasker, and having Zara plus finding his family's heirlooms would be the icing on the proverbial cake.

After a fun romp and hopefully discovering his family's scrolls, Braden would be on his way, and she'd never even have to know his true intentions. Nobody would get hurt, and everything about this situation was legal. See? He did have a moral side, after all.

She could deny wanting him, but he was a master at lying and recognized that trait in others. So, let her think what she wanted…he knew the truth, and he'd completely use her attraction to his advantage.

"Fair enough," he told her. "I'll not mention it again."

That didn't mean he wouldn't touch her or seduce her with his actions. The darkness provided the perfect setting for seduction, but it could make it a bit harder to snoop. Granted, the darkness could also provide him the cover he needed to look without being seen.

So, as far as he understood, the nine scrolls, which had been in his family since his ancestor transcribed them from Shakespeare himself, were last known to be in this house. The history ran deep with his Irish family, and the precious scrolls were lost in the chaos of the fall of the O'Sheas during the 1930s. The trunk that had been recovered from this home after the Depression had shown up empty, so it only made sense the scrolls were here…somewhere.

Decades had passed, and Braden's family had attempted to purchase the property, but Zara's family had owned it since the O'Sheas lost it and they were adamant about not being bought.

Several attempts were made by Braden's father to purchase the place, but the efforts were always blocked. Eventually Patrick opted to go about things the illegal way. Ryker had even broken in a couple of times when Zara's grandmother had been alive. The old lady had been sharp, and Ryker had been forced to dodge the cops, but they were still left empty-handed. Patrick O'Shea had even mentioned waiting until the elderly lady passed and trying again to purchase the property, but Patrick had passed before Zara's grandmother.

So, Braden would get the job done himself. Failure was not an option, and buying the place wasn't necessary at this point.

Would the scrolls be somewhere obvious? Doubtful, or someone would've found them by now, and if those scrolls *had* been found, they would've made headlines around the world. His ancestor, a monk, had transcribed original works, supposedly plays that never came to be.

Zara sank to her knees in front of the fireplace. "Shine that light a little closer."

He did as requested, waiting while she fidgeted with getting the pilot light going.

"Need help?" he offered.

"Damn it." She sat back on her heels and shook her head. "This one isn't working. It was always causing Gram issues, but I'd assumed it was fixed. I know the unit in my bedroom works fine because I've used it."

Braden shouldn't delight in the fact her bedroom had gas heat and nowhere else in the house seemed to, but he was a guy, and, well, he couldn't help himself.

"Then maybe we should find those flashlights and more candles and head upstairs."

Zara threw him a look over her shoulder as she came to her feet and turned to fully face him. "Get that gleam out of your eye. I'm on to you."

Not yet she wasn't.

"What gleam?" he asked. "It's dark, so how can you see anything?"

"Oh, I can see enough and this can't get any more awkward than it already is."

"I'm not feeling awkward at all." He focused back on her eyes and offered a smile. "Are you?"

"Damn it, you know I am. Even if this—" she gestured between them "—wasn't making me nervous, you're my first overnight guest in this house."

Surprised, Braden shifted. "You mean Shane—damn. None of my business."

Zara crossed her arms over her chest. "After rescuing me tonight, I'd say this is your business. Shane never stayed here. We were dating when my grandmother passed, but he wasn't there for me much during that time. That's when I started reevaluating our relationship."

A pity Braden couldn't have gotten away with punching Shane in the face, but he hadn't wanted to cause any more of a scene at his home during the party. This was his first appearance as head of the family; he needed to hold tight to that power, that control.

What man wasn't there for his woman during a difficult time? Shane had always been a bit of a stuffed shirt, a man who probably polished his cuff links and didn't even know how to pleasure a woman properly. Braden knew for damn sure when he got Zara into bed, he'd know exactly what to do to her, with her and for her.

Seduction hadn't been a key factor in his grand scheme, but he wasn't looking the gift horse in the mouth. He couldn't deny the attraction, and why should he ignore such a strong pull?

"I don't want to talk about Shane." Zara maneuvered around him. "Let's go find the flashlights. I suppose you'll have to sleep in my room, but that is not an invitation to any other activity."

"I'll be a perfect gentleman." He'd have her begging before the night was over. "You won't have to worry about a thing." Except that he'd be snooping through her house once she fell asleep, and he'd be stealing back what was rightfully his.

Braden shone his light toward the steps and watched her head up. Like a predator after his prey, he followed those swaying hips snug in that killer dress. If he were totally honest with himself, he'd admit that Zara had the upper hand here. Even though she had no idea why she'd been hired and why he was so eager to be in her home, she had completely taken him by surprise with her professionalism, her kick-ass attitude and her sliver of vulnerability. She'd worked his party with a smile on her face and a firm hand where her assistants were concerned, all the while trying to keep Shane silenced and take on the difficult situation herself.

He tamped down his frustration. No personal emotions were allowed to creep in on his plan. A fling was all he'd allow.

He was on a mission, and Zara was in the crosshairs.

Three

Zara stepped into her bedroom, even more aware of the crackling intimacy. The intense stare Braden had offered, the way his eyes had darted to her lips more than once... she wasn't naive and she wasn't afraid of the rumors of him being such a bad boy.

Although he'd felt very bad in a delicious way when he'd been dancing with her earlier.

However, she was fully aware that he was her boss and no matter how much she ached for him to make a move, she knew anything beyond a professional relationship would be a mistake. Besides, she couldn't commit herself to anything other than a physical relationship with any man, so that definitely left Braden O'Shea out.

Zara suppressed a laugh as they stood just inside her bedroom. Yes, this was totally professional, especially since she had a stack of bras on her dresser she'd yet to put away. Thankfully he hadn't shone the light there yet. At least the unpacked boxes were lining her walk-in closet, so that was helpful.

"My room is the only one with a king bed, but I can sleep on the chaise and you can have the bed."

Her face flushed. Why had she said anything about a bed? Why talk about the elephant in the room? She'd been so worried about this situation becoming awkward, but she was the one making it worse. Clearly Braden wasn't nervous. And why should he be? He was well aware of how jittery she was, which only proved he held the upper hand here.

"I just meant that you're a big guy and you'd be more comfortable in my bed—er, a bigger bed." *Great, Zara. Keep babbling. When one foot goes in the mouth, throw the other one in, as well.*

Braden leaned against the door frame to her bedroom. With his light facing outward, she couldn't read the expression on his face.

"I'm making you nervous."

Clearly she wasn't convincing him that she was confident. "No… Maybe a little."

That low, rich laugh filled the bedroom, enveloping her in an awareness of just how intimate this situation was going to get, whether she wanted to admit it or not.

"Chemistry and attraction can often be misinterpreted as nerves."

Zara couldn't help but laugh. "Get off the attraction. I'm your employee, and your bold statements make this awkward."

"I see no reason not to be bold." He shifted, closing the gap slightly between them. "But I've promised not to bring up the matter again, so let's just focus on staying warm. It's late, and we both need sleep."

Really? He was just going to leave it at that? Maybe he was going to hold true to his word. Zara was almost disappointed, but she shouldn't be. Braden had to be strong, because if he continued to make remarks or advances, she didn't know how long her self-control would hold out.

Hopefully the roads would be better tomorrow, and Braden could go home. Then this would all be a memory, and they would move on with their working relationship. Because that's what they should do, right? He had another party coming up in a few months, and since she'd been hired as the O'Sheas' permanent events coordinator, she had to keep her mind focused on her career.

"I'll hold the light," he told her. "Let's get these logs on."

After the logs were on and heat started filling the room, then they went in search of more flashlights, and Zara grabbed her cell. She had almost a full battery and she hoped it held out until the electricity came back on. If need be, she could always charge it in his car if the electricity stayed off too long.

Unfortunately, the snow was still coming down just as fierce as it had been, and with the roads being a hazard, Zara had no doubt it would be a while before crews could work on the lines.

Mother Nature clearly had it out for her. First the roads, now the electricity. Throw in some darkness and watch that sexual tension skyrocket and blow their clothes off.

Zara cringed. No. The clothes had to stay on. They were her only shield of defense because she'd already imagined her boss naked, and if he actually took that suit off, she would not be responsible for her actions.

Once back in her bedroom, Braden closed the door to keep the heat in. Zara had lit a candle and sat it on her nightstand. The flickering, warm glow sent the room to a level of romance that had no business being here.

And then the fact that she was still wearing her black dress hit her. Great. So much for keeping all the clothes on.

"Um, I'm going to have to change." She hated how her tone sounded apologetic. This was her house, damn it. "I

don't have anything to offer you unless you can fit in a pair
of small sweatpants and one of my T-shirts."

"I'll be fine. Go, get out of that dress."

Those words combined with that sexy tone of his had
her sighing. He'd promised not to mention sex, but the man
practically oozed it with every action, every word.

"Can you wait in the hall for a second?" she asked.

Taking his own flashlight, Braden stepped out and closed
the door behind him.

Zara quickly shoved her bras into her drawer and whipped
her snug dress over her head. She peeled off her stockings
and tossed them into a drawer, too. She really wanted to
lose the bra, but she couldn't get that comfortable with her
sexy guest.

As she pulled on a pair of leggings and an oversize sweatshirt, Zara truly wished she'd met Braden under different
circumstances. Maybe then they could explore this attraction, but she couldn't risk intimacy when she needed this
job, this recognition too much. She'd only had her grandmother, and now she was gone. There was no husband, no
other family to fall back on if her financial world crumbled.
Her company was only a year old, and being tied to the
O'Sheas would launch her into a new territory of clientele.

Yes, the rumors of O'Shea's Auction House being the
front for illegal activity had been abuzz for years—decades,
even—but the mystery surrounding the family only kept
people more intrigued, so Zara would gladly ride the coat-
tails of their popularity.

After sliding on a pair of fuzzy socks and pulling her hair
into a ponytail, Zara opened the door. Braden was texting
but glanced up at her and slid his phone back into his pocket.

"I had to check in with the security team. I try to keep
them updated on my whereabouts."

"Oh, you don't have to explain yourself."

"You look…different."

With a shrug, Zara glanced down to her outfit. "This is me in my downtime. I'm pretty laid-back."

Why did the room seem so much smaller when he came back in from the hallway? Why did he have such a presence about him that demanded attention? And how the hell did she act? What was the proper protocol for bringing your billionaire boss to your house and then having him spend the night? Milk and cookies? Bourbon and a cigar? She honestly didn't know the man on a personal level.

Zara's cell vibrated on her dresser. With the screen facing down, she didn't see the caller before she picked it up and automatically slid her finger over the screen.

"Hello?"

"Hey, I wanted to make sure you made it home okay."

"Shane."

Zara's eyes darted to Braden. In the dim light she could see his narrowed gaze, his jaw clenched.

"I know I acted like a jerk earlier, but I want another chance with you and I was worried about you getting home in this storm."

Were his words slurring?

"Shane, it's nearly one in the morning. Are you drunk?"

He must've shifted, because there was the slightest bit of static coming through the phone before he continued. "I miss you, Zara."

She turned her back to Braden and rubbed her forehead. "I got home safe. Thanks for checking, but we really are over, Shane. Good night."

"Don't hang up." Now his voice rose, as if the real Shane was emerging. "You're selfish, you know that? I'm trying to talk to you, and you're already dismissing me. We were good together, you know it."

"No, we weren't, and I'm done with—"

Suddenly the phone was ripped from her hand. Zara whirled around as Braden hit the end button and then turned the phone off.

"You won't explain yourself to him."

Zara sighed. Damn it, why did he have to be right? "He's not been this persistent until the past week or so. I'm not sure why he wants to get back together so bad, but I swear he won't affect my work with you."

Braden closed the gap between them and stared down at her. The darkness slashing over half his face made him seem even more menacing, more intriguing.

"I don't give a damn about that. I know you're a professional. But I'm not going to stand here and listen to you defend yourself to an asshole who doesn't deserve you."

"Wow." Zara crossed her arms and tried to process Braden's words, his angry tone. "Um…thanks."

Unsure what to do next, Zara glanced around the room. "I guess I'll just grab a blanket and pillow and lie down. I'm pretty beat."

The strain of the evening had seriously taken its toll on her, and all she wanted to do was crawl on to her chaise and fall dead asleep. Okay, maybe that wasn't all she wanted to do, but doing her boss was out of the question.

By the time she'd gotten situated on the chaise, she glanced to her bed where Braden sat on the edge staring in her direction.

"What?"

"Are you going to be comfortable? I didn't expect to take your bed."

Seeing him there, knowing her sheets would smell like him long after he was gone, was just another layer of arousal she didn't need.

"I'm perfectly comfortable. You're the one still in a suit."

With a soft laugh, he shook his head. In moments, he had his jacket off and was in the process of unbuttoning his shirt.

"Uh, wait. Are you undressing? Because—"

"Zara." His hands froze on the buttons. "I'm just taking my shirt off."

Just taking his shirt off. *To which he will no doubt ex-*

pose a chest she'll want to stare at. With the light from the gas fireplace and the candle on the nightstand, she could see perfectly fine.

And yup. He'd taken his black dress shirt off and revealed an amazingly sculpted chest, smattered with dark hair and…was that ink on his arm?

"You're staring," he said without looking up at her. "You're going to make me blush."

Zara laughed. "I highly doubt you blush, let alone over a woman looking at you." Because why deny the fact she had been? She'd been caught, but she didn't care. The man was worth a good, long stare. "Good night, Braden."

Her damn floral scent mocked him as he lay on top of her plush comforter. With his hands laced behind his head, Braden stared up at the ceiling watching the orange flickering glow from the candle. He wouldn't get any sleep tonight. Besides the fact he had every intention of getting back up to check out the house after Zara had gone to sleep, how the hell could he actually rest when the object of his desire was lying only feet away?

He hadn't expected to actually want her with such a passion and fierceness. Damn it. He knew he'd been attracted, but he'd passed being attracted long ago. Now he had a need so deeply embedded within him, he was going to go mad if he didn't have her.

Zara had been knockout gorgeous in that black dress and those sexy heels earlier at his party. But seeing her in such a simple, natural way, with hair up and sweats on, had Braden questioning why the hell he wasn't coercing her into this giant bed. He could have her clothes off in record time, despite what she'd said about mixing business and pleasure. The allure was there—the chemistry was hot enough to scorch them.

But he had a mission. One that couldn't be forgotten just because he'd been sidetracked by this unexpected quest for Zara. He needed to focus. Sex was one thing, a marvelous thing actually, but she'd put up a defensive wall. He was alone in the house he'd been wanting in for quite some time. So why the hell was he lying here focused on what was denied to him instead of formulating a plan of where he'd search once she was fully asleep?

Braden suppressed a groan as he rolled to his side. He needed to start this process, so he could be ready to get the hell out when the roads cleared.

The scrolls had to be in this house. They had to be; he refused to believe any different. But at the same time, he had to be realistic. His family had lost this house and everything in it during the Great Depression—a little fact Zara most likely didn't know.

In the decades that had passed, who's to say someone hadn't found the scrolls, moved them to another location and kept the secret to themselves?

A gnawing pit formed in his stomach. What if someone had found them and thought they were trash?

No, the scrolls were supposedly rolled up in small tubes. Nine different tubes for the nine works. They were somewhere, and Braden wasn't going to leave this house until he'd searched every inch of it.

He thought of the built-in bookcases in the living room he'd spotted earlier when he'd ran his phone light over the room. He'd tried to be casual about it, no reason to raise a red flag with Zara, because, as of right now, she was totally unsuspecting and completely worried about being alone with him.

Since she'd walked into his office for the job, he knew he wanted her in his bed. No reason he couldn't enjoy a little recreational activity and search at the same time. Besides, getting Zara to open up to him may be the angle they'd needed all along, even if Ryker just wanted to break in and be done with it.

No way in hell was Ryker getting close to Zara. He was

mysterious at best, terrifying at worst. And women loved that mysterious side. He had no intention of Zara being one of those women. Zara was all Braden's...for now.

Braden knew full well what Ryker did for the family. Ever since Ryker had come to be friends with Braden and Mac in grade school, their father had taken Ryker in as another son. By the time they were out of high school, Ryker was just another member of the family. The Black Sheep was too benign a term when referring to the man who did all the dirty work.

Braden stared across to Zara and realized she was looking right back at him. This was ridiculous. They were adults acting like horny teens trying to get a mental feel for what the other one was thinking.

"You're supposed to be asleep," he told her. "Do you need your bed back?"

The image of Zara in her bed wasn't new. He didn't need to say the words aloud to conjure up a vivid image. He'd already had her in bed several times in his mind.

"I can't sleep."

He knew a cure for insomnia.

"It's too quiet," she continued. "I usually sleep with a fan because I can't handle the silence at night."

Interesting. Braden bent his elbow and rested his head on his palm. "Are you afraid to stay here alone?"

"Not really. It's just my old place was so much smaller, and this house has always had that creepy factor, you know? It's old, it creaks and groans. Then there's the rumor it's haunted." She laughed. "I guess when I'm alone with my thoughts, I let my imagination run wild."

"It's not unusual for these old homes to have some ghost story. They're either based off some truth people believe, or they make for a good resale value for those seeking adventure."

"Yeah, well, I'm not up for an adventure and I don't believe in ghosts."

Braden found he liked hearing her talk. He liked how soft her voice was, how it carried through the darkness and hit him straight with a shot of arousal. So he wanted to keep her talking.

"Since we both can't sleep, why don't you tell me the ghost story?"

He saw her lick her lips as she clutched the blanket near her chest. Thanks to the dim lighting, Braden found her even more alluring. Sleep wasn't even a priority.

"It's silly, actually. Apparently there was a young couple in love, and supposedly the man went off to the army and never returned. There are stories he died in the war, stories he fell in love with another. Who knows? She went on to marry, but the rumor is you can still hear her crying."

Braden knew that story all too well. Considering this house had been in his family at the time Zara was referring to. And the woman was his great-great...several greats, grandmother. He'd always heard the story that the man who went to the army was actually her husband and he'd been killed. She'd remarried, had children but, supposedly, never got over her first love. A tragic story, a romantic one for those who were into that sort of thing...and his Irish family most definitely was.

"But, if I ever hear a woman crying in this house, it will take me one giant leap to get out of here," Zara went on with a light laugh. "An intruder I can handle. A ghost, not so much. At least a real person I can shoot."

The more she talked, the more Braden found he didn't like her in this big house alone. But, if she had a firearm, at least she could defend herself.

What if Shane showed up? The man obviously called her drunk, and, on a good night with clear roads, what would stop him from just coming over, forcing his way in? And now that she worked for Braden, Shane would see that as a betrayal. The man was that egotistical and warped.

"But I'm not sure a woman would be crying over a man

if she was married to another," Zara went on as she shifted beneath her covers. "I mean, I can't imagine loving one man, let alone falling in love twice. Or maybe she'd just married the second guy so she wasn't lonely. I'll never be that desperate."

Braden thought to his parents. They'd been in love, they'd raised a family and they'd had a bond that Braden wanted to have someday. His mother passed when Braden had been a pre-teen, and the car accident that claimed her had an impact on the entire family. They became stronger, more unified than before because they realized just how short life was.

Not now, but one day he'd have a family of his own. First, though, he'd have those scrolls back in his family's possession and steer his family right. He refused to bring a family into his life when there were enemies, people who used loved ones as a weakness to exploit.

"You've never been in love? Never knew people in love?" he asked, easing up to rest his back against the headboard.

"I've never seen love firsthand, no." Zara turned onto her back, lacing her hands on top of the blanket. "My grandmother loved me and I loved her, but as far as a man and woman... I'm not sure true love exists. Have you been in love?"

Even though he'd removed everything but his pants, heat enveloped Braden. Granted, it could be because he was in the company of a woman he wanted more than his next breath, but honestly, the logs were doing a great job, and with the door closed, the thick air was starting to become too much.

"Would you mind if I turned the logs down a bit?" he asked.

"Nice way to dodge my question." She jumped up from the chaise and threw him a smile. "I'll turn them down. It is getting a bit warm in here."

Braden watched her move across the room. In her black, body-hugging dress she'd been a knockout, but in her sweatshirt and leggings with her hair in a ponytail, she almost seemed…innocent, vulnerable.

Damn it, he didn't want to see her that way. He didn't want this to become personal with emotions getting in the way of his quest to get her in his bed and search for the scrolls.

And when the hell had he officially added her to his list of must-haves?

Somewhere between dancing with her and settling in for their sleepover.

As she started back to the chaise, she gestured toward him. "If you're hot, you can, um…you can take your pants off. I won't look. I mean, I don't want this to be uncomfortable for either of us, but I want you to be… Sorry, I'm rambling. Go ahead, take your pants off. I'll turn around."

She was killing him. Slowly, surely, killing him.

But the lady said he could remove his pants. So remove them he would.

Four

Just as Braden unzipped and started to lower his pants, Zara cried out in pain, followed quickly by words that would've made his mama blush.

With pants hanging open, Braden carefully crossed the space. "What is it?"

"Banged the side of my ankle on this damn chaise," she said through gritted teeth. "Stupid scrolled legs on this thing."

Without thinking, Braden dropped to his knees before her. His hands ran down the leg closest to the chaise, gently roaming over her tight, knit pants.

When she hissed, he pulled back and glanced up. The light was even dimmer now that she'd turned the logs down, but the miniscule candle flickered just enough of a glow for him to make out those heavy lids and the desire that stared back at him.

Keeping his eyes locked on to hers, Braden slid his fingers around her slender ankle once again. "Does this hurt?"

"Just tender."

Trailing his fingertips to another spot, he asked, "How about here?"

"No."

Weighing his next movement, Braden moved his hand on up to her calf. Zara sucked in a breath, and he knew it was for a whole other reason. Gliding over the back of her knee, he curled his hands around her thigh as he shifted closer to her. With his other hand, he slid beneath the hem of her sweatshirt to grip her waist. Satiny skin met his palm, and he'd swear she trembled and broke out in goose bumps right that second.

"Braden," she murmured.

"Relax."

Ironic he was telling her to relax when his own body was strung tighter than a coil ready to spring into action.

"This isn't appropriate," she whispered. If her tone had held any conviction whatsoever, he would've stopped, but with the way she'd panted his name, with the way her hips slightly tilted toward him, he wasn't about to ignore what her body was so obviously telling him.

He continued to allow his hands the freedom to roam as he came to his feet, pulling her with him. With one hand settled on her hip and one just beneath her shirt, he watched as Zara stared up at him, her eyes locked on to his. He refused to break the connection, didn't want to sever the intensity of this moment.

That warm skin begged for his touch, and it was all Braden could do not to jerk this shirt up and over her head so he could fully appreciate the woman. The seduction of Zara would have to be slow, romantic and all about her. He could handle that order because right now he wanted to feel her, wanted to have her come apart.

The second he encountered silk over her breast, he wasted no time in reaching around and unfastening her bra. Now that she was freed of the restraint, he cupped both breasts in his palms and watched with utter satisfaction as her lids drifted closed, as a groan escaped from her lips.

Why did she have to feel so amazing? Why was he fighting taking what he wanted instead of giving her full pleasure? This had to be about Zara, about seduction.

Braden slid one hand down to the top of her pants. Zara's eyes snapped open. She scrambled from beneath his touch. Her eyes darted away as she righted her clothes. Damn it, he'd pushed her too far when he couldn't control his hormones.

"This can't happen," she stated, her voice shaky. "We—I…"

"Don't say you're sorry," he told her as she jerked her sweatshirt down as if she was trying to erase what had just occurred. "We're adults, and dancing around the attraction wasn't going to last for long. I've been wanting to touch you since you walked into my office."

Zara's hands came up to her face. "I can't believe I did that. I just let you…" She dropped her hands and waved them in the air. "I let you…"

"Yes?" he asked, trying not to smile as she struggled.

"Is this how you treat all your new employees?"

Braden reached for her arms, pulling her flush against his body. "I've never in my life slept with an employee."

"We haven't slept together," she retorted.

"Yet."

Her gasp had him laughing, but he didn't release her. "You're so sure of yourself, aren't you? I'm not easy, Braden. I don't want you to even think that for a minute. I shouldn't have let this go so far."

"Zara, if I thought you were easy, I wouldn't waste my time trying. I look for the challenge, the chase, the risk in everything."

Now she laughed as she shook her head. Her hands were trapped between their bodies. "You're already talking about sleeping with me and you've not even kissed me. I'd say that's—"

His lips slammed on to hers. Hadn't kissed her? Was she complaining?

For one troubling moment, Braden worried she'd push him away, but after her hesitancy, she finally opened up and accepted what he was giving.

Her hands flattened against his chest as he coaxed her mouth open and tipped her head. Kissing Zara was just another total-body experience he hadn't anticipated. Kisses were either good or bad. With Zara, they were arousing, a stepping-stone for more and a promise of all the passion she kept hidden away.

If he wasn't careful, he'd start craving more of her touches, more of her soft moans, because damn it, the woman got into a man's system and...

No. Hell, no. She was not getting into his system. Nobody was penetrating that until he was damn good and ready.

Braden had to force himself to step back, to put some distance between their heated bodies.

"There. Now you've been kissed." He licked his own lips, needing to taste her again. "If you're feeling cheated on anything else, I can oblige."

Her eyes widened as she trailed her gaze down his bare chest. "N-no. You've obliged enough."

Braden smiled. "Then we both need to get some sleep."

As if he hadn't just had her body trembling against his seconds ago, he turned and sat back on her bed. Zara hadn't moved from her spot next to the chaise.

"Is your ankle okay?"

"My ankle?" She glanced down. "Oh, yeah. It's sore, but fine. Um...good night."

He watched as she slowly sank down onto her makeshift bed. He could practically hear her thinking and he knew full well she was replaying how far she'd let him go. Hell, he was, too, but he had to push that aside and keep his eye on the main reason he was here and not how close he'd been to getting her to explode in his arms.

"Don't overthink this, Zara." She continued to lie there, looking up at the ceiling. "Get some sleep."

Because the sooner she fell asleep, the quicker he could start looking through the house.

How could the man just fall asleep? Seriously? Braden acted as if this was no big deal, as if he'd patted her on the head and sent her off to bed like an obedient lover.

And the longer she lay here, the more she was wondering how she'd lost control of that situation so fast. Oh, yeah. He'd touched her. That was it. The man touched her, looked at her with those piercing eyes, and she'd been helpless. For the briefest of moments she'd forgotten all about her job, the fact her boss had his hands beneath her shirt and was working his way into her pants. Thankfully, she'd come to her senses before they'd crossed a point of no return. She needed this job, even more than she needed a one-night stand.

Braden O'Shea was a powerful man, and she was not immune to his allure. Yet she'd told herself over and over this evening how she couldn't get intimate with him, no matter how much she wanted to. She couldn't risk losing this job because she was a sad cliché and slept with her boss. How tacky was that? She prided herself on being a professional, yet the man who'd written her a colossal check was snoozing in her bed.

Whatever his secret for flipping the horny switch, she'd like to know because she was still just as turned on as before she'd put the brakes on.

She'd never known a man who was so giving, but then she hadn't known many men like Braden O'Shea. Something told her he was quite different than any other guy she'd dated.

Zara nearly groaned as she tugged on her blanket and rolled over. Dated? She and Braden were far from dating.

He'd given her a few minutes of toe-curling excitement, and that was all. He was stuck in her house thanks to Mother Nature's fury, and that was the extent of their personal relationship.

From here on out, no more touching, no more kissing. Though she had to admit that kiss had been nearly as potent as the touching.

What would morning bring? The questions whirled around in her head. Would he act as if nothing happened? Would he be able to leave, or would he be stuck here for another night? Zara wished he weren't her boss, wished this powerful, sexy man were stuck in her house under different circumstances, but the fact was he was helping to pay her bills. And without the prestige of working for him, it would take her a lot longer to get the recognition she needed for her new company.

She wasn't worried about his questionable reputation. The O'Sheas were legends, and despite the rumors surrounding Braden's father's dealings, Zara had only heard praise about Braden. He may be tough when needed, he may even show off his brute force like he had with Shane, but none of that made him a bad guy. And the way her body was still thrumming, Zara felt Braden was indeed a very good guy.

No matter what her common sense was telling her now, Zara couldn't help but want more. Not being able to touch Braden at all left her feeling somewhat cheated. Those broad shoulders, those lean hips…a man with a body like that surely knew how to use it in the most effective ways.

Gripping her blanket beneath her chin, Zara tried not to think about the man who lay just behind her, in her bed, shirtless. She tried not to think of how he'd looked at her when he'd been kneeling on the floor. She tried to keep her body from tingling even more at the fantasy of how they'd be if she crawled in between those sheets with him.

Her best hope now would be to fall asleep and dream, because having the real thing was simply out of the question.

Braden padded from the bedroom. It had taken Zara over an hour to fall asleep. She'd tossed and turned, letting out soft little moans every now and then, and there wasn't a doubt in Braden's mind she was just as sexually frustrated as he was.

Zara was one of the most passionate women he'd ever met. And when she let her guard down…purely erotic. Knowing she was lying over there restless nearly had him forgetting the plan to search the house tonight and instead dragging her back up to her own bed and finishing what they both wanted.

But she'd finally dozed off, if the subtle snoring was any indication. Braden threw one more look her way as he gently closed the door behind him. The logs were keeping the room plenty warm, because this hallway was flat-out chilly. The temperature must have really dropped outside for the inside to get so cold, so fast. At least he'd put his shirt and socks back on, so that was a minor help.

With his phone in his pocket, Braden flicked on the small flashlight that had been on Zara's bedside table. He swung it back and forth down the hallway, finally deciding to venture into the rooms toward the end where he'd never been before.

He'd seen the layout of the home several times. The floor plan was ingrained into his mind, the blueprints locked away in his home office, but seeing the rooms firsthand was entirely different. He knew there was a third floor, but right now he was going to focus on the bedrooms that sat empty. Every inch of this home could be a hiding spot, and Braden had to start somewhere. Sticking close to Zara was the smartest move right now.

There was something eerie about an old house that was pitch-black with the sounds of whirling winds and creaking. But fear never entered Braden's mind. Nothing scared him, except the prospect of not finding these scrolls. His father had wanted them back in the family's possession, but once Patrick had passed away six months ago, Braden knew this endeavor now fell to him. That, and strategically severing the ties to an underbelly of the city he wanted nothing to do with.

Nearly a decade ago, his father had supposedly ordered a prominent businessman to be taken out, along with the man's assistant. That dangerous rumor kept filtering around, but if Braden could pull this family around, point them in the right direction, perhaps such whispered speculations would be put to rest.

Everything would take time. This was a business Braden learned to be patient in. Effective, forceful and controlling, but patient.

He'd never ordered any killings, prayed to God he never had to. Transitioning was difficult, but Braden had to. He had to secure a future for the family he eventually wanted, but at the same time fulfill his father's dying wishes.

As he entered the last bedroom, he stood in the doorway and moved his light around, familiarizing himself with the furniture layout. More built-in bookcases. Nice charm to add to each room, but a pain in the ass for someone on a scavenger hunt.

Ryker had mentioned searching the obvious places, but Braden was here now and wanted to see everything for himself firsthand.

Braden slid the flashlight beneath his arm so he could use both hands to shift books and knickknacks around on the shelves. So far no hidden door, no secret hole hidden behind a panel. Nothing. But he wasn't discouraged. Getting into this house was one of the biggest hurdles, and here he was. Now he just needed to be patient, because the scrolls were here. They had to be.

The irony that his family unofficially dealt in retrieving stolen relics and heirlooms, and they couldn't even get back their own possessions, was not lost on him. Granted, they technically stole back the items, but those words would never come out of his mouth, and Ryker was the guy who did all the dirty work. So in a sense, Braden never saw how the items were taken back. So long as it was done correctly and satisfied clients all over the globe, the details didn't matter. The auction house gave them the front they needed to play modern-day Robin Hood, but the rumors around the family gave them that edge that helped them with their tough, hard-ass image.

Generations of corruption would be hard to move past, but Braden was determined. The art dealings would continue, and there was no harm in taking back what was rightfully due to those who had lost heirlooms, as long as it didn't require any violence. But any more than lying and stealing had to cease...sooner rather than later.

Ryker wasn't too keen on Braden's new, somewhat lily-white direction, but Braden wasn't asking for permission. He was in charge now, and Ryker would have to understand that any sort of bloodshed was a thing of the past.

Which reminded him, he needed to check in with their right-hand man who was currently in London looking for a rare piece of art that needed to be returned to a client in Paris during the next auction.

By the time he'd finished the two large bedrooms at the end of the hall, Braden was no closer than when he'd started. Sleep was going to have to happen because his eyes were burning, and most likely it was nearly morning at this point. He couldn't help but wonder what all the unpacked boxes were, though. He'd seen a few in her kitchen, several in the living room, and with her closet door open, he'd spotted a good amount stacked in there. Hadn't she said she'd lived here for a few months?

Those unpacked boxes held so much potential, but how many were hers and how many were already here for years?

Using his flashlight to head back to the bedroom, Braden

flicked it off as soon as he reached the doorway. The second he stepped inside, warmth surrounded him. Zara lay on her side, her hand tucked beneath her cheek, her ponytail now in disarray as hair draped over her forehead and down the side of her face.

Slipping back out of his shirt, he sat on the edge of the bed, unable to take his eyes off the sleeping beauty. He had tried to keep his hands off her. Okay, he could've tried harder, but damn it, something about her made him want to get closer to her in the most primal way possible.

He knew she was a sexy, take-charge woman. The fact she was a businesswoman, career-driven and independent, was a definite turn-on. But after dancing with her and seeing that flash of vulnerability in her eyes when Shane had entered the picture, Braden felt even more territorial…and not in the typical employee/employer way. There was no way he could not step into her life.

Braden slid between the sheets and refused to acknowledge the arousal threatening to keep him awake. He needed sleep because when morning came, he fully intended to continue his quest for the scrolls, and he sure as hell planned on more seducing. Multitasking had never been this sweet.

Five

Zara stared at her cabinets and sighed. Was it appropriate to offer your millionaire boss a s'mores Pop-Tart or a cherry one for breakfast? Because that was the extent of her options. Well, she had other flavors because she was a junk-food junkie, and Pop-Tarts were her drug of choice.

He'd still been asleep when she'd slipped from the warm room. Now she stood shivering in her kitchen and wondering when the electricity would be restored. The snow was still coming down in big, fat flakes, and there was no sign of any cars in sight.

Grabbing three different varieties of breakfast pastries, Zara spun on her fuzzy socks and raced back up the steps. Mercy, it had gotten cold in here. When she eased open the door, Braden was shifting around on her bed, sheets slipping down a bit. His glorious chest looked even better with daylight streaking through the window. Granted, it had also looked spectacular on display with the fire flickering last night.

With boxes of food under one arm, she gently closed the door behind her, but Braden's eyes instantly popped open and zeroed in on her. Suddenly she was pinned in place. That piercing gaze penetrated her across the room. Such a potent man to be able to hold such power over someone without even saying a word.

Slowly, he sat up. The sheet fell to his waist, giving up an even more tantalizing view of all that tan skin with dark hair covering his chest. Dark ink curved over one shoulder, and Zara found herself wanting to trace the lines of that tat. With her tongue.

Down, girl.

"Breakfast," she said. "I hope you like Pop-Tarts."

His brows drew in. "I can honestly say I've never had one."

Of course he hadn't. Not only was he a bajillionaire, he had the body of a sculpted god. Someone who looked like that wouldn't fill themselves with the finer junkie things in life.

"Well, you're in for a treat." She crossed the room, trying to ignore the fact that she looked like a hot mess after last night. "I'm a connoisseur of all things unhealthy and amazingly tasty."

She sat the boxes on the trunk at the end of her bed and opened each one. She tried to focus on anything other than the fact he still hadn't reached for his shirt. Was he going to spend their entire time half naked? So this is what the saying "both a blessing and a curse" meant.

"I have s'mores, cherry and chocolate." She glanced back up as he slid from the bed and came to stand beside her. "Take whatever you want. I have plenty more downstairs."

He eyed the boxes as if he truly had no clue what to choose. "I'm a chocolate lover, so the cherry is out. Should I go all in for the s'mores?"

Zara smiled. "They're the best, in my opinion."

She handed him a foil package and grabbed one for herself before heading over to stand near the logs. She needed to keep a bit of distance, because if the shirtless thing wasn't enough to make her want a replay of last night, the fact that he had sheet marks—*her* sheets—on his arm and face and he smelled musky and sexy was more than enough to have her near begging. And Zara wouldn't beg for any man, especially one who wrote her checks.

"You can have all you want, though." She was babbling. Nerves did that to a woman. "I forgot the drinks. I'm sure the fridge kept things cold, but I'll need to—"

"Zara. Breathe." Braden's hand gripped her shoulder. She hadn't even heard him come up behind her. "I'm making you nervous again."

Swallowing, she turned to face him. Holding his heavy-lidded gaze, Zara tried not to look at the sheet mark on his cheek. A minor imperfection that made this man seem so... normal.

"I'm not nervous," she said, defensively. "Why would I be nervous? I mean, just because you... I...last night...and now your shirt is still off, so I'm not sure what to do or how to act. I've never had a man here, let alone my boss. So this whole morning-after thing is different, not that we did anything to discuss the typical morning after..."

Closing her eyes, Zara let out a sigh. She shook her head to clear her thoughts before looking back up to Braden. "I'm rambling. This is just a bit awkward for me, and I didn't want to make a total fool of myself, but I'm doing just that."

Braden took the package from her hands and tore it open. After pulling out a Pop-Tart, he held it up to her.

"Why don't you eat?" he suggested. "I'm not worried about what happened last night, but if you want to run through it again, that's fine with me. Maybe we can discuss how much farther I wanted to go."

"No, we shouldn't." Zara took the pastry he held up to her. "Maybe we should just check on the road conditions instead of reliving anything."

Braden laughed as he tore open his own package. "Whatever you want. I'm at your mercy here."

Did every word that came out of his mouth have to drip with sex appeal? Was he trying to torment her further? Because if this was him putting forth no effort to torture her, she'd hate to see when he actually turned on the charm.

Zara didn't want to think about staying in this room with him for another day. If she didn't get out of here, her hormones may explode.

They ate their gourmet breakfast, and Braden muttered something about them being amazing before he went and grabbed a different flavor. Traditional chocolate this time. While he had round two, Zara went to dig out her old boots. She was going to have to get the frozen food outside and put it into the snow to stay cold. There was no other way, not if she wanted to salvage her groceries.

After she shoved her fuzzy-socked feet into her boots, Zara headed for the door. "I'll be right back."

Braden swallowed his last bite and crumbled his foil in his hand. "Where are you going?"

"I'm going to run downstairs and get the food from the freezer and fridge and set it out in the snow. It will stay cold there. I don't know what else to do with it."

Crossing to the bed, Braden reached for his shirt and shrugged into it. "I'll help."

"You don't have to. I've got it."

Ignoring her, he buttoned each button with quick, precise movements. "What else do I have to do?"

Keep that potent, sexually charged body away from hers? Stay in the warm room while she went outside and cooled off?

Zara knew she wasn't going to win this argument, so she turned and headed from the room. Braden closed the bedroom door behind them. The cooler air in the hallway slid right through Zara, helping her to focus on something other than the man who pretended like make out sessions were passed out each night before bedtime like a hug good-night.

Should her body still be humming, given they hadn't even gotten to the good part? Seriously?

As soon as she went into the kitchen, she turned to Braden, only he wasn't there. Zara backtracked a couple steps to find him in the living room staring at the built-in bookcases.

"This house has a lot of the same old-Boston charm mine does," he told her without turning around. "The trim on the top of these cabinets, the detailed edging. It's all so rare to find in homes these days. I appreciate when properties have been taken care of."

"I imagine you see quite a variety of homes with various decor in your line of work."

Throwing her a glance over his shoulder, he nodded. "I've seen million-dollar homes that were polished to perfection, every single thing in them brand-new. But it's the old houses that really pull me in. Mac is more the guy who wants all things shiny and new."

Zara crossed her arms to ward off the chill. The only vibe she'd gotten of the younger O'Shea brother was that he was a player. And with his looks and charm, she could totally see women batting their lashes and dropping their panties.

Braden ran a fingertip over a small glass church her grandmother had loved. "He's working on the opening of our Miami location. That fast-paced lifestyle and the warmer climate are also more his speed."

"You guys are quite opposite, then."

"Except when it comes to business," Braden amended as he moved to another shelf and carefully adjusted a pewter picture frame holding a picture of Zara as a child. "We see eye to eye on all things regarding the auction house."

"I've always hated that picture," Zara stated with a laugh. "My grandmother took that on my first trip to the beach.

I was eleven and had just entered that awkward stage girls go through."

Turning to face her, Braden crossed his arms and offered a slight grin. "Whatever phase you went through, you've more than made up for it."

Zara shivered at his smooth words. Apparently this smooth talker liked a woman with curves.

"You didn't go to a beach until you were eleven?" he asked, moving right on.

Oh, no. She didn't want to get into her childhood. Granted, the first decade of her life wasn't terrible, but there certainly were no family vacations, no fun beach pictures or pictures of any kind, really. Her parents had been rich, beyond rich, but they couldn't buy affection. They'd tried. Zara had more toys, more nannies than any one child needed or deserved.

When her parents had died, Zara had been numb. She hadn't even known how to feel, how to react. How did a child respond to losing the two people who were supposed to love her more than anything, yet had never said the words aloud? They'd shown her in ways, material ways, but that was the only way they knew how to express themselves.

That money she'd always thought her parents possessed was suddenly gone. Her parents' overspending had finally caught up with them, and Zara was paying the price. Apparently her parents owed everybody and their brother thousands, if not hundreds of thousands. Zara's grandmother had maneuvered funds, had borrowed against this house and had paid off every last debt her parents had left. Now the money was gone after all the debts were paid.

Just another reason Zara was determined to succeed in her business. She wanted to make her grandmother proud, even if she wasn't here to physically see Zara's triumph. She didn't want to have to sell this house that had been in her family since the Depression. Her grandmother had loved this place, and Zara wanted that last piece of family to hold on to.

"Zara?" Braden took a cautious step toward her, then another. "Where did you go?"

Zara shook her head. "Nowhere worth traveling to again. Let's get this food outside and get back upstairs. I'm freezing."

Just as she turned, Braden curled his fingers around her arm. With a glance from his hand to his eyes, Zara thought she saw a flash of something other than the desire she'd seen previously. Those piercing eyes were now filled with concern, and Zara didn't want him to be concerned for her. Having compassion was just another level of intimacy she couldn't afford to slide into with this man. It would be all too easy to lean on someone, and she'd not been raised to be dependent on others.

Zara didn't want to identify the feelings coursing through her, not when her emotions were already on edge and her body hummed even louder each time he neared, let alone touched her.

"Come on, Braden." She forced a wide smile and nodded toward the kitchen. "Let's get this done."

He looked as if he wanted to say more, but finally he nodded and released her. Maybe if they could focus on food, not freezing to death and no conversations involving personal issues, they'd get through this blizzard without any more sensual encounters or touching.

As she plucked her coat from the peg by the back door, Zara nearly laughed at her delusional thought. No way could she pretend Braden being here was just like having a friend over. Where he'd gripped her arm seconds ago was still tingling, and in a very short time, she'd find herself back upstairs, closed off in her bedroom with a man who made her ache for things she had no business wanting.

"That's all of it." Milk, eggs, cheese, frozen pizzas, meat and other groceries were tucked down into the snow to keep them from going bad. "Let's get back inside before my toes fall off."

Even though she had her fuzzy socks on under her rubber boots, her toes were going numb.

Braden held up a hand. "Wait," he whispered. "Did you hear that?"

Zara stilled. All she heard was silence because no cars were out. It was as if the rest of the world had ceased to exist, leaving only her and the boss she'd dreamed of last night.

"I don't hear anything," she told him, shoving that fantasy aside. "You have to be freezing. Come on."

He still wore his suit and the dress coat from the party. At least she could bulk up in warm layers. No way was he not freezing out here.

"Wait a second." His eyes searched the ground near her house. Slowly, he took a step, then another. "Go on inside if you don't want to wait, but I heard a cat."

A cat? She didn't own a cat. Compassion was not in her genetic makeup, so she'd spared all animals and sworn to never own one. She wouldn't have the first clue what to do if left in charge of a living, breathing thing.

Just as she reached for the door handle, Braden crouched down. Zara gasped when he pulled a snow-covered kitten up in his gloved hands. Instantly he cradled the animal to his chest and swiped the snow off its back.

Braden took cautious steps toward the back door, keeping the kitten tucked firmly just inside his coat. Zara realized his intentions immediately.

"You're bringing that inside?"

His eyes went from the gray bundle to her. "Yes. He'll freeze to death out here. He's wet and shivering."

Zara glanced around. "Where's the mom? Aren't animals made to live outside? They have fur on."

His brows shot up. "You have a coat on, too. Do you want to stay out here and see if you survive?"

Swallowing, she shook her head. "Um…so what do we do once it's inside?"

Braden tipped his head to the side. "You've never had a pet, have you?"

"Never."

Braden's sharp gaze softened. "Let's talk inside. This little guy needs warmth, and so do we."

Zara opened the back door and ushered Braden in ahead of her. Once they had their coats and boots off, Braden started searching her cabinets. He seemed to be satisfied with the box of crackers he'd found.

"Grab a bowl of water and let's get back upstairs where it's warm."

Without waiting on her, he took the box and the kitten and disappeared. Okay, so he'd basically ordered her around in her own home and that was after bringing in a stray animal.

Was badass Braden O'Shea brought to his knees over a little bundle of fur? Zara nearly laughed as she pulled out a shallow bowl and filled it with water. By the time she got upstairs, Braden was sitting on the edge of the bed, the kitten at his side, as he peeled off his socks. His feet were red and had to be absolutely freezing.

"These got soaked," he told her. "The snow went right into my boots."

"Let me have those." Placing the water on the floor at the foot of the bed, Zara reached out and took the soaked, icy socks.

"My pants are wet, too."

Her eyes darted up to his. That smirk on his face had her shaking her head. "Oh, no. Don't even think of stripping. You can roll the pant legs up and come sit by the fire."

His big hand stroked over the cat as the damp animal snuggled deeper into her cream duvet. "You're no fun at all."

"Oh, I'm loads of fun. I'm an events coordinator. I get paid to be fun."

After she laid his socks by the gas logs, which she cranked

up because she was still shivering, she turned back to see Braden feeding the kitten small bites of a cracker. For a second she just stood there and stared. She'd not met many men like Braden, hard and powerful on one hand, soft and compassionate on the other.

"You're staring," he stated without looking up.

She remained where she was because the sight of him on her bed being so…adorable was not something she'd planned on. She'd had a hard enough time resisting him when he'd been flat-out sexy. Now that an adorable factor had slipped right in, she was losing what little control she had left.

How would she handle another night with this man?

Six

So now Zara was not only nervous around him, she was nervous over a cat. This woman had so many complex layers, and damn if he didn't want to peel back each one.

"I'm going to take my pants off if you keep looking at me like that," he threatened. He didn't know what was going through her mind, but he couldn't handle her looking at him as if he was some savior or something.

"I'm just trying to figure you out."

His hand stilled on the kitten's boney back. "Don't," he told her, meeting her gaze across the room. "That's not an area you want to go to."

Zara crossed to the chaise and shoved her blanket aside before taking a seat and curling her feet beneath her. "Oh, I think maybe I do want to go there. What makes a rumored bad boy go all soft with a kitten?"

"I wouldn't have left any animal out in this. Would you?"

He needed to turn the topic of conversation back to her. Nothing good would come from her digging into his private life, but he wanted to know more and more about hers. Suddenly, finding out more intimate details had less to do with the scrolls…not that finding those weren't still his top priority.

"Honestly, if I'd been alone, I wouldn't have known what to do. I guess maybe I would've brought it in, but I seriously thought animals were made to be outside."

Braden reached into the sleeve of crackers for another and broke off a piece for the kitten. "Why no pets growing up?"

He watched from the corner of his eye as she toyed with the edge of her sweatshirt a moment before speaking. She was either nervous or contemplating how much to tell— most likely a little of both. Fine by him. He would wait.

"My parents weren't the most affectionate," she started slowly, as if finding the right way to describe her mom and dad was difficult. "To be honest, I never asked for a pet. I figured they'd say no, so I didn't bother."

When the kitten turned away and stretched before nestling deeper into the covers, Braden set the crackers on the nightstand before shifting on the bed to face her.

"Were they affectionate to you?" he asked, wondering why he was allowing himself this line of questioning. Seduction was one thing, but finding out about her childhood was a whole other level he didn't need to get into in order to do the job he came to do.

"It doesn't matter."

Suddenly it did. Braden came to his feet and padded over to join her on the narrow chaise. Easing a knee up on to the cushion, he turned sideways.

"Were you abused?" he asked, almost afraid of the answer. "Is that why you had such a strong connection with your grandmother?"

"Oh, no." Zara shook her head. "I wasn't abused. There were and are kids who have worse lives. I guess I've just always felt sorry for myself because of all the things I think I missed out on. But, they gave me a nice house, toys, camps in the summer."

"Family vacations?" he asked.

"Um…no. They went on trips and cruises while I was away at camp. When they traveled during the school year, I would stay with my grandmother." A sad smile spread across her face. "To be honest, those were the best times of my childhood. I loved spending time here. Gram would make up a scavenger hunt, and I'd spend hours exploring all these old rooms and hideout areas."

"Hideouts?" he asked. Damn, he felt like a jerk for listening to her, caring what she was actually saying and now turning it around to benefit his plan. Still, the end result would be the same. He would find those scrolls, and Zara was going to have to inadvertently help. "I know my house is old and has secret areas. I assume this one does, too?"

Zara smiled and tipped her head to meet his gaze. "Yeah. There's a hidden door beneath the stairs. It actually takes you into the den at the back of the house. In the basement there's a couple of hidden rooms, but they're so narrow, they're more like closets."

He wanted to check those areas out right this second, but he had to remain motionless and let her continue. Once she was asleep he'd be able to continue his quest. Those secret rooms she'd mentioned weren't on the blueprints he'd seen, and his father had never mentioned them, so he had to assume no one had checked there, either.

"My grandmother always told me how much she loved me," Zara went on, her voice almost a whisper as if she were talking to herself. "She always told me how I was her biggest treasure. I didn't get that until recently. I look at all the antiques in this old house, pieces I know are worth a lot of money. But to know she valued me even more…"

Braden continued to watch her battle her emotions, trying to remain strong and hold back. He admired her strength, her dignity and pride.

Slowly, Braden was sinking into her world—a world he never intended to be a part of. If he could somehow get away with taking back the scrolls, maybe they could see where this attraction led.

Damn it. All this secret snooping was supposed to be Ryker's area. Braden and Mac were more the powerhouse guys who ran everything smoothly and kept a few cops and federal agents on their payroll to keep their reputation clean.

"I'm sorry." Zara let out a soft laugh. "I didn't mean to get all nostalgic and sentimental on you."

Braden reached out, placing a hand on her knee. Her body stilled beneath his as her eyes widened. "Don't apologize for talking to me. We're more than employee/employer at this point."

Zara's actions betrayed her as her gaze darted to his mouth, then back up. She may have been stiff beneath his touch, but she couldn't hold back her emotions. Those striking eyes gave everything away.

She pulled in a deep breath. "What happened last night—"

"Wasn't nearly enough," he finished. "The pace we set is up to you, but the end result is inevitable."

Zara shifted her knee and turned to face him, mirroring him. His hand fell away, but he stretched his arm along the back of the chaise as he waited for her to offer up some excuse as to why they shouldn't explore this chemistry.

"I need this job."

He smiled. "And you were the best candidate, that's why I hired you." *Well, one of the reasons.* "Your job has nothing to do with what's going on between us."

"Nothing is going on," she all but yelled, throwing her arms wide. "Nothing can go on. Not while I'm working for you."

Braden shrugged. "Fine. You're fired."

Zara tipped her head, glaring at him from beneath heavy lids. "That's ridiculous."

"I always get what I want, Zara."

"And you're that desperate for a bedmate?"

Leaning forward, his fingertips found the side of her face, stroking down to her neck where she trembled. "No. Just you."

"Why?" she whispered.

"Why not?" he retorted.

The pulse beneath his hand jumped as he leaned in a bit closer. Her warm breath tickled him, the flare in her eyes motivated him and her parted lips begged him.

His other hand came up to cup the side of her face. His thumb stroked over her full bottom lip. Never once did she take her eyes off his, and while the power appeared to be completely his right now, this woman, who had him in unexpected knots, could flip that role at any moment and bring him to his knees. And the fact that she had no clue about her control over him made her even sexier.

He continued to stroke her lip as his other hand slid around to cup the back of her head. His fingers threaded through her hair, massaging as he went. A soft sigh escaped her, and Braden's entire body tightened in response.

"You're not thinking work right now, are you?" he whispered against her lips. "You're concentrating on my touch, on how you want more."

"What are you doing to me?" she asked as her lids lowered.

"Proving a point."

Her tongue darted out to lick her lips, brushing against his thumb, instantly flipping that control. His completely snapped with that simple move.

Braden captured her mouth beneath his, not caring for finesse or gentleness. There was only so much a man could handle. Zara's hands came up and fisted the front of his shirt as she moaned…music to his ears.

Tipping his head slightly, Braden changed the angle of the kiss. When Zara leaned into him, he wanted to drag her into his lap and speed this process along. So he did.

Gripping her around the waist, without breaking the kiss, Braden shifted to sit forward as he placed her over his lap.

Instantly her legs straddled his thighs, and her hands slid up over his shoulders as the heated kiss continued. Braden hadn't wanted a woman this bad in a long time…maybe never. Zara was sexy, yes, but there was more to her than anything superficial, and he wanted more. He wanted all she would give.

His hands slid beneath the hem of her sweatshirt. That smooth skin beneath his palms could make any man beg. He was near that point. Who knew he'd actually find a weakness in his life? He prided himself on being strong, being in control.

Just as his thumbs brushed the silk on her bra, Zara jerked back, pushing against his shoulders.

"Wait," she gasped. "We—we can't do this."

Scrambling off his lap, she held her fingers to her lips and closed her eyes. Was she trying to keep that sensation a while longer? Was she still tasting him? Braden waited. She was seriously battling with herself.

"Kissing me like that…" Zara sighed, dropped her arms and looked him in the eyes. "I can't want this, Braden. Don't you understand?"

Relaxed against the back cushion, Braden eyed her, letting her stand above him, giving her the upper hand here. A smart businessman knew when to pull back on the reins in order to get ahead.

"Why are you denying yourself?" he asked. "If the job wasn't a factor, what other excuse would you use?"

He'd hit a mark. Her chin when up a notch, her eyes narrowed. "I'm not making excuses. Nothing would've happened between us at all had you not been stuck here. The next time I would've seen you would've been at the party you're throwing in five weeks for all of your employees."

Braden laughed, shaking his head.

"Now you're laughing at me?" she asked, crossing her arms.

Slowly coming to his feet, Braden crossed to her, not a

bit surprised when she didn't back up, but tipped her head back to continue to glare.

"I'm laughing at the fact you think we wouldn't have seen each other." He tucked a portion of her hair behind her ear, purposely trailing his fingertips down her cheek. "Zara, I would've found reasons to see you. The fact I'm stuck here only provided me the opportunity I needed to seduce you properly."

Silence settled between them seconds before Zara moaned and threw her arms out to her sides as she spun toward the logs and went to stand before them. "Your ego is something I hadn't taken into account. Maybe you've forgotten I just ended a relationship with a man who thought he could control me, thought he was in charge."

Braden stared at her back, deciding to let that jab about Shane roll off him. He knew he wasn't anything like that bastard. She knew it, too.

"I didn't say I wanted a relationship," he corrected. "And I know you well enough after hearing about your childhood to say you don't, either."

Zara whirled around, her dark hair flying about her shoulders. "You think you know me? Because I gave you a small portion of my life?"

"So you do want a relationship?"

"Stop twisting my words."

Why was he purposely getting under her skin? This wasn't part of his plan, but seeing Zara worked up and verbally sparring with her was more of a turn-on than he'd thought. He needed to steer things back to where she felt in control, where she felt as if he was less of a threat. He knew she wanted him, she knew it, too, stubborn woman. But for now he'd let this moment pass. The ultimate goal was still pressing, and he had work to do.

"Why don't you show me those secret rooms?" he asked, pleased when her eyes widened.

"What?"

"Those rooms. They sound cool, and I'd like to see them."

Her eyes darted to the kitten, still sleeping on the bed. "What about him?"

Braden walked over, scooped the kitten into his arm and motioned toward the door. "All set."

"It's cold in the rest of the house."

He quirked a brow. "You want to stay in here and keep dancing around the sexual tension?"

She moved to the door so fast, Braden couldn't stop laughing. Finally he was getting somewhere. He may not be getting her into his bed, but he was seeing these illusive rooms and perhaps he'd find something, anything, to hint at the scrolls. When all was said and done, and this freak blizzard was over, he'd have all his wishes fulfilled.

Seven

Zara gripped the neck of her sweatshirt as she came down the wide staircase. Trying to hold it up just a bit more to ward off the chill helped.

Eerie quiet settled throughout the house. Who knew darkness had a tone? She could hear Braden's breathing, his every step, every brush of his clothing. Every single thing he did made her even more aware of his presence.

What the hell had she been thinking kissing him back like that? Straddling his lap and practically crawling all over his body? Part of her was mortified she'd acted like that, but on the other hand, he'd been right there with her. He'd been the one to instigate every heated occurrence. But no more. If he touched her, she'd have to walk away. Even if she had to step out into the cold hall or bundle up and sleep in a chilly spare bedroom, she couldn't let him kiss her again.

Because she feared the next kiss would lead to clothes falling off and them tumbling into bed.

With the mid-morning sun shining in the windows, enough

light filtered through to make this encounter not seem so intimate.

She led him to the den and eased the door open. "This room was never used by my grandmother. She usually just put books in here. I think I'm the only one who ever came in here, and that was just because I wanted to get to the secret passageway. As a kid, that was the coolest thing in the world to me."

"Did you ever have friends over?" he asked as he stepped into the room with her. "This house would've made the greatest backdrop for hide-and-seek."

"I had a few friends sleep over," she admitted. "Looking back now, I only brought friends here. My parents wouldn't have gone for me inviting them to our house. They were always going to some party, throwing a party or worried about their next travel venture."

Braden loathed her parents. Why bring a child into this world if you didn't intend on caring for said child? He admitted he wanted kids, when the time was right. Having them now would be ridiculous because he didn't have the time to devote to them. And children needed structure, needed family and a bond that provided security.

Zara was a strong woman, but he could see the vulnerability, the brokenness of her childhood still affecting her today.

Stepping around him, she pulled the flashlight from beneath her arm. "Follow me."

One of the built-in bookcases had a small latch. Zara jerked once, twice, and finally the hinges creaked open. As she flicked on the light and angled the beam into the darkness, Braden's heart kicked up. He desperately wanted to find what he came for, though realistically he figured things wouldn't be that easy.

The kitten purred against Braden's chest. He'd never owned a cat, but he loved animals. His sister would be so happy to take in another stray. She was the proverbial cat lady, though she'd never own up to the term. Laney would take this kitten in with a squeal of delight. He could already envision her snuggling the thing.

Braden stepped into the narrow hallway behind Zara. "Don't worry if that door closes behind you. We can't get trapped in here. I guess whoever owned this before my grandmother had a latch installed on both ends of the tunnel. My guess is someone got locked in, so they learned their lesson."

Locked in a dark place with Zara…not too far off the mark of how they'd spent last night. And not a bad predicament to be in.

The kitten perked up at Zara's voice and leaped out of Braden's arms. The little thing moved so fast, Braden worried he'd hurt himself, but when the kitten slid against Zara's ankles, he figured the animal was just fine.

Zara's flashlight held steady on the stray. "What is he doing?"

With a laugh, Braden continued to watch the cat seeking affection. "Looks like he wants to be friends."

"I have enough friends," she muttered and tried to take a step. When she tripped over the kitten, Braden held out a hand to steady her. "Will she stop trying to be an ankle bracelet anytime soon?"

"If you pick her up," Braden stated. "Cats have a tendency to cling to one person. You may be the chosen one."

With the light casting enough of a glow, Braden saw her eyes widen. "You're kidding."

"Nope."

Reluctantly, Zara plucked up the kitten, held her in a bit of an awkward way, but the little fur ball didn't seem to mind. Braden felt it best not to mention the obvious that the cat seemed to love Zara. Best move on to the point of this tour.

"Is this just a hallway?" he asked, trying to look on the

walls for any compartments or doors…hell, anything that would be a clue as to where he could search.

"It opens up into a little room before letting you out into the kitchen."

Zara let out a grunt, the flashlight bobbed and Braden used his free arm to reach out as she tumbled forward. His arm banded around her waist, his hand connected with her breast as he supported her from falling. Thankfully the kitten was snuggled tight, and Zara had a good grip on the oblivious little thing.

When Zara fell back against him, he didn't relinquish his hold. How could he when she felt too perfect with her body flush against his?

"Thanks," she whispered. "I forgot there's a bit of a dip in the floor right there."

"Are you all right?" he asked.

She nodded, her hair tickling the side of his face. "Um… you can let me go."

Her body arched, betraying her words. He couldn't stop himself. His thumb slid back and forth across her breast before he reluctantly released her. He wanted her aching for him, for his touch. If he kept pushing, she'd completely close off, and he'd look like more of a jerk that what he was. But keeping her body on high alert, having her wonder about what would happen next between them would inevitably have her in his bed. Well, technically her bed.

She said nothing as she continued on, slower this time. Finally they came to the room she'd mentioned, which wasn't more than a walk-in closet in size. Her light darted around, and she gasped. His eyes followed the beam and landed on a little yellow chair; a book lay open, cover up to hold the page. Zara turned and handed him the kitten.

"I used to sneak in here to read." She moved forward and picked up the book, flipping it over in her hand. With a laugh, she laid it back down. "This was one of my favorites."

Braden crossed the space and glanced down to the book.

He couldn't see the title, but the embracing couple on the cover told him all he needed to know.

"You read romance as a kid?"

"I was a teenager and curious," she said. Even in the dim light he could see her chin pop up a notch. "Maybe I wanted to know what all that love stuff was about, because when I was sixteen I thought I'd found love. Turns out I found a guy who'd made a bet with his buddies on who would take my virginity."

That entire statement told him more about her than she'd ever willingly reveal. She was bitter, she'd been used. She was raised by parents who were never affectionate, and other than her grandmother, she didn't have anyone she could depend on in her life.

Coming from a large Irish family, Braden had no clue what that felt like. Granted he'd never fallen in love, but he believed it existed. He'd witnessed it firsthand from his parents. While he'd had so many levels of love, Zara had emptiness.

"So you would sneak in here and read dirty books?" he asked.

"They weren't dirty. They were sweet, and now that I know how life really is, I see why they're labeled as fiction."

Yeah. Definitely bitter.

He scanned the rest of the area. There were a few empty shelves along one wall, a door on the other and absolutely nothing of use for him in here. Except for the bundles of information he'd just gathered on Zara.

"That concludes the tour," she stated. "Not as exciting as you thought, right?"

Braden shifted the kitten to his other arm, careful not to wake him. "Oh, I wouldn't say that. I got to cop a feel. I wouldn't call this venture a total loss."

For a second she said nothing, then she reached out and smacked his shoulder. "You're a smart-ass."

Braden wanted to see that smile she offered. He craved

it. Knowing he pulled her from those past thoughts with his snarky comment and put her in the here and now with a laugh was exactly his intent.

"Why don't you show me the other hidden rooms, and I'll see what other smooth moves I can come up with?" he suggested, which earned him a light right to the face. Squinting, he shielded his eyes with his free hand. "All right, I promise to be on my best behavior."

Turning away, Zara pushed open the door to the kitchen. "You'll have to do better than that," she muttered.

Nothing. He'd not found a damn thing that indicated where the scrolls were. He didn't even know if they were all together at this point. At one time there were nine, stored in the infamous trunk that now sat in his office as if to mock him on a daily basis. They could be long gone, but Braden refused to give into that line of thinking, because if they were gone, he had absolutely nowhere to look. They had to be here.

Before they'd headed back up to the bedroom, Zara had stepped out the back door and plucked some cheese and fruit out of the snow. She pulled a loaf of bread from the cabinet and got a few bottles of water.

Now they were sitting in the floor in front of the fire having a gourmet lunch while the kitten roamed around the room. Occasionally he would come back, rub against Zara as if to make sure she was still there, then he'd roam a little more.

"Is he going to pee on my things?" she asked, popping a grape into her mouth.

Braden shrugged. "Maybe, but I found a box in your kitchen and brought it up. Put a towel or something over there and he'll be very happy. Cats love boxes."

"Really?"

Nodding, he tore off another hunk of cheese. "Trust me on this. Granted, he's still a kitten, so he'll stick close to us, or you as the case may be, but once he gets comfortable here, that box will be his new home."

Zara stared as the kitten snuck beneath her bed. "I'd rather he find a new home."

"Aww, now don't be like that with your new best friend."

By the time they'd devoured the assortment, Zara leaned back and stretched her arms high above her head, pulling her sweatshirt up just enough to draw his gaze down to her creamy skin and the slight roll over the band of her pants.

"I wish the electricity would come back on," she stated, dropping her arms, oblivious to the knots in his gut. "I have so much work to do. My laptop may only have a couple hours left of charge."

"What are you working on?"

"I have an event scheduled for a client in four weeks. I need to adjust some things on the spreadsheets and set up another schedule for an event I'm working on for a bridal party." Zara started picking up the garbage and bundling it all in the empty bread sack. "Plenty of work to do with no Wi-Fi, but I'm going to get backed up if I can't get some emails done in the next few days."

Braden listened to her talk of the event scheduled a week before his next party. Zara was efficient, and the passion for her work came through in her tone. She definitely was career driven, but was that all there was to her life? He'd not heard her mention friends and he knew there was no boyfriend. He'd never met a woman who remained so closed off on a personal level.

"Why don't you work?" he suggested. "I'm going to head to my car, charge my phone and turn it on to make some calls."

He needed to check in with Ryker to see if he'd located the missing art piece in London. Then he needed to see if Mac was stuck at the main house, most likely since Mac's flight back to Miami would've been canceled with this weather. Braden would have to call his sister, too, because…

well, he worried about her even though she hated her older brothers fussing over her.

Hopping to her feet, Zara nodded. "Yeah. I need to do something. I'm not one to sit still and do nothing. After I draft my emails I'm grabbing a shower."

"With cold water?" he asked.

She smiled down at him. "I have a gas hot water heater."

His eyes raked over her body, and the very last thing he needed was an image of her naked, soapy and wet body with only a thin door separating them.

Rising to stand before her, he took the trash from her hands and headed for the bedroom door. "I'll be in my car for a while. I'll throw this away on my way out."

He left the room before he would give into temptation and join her in the shower. He needed to let Mac know that, so far, nothing had turned up. This house was damn big, but the secret hidey-holes were literally bare, save for the yellow chair and romance novel.

After throwing away the trash and bundling up, Braden tried to get through the mounds of snow to his car. There was no way to get there without soaking his feet once again because the snow was up to his knees; but he needed to check in, and once the engine warmed up, he could put the heater on full blast.

Most likely his battery would've been fine to talk inside the warm house, but he couldn't risk Zara overhearing his conversations.

Powering up his phone as he slid behind the wheel and tried to ignore his freezing wet feet, Braden watched as seven texts popped up on his screen. Mac had sent two, and the other five were from a frantic Laney asking if he was all right.

He decided to call her first because an angry woman, especially an angry Irish woman who happened to be his sister, was not someone he wanted on his bad side.

"You better be in a ditch with little cell service," she answered.

Braden laughed. "Not quite in a ditch, but I'm stuck at a friend's house and the electricity is out."

"What friend?" she asked, skepticism dripping from her voice.

"You don't know her."

"Her? So you're shacking up and can't return my texts? I had you lying in a ditch bleeding and with the roads closed, and no one saw you and you'd died all alone."

Braden pinched the bridge of his nose and sighed. "I assure you, I'm fine, and I'm not shacking up. To be honest, I'd feel better if I was."

Laney laughed. "Whoever she is, I want to meet her. Someone has you in knots. I like her already."

He wasn't in knots. Really, he was completely knot free and in total control. Just because he'd had to physically remove himself from the house since Zara was going to shower didn't mean he couldn't keep his wits about him.

"I'm at Zara's, okay?" He tried to keep his tone level so she didn't read any more into what he was saying. "I was worried about the roads, so I offered her a ride home. On the way, I got pulled over by a deputy and was informed there's a level two snow emergency on the roads and I was to stay put. So here I am."

"Aww, poor baby. Stuck in a house with a beautiful woman. Don't think I didn't see you two dancing at the party. And great job getting into the house, by the way. If I didn't know better, I'd think you had some weather god on your payroll, as well."

"Yeah, I've turned up nothing. But I'm not done yet. I'm hoping to loosen Zara up enough to get her talking. She may not even realize she knows something useful."

"You sound crankier than usual," Laney mocked. "No scrolls, no sex. I hope you're not acting like a bear toward your hostess."

Cranking the heat up, Braden dropped his head back against the seat. "Now that you know I'm alive and sexually frustrated, can we be done with this call?"

Laney laughed even harder. "Only because I love you am I letting you off the hook. Don't think I won't be discussing this with Mac."

"I've no doubt you'll do so as soon as we hang up," he muttered. "Are you okay? You're home?"

"I'm fine. Carter stayed over last night, which was a good thing because I couldn't get my generator started."

Well, at least Carter was good for one thing, but Braden still considered Laney's boyfriend a prick.

Braden bit his tongue, because if Carter kept treating his sister as if she should be thanking him for a relationship, Braden was going to step in. He'd seen too many times how Carter would act as if he was doing Laney a favor by being with her. He'd even hinted once that she'd be lonely without him. No way in hell would Delaney O'Shea be lonely. She was gorgeous, she was successful and she was a member of the most powerful family in Boston. They were never alone.

He said his goodbyes before he said something that would drive a wedge between them. He'd much rather deal with Carter on his own terms. But, at least the guy had been there during the storm, and his sister was safe. Braden would keep that in mind when he actually confronted him…and that day was coming sooner rather than later.

Braden turned the heat down, now that he was thawed out and his feet weren't so chilled. He quickly dialed Mac, only to get his voice mail.

"Hey, man. I'm stuck at Zara's house, little cell service. I'll call back when I can, but nothing has been found yet."

He disconnected the call and stared back at the house. He wondered just how long he'd have to sit out here to avoid seeing her glowing, damp body from the shower all under the pretense of letting his phone charge. He had plenty of charge to go back in, but he figured he'd let it fill up.

He needed to keep a little distance from her because he was having a hard enough time controlling this ache. He didn't like the unfamiliar need that seemed to grow stronger with each passing moment.

No need in going back in just yet, because he knew without a doubt that once he saw Zara partially nude again, there would be nothing holding him back.

Eight

Feeling refreshed after her shower, Zara found another pair of sweats and fuzzy socks. More armor to fight off the sexy man with seduction on the brain.

Okay, fine. Sex was on her mind, too, but she couldn't let herself settle too far into that part of her brain because, honestly, the sex she'd had with guys in the past had just been…meh. And she wasn't about to risk her job on some mediocre moment. Besides, if they had sex now, what if he was stuck here for two more days? Seriously. Talk about a new level of awkward. Added to that, would he expect a replay? Was he a one-and-done man?

Zara groaned as she took out her frustrations by towel-drying her hair. Why was she overanalyzing this? She wasn't shedding her fleece, no matter what tricky moves he put on her.

Zara hung her towel on the knob of her closet door. No way was she going back out to the bathroom. While the water had been nice and hot, the room itself was an icebox. There was no master bath in this house, but the bathroom was right outside her bedroom door. Still, given she was damp and her hair was still drying, that would make for one cold walk.

Grabbing her brush from the dresser, she took a seat on her bed and crossed her legs as she pulled her hair over her shoulder and started working out the tangles at the bottom.

That kitten darted out from beneath her bed, and Zara just knew that thing was making a litter box out of the space. Once again the bundle of fur slid against Zara's ankles and feet, purring as he went. Even though she'd never had an animal, she honestly didn't mind that it was in her house. She may not have a clue how to care for a pet, but she didn't want the thing outside freezing to death. Okay, and maybe she kind of liked knowing something was looking to her for care and support. She didn't necessarily love it, but she had a kernel of like.

The bedroom door opened as Braden came sliding back in. Immediately he went to the fire and peeled off his wet socks once again. Zara sighed, tapping the brush against her thigh.

"Why don't you go hop in the shower and warm up your feet? And when you're done, I'll give you a pair of my socks. They're small, but they're warm and dry." When he didn't say anything, he merely turned and stared at her, she went on. "Maybe stop going outside. Whatever you need, I can go. I at least have taller boots."

Raking a hand through his hair, Braden strode back out the door. Apparently he was taking her up on the shower. But what had happened in the time he'd walked out until now? He seemed quiet, wouldn't quite look her in the eyes. Something was wrong.

The O'Sheas were mysterious and closed off, so she'd never know. But she didn't want him upset or angry. It was freezing, they were stuck. Oh, yeah, and sexually frustrated. That made for a nice combo.

While he was gone, Zara got an idea and snuck out to the kitchen. Finding exactly what she needed, she raced back up to the bedroom. The shower was still running, so she had time to set up. Apparently he'd found towels and was making himself at home. Granted, all she had were floral specialty soaps, but she'd not exactly prepared for male guests.

Zara moved the chaise back closer to the wall to open up the middle of the floor. She settled down, crossing her legs and had the necessary items in front of her just as Braden came back in...wearing only a towel.

"You've got to be kidding me," she muttered.

Without a word, he crossed the room and laid his clothes out in front of the fire. "Unlike you, I don't have the luxury of throwing on different clothes. I've been wearing these since yesterday morning."

She glanced over and seriously wished she hadn't. Were those...yeah. He was a black boxer brief man. No tighty-whities for this alpha male...and seeing his underwear made it crystal clear he was commando beneath that terry cloth.

Braden cleared his throat, and she realized he'd turned and was staring at her. Great. Way to really hold her ground about not getting intimate when she's caught staring at the man's underwear.

"What's this?" he asked, motioning down to her stash.

She ignored the items she'd brought up from the kitchen and continued to stare up at him as if having a conversation wearing only a towel were perfectly normal.

"So you're going to be like this until your clothes dry?" She motioned with her finger up and down his body.

Clutching one side of the towel over one very muscular, very exposed thigh, Braden shrugged. "I can lose the towel, but I thought you'd be more comfortable like this."

Zara rolled her eyes. The man was proving to be impossible to resist, and she truly didn't know how much longer she could hold out.

"I'm comfortable with your clothes on," she muttered. "Anyway, I thought we could play cards, and since I'm not one to gamble, I brought up pretzel sticks we can use instead."

He quirked a brow. "You play poker?"

Zara laughed. "You didn't know my grandmother. That woman could outwit the best of the best when it came to seven-card stud. She taught me how to play when I was still learning how to write my name."

Braden quirked his brow, then headed over to the chaise and pulled off the blanket she used to sleep with. He wrapped it around his waist and sank to the floor in front of her.

That bare chest with dark hair and just a bit of ink showing over his shoulder held her captive, and she would have to concentrate on this game if she wanted to control her urge to rip that blanket and towel from his deliciously sculpted body.

"Can you play?" she asked, pulling the cards from the box.

Piercing eyes held hers. "I can play whatever game you want."

Of course he could, and he could make everything sound sexual with that low, intense tone that had her stomach doing flips.

When she offered the cards to him to shuffle, he waved a hand. "Ladies first."

Shuffling them with quick, precise movements, Zara finally felt comfortable. Cards was something she could handle, something she could somewhat control. A hobby of hers from long ago, she hadn't played for a while, but she needed the distraction, and there was only so much they could do stuck in this room.

"What's the ante?" he asked, tearing open the bag of pretzels.

"Your choice."

"Ten."

Zara dealt their first hand while he counted out twenty pretzel sticks for each of them. As soon as she laid down the door card, she smiled when his was lower than hers.

"Your bet," she told him.

He smirked. "I'm aware of the rules."

"Just making sure you know you're dealing with a professional."

There. Maybe if she kept throwing verbiage out like that, he wouldn't be so determined to cross territory they could never return from.

Braden raised the bet, but Zara didn't think he had anything worth raising for. She'd call him on his bluff. He had a poker face, that for sure. No doubt he'd used that same straight, stoic look in the business world. As the oldest son of the late Patrick O'Shea, Braden had big shoes to fill, and being the powerful man he was, he'd have no problem at all, Zara knew.

By the time the last card was dealt, Zara was looking at a full house with aces on top. Not the best hand, but still better than whatever he was lying about.

"I'll raise you," she told him, throwing in three more sticks.

When he flipped his cards over, Zara gripped her cards and simply stared. Seriously? She'd dealt him a flush? There hadn't been a gleam in his eye one time during the entire game, and she'd thought he'd been bluffing.

Narrowing her eyes, she tossed her cards down as he raked in his pretzels. The kitten chose that time to dart over and walk right through the cards and the pretzels as if he owned the place. He swatted at a pretzel and kept swatting it until he was moving too close to the logs. There was a screen around the fireplace, more for looks, but she still didn't want the little guy rubbing against it and singeing his fur.

Zara reached out, stretching to grab hold of him and his

pretzel, then deposited him on the other side of her away from the heat.

"I believe it's my deal," Braden stated with a smirk. "Hold tight. We're about to take this to a whole new level."

She tipped her head in a silent question.

"We're playing for answers now," he told her as he reached down, grabbed a pretzel and popped it into his mouth. "Whoever wins the hand can ask the other player anything, and they have to answer."

Still eyeing him skeptically, Zara asked, "Just questions? No touching, no clichéd strip poker?"

Shuffling the cards, he smiled. "I'll touch and strip if you want. Hell, that can even be one of your questions. Up to you, so ask what you want."

Mercy, the man was incorrigible, and she was finding that she loved every second of his quick wit, his flirty side and the fact he made no secret that he wanted her.

Thankfully, she won the next hand with a pair of kings, beating out his jacks. Zara reached to push the cards back in order to shuffle them as she pondered her question.

Staring down at the cards as they shuffled and fell into place, she asked, "If you believe in marriage and family so much, why are you still single?"

That sexy laugh filled the room. "I'm so glad you didn't ask something as boring as my favorite color or movie."

Risking a glance, she looked him in the eye. Okay, fine, her eyes may have lingered a little longer on his bare chest, but they eventually hit his eyes, where she saw amusement staring back at her.

"Well?" she asked, raising her brows as she started dealing.

"Haven't found the right one."

He studied his cards, offering nothing else with his response. Zara gritted her teeth. If he was going to be vague, then so could she when the time came…though she didn't intend to lose.

As she stared at her cards, though, a pit grew in her stomach. Unless she was dealt something spectacular in the next round, she was going to be answering a question, and she was almost afraid to see what he'd come up with.

The second he realized he won, he dropped a question she definitely hadn't expected.

"Why do you choose assholes to date? Because of commitment issues?"

Zara refused to be rattled. "That's two questions, so your round is disqualified."

Just as she reached for the cards, Braden's hand covered hers. As if knowing he was naked beneath that blanket weren't enough to sizzle her mind, his warm touch only added fuel to the proverbial fire.

"I'm not disqualified." Gently squeezing her hand, he turned her palm over and laced their fingers, holding their joined hands up between them. "Tell me why you only date jerks."

"How do you know I date jerks?"

His thumb stroked hers as he spoke, as if the man were trying to put her under a spell. Too late. He'd done that the moment she'd walked into his office months ago. But once he'd held her at the party, once he'd shown a more personal side, she'd turned a corner and she wasn't sure she could ever get back.

"Who did you date before Shane?" he asked.

Zara stared at him for a second before laughing. Damn. That came out sounding nervous. She wasn't nervous. Just because he was holding her hand, looking at her as if he cared and asking about her love life. Why should any of that worry her?

And even as much as all of that worried her, it was the desire, the lust staring back at her that had her stomach in knots.

"You're asking way too many questions," she whispered.

"Your silence tells me all I need to know." Inching closer,

he set the cards between them and kept his eyes locked on to hers. "You don't like commitment because your parents weren't loving or affectionate. You didn't get the attention a child deserves. Now as an adult you're dating jerks because you know you won't get attached. Same reason you haven't unpacked, if I'm guessing right. You can't even commit to this house."

Zara jerked her hand back. "Whatever you're trying to prove, stop. You don't know me well enough to analyze me."

Coming to her feet, she smoothed her hair back from her face. "I'm done playing."

Before she could turn away, Braden slowly rose. That predator look in his eyes as he closed the space between them held her firmly in place. The fact he could be so menacing, so arousing while holding on to a bulky comforter at his waist with one hand proved just how far she'd fallen from her initial mind-set. She was crumbling right at this man's feet.

And the more her resolve deteriorated, the more she wondered, why was she holding back? He'd pegged her perfectly when he said she wasn't looking for any commitment. First, she didn't have time with her business soaking up her life. Second, well, she just didn't want to. She wouldn't have any idea how. Since she'd signed on with the O'Sheas, she'd seen the close-knit family they were. A piece of her wondered what a connection that strong would be like. Leaning on someone else, expecting support was too much of a risk. But she didn't need a man.

He'd made it clear he didn't want a commitment, though. Once the roads cleared he'd be gone, and whatever happened here would stay right here. Braden wasn't one to talk, of that she was sure. Her reputation wouldn't be tarnished, she wouldn't be known as the woman who slept with her clients or her boss. Honestly, what was holding her back?

From the look in Braden's eyes, he wasn't looking for a walk down the aisle…just a walk to the bed.

Nine

Braden didn't know what changed, but the look of determination and stubbornness was wiped clean. Now Zara stared back at him with passion blazing in those striking eyes. She didn't step forward to meet him, but she no longer looked as if she wanted to flee the room.

As he stood within touching distance, Braden took in the rapid pulse at the base of her throat, her shallow breathing and wide eyes. She wasn't thinking how angry she was now.

"You're not running," he muttered, delighting in the fact she tipped her head up to look at him instead of backing up. Braden reached out, tucking her hair behind her ear and sliding his fingertip along her jawline. "Why is that, Zara?"

"Because this is my house, and I'm not afraid of you."

For such a petite woman, he was impressed. He intimidated men twice her size, yet this woman wasn't backing down. He admired her—more than he should, because all he wanted from her on a personal level was right here and right now. The scroll business had no place in this bedroom.

"Or maybe you're finally giving in," he stated, raking his finger over her bottom lip. "Maybe you see that we're both adults, we're stuck here together and this attraction isn't going away."

Her chin tipped up a notch. "Maybe I am."

Braden smiled at her bold statement. How could he not find her charming and sexy and confident all rolled into one perfect package?

Wait. Perfect? No. Nobody was perfect, but she was perfect for him right at this moment.

In all of his thirty-five years, Braden had been taught to take chances to get what he wanted. There was no greater time to test that theory than right now.

Braden dropped the comforter and the towel. Both fell to his feet without a sound. The light coming through the plantation shutters gave enough for her to see that he was completely ready for her.

"You have all the control now," he told her. "Whatever you want to do from this point on is your call. You can humiliate me and reject me, you can quit your job and claim I'm just like the jerks you dated, or you can start stripping out of those clothes and join me by the fire so I can show you exactly how much I want you."

He didn't wait on her response. Braden stepped out of the mess of comforter and tugged the blanket toward the fireplace. As he spread it out, he thought for sure he heard her shifting behind him. She wouldn't deny him or herself. That longing look in her eyes, the way she was speechless and flushed were all telling signs of what she was afraid to admit aloud.

He stilled when her hand settled on his shoulder blade. Slowly, as if to drive him completely out of his mind, she started trailing her fingers over his bare skin. She was tracing his ink, and he wasn't about to turn around and stop her no matter how much he wanted to see her, touch her. He meant it when he'd told her she was in control.

Even though he only wanted something physical from Zara, he still wasn't about to prove to her that he was like the other men she wasted time with. He would put her needs first, let her know she mattered here and what was about to happen didn't have to be ugly.

"Why did you get this?" she asked as she continued to trace the pattern. "I always wonder why people choose certain images to mark their skin for life."

On this he could at least tell her the truth. "It's a symbol that has deep meaning to my family. It dates back to the sixteenth century."

"It's beautiful," she whispered.

He couldn't wait another second. Braden turned, causing her hand to fall away, but the loss of her touch was made up for with the sight of her standing before him completely bare, completely giving and completely trusting.

"We need to set some rules," she told him.

Braden snaked an arm out around her waist and pulled her flush against his body. From chest to knee they touched, and there was no way in hell he was going to start in on some ridiculous conversation now.

"To hell with the rules."

He crushed her mouth beneath his. Zara stiffened for a second. Then, as if she couldn't deny herself anymore, she wrapped her arms around him and returned the kiss. Her passion came alive, bursting on to the scene in ways he hadn't experienced before.

She matched his desire, raising the bar to a level all her own, and Braden was the one who was nearly brought to his knees. He allowed his hands to roam over her, wanting to memorize the feel of her body, wanting her to get used to his touch because he planned on doing a whole lot more.

Braden eased back from the kiss, ignoring her protested groan which turned into a moan when his mouth traveled down the column of her throat and continued lower.

She gripped his hair as he palmed her breasts. Arching

her back, she silently offered herself up to him. Braden's lips covered her breast as he lowered her to the floor. He couldn't get enough of her, not her gasps, not her kisses, not her touch. He wanted it all, and willpower and trying to hold back were going to be a struggle.

"Do you have protection?" she asked.

Braden froze. Considering he'd only come here in his party attire, he hadn't planned on getting lucky that night. Damn it.

A smile spread across her face. "Go to my nightstand."

Thankful she was prepared, Braden made a mad dash to the drawer and found what he needed. Also thankfully, the cat stayed out of sight.

By the time he'd stepped back to the comforter, Zara was practically on display. Her arms on either side of her head, hair fanning out all around her. But it was those eyes that watched him so cautiously that made something twist in his gut. She may be trusting him with her body, but she was still not letting him in.

That fact should have given him a sense of relief, considering he was technically using her, but it didn't. He didn't want to just be some prick who proved to her that all guys were jerks.

But when she reached her arms out to him in a silent invitation to join her, there was no way in hell he could deny her or himself. Consequences be damned. Yes, this started with the scrolls, but the moment she'd walked into his office he'd wanted her, and he refused to feel guilty now. Allowing feelings to override what he was literally aching for would just leave a void that only Zara could fill.

Braden reached for her hand and settled down beside her, propping himself up on one elbow. While he wanted to devour her all at once, he also wanted to take his time, because this was a one-time thing and he wanted to savor every single second.

Trailing his hand up and down her abdomen, watch-

ing her muscles contract beneath his touch and hearing her
swift intake of breath, had him appreciating the fact he was
practicing that self-control now. He had a limited supply of
it and was using it all up on her, on this moment.

Braden watched her, studied her. He wanted to know
what she liked, what she responded to. The moment his
hand started trailing down her stomach, her lids fluttered
closed, her legs shifted in response and he was damn near
crawling out of his skin.

As his fingers found her most intimate spot, he captured
her lips, swallowing her moan. Zara's arms wrapped around
his neck, her hands sliding up into his hair, holding him
still…as if he would be anywhere else.

Braden eased back, enough to get protection in place,
before he settled between her legs.

"Don't look away," he commanded. "Your eyes are only
for me."

Why the hell did he want her to be so focused on him?
Why did he have that overwhelming primal feeling to keep
her all to himself?

Because he was selfish. Plain and simple and for right
now, Zara was his. He wanted to leave an imprint in her
mind of this moment and have her compare every single
man to him. He wanted to ruin her for others…and if he
thought too much about that, he would scare the hell out
of himself.

Braden pushed all other thoughts aside as he joined their
bodies. When her eyes closed, he shifted to his elbows,
using his hands to frame her face as his lips hovered over
hers.

"Only me, Zara."

When he started to move, she held on to his shoulders,
keeping her gaze on his. "Braden," she whispered.

Hearing his name on her lips as he filled her only exac-
erbated this unwanted emotional ache.

The second her body started pumping against his, her

face flushed, and Braden slid his mouth over hers, pushing her even further. Her fingertips dug into his shoulders as her body tensed. Braden lifted his head, wanting to watch her as she peaked. With Zara's head thrown back, a sheen of sweat covering her face and neck, Braden couldn't resist gliding his lips over her heated skin as she came undone around him. As he gripped her hips and tasted the saltiness of her skin, his own body started to rise.

Her trembling slowed, and Braden rested his forehead against hers. "Zara," he whispered, wanting her name to be the one he cried out, needing her to know he was fully aware of the woman he was with, that she mattered.

Before he could delve into that too much, his control broke. Braden covered her lips with his, wanting to join them in all possible ways. Her tongue met his as he shattered. Wave after wave washed over him, leaving only one thought, one thing that mattered at that moment…and it wasn't his family or the scrolls.

It was Zara.

Zara didn't do regrets, and there was no way she was going to start now. How could she when her body had lit up and was still tingling? Was tingle even the proper verb? She couldn't pinpoint what her body was doing, but the thrill that kept pulsing through her had everything to do with the man whose body still covered hers. Those long, lean legs rubbed against hers, the coarseness of his hair tickling her, sending new sensations throughout.

Part of her wanted to get out from under him, to get dressed and go on like nothing happened. He was her boss, for crying out loud, and she'd been so clichéd as to sleep with him.

But the other part, the part of her that was still lit up with passion, wanted to lie just like this wearing nothing but the weight of a powerful man.

"I can hear you thinking." Braden's warm breath tickled her ear. He eased up, propping himself on his elbows on either side of her face. "Maybe you need a replay so you can relax."

There was no way she could replay anything that just happened because then she'd want more. She'd want him. Sex was one thing, but wants were an entirely different matter she couldn't afford right now...and not with this man.

Zara pushed on his shoulders and slid out from under him. "No replays," she told him as she gathered her clothes. She tried like hell to not think about the fact she was walking around naked in front of her boss, but after what they'd just done...

"Already running, Zara?"

She risked a glance over and wished she hadn't. With a wrist dangling over one bent knee and his other hand holding is body upright, Braden's intense gaze pinned her in place. She clutched her sweats to her chest as if she could use them as some sort of defense against feelings. Damn emotional womanly feelings. Why did this have to be the man to stir something within her?

"I'm not running," she said. "I'm getting dressed and checking on the cat that's probably peed all over my floor."

"The cat is fine, and there's no rush to get dressed." He came to his feet and crossed the space between them. Just like he had before they'd gotten intimate. Only this time, Zara backed up.

"Braden." She held up a hand, thankful when he stopped. "I don't regret what just happened, it was amazing, but we can't do that again."

"If you're going to pull the whole boss/employer card, we're past that." His kissable mouth quirked.

"Yes, we are," she agreed. "But we're done. Nothing more can come of this."

There. She'd had a fling, she wasn't having regrets and now they could move on.

Crossing his arms over his broad chest as if he hadn't

a care in the world, Braden shrugged. "I'd had the same thought, but then I decided that wasn't right. Why should we deny ourselves what brings us pleasure?"

Zara listened to him, processed the justification, but in the end, she knew she'd get hurt because Braden was the type of man she could fall for…if she would ever let herself fall. One and done was the only way she could justify this encounter.

"It's best if we stop here and try to live with each other until you are able to leave."

The muscle ticked in his jaw, and Zara wanted to take back her words, ignore all the warning bells going off in her head and wrap her arms around him and have him give her that replay he'd suggested.

"I'll do what you want, Zara." He stepped closer, so close she could see the flecks of black in his deep brown eyes. "I'll honor your wishes, but that doesn't mean I'll stop trying to convince you that we were good together, and now that we know all about each other's bodies, we could be even better."

Those promising words delivered by a low, sexy tone did not help her cause. She clutched her clothes and watched as he wrapped up in that damn comforter again. He picked his cell up from the accent table and threw her a smile.

"I'm going to call the sheriff's department and see when travel is expected to resume."

And he walked out the door. Now the cat darted from beneath the bed and slid across the hardwood, bumping into her feet, but Zara remained frozen in place, still naked, still holding on to her clothes.

Still wanting him just as much, if not more than she had before they were intimate.

What had she gotten herself into? Because now she had a sense of what it meant to belong, just an inkling of how powerful a bond with someone else could be.

Ten

"**Y**ou've got to be missing something," Mac stated.

Yeah, common sense.

"I've searched the hidden areas," Braden explained for the third time. But Mac was understandably frustrated, as was Braden.

He felt utterly foolish with this damn comforter as he stood at the base of the steps. He watched the landing for any sign of Zara, but she was most likely still up in her room replaying everything that had just happened between them.

"I'm telling you, if they're here, they're well hidden."

Mac's sigh carried through the phone. "Maybe her grandmother sold some things before she died. Hell, I don't know. Put more pressure on Zara. We need this, Braden."

Yeah, like he wasn't aware of that. "I'm doing what I can. Pressuring Zara will only make red flags go up."

"Is she suspicious of you?"

"No."

How could she be? He'd snooped either in plain sight of

her or when she'd been sleeping. And the fact that he still needed to do more searching and his time was running out only irritated him even more because, while he wanted to find the scrolls, he wanted to go back upstairs and talk Zara into spending the entire day in bed.

"Damn," Mac muttered. "Tell me you're not actually falling for this woman."

Braden gripped the wad of comforter and sank down on to the bottom step. "I'm not."

"You don't sound convincing."

Braden gritted his teeth. "I'm not trying to convince you, so drop it."

"Keep me posted when you can," Mac said. "I changed my flight to next week. Obviously with the weather I'm not getting back to Miami anytime soon. And Ryker is stuck in London. He had a slight run-in with the cops."

Braden rubbed his forehead and cracked his neck. "Define a slight run-in."

"No charges were filed and the art is now in our possession. The rest of the details can wait."

"There will be no backlash on us?"

"It's taken care of," Mac promised.

At least one thing was going their way for now, but Braden wasn't giving up on his hunt for the scrolls. And he wasn't giving up on this need that only Zara could fill. He'd thought for sure she would be out of his system, but she was in deeper than ever.

"I'll text you if I find out anything," he told Mac. "Hopefully I'll be home by tomorrow."

"Don't come back without the scrolls."

Braden disconnected the call just as he heard Zara behind him. Jerking to his feet, he replayed the conversation he'd just had with Mac and was positive he hadn't said anything to give himself away.

She descended the stairs and barely threw him a glance.

"I'm just grabbing a notebook from the office. Do you want me to take any food back up?"

She continued by him without even stopping. So she wanted to put this awkward wedge between them? He could work with that. He could handle anything she wanted to throw his way.

"I'm fine. I'm going to head up and check on my clothes."

He didn't wait for her to turn around or reply. Shuffling back upstairs, Braden was eager to get out of this makeshift skirt because he was going to have to revoke his man card if he didn't get back into pants soon.

Once he was dressed, they needed to talk. Zara was closing back in on herself, and there was no way he was going to let that happen. He may not be the man in her life, but he wasn't about to let her think that her feelings, her emotions meant nothing. Whatever pricks had taken her to bed in the past had let her think less of herself. Most likely they'd been selfish, too, and Braden refused to be lumped with those guys.

Regardless of what happened after he left this house, he wanted Zara to know her self-worth.

Braden placed the comforter back on the bed, smoothing out the edges, and pulled on his boxer briefs. They were damp but better than nothing. His pants were still wet, so he turned them and placed them even closer to the fire.

He'd called one of his contacts at the sheriff's department before calling his brother. Apparently the road crews were working around the clock, but with the layer of ice beneath the snow, there wasn't much chance of getting out within the next two days because the temperatures were still hovering below zero.

Perfect opportunity for him to keep up his search and prove to Zara that they were good together in bed. He wasn't asking for her hand in marriage; he just wanted to enjoy her company while he was here, and who knew, maybe after he left.

He chuckled at the fact he was strutting around her room in his underwear. She may not find the matter funny at all, but it was. Braden was snooping like Ryker and seducing like Mac…a position he never thought he'd find himself in as head of the family.

As he took a seat on the bed and sent off a quick text to Ryker, the cat rubbed against Braden's ankle. Reaching down, Braden lifted the fur ball on to the bed and started stroking his back.

The kitten let out a soft purr and flopped over on to his back. Braden continued to show affection, and his mind started drifting. He had no clue what he expected from Zara. Somewhere along the way he'd gone from wanting to use her, to wanting the hell out of her, to wondering more about her and wanting to uncover those complex layers she kept so guarded.

But he couldn't let himself get too involved. He wasn't ready to start looking for "the one." What he felt for Zara had nothing to do with forever and everything to do with right now. When she'd actually let go, let him close, he'd seen a woman with pent-up passion. All of that desire she kept locked away was a shame. She deserved to be…

What? Used? Because that's where he was right at this point. He was using her and justifying it by saying they had a physical connection. But damn it, he'd never denied himself anything before and he wasn't about to start now. He still wanted Zara, but she deserved more than a man who wanted her in bed and to technically steal from her.

The bedroom door swung open, and Zara came in juggling an oversize box. Braden leaped off the bed and crossed the room, taking the box from her hold.

"Let me have it," he said when she hesitated to let go. "You carried this up the steps when I could've done it." Once he set the box down at the end of the bed, he turned back to Zara. "You should've asked for help."

Her eyes took in his body, and he couldn't help the instant male reaction. "Zara—"

Those heavy-lidded eyes snapped up to his. "You have got to put clothes on."

"If I thought you really wanted me to, if you weren't just looking at me like you wanted me again, I would throw on those damp things and put you at ease."

She stared for a moment before a bubble of laughter escaped her. "At ease? That's the last thing you're trying to do here."

When she tried to step around him, Braden moved to block her. His hands gripped her shoulders, and he tipped his head down to look her in the eye.

"You're even more withdrawn than you were before we slept together. Care to tell me what's going through your mind?"

Those bright eyes darted to his, then to the bed where the kitten lay stretched out. "I'm just trying to keep this from getting too awkward. Okay? We need to go back to boss/employee."

Braden released her, took a step back and nodded. "That doesn't mean I wouldn't have helped you with the box."

For now he let the subject drop, but he wasn't leaving anytime soon, and no doubt they'd revisit their status again. Whether he had clothes on or not, she was strung so damn tight no matter how he looked. And now that he'd had her in every way, he wanted her again. So much for getting her out of his system.

"What's in the box? I thought you were going down for a notebook."

She maneuvered around him and pulled on the folded flaps until they sprang open with a puff of dust. Coughing and waving her hand in front of her face, Zara turned to face him. "I've been putting off going through some of my grandmother's things. They've been boxed up for a while. Long before her death, she wanted to downsize, so she started packing things away and putting them in a storage unit. I only had them brought back so I didn't have to keep paying the unit fee. This house is more than big enough to hold all her things. I have no clue what all she's put away and I've been too busy to look through them. I figure now would be a good time since I'm stuck here. Maybe after I go through her stuff, I will start unpacking my own."

Braden heard every word, but he focused on the fact her grandmother had boxes packed away, and now they were back in the house. These boxes wouldn't have been in here during the search Ryker did. Did he dare hope he could uncover the scrolls that were somewhere so simple as packed away in a box?

Braden leaned forward, glancing into the box. "I can get the other boxes and bring them up here for you."

Zara knelt down on her knees and started sorting through the newspaper-wrapped goods. "They're actually down in the basement. And let me just say, if you think the first floor is cold, that basement is frigid."

Braden laughed, more out of his own anxiety and nerves over the potential in the basement, but Zara relaxed at his actions. "Tell you what, I'll go down and bring up more. You start going through this box."

She crossed her arms and rubbed them, most likely trying to get rid of the chill from being downstairs. "I hate to have you do that. I can get them later."

No way in hell was he backing down on this, not when everything his family had wanted could be right within his reach. "Which boxes am I looking for? Are they all needing to come up?"

"Now who's stubborn?" she asked, lifting her brows and smiling. "Fine, you can get them. They're on the far wall. I believe there's about five more. All the others are mine, but they're under the steps."

Braden nodded and barely resisted the urge to rush out

the door. Then he remembered he was wearing only his underwear.

Zara glanced up at him; her gaze roaming over his body only heated him even more, making him want to put those boxes on hold and give into that look of desire staring back at him.

"You're going to freeze your important parts off if you don't put something on."

His inflated ego took control as Braden propped his hands on his hips and grinned down at her. "Worried about my parts?"

"You'll be needing them again."

He continued to stare until her face flushed.

"With someone else, I mean. Not with me," she quickly added. "I just meant… Wipe that smug look off your face and put your damn pants on."

Laughing, Braden went over to check, and sure enough his pants were nearly dry except for the damp waistband. He could handle that. After dressing, he glanced at the items she was pulling out of the current box. So far just a few old pieces of pottery. Not the scrolls.

Maybe they were hidden in the basement. Maybe they were in the boxes he was about to bring up…not before he searched through them, though.

And if that was the case, if he did indeed find the centuries old treasures, he could finally give back to his family what they'd been searching for.

He could also pursue Zara with his full concentration, because the way she'd been looking at him moments ago— yeah, she wasn't over whatever they'd started, and he'd barely scratched the surface of all he wanted to do with her.

As soon as Braden was out the door, Zara blew out a breath. Mercy, but that man strutting around in his black boxer briefs was a sight to behold. He could easily put models to shame with that broad chest, those lean hips and those muscles…she'd felt every single one of them, and if she were totally honest, she wanted to again.

No matter what she told herself, no matter the common sense that normally kept her grounded, all she could think of was how amazing Braden would be if they actually took advantage of this situation and stayed in bed exploring each other.

But what would happen once the roads cleared and Braden went home? She'd work his party in a few weeks, and they'd be professional…sure. How could she watch him from across the room, knowing full well what an attentive lover he was while she should be focusing on the hors d'oeuvres and making sure the Riesling fountain kept flowing?

Zara closed her eyes and willed herself to gain some sort of control over her emotions before he came back. She needed to concentrate on sorting through these boxes. Who knew, with all of the antiques and treasures her grandmother hung on to, maybe Braden would be interested in some pieces for the auction house.

There. When he came back, they would focus on work and not the fact they were going to spend another night together. Granted, it didn't matter whether it was night or not—they'd had sex in the middle of the day.

Day sex. That was new for Zara. Not that she had some big grand arsenal of partners and experiences, but she'd always been a night, dark room, vanilla type. Maybe that's why she wanted to explore more with Braden. He'd awakened something in her, and she wasn't sure she could ignore it now. What else could he show her? Braden O'Shea was a full-body experience, that was for sure.

Zara shook her head, hoping to clear some of these crazy thoughts. She reached into the box and pulled out another paper-covered object. As she unwrapped the oblong container, she wondered what could be in this tube she'd never seen before.

Zara set the paper to the side and concentrated on the silver caps on each end. She pulled on one, then the other. Either they didn't open or they were seriously stuck. Whatever was in there was extremely light. She shook the tube, but nothing rattled.

"I forgot a flash—"

Zara turned toward the door just as Braden's eyes zeroed in on the container she held.

"Don't touch that." One second he was by the door, the next he was kneeling at her side, taking the tube from her hands. "Did you look inside?"

Stunned at his reaction, Zara stared at him and shook her head. "The caps are stuck."

He ran his hands over the outer shell as if he was dealing with the most precious of gems. She'd never seen this side of him. She could sit here completely naked, and he'd not even notice she was in the room. For a man who was hell-bent on seduction and succeeding rather well at it, he was completely focused on this container.

Which made her wonder, what the hell was in that tube, and why was he so mesmerized with it?

Eleven

Braden had no idea if he was actually holding one of the coveted scrolls. All he knew was he wanted to get inside this tube now, but he didn't want to break anything or cause damage. This container was old, not as old as the scrolls themselves, but he had no idea what they would be stored in at this point. And with the way the caps were so secured, they'd obviously been in place a while. Which only added to that layer of hope.

Holding on to the tube, he glanced toward the box.

"Anymore like this in there?"

Zara reached in but only brought out a wrapped vase that was rather valuable with familiar etching. He'd worry about the other treasures later, because if he was truly holding a scroll that dated back to the time of Shakespeare, that meant the others could be in the boxes in the basement.

Braden lifted the tube and pulled gently on one of the caps again. It was sealed good and tight. While he was maneuvering as cautiously as he could, Zara got up and went out the door. He had no clue where she was going or what she was doing; all he knew was he needed to get in this compartment right now.

Both ends were good and stuck, and all he could think of was how fast he could search the other boxes for more tubes and how quick he could get Ryker to look into this. Something akin to elation flooded him as he gripped this container. Could he have found what his father hadn't been able to? Could he finally bring these back to the O'Shea family? As head of the family, he felt the pressure to do what his father hadn't been able to.

His family prided themselves on their business, yet they hadn't been able to relocate their own inheritance after decades of trying. All the frustration and anger and stomps on their pride may finally be coming to an end.

They'd hunted down so many false leads over the years, but now Braden wanted to focus on the last point of origin. This house held the answers; he just had to know where to look, and he may have struck gold.

Braden held on to the tube and stepped into the cool hallway. Where had she gone? He called her name, waiting to hear her reply. Silence greeted him, but then she appeared at the top of the stairs with the kitten beneath her arm. Even though the little guy nestled against her, Zara still didn't look comfortable with her new friend.

Maybe Laney shouldn't get this kitten, after all. Perhaps Zara needed this bonding experience to get her to open up, to not be afraid of any type of a relationship. Animals had that effect on people.

"What were you doing?" he asked.

"You left the door open, and he darted out." She stopped before him and held the cat out to his chest. "You were too preoccupied with whatever is in that cylinder and didn't see him run out the door."

Braden winced at the harshness of her tone and knew he needed to come up with a quick cover so she didn't get too suspicious. He'd never expected her to be around when he found something of interest, so holding back his emotions hadn't crossed his mind.

"Sorry. Occupational hazard. Old treasures get the best of me."

She quirked a brow as if she wanted to argue, but didn't say a word as she brushed by him and went into the bedroom. Braden followed, closing the door and placing the cat back down on the rug. He immediately went to the paper and packaging beside the box and started swatting and playing.

"Did you get that open?" she asked, pointing to the tube.

"No." He needed to be careful how he approached this. The last thing he needed was for Zara to distrust him. "I'd like to have Ryker look, if you don't mind."

She shifted slightly, and her brows drew in. "Ryker is a friend of yours?"

"He's more than a friend." How did he even explain Ryker? Ryker was more of an experience than a person. The man was a force to be reckoned with. He butted heads with Braden more often than not, but the man was loyal to a fault. "If anyone can get into this and not do any damage to the container, it would be him."

Zara stared at him before her eyes darted to the tube in his hand. "What do you think is in there that's so important? It felt empty to me."

A paper wouldn't weigh much, and if this was indeed one of his family's scrolls, Braden wanted it to be opened without Zara present. Waiting to get this to Ryker would be a true test of self-control, but Braden had come this far; he wasn't about to destroy the tube by breaking it to get in.

"Old documents could be hidden," he told her. "You never know what you can find stored away. We've uncovered some pretty important things from all over the world when people thought containers were empty."

"I don't care if you take it to look in, but you'll let me know what's inside, right?"

"Of course." He refused to feel guilty about lying to her face. If the scroll was indeed inside, it would be of no use to her.

Well, she could sell it for a ridiculous amount of money, but the worth to the O'Sheas was invaluable. Braden was so hyped up on adrenaline with the possibilities, he could hardly stand still. He needed to contact Mac.

Braden set the tube on the side table by the door and pulled his cell from his pocket. He quickly shot Mac a text that he'd found an old tube, but couldn't confirm the contents.

"I'm going to head back downstairs." Braden glanced around the room, searching for the flashlight. "I'll get those other boxes."

"I'd like to talk to you about selling some pieces." Zara had taken a seat back on the floor and was wrapping items back up and placing them in the box. "I'm not sure how that works or even if you'd be interested for the auction house, but…"

She was back to being nervous. And to be honest, he was a bit nervous, too, because he had no clue how to proceed from here. He'd never been in this position before. Sex with women was something he'd always enjoyed, yet he'd never gotten emotionally attached. Casual relationships worked fine, but in his line of work, getting too close to someone was difficult. One day he wanted a family, but he truly had to find the right woman who would fit into his life…first he had to steer the business into a bit more legit territory.

But he kept feeling this pull toward Zara, a pull he'd not experienced with any other woman.

So why Zara? Why now? Did it all stem from needing to gain trust? He'd never had to rely on someone like this before. He'd never placed himself at the mercy of needing anyone; he purposely didn't leave himself vulnerable.

"I can look through whatever you want," he replied. "If

we agree on certain items, you have a few options we can go over."

She nodded, and the tension in her shoulders seemed to lessen as her body relaxed. "Good. I hate getting rid of her things, but at the same time, I can't keep everything."

Braden knew that ache, that need to hang on to possessions of lost loved ones. He'd still not gone through his father's belongings and he wasn't sure when he'd be ready to face that daunting task. Mac and Laney weren't ready, either. Thankfully, they were all there for each other because family meant everything to the O'Sheas. They clung to each other in times of trial. Ryker may be a hard-ass, but the man was just as much family as any blood relative, and he'd grieved right along with the rest of them after Patrick's death.

"Let me get those boxes, and we can spend the day looking through them and deciding where to go from there." When she smiled up at him, Braden had to ignore that punch of lust to the gut. She was trusting him...and he was betraying her. "Be right back."

Before he could be swept under by those mesmerizing eyes, he snatched the flashlight off the bed and headed back to the basement. Right now he needed to focus on what they would uncover, on how this could possibly end his family's hunt for what was rightfully theirs. He couldn't think how Zara was slowly getting under his skin, how she was softening toward him and opening and driving him out of his ever-loving mind.

Because if he started letting Zara have control over his mind, she'd start silently taking control over other aspects of his life. And he couldn't afford to be sidetracked right now. Not when he was so close to getting everything he'd ever wanted.

Zara ran her fingers over the pewter picture frame. "I remember this picture sitting by her bed."

The black-and-white photo of a young, newly married couple stared back at her. Her grandparents on their wedding day, standing outside the courthouse because they hadn't wanted to wait for a big ceremony in a church. They'd fallen in love and hadn't wanted to spend another minute apart.

Tears pricked Zara's eyes. "Sorry," she said, smiling as she blinked back the moisture. "I get a little sentimental when it comes to my gram."

Sitting with his back against the headboard on the bed, Braden stretched his legs out as he stared down at her. Zara sat on the floor, legs crossed, looking through yet another box. Every now and then she'd pass a piece up to him to get his opinion on selling, but now she'd found a box of photos.

Braden extended his hand toward the picture, so Zara passed it over. "My grandfather was the love of her life. She never quite got over his death, even though she lived without him for nearly twenty years."

Braden studied the picture, then glanced back down to her. "And you still don't believe in true love?"

Zara rolled her eyes and swiped at the tear that escaped. "I believe my grandparents found it, but my parents sure as hell didn't. They were more concerned with making money and traveling than they were with love or family."

Propping the photo up on the nightstand, Braden adjusted it so it faced at just the right angle. "Love exists, Zara. If you want it, you just have to wait until it finds you."

Zara had always been sure that if she ever heard a man mention love, she'd run fast and far because he only wanted something from her.

This wasn't like any scenario she'd planned in her mind. For one thing, Braden wasn't professing his love by any means. Second, even if he was, he couldn't use her for anything. He was an O'Shea. One of the most powerful families in Boston and known around the world. There was nothing he could gain from getting involved with her.

"You're unlike any man I've ever met," she told him, trying not to think too hard about how amazing he looked taking up so much space in her bed. "I don't know many men who are so open at discussing love and relationships, let alone a man who claims he's wanting a wife and marriage."

"Family is everything to me. I want kids and a wife." He shrugged as if the explanation were so simple and not to be questioned. "When I find the woman for me, I'll do anything in my power to keep her safe and to make sure that she knows she's loved at all times. My woman will never question where I stand."

The more he spoke, the more stern he became. Zara knew without a doubt that he believed love existed, and she also believed there would be one woman who would come along, capture his attention and live happily ever after because she truly didn't think Braden failed at anything he set his mind to.

"Well, there is one lucky lady in your future."

Zara pushed off the floor and scooted the box to the wall. Turning, she scanned the other unopened boxes and finally decided on one that wasn't marked. Grabbing it, she took a seat at the foot of the bed on the opposite side. She faced Braden and pulled the lid off the box. Breath caught in her throat as she reached in and ran her hand over the silky yarn. Slowly, she pulled the crochet item from the box.

Zara smiled as she laid the bright red throw across her lap. "I remember when she made this," Zara murmured, running her fingers across the tight weave. "She'd asked me what color she should make, and I told her red. I remember thinking she was such a lively woman, brown or gray wouldn't do. When she was finished, she held it up and wrapped it around my shoulders. I was sitting on the couch doing homework."

Zara pulled the piece up to her face and inhaled. That familiar vanilla scent she associated with her grandmother hit her hard. A vice gripped her heart as she willed back the emotions. The bed dipped just slightly before a hand settled on her bent knee.

"It's hard losing someone you love, someone you've depended on."

His soft words washed over her, offering comfort when she really had no one else. How pathetic had her life become that she slept with her boss and had no close friends to turn to for support? Had she seriously alienated herself because she'd been so engrossed with work?

No, she could admit the truth to herself. Commitment terrified her. Being dependent on someone, knowing they could leave at any moment and take her heart with them had her refusing to allow herself to open up to anyone. She didn't care if she was lonely. She'd rather be alone than broken.

Dropping her hands back into her lap, Zara lifted her gaze to Braden. He'd been so passionate earlier, so attentive to her needs sexually. But now he looked at her with care and compassion, and she truly had no idea what to think of him or even how to act. He could make her want things... things she'd never wanted before.

"This is all so strange to me," she admitted. "Before I started working for you, I'd heard rumors of how badass you were. Then I saw it firsthand when you threw Shane out of the party. Then you take in a kitten, snuggle with it, for crying out loud, and you look as if you want to hug me, and not for anything sexually related. I'm not sure which Braden I'll see from moment to moment."

His eyes hardened, his jaw clenched, but he didn't remove his hand. "The badass Braden trumps the nice one. I'm not a nice guy, Zara. I'm selfish, and I take what I want when I want it."

Shivers raced through her. He'd taken exactly what he'd wanted where she was concerned...not that she was complaining.

Zara covered his hand. "You're a nice guy when it counts. You'll never convince me otherwise."

He looked as if he wanted to say more, but he eased back and slid off the other side of the bed. She watched as he surveyed the boxes littering her bedroom.

"So you only have one more to go through," he stated as he headed for the largest box he'd brought up from the basement. She knew he was changing the subject, which had been her tactic all along. "It was heavy, so you may want to come over here to look through it, or I can pull out items and bring them to you."

Zara swung her legs off the bed and headed toward the box. "Let's see what this one has, and then we can discuss what I'll be selling."

Because the tender moment that had just happened couldn't happen again—clearly it had left them both shaken. She needed to keep her wits about her and remember that she was still his employee, she was still needing this reputable job to keep her business going in the right direction, and she needed to forget how this man made her body tingle in ways she never knew possible…and how he was acting as if he truly cared.

Twelve

They'd had a gourmet dinner of crackers, lunch meat, cheese and some fruit. Zara had grabbed a bottle of wine from the cellar, and now she sat on the chaise, legs stretched before her, her back against the side arm as she twirled the stem of her wineglass.

The poor kitten was going stir-crazy, so Zara had taken him for a walk through the house. Braden was already seeing their bond form, but he wasn't about to call her on it. She'd realize soon enough.

As the kitten pounced on her shoe, Zara watched him. "Should we give him a name or something?"

"Does this mean you're keeping him?"

Zara threw Braden a look. "I didn't say that. I just feel like he should be called something other than *Cat*."

Braden laughed. "Admit it, you like him."

"I'll call him Jack while he's here," she decided.

"Jack?"

Zara nodded. "Jack Frost."

Braden smiled at the perfect name. "Jack it is."

Zara didn't want to make commitments, didn't want to have to worry about anyone else but herself, and Braden understood her reasons. But at some point she'd have to put herself out there, even if it was with a cat. She was going to be one lonely person if she kept herself so distanced. He wouldn't know what he'd do without his family.

"So, what's it like having siblings?" she asked, staring into her glass…her fourth glass if he was counting correctly. "Being an only child sucked sometimes."

Braden shifted his back against the side of the bed, brought his knee up and reached out to pet Jack as he came over and slid against Zara's leg. Braden had stopped at three glasses of wine. He was a big guy, so he wasn't feeling anything, and one of them had to keep their wits about them. Apparently that responsibility fell to him.

"We had our moments," he admitted. "Laney is the baby, and she gets a bit angry when Mac and I look out for her. She's determined, stubborn, always putting others first, even at the sacrifice of her own happiness." He narrowed his gaze, which he knew she could see since they had lit candles and she was only a few feet away, staring right at him. "Sounds like someone else I know."

Zara took a sip of wine. "I prefer career driven."

Braden laughed as went on. "Mac and I tend to get along now, but when we were younger we pretty much caused havoc in the house. Mom passed when I was ten, Mac was seven and Laney was only four. That was about the time Ryker started coming around, too."

Propping her elbow on the arm of the chaise, Zara rested her head in her hand and settled the base of the wineglass in front of her, still holding on to the rim with those delicate fingers. "You speak of him quite a bit. You all are really close. I can hear the affection in your tone when you talk of your family."

When she discussed her parents, all that had laced her

tone was disdain. The only love he heard from her was when she told stories of her grandmother.

"We've always been a close family. My parents were adamant about that. We may fight, yell, even throw a few punches, but when it comes down to it, I know my family always has my back, and they know I always have theirs."

Zara smiled. "Unconditional love." She drained the rest of her glass, then sat it on the small accent table on the other side of the arm. "I bet when you all were younger you had snowball fights in weather like this."

Braden nodded, his hand stilled on the kitten's back as he replayed one particular day. "My brother, Mac, has a scar running through his brow as a souvenir from one of our snowball fights."

Zara's eyes widened. "He got cut from snow?"

"He got cut because our sister threw a snowball that had a rock in it. She's a lot stronger than she looks, but she had no idea about the rock. Trust me, she felt awful, and Mac played on her guilt for years."

She made a soft noise of acknowledgment, nearly a tender tone that had him almost hating how he was reliving these memories when she didn't have too many happy ones. But she wanted to hear them, and he actually enjoyed sharing stories of his family…so long as people didn't start butting into the family business and asking unnecessary questions.

"I bet you all had a big Christmas tree, family vacations, huge birthday parties."

"Yes to all of that," he confirmed. "The downfall of the siblings, when you're a kid, no matter what you got for a present, you had to share. I never liked that rule. When something belongs to me, it's mine for good."

Zara's lids lowered a touch, from the alcohol or from the double meaning she'd taken from his words. Had he subconsciously said that just for her benefit? Maybe, maybe not, but he wasn't sorry now that the words were out.

"This morning, when we…you know…"

"Had sex," he finished when she trailed off. He had no clue where she was going with this, but he knew exactly what topic she was dancing around when she couldn't even say the words.

"Yes. I didn't handle that very well." Her fingertip toyed with the binding running along the outer cushion; her eyes remained fixed on his, though, which only made her sexier, to realize that she wasn't afraid to face this head-on.

"I don't know," he amended. "I think you handled the sex perfectly."

A flirty smile spread across her lips. "I meant afterward. I'm not used to such a giving lover. I didn't know how to react, and with you being my boss, I thought it was easiest to just ignore everything and try to pretend we were on the same level playing field as before we stripped out of our clothes."

Braden didn't say a word. The wine was apparently making her more chatty than usual, and now that she was discussing the proverbial elephant in the room, he wanted to know what she had to say.

"I guess I should've said thank you," she added quickly. "Circumstances have us here together, and you could've been selfish, you could've totally ignored me after, but you didn't. You were…"

"If you say nice I'm going to be angry."

"Sweet."

Braden groaned. "I would've rather been nice."

He eyed her for another minute, more than aware of the crackling tension that had just been amped up in the past two minutes.

"I'm trying to thank you," she went on, talking louder to drown out his mumble. "It's refreshing to know there are guys like you out there."

Guys like him? He wanted to laugh, he wanted to confess just how ruthless he truly was and he wanted her to never look for a man like him in the future. Yes, he'd been caring in bed; yes, he'd rescued a cat. Those were qualities any man should possess. Braden didn't go above and beyond. For one thing, her pleasure brought him pleasure. Call it primal, territorial, whatever. When Zara had been turned on, that made him all chest-bumping, ego-inflated happy because he'd caused her arousal, her excitement.

"Does that mean you're looking for a guy who will treat you right, and you're done with the asshats you've been dating?" he asked.

"Maybe it means I want you to show me again how a woman should be treated."

Braden froze. The bold statement slammed into him. Nothing much could catch him off guard, but this woman kept him on his toes.

"Your wine is talking," he stated, attempting to blow it off, give her an out in case she hadn't meant to say that aloud.

"Maybe so," she admitted. "Or I'm just saying what I've been thinking all day. Every time I'd look at you or accidentally touch you, I'd think back to how amazing this morning was. Even though a relationship would be a huge mistake, I'm finding it rather difficult to stay over here while you're in my bed."

Had the heat cranked up more in here? Braden was sweating after that speech she just delivered.

Zara stretched out even more on the chaise and rolled on to her back, staring up at the ceiling as she continued to talk. "Wanting you isn't new, though. You know what you look like. I'm sure women throw themselves at you all the time. I don't want to be that typical, predictable woman."

"Baby, you're anything but typical and predictable."

Her soft laugh wrapped him in warmth. "I'll take that as a compliment and I like when you call me baby. But I meant that I wanted you when I first saw you, but this job had to take precedence and I refused to be so trite as to hit on my boss."

Oh, he would've loved had she come into his office that first day and had her way with him. Before his fantasy carried him away too much, Braden concentrated on her as she continued.

"Then I was mortified you had to see that whole incident with Shane, but when you and I were dancing, I wasn't thinking about Shane. I was thinking how great you smelled, powerful and manly."

Braden smiled into the dim light. She would be so embarrassed tomorrow when she woke and realized all she'd verbally spewed out tonight. But there was no way in hell he was stopping her.

"Now that you're stuck here, all I can think about is how amazing this morning was and how I'm going to lie here tonight and replay it in my mind."

Braden came to his knees and slowly closed the space between them. He laid a hand across her abdomen, startling her as she jerked to stare him in the eyes. Their faces were inches apart, so close he could ease forward just a touch and have that mouth beneath his in seconds. From this closer vantage point, he could see the slight flush in her cheeks from the wine, the moist lips where she'd licked them from being nervous, the pulse point at the base of her neck.

"Who said you had to lie here and replay it?" he asked, easing his hand beneath her shirt. His palm flattened out on her stomach, and the quivering beneath his touch only added to his desire for her. "Maybe that bed was lonely last night. Maybe I got sick of rolling over and inhaling your jasmine scent. Maybe I was awake all night wondering when you'd come to your senses and join me."

Zara lifted her arms, her hands resting on either side of her face. The innocent move, or maybe not-so-innocent, arched her back and pressed her breasts up.

"I couldn't join you, Braden. I don't have a good track

record with men, not that I'm looking for one right now, and I couldn't risk my job no matter how much I wanted you. Besides, I would've died had you rejected me."

That right there was the crux of her issue. Rejection. She'd been rejected by so many people. Well, maybe not so many in quantity, but definitely all of the important people, save for her grandmother. She feared rejection, and here he was using her. Taking advantage of a vulnerable woman was a straight ticket to hell.

"I wouldn't have rejected you," he murmured. "I was battling myself back at my party because I just wanted to drag you into a room, a closet, anywhere that we could be alone, and I could show you how much I wanted you."

He trailed his fingertips over her heated skin, earning him a swift intake of breath as her eyes drifted closed. "That wouldn't have looked very good for my reputation," she muttered. "I'm a professional and I can't afford for people to think I slept with you to get the job."

"Nobody will think that," he assured her. He'd make damn sure she had more jobs lined up than she could handle. He'd make sure she could choose the ones she wanted and didn't have to worry about taking them all.

"Keep touching me, Braden." Her voice, a throaty whisper, washed over him. "Your touch feels so good."

She was killing him. Those soft moans, her body all laid out on display. He'd told her he wasn't a nice guy and he was primed and ready to snap and take what she was blatantly offering. But he wouldn't want anyone else treating Zara disrespectfully. She deserved better than a man who couldn't control his hormones and took advantage of the fact she loved wine and couldn't hold it like the rest of his Irish family.

"Zara." He stilled his hand to get her attention, to let her know he couldn't take her to bed. But her soft snore greeted him. Braden sat back on his heels, kept his hand on her stomach and simply stared.

When was the last time she'd fully let go and relaxed? Did she trust anyone in her life on a personal level, or were all of her acquaintances the closest things she had to family and friends? Dating men who were users, jerks and not looking for commitment was a surefire way to keep yourself closed off from the world. Zara was excelling at being a loner. The irony wasn't lost on him that she planned parties and lavish bashes for people to mingle, socialize and enjoy the company of others, yet she refused to put herself in a position to enjoy anyone.

From the investigating he'd done before hiring her officially, he'd learned she'd had a small apartment in Boston, mostly kept to herself and rarely dated. She threw herself into her work, and it showed, but wasn't there more to life?

Braden snorted. Yeah, there was, and he was going to find it as soon as his family business was a bit more secure in a new territory.

As he watched her sleep, something shifted inside him. He didn't want that damn shift. He didn't want to care so much about Zara, about her loveless childhood and how it molded her into the fierce woman she was today.

All Braden wanted to do was wake her up, take her to bed and make love to her all night. Then he wanted to get home tomorrow and show Mac that tube so they could figure out how the hell to proceed from here.

Yet none of that was going to happen, so here he sat staring at the most complex, beautiful woman he'd ever known. Parts of her reminded Braden of his sister. He hadn't been feeding Zara a line of bull earlier when he'd said that, either. But Laney had something Zara didn't, and that was the strength and backing of a family.

It bothered him more than it should that Zara had nobody. He'd been fully aware of her living situation and family life before he'd hired her. He'd made a point to know exactly who Zara Perkins was so he could come at her the right way, the way that would ensure she trust him, work for him and allow him access into her home.

Granted, he hadn't planned on a snowstorm, but he wasn't looking a gift horse, or Mother Nature, in the mouth.

Braden sighed and raked a hand through his hair. He should rest, he should get back up and start searching. But he didn't want to do any of that. Not when Zara's body felt so warm beneath his palm, not when she was sleeping so peacefully and beautifully.

For once, he wasn't thinking work or how to get those coveted scrolls. No, for once Braden O'Shea was soaking in all of the goodness from another, hoping it would somehow rub off on him and make him not so much of a bastard. Because if Zara ever found out what he'd done, she'd hate him forever.

And that chilling thought scared the hell out of him.

Thirteen

Zara rolled over onto her side, coming to rest against a warm leg just as her arm crossed over a taut chest. She stilled, blinking into the darkness. No candles were burning, but the soft glow from the logs helped her get her bearings. She wasn't on the chaise where she'd been drinking her wine.

Wine. Zara froze. She'd gotten pretty chatty if she recalled correctly, but thankfully she was still dressed. So nothing had happened between Braden and her, but she was lying in bed beside him. Had he put her here?

Zara slowly started easing back to her side instead of crawling all over her temporary roommate.

"And here I thought you wanted to touch me."

Braden's thick tone filled the room.

"I didn't mean to… I had no idea we were…that you were…"

Lightning fast, Braden grabbed her arm and held her still. "Don't move. I put you here because I want you here."

Zara had to admit being in her own bed with her feather-down duvet was like heaven. Okay, fine, she loved being next to this man, knowing that he carried her and put her in bed, then climbed in beside her. What woman wouldn't get all giddy over that fact?

"Did I ask you to have sex with me again?" Mercy, the fact she had to even ask that question was even more embarrassing than the actual question.

"You implied you were willing."

Pathetic, party of one?

"Which just proves my theory that you're a nice guy."

In an instant, Braden had her on her back, her hands above her head, the entire length of his body on hers. "Do you feel light-headed at all? Headache? Dizziness?"

Breathless from their current state, Zara shook her head. "Why?"

"Because I'm about to strip you and take you up on that offer now. I want you to be fully aware of what I'm doing to you."

His lips captured hers before she could even comprehend what he was saying, but words were moot at this point. The fierce kiss, the tilt of his hips against hers and the way he gripped her wrists above her head were all very telling signs as to what he wanted. Added to that, her body had lit up from within, and she wanted everything he was willing to give her. She wasn't denying herself, not now, not with Braden.

He was right. She dated jerks. She did so to keep a distance and not form any relationship. So why shouldn't she sleep with a man who was considerate, obviously wanted her and wasn't asking for any type of commitment?

Oh, right. He was her boss. Well, at the moment, her boss was removing her pants and panties right along with them. Even as Zara's mind told her to put a stop to this, her body shifted so he could continue ridding her of the unwanted clothes.

She kicked the pants off her ankles and groaned when

Braden placed open-mouth kisses on her stomach. She threaded her hands through his hair. She'd already slept with him once; stopping now wouldn't change what had already happened. And Braden's promise of stripping her down was already proving to be amazing because he currently had his teeth on the hem of her shirt, sliding it up her torso.

When the material bunched at her breasts, she tried to pull her hands free to help.

"I've got this," he whispered. "Your only job is to relax and let me work."

Who was she to argue? He was her boss, after all.

He eased back enough to jerk the shirt over her head and toss it to the floor.

"If that cat pees on my—"

Braden's tongue trailed down her throat and into the valley of her breasts, cutting off any thought she'd had. Zara's back arched—she couldn't move much with his weight on her, but she wiggled beneath him enough to let him know he was absolutely driving her mad with this slow pace he'd set.

"Braden," she whispered. "Please."

"Anything."

He cupped one breast, stroking her skin with his thumb, his other hand trailing down her side and settling on her hip. His mouth, his hands—he seemed to be touching her all over at once. Zara's legs shifted anxiously, waiting for his next move. How could he be so thorough when she just wanted him to touch her where she ached the most?

Finally he slid his fingertips over her thighs, inching higher. Zara tilted her hips, near ready to beg him for more when he finally covered her with his hand. She eased her legs wider, giving him the access he needed.

While his fingers stroked her, he moved his other hand to lace their fingers together over her chest. His lips slid over her abdomen, and Zara thought she was going to shoot up off this bed if he didn't finish her soon.

"You're squirming," he murmured against her stomach. "You're going too slow."

His soft laughter filled the room. "I'm hanging on by a thread trying to give you pleasure, and you're complaining."

Zara pulled her hand from his and framed his face, forcing him to look up at her. "Put us both out of our misery. I want you. Now."

Braden crawled up her body, leaned over to the nightstand and pulled out a condom, quickly sheathing himself. When he rested his hands on either side of her head and hovered right above her, Zara's gaze locked on to his. Something flickered in his eyes, something she'd never seen from him before...or any other man for that matter. Before she could read too much into it, he plunged into her, making her cry out.

Gone was the slow, patient Braden. This Braden had snapped, was staking his claim and pulling her into his web of passion and desire.

His lips trailed over her shoulder, her neck, up her jawline as he continued to pump his hips. Zara could only grip his biceps and arch into him because he was in total control and doing everything absolutely perfectly.

Perfect. That was the one word that kept coming to mind every time she thought of Braden and how they were together.

When he kissed her, roughly, passionately, all thoughts evaporated. Her entire body heated, rising higher and higher as he increased the pace.

"Braden," she panted against his mouth. "Braden... I..."

He kissed his way to her ear and whispered, "Zara."

Her name softly on his lips when his body was so hard, so intensely moving against hers was enough to set her over the edge. She couldn't control the tremors racking her body; she couldn't control the way she screamed his name, clawed his shoulders.

Braden's entire body tensed as he arched back. Clenching his jaw, he stared down at her as he climaxed. The intensity of his stare stirred something so deep within her, so deep she was positive nobody had ever even uncovered that area before.

But Braden had. He'd uncovered so much about her, even more than she knew about herself.

When Braden eased on to his back, pulling her to sprawl on top of him, Zara could no longer deny the fact she was falling for her boss. And she could say that with certainty because he was the only man to ever care, to ever put her first, to ever pull feelings from her she hadn't even known she'd possessed.

The best part was that he did every bit of that without even trying. He just…was. He was everything she hadn't known she was looking for, and here he was, holding her so tightly after he'd made love to her in her own bed. His heart beat against her chest, and Zara had never been more aware of another the way she was with Braden.

The question now was what did she do about these feelings she never wanted? They were too strong to ignore, they were too scary to act on, but she'd never backed down from fear before.

Now she just had to figure out how to be strong, keep her business with the O'Sheas and keep Braden in her personal life for good.

Braden woke to a sleeping Zara on his chest, her hair spread all around him. Something had happened in the middle of the night…something that had nothing to do with the sex. There had been a new level introduced. How the hell had that happened? He'd seen something in Zara's eyes and he knew full well it was more than desire, more than lust.

But what scared him most was what she may have seen in his own eyes. He knew what he'd been feeling when they'd been together. Even if he was only admitting it to himself, he was feeling more for Zara than just physical attraction.

Raking a hand over his face, he reached to the bedside table for his phone and turned it on. The battery was starting to get low, but as soon as the phone powered on, his texts lit up. Apparently the road level was downgraded, and he could get out now. Did he tell Zara, or did he continue to stay here and search her house? He'd found the one tube that could be holding a scroll and he desperately wanted to get it into Mac's hands.

The electricity was still out, but maybe the electric company would be coming through soon, since there were no driving restrictions now.

His entire home had a backup generator. Possibilities swirled around in his mind. Zara nestled closer to his side, a soft sigh escaping her lips. When her warm breath fanned across his bare chest, he knew right then that he would be going home today…and she'd be coming with him.

That primal, territorial need he had for her had intensified. The ache to see her in his home, in his bed was nearly all-consuming.

Braden shot off a quick text to Mac that he would be home later with Zara and the container. Yes, it was presumptuous to assume she'd be coming with him, but he wouldn't take no for an answer. He saw exactly how much he affected her, he felt it, and after last night, she may wake up more confused than ever; but until Braden knew what the hell was going on between them, he wasn't about to leave her alone to start thinking of all the reasons they wouldn't work.

Not to mention he didn't want her out of his sight until he learned what was in this tube, because if it did indeed hold one of the scrolls, he would have to search this house again.

Braden set his phone back on the nightstand and turned toward Zara, wrapping both arms around her. As he pulled her body flush against his, he couldn't help but wonder how he'd gotten so far into her world. He'd started with wanting to gain enough trust to get into her home, and while she'd interested him from the start, he'd be lying if he said he hadn't wanted to sleep with her; but no way in hell had he planned on getting emotionally involved.

Damn it. This complicated things.

"I'm getting spoiled," she mumbled against his chest. "Waking to a warm, naked man who's holding me. Not being able to work, eating junk all the time."

Braden raked his hands up her back, loving the feel of all that smooth, silky skin beneath his palms. "Get dressed. The roads are better so we're heading to my house."

Zara jerked back. "Your house? Are you going to ask or just demand? I'm fine right here, you know."

"My house has a backup generator, so we'll have full amenities." He kissed her temple, hoping to soften her even more. "You're more than welcome to stay here, but why don't you come with me until your house is up and running?"

She tensed beneath him, and he wasn't about to give her the chance to back out. Softly he covered her lips with his. "I want you in my bed, Zara," he murmured against her. "I need you there."

Knowing he was fighting dirty, he allowed his fingertips to trail back down. Cupping her bottom, he pulled her against his hips. "But if you don't want to join me, just say so."

Zara groaned. "You're not playing fair."

"I'm not playing at all." He nipped at her lips. "I have some work to do, but I promise we'll pick up right here later."

Her brows drew in slightly. "I don't know, Braden."

"I do." He rested his forehead against hers, knowing she needed tenderness. "If we didn't work together in anyway, would you come to my house?"

She hesitated.

"I'm not asking for anything more," he added. "I'm just not ready to let you go."

"You make it impossible to say no."

Braden laughed, kissed her softly and tipped her face up. "That's my plan. Now let's get dressed and get out of here."

As he rolled over and came to sit on the edge of the bed, the cat darted out and rubbed against Braden's ankles. His sister would definitely take this little guy in if Zara didn't. That girl took in so many stray animals, she needed to live out in the country where she had land for such things. Having a home in the middle of Boston wasn't ideal for a make-shift animal shelter.

Braden rubbed the cat's back before coming to his feet. He'd pulled on his boxers and pants when he realized Zara was still in bed, the sheet pulled up beneath her arms, covering all the delicious spots.

"What's wrong?"

She toyed with the edge of the pillowcase. "What will your family say about me coming home with you? I mean, they know me as the events coordinator. Are they going to think I'm… I don't know."

He wanted to put her uncomfortable state to rest and move on. "Just say it. What are you afraid they're going to think?"

Her eyes met his. "That I'm using you for this position."

Guilt weighed heavy on him, but he brushed aside the unwanted emotion and crossed back to the bed, taking a seat on the edge and reaching out for her hand.

"First of all, you were hired long before we slept together. Second, it's nobody's business what we're doing. And lastly, they would never think that."

Zara's eyes searched him as if she were trying to tell if he was lying or hiding something. He couldn't very well tell her his family would never think she was using him because he'd been the one to use her in the first place. She could never know the real reason he'd hired her new company. No way in hell would he want her hurt in such a manner.

Because even if the scrolls were discovered in this house, Braden wasn't so sure he wanted to give up seeing Zara.

Suddenly the quest for his family's heirlooms and the need to be with this woman were totally separate issues, both important and both he refused to back down from.

Fourteen

Zara walked through the hallway of the O'Sheas' home. Unlike the other night when she was working and in the ball-room, now she was on the second floor, following Braden to her room…which she had no doubt would actually be his room.

In one hand he pulled her suitcase, in the other he held the kitten. Everything about this seemed a bit domestic, a bit too personal. Yes, sex was personal, too, but what they'd shared last night had gone so far beyond sex, but she had no clue about the territory she'd entered and she couldn't spend too much time thinking on it or she may run screaming.

And had Braden asked her to come to his home when he'd been dressed and not rubbing all over her body, she could've used some common sense and told him this wasn't the smartest of ideas. She was safe staying in her house with the gas heater. She'd eaten just fine, thanks to the stash of Pop-Tarts, and she'd been warm. What more did she need?

Zara adjusted her laptop bag on her shoulder. Braden

had stepped into the house and promptly handed the mystery tube to Mac. They'd exchanged a look, and Zara knew they'd just had some silent conversation that only worked when such a deep bond was formed. She had no idea what was so important about this find, but whatever it was, she trusted him to clue her in since the item was from her grandmother's house.

"You can work in here." Braden stepped aside, gesturing for her to enter the room first. "There's a desk in the corner by the double doors. I need to speak with Mac, and I could be a while."

He pulled her suitcase over to the closet and turned to face her. "Will you be all right?"

Zara glanced around the spacious bedroom. The king-size bed sat on a platform on the far wall. The dark, rich four posters were masculine, matching the deep blue bedding. Of course a man like Braden would have his bed be the dominant feature in his master suite. The sitting area with leather club chairs and a mahogany coffee table only added to the overall masculine theme of the room.

"This is your bedroom." She didn't ask as her eyes met his.

Still holding the kitten in one arm, he crossed to her. Each step he took seemed to be in tune with her heartbeat.

"I told you this is where I wanted you. Nobody will bother you in here. The staff knows to stay away from my quarters, and Mac keeps a guest room on the other side of the house. We have total privacy here."

Zara shivered at the veiled promise, but at the same time, the prospect of being totally alone with him, on his turf where she may be able to learn even more about him, held so much appeal.

"Go on," she told him with a smile. "I'll be fine. I actually have several things to work on, and now that I don't have to worry about my battery, I can focus for several hours. Do you need to leave the kitten with me?"

Braden shook his head. "Nah. He likes me. Not as much as he likes you, but I'll let him run around for a bit." Stopping at the doorway, Braden turned, offering her a lopsided grin. "I'll have dinner brought up later. I plan on spending the entire evening with you and no interruptions, so make sure you get that work done because you're mine."

That man did have a way with delivering promises. The impact he could make on her body without even touching her was astounding. But she couldn't stand in the doorway all day and daydream about how sexy and amazing Braden was.

For one thing, she wasn't moving in. She was here temporarily, and she needed to remember that. For another, she was behind on work. She had to get her spreadsheets updated for the upcoming events, Braden's included. In the next two months, she had seven events planned, some big, some small, but Zara prided herself on treating each event as if it was the only one she worked on. She wanted her clients to feel special, to feel as if she cared only for them and no one else.

Zara headed to the antique desk in the corner near the doors that led out on to a balcony. The thick snow blanketed the open space, but Zara's imagination worked just fine. What she wouldn't give to work on a terrace during the warmer months. How inspiring and refreshing to be outside on the days she worked from home.

Once she booted up her computer, she tried not to focus on the giant bed directly across from her line of sight. If she stared too long, she'd start fantasizing even more about what would take place there later, and since she already knew how talented the man was in bed, her fantasy just sprang into mind without her even trying.

Zara closed her eyes and sighed. She seriously had to get a grip on this situation and her feelings. Right now he was downstairs working with his brother, and Zara needed to remember she had a job to do, as well. The weekend was over. Even though the snow still covered a good portion of the area in Boston and the surrounding towns, Zara still had to think ahead. When these upcoming events rolled around, the snow would most likely be gone, and her clients were expecting a spectacular party.

Zara pulled up her schedule and made mental notes as well as jotting down some handwritten ones. She did nearly everything online, but still reverted back to pen and paper at times. She might do some things old-school, but that was okay. She attributed those skills to her grandmother.

And thinking of her grandmother brought her mind back around to Braden and what he'd found, if anything, inside that tube.

"Damn it." Braden slammed his fist on the desktop. "Where the hell did it disappear to?"

"You don't even know one of the scrolls is what was in here." Mac carefully put the cap back on. "There were no other tubes?"

Braden rested his palms on his desk and shook his head. "Nothing. There were still some boxes, though. Zara hadn't even unpacked her own things, yet. Between all of that and her grandmother's things, I could've spent days searching that house."

Standing on the other side of the desk, Mac laid the tube down and crossed his arms. "You were there for two days, and from what I can tell you managed one empty tube and sleeping with the woman you're using. You're in quite a mess, brother. We'll get the scrolls eventually, no need to seduce your way to them."

Fury bubbled within Braden. He leaned forward, holding Mac's gaze. "Don't be an ass. What Zara and I do is none of your concern, and I'm more than capable of searching. I know my position here."

Mac smiled, completely uncaring as to Braden's building anger. "Sounds like your lady's gotten to you. Why don't you just tell her what you want? At this point she trusts you. You guys played house for two days, you brought back a damn cat and now she's up in your room. If you tell her you need to search her house, I doubt she'd turn you away."

Braden pushed off the desk. He couldn't tell her. Not now. It was because she trusted him that he couldn't come clean with what he needed. Once she discovered he'd lied from the beginning and only initially hired her so he could get close, she'd start to question everything between them, and he couldn't have that.

"I'll find another way," Braden assured Mac. "When will Ryker be back?"

"He made it back to the States, but the airport is closed. He flew into Provincetown and rented a car. He should be here this afternoon."

Turning to face the floor-to-ceiling window facing the snow-covered property, Braden racked his brain on a solution. He'd been so damn sure there was a scroll inside that tube. He had to focus, keep his head on straight or he'd find himself in an even bigger mess. He was the O'Shea in charge now, and he needed to damn well act like it.

"Ryker needs to get into Zara's house while she's here," Mac stated simply.

"No." Braden shook his head, tossing his brother a glance over his shoulder. "I won't do that."

Damn it. What had happened to him? Three days ago Braden would've jumped at the chance to have Zara here preoccupied in his bed while Ryker went through her house. But now…well, now he couldn't go through with it.

"You're falling for her."

Braden jerked around. "I am not."

"I can't blame you," Mac went on as if Braden's denial meant nothing. "She's beautiful, sexy, a businesswoman. Clearly everything you'd ever want in a woman."

Yeah, she was. That was part of the problem, because he couldn't take things to the next level with her. For one thing, he'd only just gotten to know her, and when he said he wanted a wife and a family, he meant it. He didn't just want a woman to keep his bed warm. Braden wanted that bond his parents had. But the obvious reason Zara couldn't be that woman was because he'd lied to her from the get-go. Braden wanted a wife, a family, yes. But he wanted it to be the real deal, and there was no way he could start a relationship with someone he'd lied to, was continuing to lie to.

And how the hell had his mind gone into wife mode when he thought of Zara? That was ridiculous. She didn't do relationships, and he was using her. Definitely no happily-ever-after for them.

"Don't get carried away." Braden rounded the desk, pulling his phone from his pocket to check his messages. "Have you heard from Laney?"

"Yesterday I did. I guess Carter is staying with her during the storm."

Braden grunted as he scrolled through his email. "I need to take a shower and change from these clothes. Once Ryker gets here we all need to have a meeting."

Mac nodded. "And what about your houseguest?"

Braden gripped his phone and eyed his brother. "She's not your concern."

"You know she's going to find out what's going on. You've brought her here, she's going to hear talk or get suspicious as to why you want back in her house."

Gritting his teeth, Braden was well aware of all the concerns in having Zara here, but he wasn't ready to let her go.

"You let me worry about Zara," Braden warned. "Once Ryker gets here, we'll work on a plan. I'd be more comfortable if Laney was here, too, but she's stubborn."

"Carter wouldn't let her come."

Braden laughed. "The day that schmuck keeps my sister away from me is the day he disappears from her life for good."

Mac nodded in agreement. "I'll text her and tell her I'm

having Ryker pick her up on his way here. She needs to be in on this meeting anyway."

"Give me fifteen minutes. We'll just meet in here. I'll have the cook prepare a late lunch for us."

Braden headed toward the doorway, then stopped and glanced over his shoulder. "Don't argue if Laney acts like it's a problem to come. Ryker will take care of any issues. Just text him."

Mac laughed. "You know Laney and Ryker are like oil and water, right? Are you wanting a fight? It's best if I try to run interference before he gets there."

Braden shrugged. "I trust Ryker to take care of it, and Laney will know why we need her here. It's none of Carter's business, and I don't give a damn if Ryker offends him."

"Our little sister is going to arrive, and I'm pointing her in your direction when she unleashes her anger."

Braden thought of the woman currently upstairs in his bedroom. "I can handle an emotional woman." He hoped.

Fifteen

"I didn't need to be manhandled by the family bouncer."

Braden sat behind his father's old desk, now his, and looked across to his sister who refused to take a seat. With her arms folded, she shot death glares between Braden, Mac and Ryker. She may not be happy, but she was here.

"If you'd just said we needed to have a family meeting, I would've had Carter bring me," she continued, zeroing in on Braden. "I don't appreciate being told I was coming and my ride would be Ryker."

The man in question leaned against the wall by the door. His thick arms crossed, he'd yet to take his coat off, and he'd not said a word. Braden knew the man was processing everything, but he also didn't have a care in the world…least of all an angry Laney.

"Carter isn't invited to my house." Braden eased back in his chair and met his sister's fiery gaze. "I know you like him, but I don't, and you're well aware of my feelings on that matter. Ryker was coming in from the airport, and it was easier for him to get you. Now, are you going to have a seat or stand there and pout because you don't like your mode of transportation?"

Laney narrowed her eyes. "It's the lack of respect I'm pissed about."

"I respect you, Laney." He smiled when she finally took a seat next to Mac on the leather sofa. "If I didn't, you wouldn't have been called to this meeting."

Braden glanced up to Ryker. "Close that door."

Once the door was closed, Ryker moved on into the room, sinking into the oversize leather chair next to the sofa. Braden eased forward, resting his forearms on the desk.

"We'll discuss what happened with you in London later," Braden promised, nodding to Ryker. "First, we need to discuss the scrolls. I've spent the last two days in Zara Perkins's home, and so far all I've found is an empty tube that may or may not have held one or all of the scrolls. I'm sure they're stored separately, because together they could be ruined."

Laney shifted, leaning onto the arm of the sofa. "Did she know you were looking?"

"No. We were going through some of her grandmother's boxed-up things, and that's when I found this tube."

He pulled the container from below his desk and sat it up for them to see. "I was unable to get it open, but when I brought it back, Mac managed to get into it. There was a miniscule section that looked as if it had been broken before, so he pried that part open."

Ryker was first to reach for the tube. He examined it thoroughly before resting it on his leg. "Tell me where you looked in her house, and I'll start my search in other areas."

Because Ryker assumed he'd be the next plan of action. He never questioned his duties, his position. He'd been the muscles, the enforcer, the behind-the-scenes man for the O'Sheas for years. Braden knew Ryker felt an intense sense of loyalty because he'd been taken in when his home life was extremely lacking.

"I don't want you going in again," Braden countered, earning him raised brows from Ryker. "Zara trusts me, and I don't want you going into her house while she's here."

"You've got to be kidding me," Laney stated, eyes wide. "We need to find these and get them back where they belong. Either tell her what's going on or let Ryker look. And what the hell is she doing here?"

Braden ignored Mac's smirk. "She's staying here until her power comes back on, and that's all you need to know."

"So you're sleeping with her, and you've earned her trust, you say, yet you can't ask her to have a look around?"

That pretty much summed up his predicament, but he wasn't going to get into this with his baby sister. Whatever was going on with Zara was private.

Besides, the guilt that slid through him was getting quite uncomfortable. He was using Zara, no way to sugarcoat that. If any man treated Laney like this, Braden would destroy him.

"She doesn't have to know," Ryker chimed in. "I'm quick and thorough."

Mac eased forward to face Ryker. "Braden has suddenly developed a conscience where his woman is concerned."

Angry that his credibility was coming into question, Braden fired back at his younger brother. "Would you betray Jenna?"

Mac's eyes narrowed. "Jenna is my best friend, nothing more. I've known her for years. And, no, I'd never betray her for any reason."

"Then shut the hell up, and let me handle this."

Raking a hand over his face, Braden truly had no idea how to deal with the situation. "The scrolls may not even be in the house at this point. They could've been moved or accidentally tossed out. But, I have to believe had they been sold, we would've heard about it. Documents with Shakespeare's earliest works would've hit the media worldwide. Even if sold on the black market, we would've heard whispers. Our reach is far enough in the underground world."

"So how are you going to search the house?" Ryker asked.

"When I take Zara back home, I'm going to find a reason to stay." That wouldn't be too hard, considering their current state. "I'll search where I haven't. I won't leave anything untouched. I don't want to lie to her any more than necessary, so we're not breaking in."

"And what are you going to do if Zara finds out you've lied to her?" Mac asked.

"She won't find out," Braden assured him. She couldn't find out, because if she did, all this work would be for nothing. Not only would she permanently block him from searching, she'd never trust again. He'd made so much progress in only two days, he refused to believe anything bad would happen. And it was a risk he was willing to take to get all he wanted.

Zara had become too important too fast. He wasn't ready to sever their personal tie. Scrolls aside, he wanted her. And, if he told her even a portion of the truth, she was so distrusting that he wasn't sure she wouldn't cut him out of her life. She had every right.

"The cook has prepared a late lunch," Braden stated, coming to his feet. "I need to speak with Ryker privately."

Mac and Ryker stood, but Laney remained seated, stubborn as ever. "And when can I go home?" she asked.

"Whenever Ryker wants to take you."

Ryker glanced to Laney. "Might be a while. I still need to eat and crash. I had a bit of a run-in with the London police, and I'm jet-lagged."

"I'll call a cab," she said through gritted teeth.

"No, you won't," Ryker commanded.

Braden bit the inside of his cheek to keep from smiling. Mac turned his head to hide his smile, as well. Ryker could go without sleep for days. He was a force to be reckoned with, and if he wanted to do something, he'd do it. Apparently he didn't want Laney to leave yet, which was fine with Braden. The more she was away from Carter, the better.

Before Laney could protest, because she no doubt would, her cell rang. Pulling her phone from the pocket of her jeans, she glanced at the screen, then up to Braden. Without a word, she came to her feet and moved to the opposite side of the room where she answered with her back to them.

"You know he's calling to check up on her," Mac whispered.

Braden nodded in agreement. "I don't see what the hell she puts up with him for."

"She's defiant." Ryker's eyes remained on Laney. "She may see something in him, but she's staying with him out of spite because you two make a big deal about it."

Braden eased a hip on his desk and crossed his arms. "And you don't? I'm sure you didn't get out of her house without a verbal sparring match with Carter."

Ryker sneered. "I can handle that prick."

"I don't know when I'll be home." Laney's slightly raised voice carried across the room. "Of course I'm at my brother's house. Where else would I be?"

Braden's blood boiled, and a little of what Ryker said started to ring true. Maybe in Mac and Braden's attempt to protect her, they'd driven her deeper into the arms of a controlling asshole. Damn it. He needed to talk to her one-on-one.

Mac headed for the door. "I'm getting something to eat. I'll be around if you need me."

Braden pulled his gaze from his sister and stepped closer to Ryker. "Do I need to know anything about London?"

Ryker's dark eyes met his. "I handled it."

"With no trace back to us?"

Nodding, Ryker's jaw clenched. "I even managed to gain

the trust and cooperation of two of the boys in blue. Next time I go back, we'll have no worries."

Relief slid through Braden. He knew whatever Ryker had done, he'd done his job well. "And the item is secured?"

"It's in the Paris office, ready to go back to its rightful owner."

Braden slapped Ryker on the back. "Go eat. I'll clean things up with Laney and take her back home."

Ryker's brows lifted. "You're taking her back willingly?"

"She makes her own decisions. I'm just hoping she sees Carter for who he is before it's too late, because if he crosses the line more than he has, he'll have bigger problems on his hands than just checking up on her."

Ryker's thin lips pulled into an eerie grin. "I'll take her back after I eat. I'd like to have a talk with him."

Braden shook his head. "I'll take care of it. You go relax."

Ryker looked as if he wanted to argue, but finally he nodded. After throwing Laney one more glance, he left the room.

While waiting for her to finish her call, Braden put the tube in the lock cabinet by the door. He didn't want that container going anywhere for now.

Finally Laney turned, slid the phone in her pocket and started toward the door. Braden stepped in her path and hated that look of sadness that stared back at him. While he wanted to unleash his anger and tell her to drop that jerk, he knew she wouldn't listen to words.

In a move that surprised both of them, Braden glided his arms around her shoulders and pulled her against him. He kissed her on the head and whispered, "I'm sorry I was a jerk to you."

Laney squeezed him back, resting her head on his shoulder. "You're always a jerk, but you never apologize."

Laughing, Braden eased back and smoothed her dark hair away from her face. "I just want you happy and to be with someone who deserves you. I just don't like how Carter treats you."

"He treats me great when we're together," she said with a slight smile. "His ex cheated on him, and he's leery. I can't blame him after hearing the stories."

Braden would save his opinion on that topic. From the rumors he'd heard, it wasn't Carter's ex doing the cheating at all. But Braden still had a tail on Carter, so time would tell.

"You can stay and eat, or I'll take you home. Whatever you want."

Laney tipped her head and narrowed one eye at him. "Who are you and what have you done with my big brother?"

He shrugged. "I told you, I just want you happy."

Her features softened as she ran a finger between his brows. "Your worry lines aren't as prominent as they normally are. If I had to guess, I'd say Zara is to thank for the new Braden."

"Zara is…" Hell, he didn't even know what to say.

Laney patted his cheek. "It's okay. I can tell your feelings for her are strong, and I won't say a word. Just promise me you won't hurt her. I don't know her personally, but if you're having these emotions, then I'd say she is, too. Be careful where your hearts are concerned."

Braden swallowed and feared that when all was said and done, someone's heart would be hurt.

Ignoring that lump in his throat, he looped his arm through Laney's. "Why don't you stay and eat? Then I'll take you back."

Laney looked up at him with bright eyes. "I love you, Braden. Dad would be proud of you."

Another point that worried him. He hoped like hell he did the O'Shea name proud, because his father, grandfather and great-grandfather had done an impeccable job of building up a reputation. Some may be skeptical, but the name was respected and sometimes feared. No one messed with the O'Sheas. And once Braden guided the family into an even more reputable area, he could hold his head high, knowing he'd done the right thing.

Braden led Laney toward the kitchen. Once he got her back home, he could focus on Zara. Their time alone couldn't come soon enough.

Sixteen

Braden was surprised when he stepped into the master suite and Zara was nowhere in sight. A hint of her signature jasmine perfume lingered in the room.

He turned toward the attached bath and smiled. Looked as if she was a step ahead of him. He undressed as he moved toward the wide doorway. His shirt fell off his shoulders to the floor, he stepped out of his shoes, hopped out of his socks and shed his pants and boxers. By the time he stepped into the bathroom, he was more than ready to join Zara.

But he stopped as soon as his feet hit the tile. There in the sunken garden tub was Zara. She'd apparently packed bubbles because she was neck deep into them, her head tipped back, hair piled on her head and eyes closed. Was she sleeping? She wasn't moving.

Braden took a few moments to take in the sight of Zara relaxing in his tub. He'd never used it, never had a need. He grabbed a shower and that was it. This sunken bubble bath never looked so good.

Damp tendrils clung to the side of her neck, her pink lips parted on a soft sigh. Braden could barely restrain himself. He'd never wanted a woman with such a fierce ache before, and the knot in his gut told him this need wasn't only physical anymore. If everything between them were merely physical, Braden would've let Ryker go into her place and look around. But he couldn't do it.

Zara shifted, her eyes opened, instantly locking on him. A slow, seductive smile spread across her face.

"I meant to be done by the time you came up. But this is too relaxing." She lifted one bubble-covered arm, reaching out to him. "Join me?"

Braden wasn't about to turn down an invitation like that, even if he'd smell like flowers when he got out. Being with Zara, no matter the circumstances, was totally worth it.

Zara scooted forward, giving him room to step in behind her. When his legs stretched out on either side of her, Braden pulled her back against his chest. She rested her head on his shoulder and peered up at him.

"Did you get your meeting taken care of?"

He scooped up bubbles and swiped them over her bent knees. "I did and now I'm all yours. Did you manage to work?"

"I added another event," she stated, her voice lifting with excitement. "Parker Abrams was at your party the other night. His assistant sent me an email about working on his corporate event he hosts once a year for his employees. Apparently their last coordinator was caught making out with Parker's intoxicated son. Great news headline, bad for business. But how am I any different? I'm sleeping with my boss."

Braden smiled. "That's great news for you. I promise to keep our fling a secret."

Her lids closed, and Braden wanted to take back the words. This was starting to feel like more than a fling. He knew it, even if he didn't admit it out loud. There was something deeper than intimacy going on here. Short-term was the only way he'd worked before, but now...he didn't necessarily want to keep Zara a secret. She deserved more... they deserved more.

Zara rubbed her hand along the arm he had wrapped around her stomach. "I feel weird discussing business with you when we're naked. It's wrong...isn't it?"

Nothing about this moment was wrong. Nothing about having Zara smiling, happy and naked was wrong.

Braden nuzzled against her neck. "Then maybe we shouldn't talk."

Zara's slight groan had him reaching up to cup the side of her face, turning her so he could capture her lips. But the woman in his arms went a step further and turned until she faced him. Braden straightened his legs when she straddled his lap.

"I was lying here dreaming of you," she told him as she poised herself above him. "I have no idea how we got to this point, but I don't want to be anywhere else."

Encircling her waist with his hands, Braden stroked her damp skin with his thumbs. "I don't want anything between us, Zara."

"I've always used protection, and I'm on birth control." She tipped her hips, enough to nearly have his eyes roll back in his head. "What about you?"

"I'm clean and I've never been without a condom."

She quirked a brow in silent question. Braden eased up enough to claim her mouth at the same time he thrust into her. That instant friction, skin to skin, no barriers, was so new, so all-consuming, he wanted to take a moment and just...feel.

But Zara started moving, starting those pants as she tore her mouth away and gripped his shoulders. When she tipped her head back and bit her lip, Braden was absolutely mesmerized by the woman who'd managed to have complete and total control over him. So much so he was letting her into his private life, into his home. He'd never brought a woman into his bed.

Zara was different. He'd known it from the moment she'd stepped into his office. And now she was his. Would he ever let her go?

The thought of losing her chilled him, but he refused to think on that now.

Braden slid his hands up her soapy sides and cupped her breasts. Sliding his thumbs back and forth earned him another groan as she arched her back.

"Look at me," he demanded. He needed her to see him, to see them. Every primal part of him suddenly took over. "You're mine."

Those wide eyes locked on to his, and her mouth opened in a silent cry as he quickened the pace.

"Say it." Braden went back to gripping her waist, holding her still so he could gain back control. "Say you're mine, Zara."

"Yes," she cried. "Only yours."

When his hand dipped in the water and touched her intimately, she shattered all around him. Braden would never tire of seeing her come undone, of knowing he caused her pleasure. This was his, she was his. No other man would experience Zara so long as Braden was around, because he wasn't kidding and he hadn't been swept into the heat of the moment when he'd demanded she say she belonged to him.

Just as her trembling stopped, Braden squeezed her waist and let himself go. Zara leaned down, whispering something into his ear. He didn't grasp what she was saying; it didn't matter. This woman in his arms was all he needed for tonight, for tomorrow.

And now Braden was starting to wonder if she was the woman he needed forever. If she was, how the hell would he ever be able to build on anything when their initial meeting was all based on a lie? On him using her?

As Zara lay spent against him, Braden knew one thing

for certain. He either needed to let her go once he searched her home, or he needed to come clean with how they'd met in the first place.

Either way was a risk. Would she understand? Would she see that he'd had no choice in the matter, but once he'd gotten to know her all bets were off?

She had to understand, because Braden refused to lose her. Having her walk away wasn't an option.

Someone smacked her bare backside.

Zara jumped, twisting in the silky sheets and thick duvet. Sweeping the hair out of her eyes, she glared up to see Braden staring down at her, a wicked grin on his face and a twinkle in his eye.

But he was holding a cup of coffee. "That better be for me," she grumbled, reaching for the mug. Jack clawed at the side of the bed until Braden lifted him up.

"Of course. I also managed breakfast."

He reached to the nightstand and presented her with a plate. Zara eyed it before pulling the napkin from the top. A laugh escaped her.

"I know full well you do not stock s'mores Pop-Tarts in your house, considering you hadn't had them before I introduced you to them." She plucked one off the plate as she took a sip of the steaming hot coffee, black, just the way she liked it. "So how did you manage this?"

He cocked his head and raised his brows as if her question was absurd. Of course he had someone go out in this ridiculous weather just to get her a box of Pop-Tarts. The idea warmed her more than it should. It was a box of processed junk that cost a couple bucks, but he'd done so out of…what? Love? No, he didn't love her, but he obviously cared for her.

"Hurry up and eat," he told her. "I have another surprise for you."

With the Pop-Tart between her teeth, she narrowed her

eyes and bit off a hunk. Jack stretched out on Braden's pillow next to Zara. "What?"

He stepped back from the bed, and she took in the sight of him wearing—a ski suit?

"I hope you brought warm clothes. If not, I'll find something for you. Laney most likely has some clothes in her old room."

"Where are we going?" she asked, a bit nervous at how energetic he was this morning. Apparently the two times he'd woken her in the middle of the night hadn't worn him out.

"Just eat, put on warm clothes and I'll go see what else I can find." He leaned down, kissed her on the forehead and eased back just enough to look her in the eyes. "Trust me?"

Zara swallowed, nodded. "I wouldn't be here if I didn't."

Something flashed through his eyes, but just as quick as it appeared, the image was gone. Braden nodded down to her plate. "Eat up. You're going to need your energy."

"After last night, I'm exhausted."

His mouth quirked up in a grin. "Compliments will get you everything."

Zara rolled her eyes. "Easy there, tiger. Your ego is showing."

"My ego is never hidden," he countered as he walked to the door. "I'll have a heavier coat and thick gloves for you downstairs. Meet me by the front door in twenty minutes."

Zara gave him a mock salute, which earned her a chuckle as he walked out and closed the bedroom door behind him. She had no clue what he had planned, but obviously something outside. Was Braden an outdoorsy type? What did she truly know about the man she was falling for?

She broke off another piece of her pastry and smiled. She actually knew quite a bit. He was loyal and he was caring, though he'd never admit it. Family meant everything to him, and he wanted his own one day. He may have a reputation as a hard-ass, a man to be feared in the business world, but the Braden O'Shea she saw was loving.

Zara finished her breakfast and coffee, then set her dishes on the bedside table. She unplugged her phone from the charger and checked messages. Then she wished she hadn't. Three texts from Shane asking if she was all right. The first one was a simple question, the second was more demanding and the third was flat-out demanding. Arrogant jerk. Without replying, she laid her phone back down and started getting ready for…whatever it was she was doing this morning. She had emails to get to, but for now she wanted to be with Braden because he'd gone to the trouble of surprising her, and he seemed excited. Zara didn't know if she should be scared or worried.

The sooner she got dressed, the sooner she'd find out what Mr. O'Shea had planned.

Seventeen

"You're kidding."

Bundled up like an abominable snowman with layers upon mismatched layers, a bright yellow cap on her head and red snow boots, Zara stared at Braden as he knelt down in the knee-high snow and started forming a ball. The man may be a ruthless businessman, but this playful side was just as sexy and appealing.

"Do I look like I'm kidding?" he shot back over his shoulder. "We're building a snowman. Get down here and make balls."

Zara snorted. "You're going to freeze yours off," she muttered.

"Cute. Now help me."

Surveying the pristine blanket of snow, Zara squinted her eyes at the glare from the sun's reflection. She shoved her gloved hands into the pockets of Laney's old ski coat. Apparently she'd had some old things in her closet, and Braden claimed his sister wouldn't care.

Zara wasn't sure what had her more scared, the fact that she was getting in deeper with this family or that Braden was showing her his playful side.

It was the snowman. Something so simple, so traditional hit her right in the gut.

Braden glanced back over his shoulder, then pushed to his feet. "You're frowning."

"You probably did this all the time growing up," she stated, looking at the mound he'd started. "It's ridiculous how something like this freaks me out."

Braden stepped closer, peered down at her until she met his gaze. "You're supposed to be having fun. I want you to experience all the simple things, and I want to be the one to experience them with you. For now, we're starting with a snowman. Maybe later we can make snow cream or have hot chocolate with little marshmallows."

What did he mean he wanted to be the one to experience things with her? Was he thinking long-term? Was he saying he wanted something permanent?

"Where are we going with this?" she asked.

Braden braced his hands on her shoulders. "Wherever we want." He nipped at her lips. "But right now, we're making a snowman, and we're going to have fun. Then I'm going to kick your butt at a snowball fight."

Zara laughed. "You can try, but don't take inexperience for weakness."

"Is that a challenge?" he asked.

"Consider yourself warned." Zara took in a deep, cool breath and sighed. "Now, let's get to making some big balls."

Laughing, Braden smacked another cold kiss on her lips. Together they worked rolling one giant ball. Zara had no idea building a snowman was so much work. Despite the twenty degree temps, she was actually starting to work up a sweat. By the time they got the third ball rolled and on top of the middle one, Zara was nearly winded. Her muscles were hurting, and for mercy's sake she was clearly out of shape. Apparently eating junk and planning parties didn't help build up the endurance.

And here she thought her running regimen kept her endurance up. Apparently, she needed to change her workouts to walking in deep snow and using her core to keep her balanced.

"I'm going to need to soak in that tub again," she told him as they stood back to admire their work. "My muscles are crying."

The wicked grin he shot her sent shivers of arousal coursing through her. "I could be persuaded to give you a massage."

"During the bath?"

"I'd say we both deserve to soak our tired muscles."

Zara glanced back to the snowman. "This thing doesn't look finished. Should we have a carrot or something?"

Braden laughed. "I brought out a bag of various things. It's on the porch."

As he maneuvered through the snow to the porch, Zara got the most wonderful idea. Before he could turn back to see her, she quickly made two snowballs. Compact in each of her palms, she held them until just the right time.

The moment he turned around with the bag in his hand and stepped off the porch, Zara pelted him right in the face. She couldn't even fully enjoy his look of shock because she was doubled over with laughter and trying to gather more ammunition.

Before she could straighten, a wet, cold blob smacked her on the side of her head, barely missing her exposed cheek.

Zara tried to get to the snowman to use as a shield, but she ended up slipping in the snow and falling headfirst into the snowman, sending it toppling.

"No," she screamed as her body landed on the head.

Braden tackled her from behind. "That's what you get for fighting dirty."

He rolled her in the snow and pinned her down. She couldn't catch her breath for laughing. Braden straddled her as he trapped her hands beside her head.

"Still laughing?" he asked. "You may have got the jump on me, but who's in charge now?"

"It was worth it." Zara attempted to control herself, but his face was wet from the snowballs that had assaulted him. "I'm sorry I killed our snowman, though."

"You don't look sorry. You look smug."

"And you look cold," she countered. "I guess I kicked your butt at the snowball fight since you only got my hat."

Braden leaned down, his lips hovering just over hers. "You know what they say about paybacks," he muttered before he kissed her thoroughly, passionately…promisingly.

She hadn't even noticed he released her hands until icy cold snow was shoved into the top of her coat.

"Braden," she yelled as he jumped off her. "You put snow down my top."

She hopped up, dancing around, trying to get the blistering snow off her bare skin. "That's not playing fair."

"I gave you a warning about paybacks," he called as he scooped up another snowball.

Zara ducked as the ball flew over her head. "Oh, buddy. It's on."

Soaking in the garden tub had definitely done wonders for the sore muscles. Not to mention the fact Braden took full advantage of massaging every inch of Zara before he made love to her.

After their epic snowball fight, which they finally declared a tie, they came back in, and thanks to the chef, who was now going to get a raise, Braden and Zara had steaming cups of hot chocolate with marshmallows. Braden hadn't even had to request the treat.

Now they were spent in every way as they lounged beneath the covers in his massive bed.

"You're going to make it hard for me to go home," she muttered, snuggling deeper against his side. "Besides the hot sex, I've been undressed so much here, I may never want to wear pants again."

Braden's hand slid over her bare backside. He wasn't ready for her to leave. "Fine by me. Keeping you in my bed won't be a hardship."

Zara trailed her fingertips over his taut abdomen. "It's going to be a bit unprofessional of me to host parties while naked in your bed."

"You'll definitely be remembered."

These past few days had been more than he'd ever thought possible. Zara had embedded herself so deep into his life, he needed to come clean because he wanted to build something stronger, something permanent with her.

Once he explained why he'd needed to get into her house, she'd understand. They'd forged a bond so intimate and so fierce, he knew she would understand. Her grandmother had meant the world to her, so that family loyalty she would be able to relate to. Even though her parents hadn't been the most stellar of people in her life, Zara would see where he was coming from.

Then they could discuss the future. He just wished like hell his hand hadn't been forced, because he didn't want to tell her he'd lied to her. Right now she looked at him as if he were everything she'd been searching for but afraid to hope for. He didn't want to be the one to disappoint, to crush her and make her untrusting again.

"I need to tell you something." The words were out before he could fully gear himself up for this talk. "I'm not sure where to start."

Zara stilled against his side. Damn it, he hadn't meant to start out like this, instantly putting her on the defensive.

"You've asked before where this is going." Braden shifted to his side so he could face her. Lying in bed wasn't the ideal place to start this, but she was naked so she wouldn't run out angry. "I don't want you just in my bed, Zara. I want more."

Her eyes widened, either in panic or in shock he wasn't sure.

Reaching for her hand, he brought it to his chest and held her palm flat over his heart. "I know this has been fast, but the attraction was there the moment you came into my office. Seeing you at the party the other night only intensified things. But spending so much time with you over the past few days, I've realized that I care for you more than any woman I've had in my life other than my sister and my mother."

"Braden." Zara closed her eyes. "I want this, so much. But everything about long-term scares me. I mean, I can't even unpack all of my clothes at my new house. I want things, I want stability and a foundation. I've just never had that in my life, and... I'm scared."

Her words came out on a whisper, her breath tickling his bare chest, her declaration slicing him in two.

"I know you are, and that's why I want to be completely honest with you." Damn it, was that him trembling? "You're the woman I want in my life because you make me want to be honest, you make me want to be that guy you trust and think is such a good person."

Zara slid her hand from beneath his and eased back. "What do you mean be honest?"

"There's so much you need to know, and I have no idea where to start."

Braden sat up, rubbing his hands over his face. He was either the stupidest man alive or he was brilliant for coming clean like this and risking her trust. Surely once she learned the truth, the truth that came straight from him, she'd understand. Finding out any other way would make him look like a jerk, and understandably she'd be pissed. But by confessing his sins straight to her, Braden was confident she'd forgive him and they could move forward.

Could things be that easy?

Her hand rested on his shoulder blade. "Braden. You're scaring me."

Yeah, he was scaring himself, too. But this was worth it; *she* was worth it.

"My family has had some priceless heirlooms missing for decades." He opted to start all the way back at the beginning as opposed at the end when he'd started using her. "We had an ancestor who was an Irish monk during the sixteenth century."

"I have no idea how this affects us," she stated, coming to sit up beside him.

"Just listen."

Braden turned, facing her because he'd never backed down from what he wanted, and he was facing Zara head-on because he'd never wanted anything more.

"My ancestor transcribed nine of Shakespeare's works and they were written on scrolls. They were passed down from generation to generation, but during the Great Depression they were in a house that belonged to my family. They lost everything and were forced out before they could get the scrolls."

Braden searched her eyes as he grabbed her hand. "Those scrolls were left in the house, and we've been searching for them since."

"I still don't get any of this," she told him, shaking her head. "What do these scrolls have to do with us?"

"The house that belonged to my family until the Depression is yours, Zara."

"What?" she gasped. "Wait a minute, you think I have some documents that supposedly have works by Shakespeare hidden in my home?"

He watched as she processed all the words, then her shock morphed into hurt right before his eyes. Before she even spoke, his heart clenched in pain for her. He never knew he could physically hurt simply because someone he cared for was in pain.

"Did you search my house?" she asked, agony lacing her voice as she scooted back from him and clutched the sheet up around her neck as if she needed a shield of protection.

Braden swallowed the lie that could easily slip out. He wasn't that guy, not with her. Not anymore. "Yes."

Her lips clamped together as moisture gathered in her eyes. "And helping me go through my grandmother's things. That was another way for you to search?"

He nodded as lead settled in his gut.

"That was why you flipped out when you saw me holding that tube." Her eyes darted away as she spoke, as if she were playing the day back through her mind and realizing what he'd done. "You were in such a hurry to get back here, you wanted that opened so you could see inside it."

"There was nothing in it."

Tear-filled eyes swung back to him. "So now what? You need to do another search? Why didn't you just ask me in the beginning?"

Another gasp escaped her seconds before a tear slid down her cheek. She didn't bother to swipe it away, and that wet track mocked him. He'd done this to her. He'd hurt her, on purpose, but he'd had no other way initially. Not only that, he'd justified his actions.

"You hiring me wasn't because of my abilities at all," she whispered, scooting back. "You were using me from the start."

Before he could defend himself—and what could he say that wouldn't sound terrible—Zara sprang from the bed and started pulling clothes from her suitcase.

"I've been such a fool," she declared as she pulled on a pair of panties. "You've been playing me for months. I refused to believe the rumors about your business, about how ruthless and conniving the O'Sheas are. Now I know the truth. I won't let you use me again."

Eighteen

Zara's hands shook—from anger, from hurt, from the urgency to get the hell out of here. She couldn't get dressed quick enough.

"You're not leaving."

Zara yanked a sweatshirt over her head. "If I have to walk home, I'm not staying with you another second. I refuse to be with a liar and a manipulator, with a man who claims to care for me, yet you lie about everything."

Braden stood, grabbed a pair of boxer briefs and jerked them on before coming around the side of the bed. "There's so much about my business I can't share with you, Zara. We do what we have to do, and, yes, we use people, we've lied, we've cheated. But everything you and I have shared was genuine and real."

"Real?" she cried as she turned to him, her hands propped on her hips. "How can anything be real when the trust was clearly one-sided? Do you know how hard I fought what was happening between us? I kept telling myself that we couldn't get involved, that anything I felt for you was all superficial. Your power, your charm, everything about you drew me in, and then you went and showed me that sweet, caring side that had my guard coming down."

Zara refused to give into the sting of tears. She blinked them away before continuing, because if he wanted honesty, he was about to get it.

"I believed everything you said to me," she went on, her tone softening because the fight was going out of her. "I believed every touch, every promise. The fact that you sought me out to purposely use me cuts me like nobody else's actions or words ever has. How did you plan on getting into my house once you hired me? Seduction? You succeeded. I guess this storm really played well into your hands."

Another thought gripped her. "Shane warned me your family were liars and manipulators. I ignored him because I thought he was jealous. Looks like he might have had my best interest at heart after all."

"Zara."

He started to reach for her, but she stepped back, bumping into the small table her suitcase laid on. She skirted around it, never taking her eyes off him.

"Do you think I'm going to let you touch me? You did this. You destroyed something I was starting to hope for, something I'd already settled into. Damn it, Braden, I was falling for you, and you betrayed everything good that I had in my life. My self-confidence, my business, us."

She let out a lifeless laugh at his pained expression. "There never was an *us*, though. There was you sneaking behind my back, using me, and then there was me being naive and hopeful."

"Would you listen to me?"

Braden took a step forward and came within inches of her. Zara refused to back up, back down. She would put up a strong front before him if it killed her. She could collapse later in the privacy of her empty home.

"The deceit started when I hired you for who you were. I can't deny that. And, yes, I wanted to find a way into your house by gaining your trust. But the moment I got into your house, the second I touched you intimately, something changed for me. I still wanted to find what I came for, but I also wanted you and not just in bed. You did something to me, Zara. I can't let you go."

He seemed so heartfelt, so genuine, yet none of that mattered because it all came down to the fact he'd lied and betrayed her.

"You have no choice," she retorted, crossing her arms over her chest to keep more hurt from seeping into her heart. "You should've come clean before you took me to bed, because now all I think is you slept with me to gain my trust. You manipulated me, used my feelings."

Zara glanced around the room and let out a sigh. Ignoring Braden, she pushed past him to gather her things from the bathroom. Her eyes darted to the garden tub where memories had been made. Never again would she be a fool over a man. She should've listened to her heart in the first place.

Grabbing her lotion, toothbrush, bubble bath and razor, Zara came back out and dumped it all into her suitcase. She didn't care if anything leaked over her clothes; she had bigger issues at the moment.

With a swift jerk, she zipped up her luggage and turned back to Braden, who still hadn't moved. "I want someone to take me home. Not you."

The muscle in Braden's jaw ticked as he nodded. "Ryker is still here. I'll have him take you."

Zara extended the handle on her suitcase and started for the door. When Braden reached for it, she shot him a look. "Don't touch it. From here on out, I need nothing from you."

Before she could open the door, Braden slapped his hand on it, caging her between the wood and his hard body. "I'm letting you walk away because you need to think about this, about us. But I'm not giving up on you, Zara. You know in your heart everything between us was real. You felt it in my touch. That's something even I can't lie about."

Zara closed her eyes, wishing she could stop his words from penetrating so deeply into her heart. He'd already taken up too much space there. Surrounded by his heat, his masculine scent, Zara needed to get out of here where she could be alone and think without being influenced by this sexy man…a man she'd thought had a heart of gold. He only proved those men didn't exist.

"Let me go," she whispered. "I can't be here. I can't do this. Romance isn't real after all, is it?"

When his hand settled on her shoulder, she nearly lost it. Because no matter what he'd done to her, she couldn't just turn off her feelings.

"Don't shut me out," he whispered against her ear.

Steeling herself against his charms, his control over her, she shifted so his hand fell away. "You shut yourself out."

"Let me get dressed and I'll find Ryker for you."

Zara threw him a look over her shoulder. "I'll find him. I've already told you from here on out, you're not needed."

Pushing away, she opened the door and headed out into the hall. She'd never met this Ryker Braden had talked about, but surely she could find him and get the hell out of here.

She'd wait outside in the freezing cold if she had to. It couldn't be any colder than the bedroom they'd shared.

Awkward was such a mild word for this car ride back to her house. And because the roads were still covered, the trip took twice as long.

Zara didn't dare glance over to her driver. The man was built like a brick wall with coal-black hair and dark eyes. She could easily see why he was the O'Sheas' go-to guy. He had that menacing, brooding look down perfectly. Fitting for being the right-hand man for a lying, cheating family.

And the scar running along his neck? The man had barely

said a word to her other than "hi" and "the truck is over here," but he had badass written all over him.

"I've never pried into Braden's personal life."

Zara jerked in her seat at the deep tone and the fact he was actually going to bring up the proverbial elephant parked in the truck with them. "Then don't start now," she countered.

"I owe him," Ryker said simply before continuing. "He's never brought a woman back to the house, so whatever is going on between the two of you, it's serious. The O'Sheas are a private family. Other than the parties in the ballroom, no outsiders come into their home."

And that told her more than she needed to know. They were all hiding something.

Zara stared out the window. "You may owe him loyalty, but I owe him nothing. He's a liar."

Silence enveloped them once more. Zara folded her arms, pulling her coat tighter around her. She couldn't get warm, and it had nothing to do with winter hanging on for dear life.

"What did he tell you?" Ryker finally asked. The cautious way he phrased the question put Zara on alert.

She turned in her seat to face him, no longer caring how menacing this man was. "I assume you know full well why he wanted in my house, since you're like a brother to him."

Ryker's silence told her everything she needed to know. She refused to discuss this further with a stranger—not only a stranger, but one who was devoted to Braden.

As they neared her house, Zara's anger bubbled and intensified. Not only had Braden lied to her, he'd had a whole damn team of people in his corner. She hadn't thought of this sooner, but no doubt his brother and sister knew, too. She'd been made a fool by the entire family.

Ryker pulled on to her street, rounded the truck into her drive and put the vehicle in Park. Just as she reached for the handle, he spoke up once again.

"I offered to break into your house while you were staying with Braden." Ryker's dark eyes met hers, holding her in place. "He refused because he didn't want to betray you anymore."

A lump formed in her throat. "I'm glad he feels guilty."

"That wasn't just guilt. You know exactly what he feels for you."

Zara didn't want to think about what Braden's true feelings for her were because he had a warped way of showing them. Added to that, was she seriously sitting here having a heart-to-heart chat with a man who looked like an extra from a mafia movie?

Jerking on the handle, Zara stopped. She wanted to keep the upper hand, she wanted Braden to know she was in control of her life. What better way than to call him on his betrayal?

Zara glanced back to Ryker. The man's intense gaze still locked on her.

"Come on in," she invited. "You want to know if those coveted scrolls are here. I have no idea, but if they are, they're technically mine since I own the house. But you're more than welcome to come and look."

"And if I find them?"

Zara shrugged. "Then it sounds like Braden and I will have some business to discuss."

Ryker eyed her another minute, and she didn't know if she was more afraid if he came inside or if he didn't.

Nineteen

"The hell you say?"

There was no way Braden heard right.

"She invited me inside to look around," Ryker repeated.

Braden sank down into his leather office chair and processed Zara's shocking actions. Ryker remained standing on the other side of the desk, the man never ready to fully relax.

"I didn't go," Ryker added. "Whatever is going on between the two of you is something I want no part of, and it's so much more than the scrolls at this point."

Braden didn't want to be part of this mess, either, but unfortunately he'd brought it all on himself and he was screwed.

"I'll take care of this," Braden promised. "You have more work to do. We have a piece in Versailles that needs to be acquired before the May auction, too. I have the specs here."

Braden slid the folder across his desk. Without picking it up, Ryker flipped it open and started reading. Laney had done all the online investigating. She was a whiz at hacking without leaving even the slightest clue anyone had done so. She was invaluable to the family.

Braden knew Ryker would take things over from here, which was good because Braden had no energy to put into this project right now. His mind was on Zara and the fact she'd so easily invited Ryker into her home to search.

Was she playing a game? Mocking him? Was she seriously just going to let him search with no strings attached?

As much as Braden wanted to rush over and figure out what the hell she was thinking, he also wanted to give her space. He wouldn't give her too much, but he wanted her to miss him, to realize that they were good together and his actions had been justified in the beginning.

Ryker tapped the folder on the desk. "I'll take care of it. I'm heading to my apartment, if you need me for anything."

Braden nodded and waited until Ryker had stepped out before he braced his elbows on his desk and rested his head in his palms. What the hell was he going to do? He'd messed this up. In the beginning, had he known he would've fallen for her, he would've confessed what he wanted. But he'd never known any other way than to take what he wanted and not worry about feelings or personal issues cropping up.

Braden cursed himself as he slammed his fists on to the glossy desktop. Just as he pushed away, his cell vibrated. Glancing at the screen, Braden didn't recognize the number. He wasn't in the mood to chat, but he never knew when it was a business call. For the O'Sheas, business always carried on, no matter what was going on in their private lives.

Braden grabbed the phone and slid his fingertip across the screen. "Hello."

"What the hell did you do to Zara?"

Stunned by the rage-filled tone, it took Braden a minute to place the caller. "Why are you calling me, Shane?"

"I went by her house to check on her, and she'd been crying."

Braden wasn't stupid; he figured Zara had cried, but he

wanted to give her space. Still, the thought of her alone in that big house, crying with no one to hold her, comfort her, other than the cat, gutted him.

No one, but the prick Shane.

"How the hell do you know I did anything?" Braden asked.

"Because I know you, O'Shea. And now that she's done with you, I'm moving full-force into winning her back. Just thought you should know."

That arrogant, egotistical tone slammed into him.

"You went to her house?" Braden jerked to his feet. Gripping the phone, he started for the door. "Stay away from what's mine. You won't be warned again."

Braden disconnected the call and quickly shot off a text to Ryker. Yes, he was in the same house, but Braden wasn't wasting any time. He wanted Shane dealt with right now, and while Braden would love being the one to do so himself, Braden had someone else who needed his attention even more.

Zara tugged on the old bed until it was beneath the window. She'd worked up a sweat, but finally her bedroom was rearranged. She needed it to be different, because every time she'd walked in here, she'd seen Braden. He consumed her entire home, and Zara was trying like hell to rid the house of memories. Unfortunately, they were permanently embedded into her mind, her heart.

She'd only been home an hour when her electricity kicked back on. Making good use of the time, she washed her sheets and comforter. There was no way she would've been able to crawl into bed surrounded by Braden's masculine scent... and she was almost positive Jack had an accident.

She stared over at the chaise she'd pushed near the door. She truly had no idea where to put that now that she'd changed the bed.

Zara circled her room, stopping when her eyes zeroed in

on a sock, a piece of cardboard and a small towel where her bed used to be. That kitten had started a stash.

Just the thought of the kitten, of how Braden hadn't thought twice about rescuing it, had her eyes burning all over again. She'd experienced a wide variety of emotions in the past few hours. Anger, sorrow, fury and then emptiness.

All of that stemmed from Braden. She refused to even think of all the emotions she'd felt when Shane had stopped by. Unfortunately, he'd caught her during the sorrow stage.

Zara headed down to the first floor to check on the status of her sheets. They should be dry by now, and she needed to keep focused and stay busy. She didn't want to contemplate how bored she would be once she ran out of things to do. Even work wasn't appealing to her right now.

Just as she hit the bottom step, her doorbell rang. The last thing she wanted was a visitor, especially if Shane decided to come back. Now she'd hit her anger stage, and he'd be sorry if he decided he still couldn't take no for an answer.

The stained-glass sidelights provided no clue as to who her visitor was. Zara checked the peephole in the old door and gritted her teeth. She didn't want to get into this. She truly did not want to rehash all the good, bad and sexy with the man on the other side of the door.

But she knew Braden O'Shea well enough now to know he wasn't going away without a fight. Well, if he wanted a fight, she was ready to give him one.

Jerking the door open, Zara blocked the entrance and stared at her unwelcome guest.

"Ready to search the house?" she asked sweetly.

With his hands shoved in his black wool coat, collar up around his stubbled jawline, Braden still looked sexy. Why did he have to be so damn perfect to look at?

"I don't want to search your house," he told her, his jaw clenched. "I want to talk, and if you don't want me inside, I'm more than willing to stand on your porch. The choice is yours."

She gripped the edge of the door. "I could slam this door in your face and not give you a second thought."

"You could," he agreed. "But you're not a heartless woman, Zara. And no matter what you feel now, you also still have feelings for me. You're not the type of person who can just turn those off."

Hesitating, trying to figure out what to do, Zara gave in and pushed the door wider. Turning on her socked feet, she headed into the living room. The door closed behind her, but she kept her back to the doorway because right now she couldn't even face him. If he wanted to talk, he was more than welcome to do so, but Zara didn't know if she had the strength to face him head-on.

So much for that fight she'd geared up for. Just seeing him, hearing that sultry voice thrust her back into the sorrowful stage.

"Why are you here?" she asked, wrapping her arms around her waist. "Haven't we said enough?"

"Are you going to look at me?"

Swallowing, Zara shook her head. "No."

"Fair enough."

Braden's footsteps shuffled behind her, and she braced herself for his touch, but it never came. Still, the hairs on her neck stood on end. He was close, definitely within reaching distance, yet he didn't reach for her.

"There's nothing I can say to undo what I did."

Yeah, he was so close, she could feel the warmth of his breath when he spoke. He wasn't going to make this easy on her.

"When my father was in the hospital, the doctors weren't sure if he'd make it through the heart surgery. Dad knew, though. He knew the outcome. I could tell by the way he took my hand, asked me to find these scrolls no matter what."

Zara bit her lip to keep it from trembling. Braden's words, thick with emotion, were killing her. He did all of this for

his family, the family he loved and a family that stood together through life's trials. Even though she didn't have this
type of bond, she was starting to see just how important
it was, and maybe Braden had been put in a rough place,
torn between what he wanted and what he was bound to.

"I knew I was next in line to be in charge of everything, legal or otherwise." Braden laughed. "You're the only
woman I've ever become this close to. That scares the hell
out of me, Zara. My family is… We have secrets. To know
you have that much power over me, to know that at any
moment you could turn on me and ruin my family if you
knew everything. I'm willing to risk it. That alone tells me
how much I love you."

Zara whipped around, but Braden held a finger over her
lips.

"I'm not done," he told her. "I saw how hard my dad
searched for these scrolls. We believed they were still here,
somewhere. We recovered an old trunk that had been here,
but it proved to be a dead end a couple months ago. But
when he died, I vowed to honor his wishes, to be head of
the family and someone he'd be proud of. I made it my mission to find them, no matter the cost. And I knew I had to
start with your home."

His hand slid from her lips, and she had to stop herself
from licking where he'd touched. She was still reeling from
his confession of love. Did he mean those words? Or was
he just sorry he'd actually lost at something? The scrolls…
and her.

"I knew a young woman lived here, and once I found
out your profession, I knew it would be easy to meet you.
Everything after that fell into place so fast…"

Braden shook his head, ran a hand over his face. The
stubble on his cheeks rasped against his palm. He shut his
eyes for the briefest of moments before opening them. Closing the miniscule gap between them, Braden placed his
hands on her shoulders.

"If I'd know how fast, how hard I was going to fall for you, I would've done things differently. But the past is something even I'm not powerful enough to change. All I can do is promise you I won't lie to you again."

Zara wanted to be tough, to step away from his touch, but she couldn't bring herself to move.

"What makes you think I'll believe anything you're saying?" she asked, surprised her voice came out stronger than she actually felt. "Maybe you're just upset that you didn't find the scrolls. Maybe you still need me for this house, and you want my trust back for that reason alone."

"If I wanted this house searched tomorrow, it would be done without you knowing about it."

Zara knew he was telling the truth. And yet, he hadn't sent Ryker when she'd been at Braden's house. That had to count for something…didn't it?

"Right now, all I care about is you," he went on. "I've never begged for anything in my life. I've never had to. Damn it, Zara. I have no idea what to do to get you back. I'm in territory I've never been before."

His raw honesty paralleled her own. "You think this is familiar to me?" she cried. "I've never had a man tell me he loved me. I have no idea whether or not to believe you."

Those powerful hands slid up to frame her face. Braden tipped her face up. She had no choice but to look him straight in the eye.

"You want to believe me," he murmured. "You want to believe it because your feelings are so strong and you want to hold on to that happiness… A happiness only I can give you."

Zara reached up, gripped his wrists. She wanted to pull them away, but she found herself hanging on. "I want to be done with you, Braden. I want to be over you, but I can't just ignore what I feel. You hurt me so deep. I've never been cut that deep before. My parents, guys I've dated, I've always known where I stood with them. But with you, I thought I was in one place, but I wasn't even close."

Braden's thumbs stroked her skin, sending her nerves into high gear. Why did he have to come back? Why couldn't he have just let the break be clean?

"Never again," he promised. "You'll never wonder where you stand with me. You're it for me, Zara. I know you have a fear of commitment, I know where we stand right now is shaky, but I'm not giving up. I want you in my life permanently."

One second she was listening to him profess his love, his loyalty, the next she was leaning against him, kissing him. Her mouth moved over his, her hands still gripped his wrists, but she'd needed more contact, needed Braden.

When she eased back, she licked her lips and looked into his eyes. "I can't promise you anything. All I can promise is that we work together to see where this goes. You hurt me, Braden. That's not something I can forgive so easily."

He nodded, sliding his thumb across her bottom lip. "I can understand that, and it's more than I deserve. But I'm going to be patient where you're concerned. I don't want anyone else with me. I don't want to spend my life with another woman, so if we have to take this slow for you to see how serious I am, then so be it."

She hated to bring up the bone of contention between them, but she couldn't leave it hanging in the air.

"If you want to search this house, you can."

The muscle in Braden's jaw ticked, his lids lowered and he let out a sigh. "I'm not doing anything with this house or the scrolls until you and I are on solid ground."

Zara gasped. "You're serious," she whispered.

"I've never been more serious about anyone in my life." His lips slid over hers again for a brief second. "I meant what I said about loving you. I want to fulfill my father's wishes, but I will love you first and always."

Zara threw her arms around his neck, the thick coat getting in her way when she really wanted to feel him without barriers. "I hated you," she sobbed, hating how her emotions had betrayed her, and now she was an emotional wreck. "I moved my bedroom furniture around, I washed all the blankets and sheets trying to get you out of my room."

His soft chuckle vibrated against her. "You wasted a lot of time and energy, because I'm about to take you back upstairs and make love to you."

She eased back, swiped at her face and smiled. "Everything is still in the dryer."

In a swift, unexpected move, Braden scooped her up into his arms and headed for the steps. "If I recall, our first time wasn't in the bed anyway."

Zara toyed with the ends of his hair. She didn't care where he took her, she would go. They were starting fresh, and she knew in her heart this was meant to be. He was the man who would show her what love was, show her what loyalty and commitment were.

This was the man she'd spend the rest of her life with.

Epilogue

"Calm down, Laney. What happened?"

Zara sat up, pulling the old quilt around her as she listened to the urgency in Braden's tone as he talked to his sister on the cell. The kitten snuggled against her side.

"Don't go anywhere. I'm sending Ryker. He's closer than I am."

With a curse, he disconnected the call and punched in another number.

"Is she okay?" Zara asked.

"No."

Braden reached around, tucking her against his side as he held the cell to his ear. The fact he was still seeking her during a family crisis only added to the promise he'd made only hours ago to keep her first in his life.

"Ryker." Braden's bare torso tensed as he spoke. "Go to Laney's house. She needs you to help pack some things and get her back to my house safely. Carter cheated on her, and now he's trying to get her to open her door. I just hung up with her, and she's hysterical. You're closer than I am, which means you'll need to be nice. I'll be home shortly and meet you guys there."

Once he disconnected the call, he turned into her arms. "I'm sorry."

Zara smoothed her hand over his forehead, pushing away a strand of hair. "Don't be. The fact that you're helping your sister makes me love you more."

Braden froze. "You love me?"

"I fell in love when you brought the kitten inside," she confessed. "I didn't want to admit it then or when you told me. But I can't keep it inside. I know you had your reasons for lying. I don't like them, but I understand them. I know your family loyalty runs deep, and I know when you say you love someone, you mean it."

He rested his forehead against hers. "You have no idea how relieved I am to hear you say that. To know that you believe I love you, and it has nothing to do with my family's history, this house, or those scrolls."

"Is your sister okay? Maybe we should get some clothes on and head to your place."

Braden kissed her before easing up. "Would you want to pack some things and stay with me for a while?"

Zara stared up at him, marveling at the way that body always had her complete focus. "Define a while."

He shrugged. "We can start with one day and gradually ease you into forever."

Zara smiled, jumping to her feet. "Forever. That word always scared me before."

"And now?" he asked, wrapping his arms around her and pulling her flush with his body.

She smacked his lips with her own. "And now I want to hold on to it, I want to hold on to you. Forever."

* * * * *

NOT THE
BOSS'S BABY

SARAH M. ANDERSON

To Leah Hanlin. We've been friends for over twenty years now, and I'm so glad I've been able to share this journey—and my covers!—with you. Let's celebrate by getting more sleep!

One

"Ms. Chase, if you could join me in my office."

Serena startled at the sound of Mr. Beaumont's voice coming from the old-fashioned intercom on her desk. Blinking, she became aware of her surroundings.

How on earth had she gotten to work? She looked down—she was wearing a suit, though she had no memory of getting dressed. She touched her hair. All appeared to be normal. Everything was fine.

Except she was pregnant. Nothing fine or normal about *that*.

She was relatively sure it was Monday. She looked at the clock on her computer. Yes, nine in the morning—the normal time for her morning meeting with Chadwick Beaumont, President and CEO of the Beaumont Brewery. She'd been Mr. Beaumont's executive assistant for seven years now, after a yearlong internship and a year working in Human Resources. She could count the number of times they'd missed their 9:00 a.m. Monday meeting on two hands.

No need to let something like a little accidental pregnancy interrupt that.

Okay, so everything had turned upside down this past weekend. She wasn't just a little tired or a tad stressed out. She wasn't fighting off a bug, even. She was, in all likelihood, two months and two or three weeks pregnant. She knew that with certainty because those were the last times she'd slept with Neil.

Neil. She had to tell him she was expecting. He had a right to know. God, she didn't want to see him again—to be rejected again. But this went way beyond what she wanted. What a huge mess.

"Ms. Chase? Is there a problem?" Mr. Beaumont's voice was strict but not harsh.

She clicked the intercom on. "No, Mr. Beaumont. Just a slight delay. I'll be right in."

She was at work. She had a job to do—a job she needed now more than ever.

Serena sent a short note to Neil informing him that she needed to talk to him, and then she gathered up her tablet and opened the door to Chadwick Beaumont's office. Chadwick was the fourth Beaumont to run the brewery, and it showed in his office. The room looked much as it might have back in the early 1940s, soon after Prohibition had ended, when Chadwick's grandfather John had built it. The walls were mahogany panels that had been oiled until they gleamed. A built-in bar with a huge mirror took up the whole interior wall. The exterior wall was lined with windows hung with heavy gray velvet drapes and crowned with elaborately hand-carved woodwork that told the story of the Beaumont Brewery.

The conference table had been custom-made to fit the

room—Serena had read that it was so large and so heavy that John Beaumont had to have the whole thing built in the office because there was no getting it through a doorway. Tucked in the far corner by a large coffee table was a grouping of two leather club chairs and a matching leather loveseat set. The coffee table was supposedly made of one of the original wagon wheels that Phillipe Beaumont had used when he'd crossed the Great Plains with a team of Percheron draft horses back in the 1880s on his way to settle in Denver and make beer.

Serena loved this room—the opulence, the history. Things she didn't have in her own life. The only changes that reflected the twenty-first century were a large flatscreen television that hung over the sitting area and the electronics on the desk, which had been made to match the conference table. A door on the other side of the desk, nearly hidden between the bar and a bookcase, led to a private bathroom. Serena knew that Chadwick had added a treadmill and a few other exercise machines, as well as a shower, to the bathroom, but only because she'd processed the orders. She'd never gone into Chadwick's personal space. Not once in seven years.

This room had always been a source of comfort to her—a counterpoint to the stark poverty that had marked her childhood. It represented everything she wanted—security, stability, *safety*. A goal to strive for. Through hard work, dedication and loyalty, she could have nice things, too. Maybe not this nice, but better than the shelters and rusted-out trailers in which she'd grown up.

Chadwick was sitting behind his desk, his eyes focused on his computer. Serena knew she shouldn't think of him as Chadwick—it was far too familiar. Too personal. Mr. Beaumont was her boss. He'd never made a move on her, never suggested that she "stay late" to work on a project that didn't exist—never booked them on a weekend conference that didn't exist. She worked hard for him, pulling long hours whenever necessary. She did good work for him and he rewarded her. For a girl who'd lived on free school lunches, getting a ten-thousand-dollar bonus *and* an eight-percent-a-year raise, like she had at her last performance review, was a gift from heaven.

It wasn't a secret that Serena would go to the ends of the earth for this man. It *was* a secret that she'd always done just a little more than admire his commitment to the company. Chadwick Beaumont was an incredibly handsome man—a solid six-two, with sandy blond hair that was neatly trimmed at all times. He was probably going gray, but it didn't show with his coloring. He would be one of those men who aged like a fine wine, only getting better with each passing year. Some days, Serena would catch herself staring at him as if she were trying to savor him.

But that secret admiration was buried deep. She had an excellent job with benefits and she would never risk it by doing something as unprofessional as falling in love with her boss. She'd been with Neil for almost ten years. Chadwick had been married as well. They worked together. Their relationship was nothing but business-professional.

She had no idea how being pregnant was going to change things. If she'd needed this job—and health benefits—before, she needed them so much more now.

Serena took her normal seat in one of the two chairs set before Chadwick's desk and powered up her tablet. "Good morning, Mr. Beaumont." Oh, heavens—she'd forgotten to see if she'd put on make-up this morning in her panic-induced haze. At this point, she could only pray she didn't have raccoon eyes.

"Ms. Chase," Chadwick said by way of greeting, his

gaze flicking over her face. He looked back at his monitor, then paused. Serena barely had time to hold her breath before she had Chadwick Beaumont's undivided attention. "Are you okay?"

No. She'd never been less okay in her adult life. The only thing that was keeping her together was the realization that she'd been less okay as a kid and survived. She'd survive this.

She hoped.

So she squared her shoulders and tried to pull off her most pleasant smile. "I'm fine. Monday mornings, you know."

Chadwick's brow creased as he weighed this statement. "Are you sure?"

She didn't like to lie to him. She didn't like to lie to anyone. She had recently had her fill of lying, thanks to Neil. "It'll be fine."

She had to believe that. She'd pulled herself out of sheer poverty by dint of hard work. A bump in the road—a baby bump—wouldn't ruin everything. She hoped.

His hazel eyes refused to let her go for a long moment. But then he silently agreed to let it pass. "Very well, then. What's on tap this week, beyond the regular meetings?"

As always, she smiled at his joke. What was on tap was beer—literally and figuratively. As far as she knew, it was the only joke he ever told.

Chadwick had set appointments with his vice presidents, usually lunch meetings and the like. He was deeply involved in his company—a truly hands-on boss. Serena's job was making sure his irregular appointments didn't mess up his standing ones. "You have an appointment at ten with your lawyers on Tuesday to try and reach a settlement. I've moved your meeting with Matthew to later in the afternoon."

She carefully left out the facts that the lawyers were divorce attorneys and that the settlement was with his soon-to-be-ex-wife, Helen. The divorce had been dragging on for months now—over thirteen, by her count. She did not know the details. Who was to say what went on behind closed doors in any family? All she knew was that the whole process was wearing Chadwick down like waves eroding a beach—slowly but surely.

Chadwick's shoulders slumped a little and he exhaled with more force. "As if this meeting will go any differently than the last five did." But then he added, "What else?" in a forcefully bright tone.

Serena cleared her throat. That was, in a nutshell, the extent of the personal information they shared. "Wednesday at one is the meeting with the Board of Directors at the Hotel Monaco downtown." She cleared her throat. "To discuss the offer from AllBev. Your afternoon meeting with the production managers was cancelled. They're all going to send status reports instead."

Then she realized—she wasn't so much terrified about having a baby. It was the fact that because she was suddenly going to have a baby, there was a very good chance she could lose her job.

AllBev was an international conglomerate that specialized in beer manufacturers. They'd bought companies in England, South Africa and Australia, and now they had their sights set on Beaumont. They were well-known for dismantling the leadership, installing their own skeleton crew of managers, and wringing every last cent of profit out of the remaining workers.

Chadwick groaned and slumped back in his chair. "That's this week?"

"Yes, sir." He shot her a wounded look at the *sir*, so she corrected herself. "Yes, Mr. Beaumont. It got moved up to accommodate Mr. Harper's schedule." In addition to owning one of the largest banks in Colorado, Leon Harper was also one of the board members pushing to accept AllBev's offer.

What if Chadwick agreed or the board overrode his wishes? What if Beaumont Brewery was sold? She'd be out of a job. There was no way AllBev's management would want to keep the former CEO's personal assistant. She'd be shown the door with nothing more than a salvaged copier-paper box of her belongings to symbolize her nine years there.

Maybe that wouldn't be the end of the world—she'd lived as frugally as she could, tucking almost half of each paycheck away in ultra-safe savings accounts and CDs. She couldn't go back on welfare. She *wouldn't*.

If she weren't pregnant, getting another job would be relatively easy. Chadwick would write her a glowing letter of recommendation. She was highly skilled. Even a temp job would be a job until she found another place like Beaumont Brewery.

Except…except for the benefits. She was pregnant. She *needed* affordable health insurance, and the brewery had some of the most generous health insurance around. She hadn't paid more than ten dollars to see a doctor in eight years.

But it was more than just keeping her costs low. She couldn't go back to the way things had been before she'd started working at the Beaumont Brewery. Feeling like her life was out of control again? Having people treat her like she was a lazy, ignorant leech on society again?

Raising a child the way she'd been raised, living on food pantry handouts and whatever Mom could scavenge from her shift at the diner? Of having social workers threaten to take her away from her parents unless they could do better—*be* better? Of knowing she was always somehow less than the other kids at school but not knowing why—until the day when Missy Gurgin walked up to her in fourth grade and announced to the whole class that Serena was wearing the exact shirt, complete with stain, she'd thrown away because it was ruined?

Serena's lungs tried to clamp shut. *No,* she thought, forcing herself to breathe. It wasn't going to happen like that. She had enough to live on for a couple of years—longer if she moved into a smaller apartment and traded down to a cheaper car. Chadwick wouldn't allow the family business to be sold. He would protect the company. He would protect her.

"Harper. That old goat," Chadwick muttered, snapping Serena back to the present. "He's still grinding that ax about my father. The man never heard of letting bygones be bygones, I swear."

This was the first that Serena had heard about this. "Mr. Harper's out to get you?"

Chadwick waved his hand, dismissing the thought. "He's still trying to get even with Hardwick for sleeping with his wife, as the story goes, two days after Harper and his bride got back from their honeymoon." He looked at her again. "Are you sure you're all right? You look pale."

Pale was probably the best she could hope for today. "I…." She grasped at straws and came up with one. "I hadn't heard that story."

"Hardwick Beaumont was a cheating, lying, philandering, sexist bigot on his best day." Chadwick repeated all of this by rote, as if he'd had it beaten into his skull with a dull spoon. "I have no doubt that he did exactly that—or something very close to it. But it was forty years ago. Hardwick's been dead for almost ten years.

Harper…." He sighed, looking out the windows. In the distance, the Rocky Mountains gleamed in the spring sunlight. Snow capped off the mountains, but it hadn't made it down as far as Denver. "I just wish Harper would realize that I'm not Hardwick."

"I know you're not like that."

His eyes met hers. There was something different in them, something she didn't recognize. "Do you? Do you, really?"

This…this felt like dangerous territory.

She didn't know, actually. She had no idea if he was getting a divorce because he'd slept around on his wife. All she knew was that he'd never hit on her, not once. He treated her as an equal. He respected her.

"Yes," she replied, feeling certain. "I do."

The barest hint of a smile curved up one side of his lips. "Ah, that's what I've always admired about you, Serena. You see the very best in people. You make everyone around you better, just by being yourself."

Oh. *Oh*. Her cheeks warmed, although she wasn't sure if it was from the compliment or the way he said her name. He usually stuck to Ms. Chase.

Dangerous territory, indeed.

She needed to change the subject. *Now.* "Saturday night at nine you have the charity ball at the Denver Art Museum."

That didn't erase the half-cocked smile from his face, but it did earn her a raised eyebrow. Suddenly, Chadwick Beaumont looked anything but tired or worn-down. Suddenly, he looked hot. Well, he was always hot—but right now? It wasn't buried beneath layers of responsibility or worry.

Heat flushed Serena's face, but she wasn't entirely sure why one sincere compliment would have been enough to set her all aflutter. Oh, that's right—she was pregnant. Maybe she was just having a hormonal moment.

"What's that for, again? A food bank?"

"Yes, the Rocky Mountain Food Bank. They were this year's chosen charity."

Every year, the Beaumont Brewery made a big splash by investing heavily in a local charity. One of Serena's job responsibilities was personally handling the small mountain of applications that came in every year. A Beaumont Brewery sponsorship was worth about $35 million in related funds and donations—that's why they chose a new charity every year. Most of the non-profits could operate for five to ten years with that kind of money.

Serena went on. "Your brother Matthew planned this event. It's the centerpiece of our fundraising efforts for the food bank. Your attendance will be greatly appreciated." She usually phrased it as a request, but Chadwick had never missed a gala. He understood that this was as much about promoting the Beaumont Brewery name as it was about promoting a charity.

Chadwick still had her in his sights. "You chose this one, didn't you?"

She swallowed. It was almost as if he had realized that the food bank had been an important part of her family's survival—that they would have starved if they hadn't gotten groceries and hot meals on a weekly basis. "Technically, I choose all the charities. It's my job."

"You do it well." But before the second compliment could register, he continued, "Will Neil be accompanying you?"

"Um…." She usually attended these events with Neil. He mostly went to hobnob with movers and shakers, but Serena loved getting all dressed up and drinking champagne. Things she'd never thought possible back when she was a girl.

Things were different now. So, *so* different. Suddenly, Serena's throat closed up on her. God, what a mess.

"No. He…" *Try not to cry, try not to cry.* "We mutually decided to end our relationship several months ago."

Chadwick's eyebrows jumped up so high they almost cleared his forehead. "Several *months* ago? Why didn't you tell me?"

Breathe in, breathe out. Don't forget to repeat.

"Mr. Beaumont, we usually do not discuss our personal lives at the office." It came out pretty well—fairly strong, her voice only cracking slightly over the word *personal*. "I didn't want you to think I couldn't handle myself."

She was his competent, reliable, loyal employee. If she'd told him that Neil had walked out after she'd confronted him about the text messages on his phone and demanded that he recommit to the relationship—by having a baby and finally getting married—well, she'd have been anything but competent. She might be able to manage Chadwick's office, but not her love life.

Chadwick gave her a look that she'd seen before— the one he broke out when he was rejecting a supplier's offer. A look that blended disbelief and disdain into a potent mix. It was a powerful look, one that usually made people throw out another offer—one with better terms for the Brewery.

He'd never looked at her like that before. It bordered on terrifying. He wouldn't fire her for keeping her private life private, would he? But then everything about him softened as he leaned forward in his chair, his elbows on the table. "If this happened several months ago, what happened this weekend?"

"I'm sorry?"

"This weekend. You're obviously upset. I can tell, although you're doing a good job of hiding it. Did he…" Chadwick cleared his throat, his eyes growing hard. "Did he do something to you this weekend?"

"No, not that." Neil might have been a jerk—okay, he *was* a cheating, commitment-phobic jerk—but she couldn't have Chadwick thinking Neil had beaten her. Still, she was afraid to elaborate. Swallowing was suddenly difficult and she was blinking at an unusually fast rate. If she sat there much longer, she was either going to burst into tears or black out. Why couldn't she get her lungs to work?

So she did the only thing she could. She stood and, as calmly and professionally as possible, walked out of the office. Or tried to, anyway. Her hand was on the doorknob when Chadwick said, "Serena, stop."

She couldn't bring herself to turn around and face him—to risk that disdainful look again, or something worse. So she closed her eyes. Which meant that she didn't see him get up or come around his desk, didn't see him walk up behind her. But she heard it—the creaking of his chair as he stood, the footsteps muffled by the thick Oriental rug. The warmth of his body as he stood close to her—much closer than he normally stood.

He placed his hand on her shoulder and turned her. She had no choice but to pivot, but he didn't let go of her. Not entirely. Oh, he released her shoulder, but when she didn't look up at him, he slid a single finger under her chin and raised her face. "Serena, look at me."

She didn't want to. Her face flushed hot from his touch—because that's what he was doing. *Touching* her. His finger slid up and down her chin—if she didn't know better, she'd say he was caressing her. It was the most intimate touch she'd felt in months. Maybe longer.

She opened her eyes. His face was still a respectable foot away from hers—but this was the closest they'd ever been. He could kiss her if he wanted and she wouldn't be able to stop him. She *wouldn't* stop him.

He didn't. This close up, his eyes were such a fine blend of green and brown and flecks of gold. She felt some of her panic fade as she gazed up into his eyes. She was not in love with her boss. Nope. Never had been. Wasn't about to start falling for him now, no matter how he complimented her or touched her. It wasn't going to happen.

He licked his lips as he stared at her. Maybe he was as nervous as she was. This was several steps over a line neither of them had ever crossed.

But maybe…maybe he was hungry. Hungry for her.

"Serena," he said in a low voice that she wasn't sure she'd ever heard him use before. It sent a tingle down her back that turned into a shudder—a shudder he felt. The corner of his mouth curved again. "Whatever the problem is, you can come to me. If he's bothering you, I'll have it taken care of. If you need help or…" She saw his Adam's apple bob as he swallowed. His finger stroked the same square inch of her skin again and she did a whole lot more than shudder. "Whatever you need, it's yours."

She needed to say something here, something professional and competent. But all she could do was look at his lips. What would they taste like? Would he hesitate, waiting for her to take the lead, or would he kiss her as if he'd been dying to do for seven years?

"What do you mean?" She didn't know what she wanted him to say. It *should* sound like an employer expressing concern for the well-being of a trusted employee—but it didn't. Was he hitting on her after all this time? Just because Neil was a jerk? Because she was obviously having a vulnerable moment? Or was there something else going on there?

The air seemed to thin between them, as if he'd leaned forward without realizing it. Or perhaps she'd done the leaning. *He's going to kiss me,* she realized. *He's going to kiss me and I want him to. I've always wanted him to.*

He didn't. He just ran his finger over her chin again, as if he were memorizing her every feature. She wanted to reach up and thread her fingers through his sandy hair, pull his mouth down to hers. Taste those lips. Feel more than just his finger.

"Serena, you're my most trusted employee. You always have been. I want you to know that, whatever happens at the board meeting, I will take care of you. I won't let them walk you out of this building without anything. Your loyalty *will* be rewarded. I won't fail you."

All the oxygen she'd been holding in rushed out of her with a soft "*oh.*"

It was what she needed to hear. God, how she needed to hear it. She might not have Neil, but all of her hard work was worth something. She wouldn't have to think about going back on welfare or declaring bankruptcy or standing in line at the food pantry.

Then some of her good sense came back to her. This would be the time to have a business-professional response. "Thank you, Mr. Beaumont."

Something in his grin changed, making him look almost wicked—the very best kind of wicked. "Better than *sir,* but still. Call me Chadwick. Mr. Beaumont sounds too much like my father." When he said this, a hint of his former weariness crept into his eyes. Suddenly, he dropped his finger away from her chin and took a step back. "So, lawyers on Tuesday, Board of Directors on Wednesday, charity ball on Saturday?"

Somehow, Serena managed to nod. They were back on familiar footing now. "Yes." She took another deep breath, feeling calmer.

"I'll pick you up."

So much for that feeling of calm. "Excuse me?"

A little of the wickedness crept back into his smile. "I'm going to the charity gala. You're going to the charity gala. It makes sense that we would go to the charity gala together. I'll pick you up at seven."

"But...the gala starts at nine."

"Obviously we'll go to dinner." She must have looked worried because he took another step back. "Call it...an early celebration for the success of your charity selection this year."

In other words, don't call it a date. Even if that's what it sounded like. "Yes, Mr. Beau—" He shot her a hot look that had her snapping her mouth shut. "Yes, Chadwick."

He grinned an honest-to-God grin that took fifteen years off his face. "There. That wasn't so hard, was it?" Then he turned away from her and headed back to his desk. Whatever moment they'd just had, it was over. "Bob Larsen should be in at ten. Let me know when he gets here."

"Of course." She couldn't bring herself to say his name again. Her head was too busy swimming with everything that had just happened.

She was halfway through the door, already pulling it shut behind her, when he called out, "And Serena? Whatever you need. I mean it."

"Yes, Chadwick."

Then she closed his door.

Two

This was the point in his morning where Chadwick normally reviewed the marketing numbers. Bob Larsen was his handpicked Vice President of Marketing. He'd helped move the company's brand recognition way, way up. Although Bob was closing in on fifty, he had an intrinsic understanding of the internet and social media, and had used it to drag the brewery into the twenty-first century. He'd put Beaumont Brewery on Facebook, then Twitter—never chasing the trend, but leading it. Chadwick wasn't sure exactly what SnappShot did, beyond make pictures look scratched and grainy, but Bob was convinced that it was the platform through which to launch their new line of Percheron Seasonal Ales. "Targeting all those foodies who snap shots of their dinners!" he'd said the week before, in the excited voice of a kid getting a new bike for Christmas.

Yes, that's what Chadwick *should* have been thinking

about. He took his meetings with his department heads seriously. He took the whole company seriously. He rewarded hard work and loyalty and never, ever allowed distractions. He ran a damn tight ship.

So why was he sitting there, thinking about his assistant?

Because he was. Man, was he.

Several months.

Her words kept rattling around in his brain, along with the way she'd looked that morning—drawn, tired. Like a woman who'd cried her eyes out most of the weekend. She hadn't answered his question. If that prick had walked out several months before—and no matter what she said about what 'we decided,' Chadwick had heard the 'he' first—what had happened that weekend?

The thought of Neil Moore—mediocre golf pro always trying to suck up to the next big thing every time Chadwick had met him—doing anything to hurt Serena made him furious. He'd never liked Neil. Too much of a leech, not good enough for the likes of Serena Chase. Chadwick had always been of the opinion that she deserved someone better, someone who wouldn't abandon her at a party to schmooze a local TV personality like he'd witnessed Neil do on at least three separate occasions.

Serena deserved so much better than that ass. Of course, Chadwick had known that for years. Why was it bothering him so much this morning?

She'd looked so…different. Upset, yes, but there was something else going on. Serena had always been unflappable, totally focused on the job. Of course Chadwick had never done anything inappropriate involving her, but he'd caught a few other men assuming she was up for grabs just because she was a woman in Hardwick Beaumont's old office. Chadwick had never done business with those men again—which, a few times, meant going with the higher-priced vendor. It went against the principles his father, Hardwick, had raised him by—the bottom line was the most important thing.

Hardwick might have been a lying, cheating bastard, but that wasn't Chadwick. And Serena knew it. She'd said so herself.

That had to be why Chadwick had lost his mind and done something he'd managed not to do for eight years— touch Serena. Oh, he'd touched her before. She had a hell of a handshake, one that betrayed no weakness or fear, something that occasionally undermined other women in a position of power. But putting his hand on her shoulder? Running a finger along the sensitive skin under her chin? Hell.

For a moment, he'd done something he'd wanted to do for years—engage Serena Chase on a level that went far beyond his scheduling conflicts. And for that moment, it'd felt wonderful to see her dark brown eyes look up at him, her pupils dilating with need—reflecting his desire back at him. To feel her body respond to his touch.

Some days, it felt like he never got to do what he wanted. Chadwick was the responsible one. The one who ran the family company and cleaned up the family messes and paid the family bills while everyone else in the family ran amuck, having affairs and one-night stands and spending money like it was going out of style.

Just that weekend his brother Phillip had bought some horse for a million dollars. And what did his little brother do to pay for it? He went to company-sponsored parties and drank Beaumont Beer. That was the extent of Phillip's involvement in the company. Phillip always did exactly what he wanted without a single thought for how it might affect other people—for how it might affect the brewery.

Not Chadwick. He'd been born to run this company. It wasn't a joke—Hardwick Beaumont had called a press conference in the hospital and held the newborn Chadwick up, red-faced and screaming, to proclaim him the future of Beaumont Brewery. Chadwick had the newspaper articles to prove it.

He'd done a good job—so good, in fact, that the Brewery had become the target for takeovers and mergers by conglomerates who didn't give a damn for beer or for the Beaumont name. They just wanted to boost their companies' bottom lines with Beaumont's profits.

Just once, he'd done something he wanted. Not what his father expected or the investors demanded or Wall Street projected—what *he* wanted. Serena had been upset. He'd wanted to comfort her. At heart, it wasn't a bad thing.

But then he'd remembered his father. And that Chadwick seducing his assistant was no better than Hardwick Beaumont seducing his secretary. So he'd stopped. Chadwick Beaumont was responsible, focused, driven, and in no way controlled by his baser animal instincts. He was better than that. He was better than his father.

Chadwick had been faithful while married. Serena had been with—well, he'd never been sure if Neil was her husband, live-in lover, boyfriend, significant other, life partner—whatever people called it these days. Plus, she'd worked for Chadwick. That had always held him back because he was not the apple that had fallen from Hardwick's tree, by God.

All of these correct thoughts did not explain why Chadwick's finger was hovering over the intercom button, ready to call Serena back into the office and ask her again what had happened this weekend. Selfishly, he almost wanted her to break down and cry on his shoulder, just so he could hold her.

Chadwick forced himself to turn back to his monitor and call up the latest figures. Bob had emailed him the analytics Sunday night. Chadwick hated wasting time having something he could easily read explained to him. He was no idiot. Just because he didn't understand *why* anyone would take pictures of their dinner and post them online didn't mean he couldn't see the user habits shifting, just as Bob said they would.

This was better, he thought, as he looked over the numbers. Work. Work was good. It kept him focused. Like telling Serena he was taking her to the gala—a work function. They'd been at galas and banquets like that before. What difference did it make if they arrived in the same car or not? It didn't. It was business related. Nothing personal.

Except it was personal and he knew it. Picking her up in his car, taking her out to dinner? Not business. Even if they discussed business things, it still wouldn't be the same as dinner with, say, Bob Larsen. Serena usually wore a black silk gown with a bit of a fishtail hem and a sweetheart neckline to these things. Chadwick didn't care that it was always the same gown. She looked fabulous in it, a pashmina shawl draped over her otherwise bare shoulders, a small string of pearls resting against her collarbone, her thick brown hair swept up into an artful twist.

No, dinner would not be business-related. Not even close.

He wouldn't push her, he decided. It was the only compromise he could make with himself. He wasn't like his father, who'd had no qualms about making his secretaries' jobs contingent upon sex. He wasn't about to trap Serena into doing anything either of them would regret. He would take her to dinner and then the gala, and would do nothing more than enjoy her company. That was that. He could restrain himself just fine. He'd had years of practice, after all.

Thankfully, the intercom buzzed and Serena's normal, level voice announced that Bob was there. "Send him in," Chadwick replied, thankful to have a distraction from his own thoughts.

He had to fight to keep his company. He had no illusions that the board meeting on Wednesday would go well. He was in danger of becoming the Beaumont who lost the brewery—of failing at the one thing he'd been raised to do.

He did not have time to be distracted by Serena Chase.

And that was final.

The rest of Monday passed without a reply from Neil. Serena was positive about this because she refreshed her email approximately every other minute. Tuesday started much the same. She had her morning meeting with Chadwick where, apart from when he asked her if everything was all right, nothing out of the ordinary happened. No lingering glances, no hot touches and absolutely no near-miss kisses. Chadwick was his regular self, so Serena made sure to be as normal as she could be.

Not to say it wasn't a challenge. Maybe she'd imagined the whole thing. She could blame a lot on hormones now, right? So Chadwick had stepped out of his prescribed role for a moment. She was the one who'd been upset. She must have misunderstood his intent, that's all.

Which left her more depressed than she expected. It's not like she *wanted* Chadwick to make a pass at her. An

intra-office relationship was against company policy—
she knew because she'd helped Chadwick rewrite the
policy when he first hired her. Flings between bosses and
employees set the company up for sexual harassment law-
suits when everything went south—which it usually did.

But that didn't explain why, as she watched him walk
out of the office on his way to meet with the divorce lawyers with his ready-for-battle look firmly in place, she
wished his divorce would be final. Just because the process was draining him, that's all.

Sigh. She didn't believe herself. How could she convince anyone else?

She turned her attention to the last-minute plans for
the gala. After Chadwick returned to the office, he'd
meet with his brother Matthew, who was technically in
charge of planning the event. But a gala for five hundred
of the richest people in Denver? It was all hands on deck.

The checklist was huge, and it required her full attention. She called suppliers, tracked shipments and checked
the guest list.

She ate lunch at her desk as she followed up on her
contacts in the local media. The press was a huge part of
why charities competed for the Beaumont sponsorship.
Few of these organizations had an advertising budget.
Beaumont Brewery put their name front and center for
a year, getting television coverage, interviews and even
fashion bloggers.

She had finished her yogurt and wiped down her desk
by the time Chadwick came back. He looked *terrible*—
head down, hands jammed into his pockets, shoulders
slumped. Oh, no. She didn't even have to ask to know
that the meeting had not gone according to plan.

He paused in front of her desk. The effort to raise his
head and meet her eyes seemed to take a lot out of him.

Serena gasped in surprise at how *lost* he looked. His eyes were rimmed in red, like he hadn't slept in days.

She wanted to go to him—put her arms around him and tell him it'd all work out. That's what her mom had always done when things didn't pan out, when Dad lost his job or they had to move again because they couldn't make the rent.

The only problem was, she'd never believed it when she was a kid. And now, as an adult with a failed long-term relationship under her belt and a baby on the way?

No, she wouldn't believe it either.

God, the raw pain in his eyes was like a slap in the face. She didn't know what to do, what to say. Maybe she should just do nothing. To try and comfort him might be to cross the line they'd crossed on Monday.

Chadwick gave a little nod with his head, as if he were agreeing they shouldn't cross that line again. Then he dropped his head, muttered, "Hold my calls," and trudged into his office.

Defeated. That's what he was. *Beaten*. Seeing him like that was unnerving—and that was being generous. Chadwick Beaumont did not lose in the business world. He didn't always get every single thing he wanted, but he never walked away from a negotiation, a press conference—anything—looking like he'd lost the battle *and* the war.

She sat at her desk for a moment, too stunned to do much of anything. What had happened? What on earth would leave him that crushed?

Maybe it was the hormones. Maybe it was employee loyalty. Maybe it was something else. Whatever it was, she found herself on her feet and walking into his office without even knocking.

Chadwick was sitting at his desk. He had his head

in his hands as if they were the only things supporting his entire weight. He'd shed his suit coat, and he looked smaller for having done it.

When she shut the door behind her, he started talking but he didn't lift his head. "She won't sign off on it. She wants more money. Everything is finalized except how much alimony she gets."

"How much does she want?" Serena had no business asking, but she did anyway.

"Two hundred and fifty." The way he said it was like Serena was pulling an arrow out of his back.

She blinked at him. "Two hundred and fifty dollars?" She knew that wasn't the right answer. Chadwick could afford that. But the only other option was...

"Thousand. Two hundred and fifty thousand dollars."

"A year?"

"A month. She wants three million a year. For the rest of her life. Or she won't sign."

"But that's—that's insane! No one needs that much to live!" The words burst out of her a bit louder than she meant them to, but seriously? Three million dollars a year forever? Serena wouldn't earn that much in her entire lifetime!

Chadwick looked up, a mean smile on his face. "It's not about the money. She just wants to ruin me. If I could pay that much until the end of time, she'd double her request. Triple it, if she thought it would hurt me."

"But why?"

"I don't know. I never cheated on her, never did anything to hurt her. I tried..." His words trailed off as he buried his face in his hands.

"Can't you just buy her out? Make her an up-front offer she can't refuse?" Serena had seen him do that before, with a micro-brew whose beers were undercutting

Beaumont's Percheron Drafts line of beers. Chadwick had let negotiations drag on for almost a week, wearing down the competitors. Then he walked in with a lump sum that no sane person would walk away from, no matter how much they cared about the "integrity" of their beer. Everyone had a price, after all.

"I don't have a hundred million lying around. It's tied up in investments, property...the horses." He said this last bit with an edge, as if the company mascots, the Percherons, were just a thorn in his side.

"But—you have a pre-nup, right?"

"Of *course* I have a pre-nup," he snapped. She flinched, but he immediately sagged in defeat again. "I watched my father get married and divorced four times before he died. There's no way I wouldn't have a pre-nup."

"Then how can she do that?"

"Because." He grabbed at his short hair and pulled. "Because I was stupid and thought I was in love. I thought I had to prove to her that I trusted her. That I wasn't my father. She gets half of what I earned during our marriage. That's about twenty-eight million. She can't touch the family fortune or any of the property—none of that. But..."

Serena felt the blood drain from her face. "Twenty-eight *million*?" That was the kind of money people in her world only got when they won the lottery. "But?"

"My lawyers had put in a clause limiting how much alimony would be paid, for how long. The length of the marriage, fifty thousand a month. And I told them to take it out. Because I wouldn't need it. Like an idiot." That last bit came out so harshly—he really did believe that this was his fault.

She did some quick math. Chadwick had gotten mar-

ried near the end of her first year at Beaumont Brewery—
her internship year. The wedding had been a big thing,
obviously, and the brewery had even come out with a
limited-edition beer to mark the occasion.

That was slightly more than eight years ago. Fifty
thousand—still an absolutely insane number—times
twelve months times eight years was...*only* $4.8 mil-
lion. And somehow, that and another $28 million wasn't
enough. "Isn't there...anything you can do?"

"I offered her one fifty a month for twenty years. She
laughed. *Laughed*." Serena knew the raw desperation
in his voice.

Oh, sure, she'd never been in the position of losing a
fortune, but there'd been plenty of desperate times back
when she was growing up.

Back then, she'd just wanted to know it was going
to be okay. They'd have a safe place to sleep and a big
meal to eat. To know she'd have both of those things the
next day, too.

She never got those assurances. Her mother would
hum "One Day At a Time" over and over when they had
to stuff their meager things into grocery bags and move
again. Then they finally got the little trailer and didn't
have to move any more—but didn't have enough to pay
for both electricity and water.

One day at a time was a damn fine sentiment, but it
didn't put food on the table and clothes on her back.

There had to be a way to appease Chadwick's ex, but
Serena had no idea what it was. Such battles were beyond
her. She might have worked for Chadwick Beaumont for
over seven years, might have spent her days in this office,
might have attended balls and galas, but this was not her
world. She didn't know what to say about someone who
wasn't happy with *just* $32.8 million.

But she could sympathize with staring at a bill that could never be paid—a bill that, no matter how hard your mom worked as a waitress at the diner or how many overtime shifts as a janitor your dad pulled, would never, ever end. Not even when her parents had filed for bankruptcy had it truly ended, because whatever little credit they'd been able to use as a cushion disappeared. She loved her parents—and they loved each other—but the sinking hopelessness that went with never having enough...

That's not how she was going to live. She didn't wish it on anyone, but especially not on Chadwick.

She moved before she was aware of it, her steps muffled by the carpeting. She knew it would be a lie, but all she had to offer were platitudes that tomorrow was a new day.

She didn't hesitate when she got to the desk. In all of the time she'd spent in this office, she'd never once crossed the plane of the desk. She'd sat in front of the massive piece of furniture, but she'd never gone around it.

Today she did. Maybe it was the hormones again, maybe it was the way Chadwick had spoken to her yesterday in that low voice—promising to take care of her.

She saw the tension ripple through his back as she stepped closer. The day before, she'd been upset and he'd touched her. Today, the roles were reversed.

She put her hand on his shoulder. Through the shirt, she felt the warmth of his body. That's all. She didn't even try to turn him as he'd turned her. She just let him know she was there.

He shifted and, pulling his opposite hand away from his face, reached back to grab hers. Yesterday, he'd had all the control. But today? Today she felt they were on equal footing.

She laced their fingers together, but that was as far as

it went. She couldn't make the same kinds of promises he had—she couldn't take care of him when she wasn't even sure how she was going to take care of her baby. But she could let him know she was there, if he needed her.

She chose not to think about exactly what *that* might mean.

"Serena," Chadwick said, his voice raw as his fingers tightened around hers.

She swallowed. But before she could come up with a response, there was a knock on the door and in walked Matthew Beaumont, Vice President of Public Relations for the Beaumont Brewery. He looked a little like Chadwick—commanding build, the Beaumont nose—but where Chadwick and Phillip were lighter, sandier blondes, Matthew had more auburn coloring.

Serena tried to pull her hand free, but Chadwick wouldn't let her go. It was almost as if he wanted Matthew to see them touching. Holding hands.

It was one thing to stick a toe over the business-professional line when it was just her and Chadwick in the office—no witnesses meant it hadn't really happened, right? But Matthew was no idiot.

"Am I interrupting?" Matthew asked, his eyes darting between Serena's face, Chadwick's face, and their interlaced hands.

Of course, Serena would rather take her chances with Matthew than with Phillip Beaumont. Phillip was a professional playboy who flaunted his wealth and went to a lot of parties. As far as Serena could tell, Phillip might be the kind of guy who wouldn't have stopped at a simple touch the day before. Of course, with his gorgeous looks, he probably had plenty of invitations to keep going.

Matthew was radically different from either of his brothers. Serena guessed that was because his mother was Hardwick's second wife, but Matthew was always working hard, as if he were trying to prove he belonged at the brewery. But he did so without the intimidation that Chadwick could wear like a second skin.

With a quick squeeze, Chadwick released her hand and she took a small step back. "No," Chadwick said. "We're done here."

For some inexplicable reason, the words hurt. She didn't know why. She had no good reason for him to defend their touch to his half brother. She had absolutely no reason why she would want Chadwick to defend their relationship—because they didn't have one outside of boss and trusted employee.

She gave a small nod of her head that she wasn't sure either of them saw, and walked out of his office.

Minutes passed. Chadwick knew that Matthew was sitting on the other side of the desk, no doubt waiting for something, but he wasn't up for that just yet.

Helen was out to ruin him. If he knew why, he'd try to make it up to her. But hadn't that pretty much described their marriage? She got her nose bent out of shape, Chadwick had no idea why, but he did his damnedest to make it up to her? He bought her diamonds. She liked diamonds. Then he added rubies to the mix. He'd thought it made things better.

It hadn't. And he was more the fool for thinking it had.

He replayed the conversation with Serena. He hadn't talked much about his divorce to anyone, beyond informing his brothers that it was a problem that would be taking up some measure of his time. He didn't know why he'd told Serena it was his fault that negotiations had gotten to this point.

All he knew was that he'd had to tell someone. The

burden of knowing that this whole thing was a problem he'd created all by himself was more than he could bear.

And she'd touched him. Not like he'd touched her, no, but not like she'd ever touched him before. More than a handshake, that was for damn sure.

When was the last time a woman had touched him aside from the business handshakes that went with the job? Helen had moved out of the master bedroom almost two years before. Not since before then, if he was being honest with himself.

Matthew cleared his throat, which made Chadwick look up. "Yes?"

"If I thought you were anything like our father," Matthew began, his voice walking the fine line between sympathetic and snarky, "I'd assume you were working on wife number two."

Chadwick glared at the man. Matthew was only six months younger than Chadwick's younger brother, Phillip. It had taken several more years before Hardwick's and Eliza's marriage had crumbled, and Hardwick had married Matthew's mother, Jeannie, but once Chadwick's mother knew about Jeannie, the end was just a matter of time.

Matthew was living proof that Hardwick Beaumont had been working on wife number two long before he'd left wife number one.

"I haven't gotten rid of wife number one yet." Even as he said it, though, Chadwick flinched. That was something his father would have said. He detested sounding like his father. He detested *being* like his father.

"Which only goes to illustrate how you are *not* like our father," Matthew replied with an easy-going grin, the same grin that all the Beaumont men had. A lingering gift from their father. "Hardwick wouldn't have cared. Marriage vows meant nothing to him."

Chadwick nodded. Matthew spoke the truth and Chadwick should have taken comfort in that. Funny how he didn't.

"I take it Helen is not going quietly into the night?"

Chadwick hated his half brother right then. True, Phillip—Chadwick's full brother, the only person who knew what it was like to have both Hardwick and Eliza Beaumont as parents—wouldn't have understood either. But Chadwick hated sitting across from the living symbol of his father's betrayal of both his wife and his family.

It was a damn shame that Matthew had such a good head for public relations. Any other half relative would have found himself on the street long ago, and then Chadwick wouldn't have had to face his father's failings as a man and a husband on a daily basis.

He wouldn't have had to face his own failings on a daily basis.

"Buy her out," Matthew said simply.

"She doesn't want money. She wants to hurt me." There had to be something wrong with him, he decided. Since when did he air his dirty laundry to anyone—including his executive assistant, including his half brother?

He didn't. His personal affairs were just that, personal.

Matthew's face darkened. "Everyone has a price, Chadwick." Then, in an even quieter voice, he added, "Even you."

He knew what that was about. The whole company was on pins and needles about AllBev's buyout offer. "I'm *not* going to sell our company tomorrow."

Matthew met his stare head-on. Matthew didn't flinch. Didn't even blink. "You're not the only one with a price, you know. Everyone on that board has a price, too—and probably a far sight less than yours." Matthew paused, looking down at his tablet. "Anyone else would have already made the deal. Why you've stuck by the family name for this long has always escaped me."

"Because, unlike *some* people, it's the only name I've ever had."

Everything about Matthew's face shut down, which made Chadwick feel like an even bigger ass. He remembered his parents' divorce, remembered Hardwick marrying Jeannie Billings—remembered the day Matthew, practically the same age as Phillip, had come to live with them. He'd been Matthew Billings until he was five. Then, suddenly, he was Matthew Beaumont.

Chadwick had tortured him mercilessly. It was Matthew's fault that Eliza and Hardwick had fallen apart. It was Matthew's fault that Chadwick's mom had left. Matthew's fault that Hardwick had kept custody of both Chadwick and Phillip. And it was most certainly Matthew's fault that Hardwick suddenly hadn't had any time for Chadwick—except to yell at him for not getting things right.

But that was a child's cop-out and he knew it. Matthew had been just a kid. As had Phillip. As had Chadwick. Hardwick—it had been all *his* fault that Eliza had hated him, had grown to hate her children.

"I'm...that was uncalled for." Nearly a lifetime of blaming Matthew had made it damn hard to apologize to the man. So he changed the subject. "Everything ready for the gala?"

Matthew gave him a look Chadwick couldn't quite make out. It was almost as if Matthew was going to challenge him to an old-fashioned duel over honor, right here in the office.

But the moment passed. "We're ready. As usual, Ms.

Chase has proven to be worth far more than her weight in gold."

As Matthew talked, that phrase echoed in Chadwick's head.

Everyone did have a price, he realized.

Even Helen Beaumont. Even Serena Chase.

He just didn't know what that price was.

Three

"The Beaumont Brewery has been run by a Beaumont for one hundred and thirty-three years," Chadwick thundered, smacking the tabletop with his hand to emphasize his point.

Serena jumped at the sudden noise. Chadwick didn't normally get this worked up at board meetings. Then again, he'd been more agitated—more abnormal—this entire week. Her hormones might be off, but he wasn't behaving in a typical fashion, either.

"The Beaumont name is worth more than $52 dollars a share," Chadwick went on. "It's worth more than $62 a share. We've got one of the last family-owned, family-operated breweries left in America. We have the pleasure of working for a piece of American history. The Percherons? The beer? That's the result of hard American work."

There was an unsettled pause as Serena took notes. Of

course there was a secretary at the meeting, but Chadwick liked to have a separate version against which he could cross-check the minutes.

She glanced up from her seat off to the side of the hotel ballroom. The Beaumont family owned fifty-one percent of the Beaumont Brewery. They'd kept a firm hand on the business for, well, forever—easily fending off hostile takeovers and not-so-hostile mergers. Chadwick was in charge, though. The rest of the Beaumonts just collected checks like any other stockholders.

She could see that some people were really listening to Chadwick—nodding in agreement, whispering to their neighbors. This meeting wasn't a full shareholders' meeting, so only about twenty people were in the room. Some of them were holdovers from Hardwick's era—handpicked back in the day. They didn't have much power beyond their vote, but they were fiercely loyal to the company.

Those were the people nodding now—the ones who had a personal stake in the company's version of American history.

There were some members—younger, more corporate types that had been brought in to provide balance against the old-boys board of Hardwick's era. Chadwick had selected a few of them, but they weren't the loyal employees that worked with him on a day-to-day basis.

Then there were the others—members brought in by other members. Those, like Harper and his two protégées, had absolutely no interest in Beaumont beer, and they did nothing to hide it.

It was Harper who broke the tense silence. "Odd, Mr. Beaumont. In my version of the American dream, hard work is rewarded with money. The buyout will make you a billionaire. Isn't that the American dream?"

Other heads—the younger ones—nodded in agreement.

Serena could see Chadwick struggling to control his emotions. It hurt to watch. He was normally above this, normally so much more intimidating. But after the week he'd had, she couldn't blame him for looking like he wanted to personally wring Harper's neck. Harper owned almost ten percent of this company, though. Strangling him would be frowned upon.

"The Beaumont Brewery has already provided for my needs," he said, his voice tight. "It's my duty to my company, my *employees*...." At this, he glanced up. His gaze met Serena's, sending a heated charge between them.

Her. He was talking about her.

Chadwick went on, "It's my duty to make sure that the people who *choose* to work for Beaumont Brewery also get to realize the American dream. Some in management will get to cash out their stock options. They'll get a couple of thousand, maybe. Not enough to retire on. But the rest? The men and women who actually make this company work? They won't. AllBev will walk in, fire them all, and reduce our proud history to nothing more than a brand name. No matter how you look at it, Mr. Harper, that's not the American dream. I take care of those who work for me. I reward loyalty. I do not dump it by the side of the road the moment it becomes slightly inconvenient. I cannot be bought off at the expense of those who willingly give me their time and energy. I expect nothing less from this board."

Then, abruptly, he sat. Head up, shoulders back, he didn't look like a man who had just lost. If anything, he looked like a man ready to take all comers. Chadwick had never struck her as a physical force to be reckoned with—but right now? Yeah, he looked like he could fight for his company. To the death.

The room broke out into a cacophony of arguments—the old guard arguing with the new guard, both arguing with Harper's faction. After about fifteen minutes, Harper demanded they call a vote.

For a moment, Serena thought Chadwick had won. Only four people voted to accept AllBev's offer of $52 a share. A clear defeat. Serena breathed a sigh of relief. At least something this week was going right. Her job was safe—which meant her future was safe. She could keep working for Chadwick. Things could continue just as they were. There was comfort in the familiar, and she clung to it.

But then Harper called a second vote. "What should our counteroffer be? I believe Mr. Beaumont said $62 a share wasn't enough. Shall we put $65 to a vote?"

Chadwick jolted in his seat, looking far more than murderous. They voted.

Thirteen people voted for the counteroffer of $65 a share. Chadwick looked as if someone had stabbed him in the gut. It hurt to see him look so hollow—to know this was another fight he was losing, on top of the fight with Helen.

She felt nauseous, and she was pretty sure it had nothing to do with morning sickness. Surely AllBev wouldn't want to spend that much on the brewery, Serena hoped as she wrote everything down. Maybe they'd look for a cheaper, easier target.

Everything Chadwick had spoken of—taking care of his workers, helping them all, not just the privileged few, reach for the American dream—that was why she worked for him. He had given her a chance to earn her way out of abject poverty. Because of him, she had a chance to raise her baby in better circumstances than those in which she'd been raised.

All of that could be taken away from her because Mr. Harper was grinding a forty-year-old ax.

It wasn't fair. She didn't know when she'd started to think that life was fair—it certainly hadn't been during her childhood. But the rules of Beaumont Brewery had been more than fair. Work hard, get promoted, get benefits. Work harder, get a raise, get out of a cube and into an office. Work even harder, get a big bonus. Get to go to galas. Get to dream about retirement plans.

Get to feel secure.

All of that was for sale at $65 a share.

The meeting broke up, everyone going off with their respective cliques. A few of the old-timers came up to Chadwick and appeared to offer their support. Or their condolences. She couldn't tell from her unobtrusive spot off to the side.

Chadwick stood stiffly and, eyes facing forward, stalked out of the room. Serena quickly gathered her things and went after him. He seemed to be in such a fog that she didn't want him to accidentally leave her behind.

She didn't need to worry. Chadwick was standing just outside the ballroom doors, still staring straight ahead.

She needed to get him out of there. If he was going to have another moment like he'd had yesterday—a moment when his self-control slipped, a moment where he would allow himself to be lost—by no means should he have that moment in a hotel lobby.

She touched his arm. "I'll call for the car."

"Yes," he said, in a weirdly blank voice. "Please do." Then his head swung down and his eyes focused on her. Sadness washed over his expression so strongly that it brought tears to her eyes. "I tried, Serena. For you."

What? She'd thought he was trying to save his company—the family business. The family name. What did he mean, he'd tried for *her*?

"I know," she said, afraid to say anything else. "I'll go get the car. Stay here." The driver stayed with the car. The valet just had to go find him.

It took several minutes. During that time, board members trickled out of the ballroom. Some were heading to dinner at the restaurant up the street, no doubt to celebrate their brilliant move to make themselves richer. A few shook Chadwick's hand. No one else seemed to realize what a state of shock he was in. No one but her.

Finally, after what felt like a small eternity, the company car pulled up. It wasn't really a car in the true sense of the word. Oh, it was a Cadillac, but it was the limo version. It was impressive without being ostentatious. Much like Chadwick.

The doorman opened the door for them. Absent-mindedly, Chadwick fished a bill out of his wallet and shoved it at the man. Then they climbed into the car.

When the door shut behind them, a cold silence seemed to grip the car. It wasn't just her security on the line.

How did one comfort a multi-millionaire on the verge of becoming an unwilling billionaire? Once again, she was out of her league. She kept her mouth shut and her eyes focused on the passing Denver cityscape. The journey to the brewery on the south side of the city would take thirty minutes if traffic was smooth.

When she got back to the office, she'd have to open up her resume—that was all. If Chadwick lost the company, she didn't think she could wait around until she got personally fired by the new management. She *needed* uninterrupted health benefits—prenatal care trumped any thought of retirement. Chadwick would understand that, wouldn't he?

When Chadwick spoke, it made her jump. "What do you want?"

"Beg pardon?"

"Out of life." He was staring out his own window. "Is this what you thought you'd be doing with your life? Is this what you wanted?"

"Yes." Mostly. She'd thought that she and Neil would be married by now, maybe with a few cute kids. Being single and pregnant wasn't exactly how she'd dreamed she'd start a family.

But the job? That was exactly what she'd wanted.

So she wasn't breaking through the glass ceiling. She didn't care. She was able to provide for herself. Or had been, anyway. That was the most important thing.

"Really?"

"Working for you has been very...stable. That's not something I had growing up."

"Parents got divorced too, huh?"

She swallowed. "No, actually. Still wildly in love. But love doesn't pay the rent or put food on the table. Love doesn't pay the doctor's bills."

His head snapped away from the window so fast she thought she'd heard his neck pop. "I...I had no idea."

"I don't talk about it." Neil knew, of course. He'd met her when she was still living on ramen noodles and working two part-time jobs to pay for college. Moving in with him had been a blessing—he'd covered the rent for the first year while she'd interned at Beaumont. But once she'd been able to contribute, she had. She'd put all her emphasis on making ends meet, then making a nest egg.

Perhaps too much emphasis. Maybe she'd been so focused on making sure that she was an equal contributor to the relationship—that money would never drive them apart—that she'd forgotten a relationship was more than a bank account. After all, her parents had nothing *but* each other. They were horrid with money, but they loved each other fiercely.

Once, she'd loved Neil like that—passionately. But somewhere along the way that had mellowed into a balanced checkbook. As if love could be measured in dollars and cents.

Chadwick was staring at her as if he'd never seen her before. She didn't like it—even though he no longer seemed focused on the sale of the company, she didn't want to see pity creep into his eyes. She hated pity.

So she redirected. "What about you?"

"Me?" He seemed confused by the question.

"Did you always want to run the brewery?"

Her question worked; it distracted Chadwick from her dirt-poor life. But it failed in that it created another weary wave that washed over his expression. "I was never given a choice."

The way he said it sounded so…cold. Detached, even. "Never?"

"No." He cut the word off, turning his attention back to the window. Ah. Her childhood wasn't the only thing they didn't talk about.

"So, what *would* you want—if you had the choice?" Which he very well might have after the next round of negotiations.

He looked at her then, his eyes blazing with a new, almost feverish, kind of light. She'd only seen him look like that once before—on Monday, when he'd put his finger under her chin. But even then, he hadn't looked quite this…heated. The back of her neck began to sweat under his gaze.

Would he lean forward and put his hand on her again? Would he keep leaning until he was close enough to kiss? Would he do more than just that?

Would she let him?

"I want…" He let the word trail off, the raw need in his voice scratching against her ears like his five-o'clock shadow would scratch against her cheek. "I want to do something for me. Not for the family, not for the company—just for me."

Serena swallowed. The way he said that made it pretty clear what that 'something' might be.

He was her boss, she was his secretary, and he was still married. But none of that seemed to be an issue right now. They were alone in the back of a secure vehicle. The driver couldn't see through the divider. No one would barge in on them. No one would stop them.

I'm pregnant. The words popped onto her tongue and tried frantically to break out of her mouth. That would nip this little infatuation they both seemed to be indulging right in the bud. She was pregnant with another man's baby. She was hormonal and putting on weight in odd locations and wasn't anyone's idea of desirable right now.

But she didn't. He was already feeling the burden of taking care of his employees. How would he react to her pregnancy? Would all those promises to reward her loyalty and take care of her be just another weight he would struggle to carry?

No. She had worked hard to take care of herself. So she was unexpectedly expecting. So her job was possibly standing on its last legs. She would not throw herself at her boss with the hopes that he'd somehow "fix" her life. She knew first-hand that waiting for someone else to fix your problems meant you just had to keep on waiting.

She'd gotten herself into her current situation. She could handle it herself.

That included handling herself around Chadwick.

So she cleared her throat and forced her voice to sound light and non-committal. "Maybe you can find something that doesn't involve beer."

He blinked once, then gave a little nod. He wasn't going to press the issue. He accepted her dodge. It was the right thing to do, after all.

Damn it.

"I like beer," he replied, returning his gaze to the window. "When I was nineteen, I worked alongside the brew masters. They taught me how to *make* beer, not just think of it in terms of units sold. It was fun. Like a chemistry experiment—change one thing, change the whole nature of the brew. To those guys, beer was a living thing—the yeast, the sugars. It was an art *and* a science." His voice drifted a bit, a relaxed smile taking hold of his mouth. "That was a good year. I was sorry to leave those guys behind."

"What do you mean?"

"My father made me spend a year interning in each department, from the age of sixteen on. Outside of my studies, I had to clock in at least twenty hours every week at the brewery."

"That's a lot of work for a teenager." True, she'd had a job when she was sixteen, too, bagging groceries at the local supermarket, but that was a matter of survival. Her family needed her paycheck, plus she got first crack at the merchandise that had been damaged during shipping. She kept the roof over their heads and occasionally put food on the table. The satisfaction she'd gotten from accomplishing those things still lingered.

His smile got less relaxed, more cynical. "I learned

how to run the company. That's what he wanted." She must have given him a look because he added, "Like I said—I wasn't given any choice in the matter."

What his father had wanted—but not what Chadwick had wanted.

The car slowed down and turned. She glanced out the window. They were near the office. She felt like she was running out of time. "If you had a choice, what would you want to do?"

It felt bold and forward to ask him again—to demand he answer her. She didn't make such demands of him. That's not how their business relationship worked.

But something had changed. Their relationship was no longer strictly business. It hadn't crossed a line into pleasure, but the way he'd touched her on Monday? The way she'd touched him yesterday?

Something had changed, all right. Maybe everything.

His gaze bore into her—not the weary look he wore when discussing his schedule, not even the shell-shocked look he'd had yesterday. This was much, much closer to the look he'd had on Monday—the one he'd had on his face when he'd leaned toward her, made the air thin between them. Made her want to feel his lips pressing against hers. Made her want things she had no business wanting.

A corner of his mouth curved up. "What are you wearing on Saturday?"

"What?"

"To the gala. What are you wearing? The black dress?"

Serena blinked at him. Did he seriously *want* to discuss the shortcomings of her wardrobe? "Um, no, actually…." It didn't fit anymore. She'd tried it on on Monday night, more to distract herself from constantly refreshing her email to see if Neil would reply than anything else.

The dress had not zipped. Her body was already changing. How could she not have realized that before she peed on all those sticks? "I'll find something appropriate to wear by Saturday."

They pulled up in front of the office building. The campus of Beaumont Brewery was spread out over fifteen acres, with most of the buildings going back to before the Great Depression.

That sense of permanence had always attracted Serena. Her parents moved so frequently, trying to stay one step ahead of the creditors. The one time Serena had set them up in a nice place with a reasonable rent—and covered the down payment and security deposit, with promises to help every month—her folks had fallen behind. Again. But instead of telling her and giving her a chance to make up the shortfall, they'd done what they always did—picked up in the middle of the night and skipped out. They didn't know how to live any other way.

The Beaumonts had been here for over a century. What would it be like to walk down halls your grandfather had built? To work in buildings your great-grandfather had made? To know that your family not only took care of themselves, but of their children and their children's children?

The driver opened up their door. Serena started to move, but Chadwick motioned for her to sit. "Take the afternoon off. Go to Neiman Marcus. I have a personal shopper there. He'll make sure you're appropriately dressed."

The way he said it bordered on condescending. "I'm sorry—was my black dress inappropriate somehow?"

It had been an amazing find at a consignment shop. Paying seventy dollars for a dress and then another twenty to get it altered had felt like a lot of money, but she'd worn it more than enough to justify the cost, and it had always made her feel glamorous. Plus, a dress like that had probably cost at least five hundred dollars originally. Ninety bucks was a steal. Too bad she wouldn't be able to wear it again for a long time. Maybe if she lost the baby weight, she'd be able to get back into it.

"On the contrary, it would be difficult to find another dress that looks as appropriate on you. That's why you should use Mario. If anyone could find a better dress, it would be him." Chadwick's voice carried through the space between them, almost as if the driver wasn't standing three feet away, just on the other side of the open car door.

Serena swallowed. He didn't have her backed against a door and he certainly wasn't touching her, but otherwise? She felt exactly as she had Monday morning. Except then, she'd been on the verge of sobbing in his office. This? This was different. She wouldn't let her emotions get the better of her today, hormones be damned.

So she smiled her most disarming smile. "I'm afraid that won't be possible. Despite the generous salary you pay me, Neiman's is a bit out of my price range." Which was not a lie. She shopped clearance racks and consignment stores. When she needed some retail therapy, she hit thrift stores. Not an expensive department store. Never Neiman's.

Chadwick leaned forward, thinning the air between them until she didn't care about the driver. "We are attending a work function. Dressing you appropriately is a work-related expense. You will put the dress on my account." She opened her mouth to protest—that was not going to happen—when he cut her off with a wave of his hand. "Not negotiable."

Then, moving with coiled grace, he exited the vehicle. And made the driver shut the door before Serena could follow him out. "Take her to Neiman's," she heard Chadwick say.

No. No, no, no, *no*. This wasn't right. This was wrong on several levels. Chadwick gave her stock options because she did a good job on a project—he did not buy her something as personal, as *intimate*, as a dress. She bought her own clothing with her own money. She didn't rely on any man to take care of her.

She shoved the door open, catching the driver on the hip, and hopped out. Chadwick was already four steps away. "*Sir*," she said, putting as much weight on the word as she could. He froze, one foot on a step. Well, she had his attention now. "I must respectfully decline your offer. I'll get my own dress, thank you."

Coiled grace? Had she thought that about him just moments ago? Because, as Chadwick turned to face her and began to walk back down toward where she was standing, he didn't look quite as graceful. Oh, he moved smoothly, but it was less like an athlete and more like a big cat stalking his prey. *Her*.

And he didn't stop once he was on level ground. He walked right up to her—close enough that he could put his finger under her chin again, close enough to kiss her in broad daylight, in front of the driver.

"You asked, Ms. Chase." His voice came out much closer to a growl than his normal efficient business voice. "Did you not?"

"I didn't ask for a dress."

His smile was a wicked thing she'd never seen on his face before. "You asked me what I wanted. Well, this is what I want. I want to take you out to dinner. I want you to accompany me to this event. And I want you to feel as beautiful as possible when I do it."

She sucked in a breath that felt far warmer than the ambient air temperature outside.

His gaze darted down to her lips, then back up to her eyes. "Because that black dress—you feel beautiful in it, don't you?"

"Yes." She didn't understand what was going on. If he was going to buy her a dress, why was he talking about how she felt? If he was going to buy her a dress and look at her with this kind of raw hunger in his eyes—talk to her in this voice—shouldn't he be talking about how beautiful he *thought* she was? If he was going to seduce her—because that's what this was, a kind of seduction—wasn't he going to tell her she was pretty? That he'd always thought she was pretty?

"It is a work-related event. This is a work-related expense. End of discussion."

"But I couldn't possibly impose—"

Something in him seemed to snap. He did touch her then—not in the cautious way he'd touched her on Monday, and not in the shattered way he'd laced his fingers with hers just yesterday.

He took her by the upper arm, his fingers gripping her tightly. He moved her away from the car door, opened it himself, and put her inside.

Before Serena could even grasp what was happening, Chadwick had climbed in next to her. "Take us to Neiman's," he ordered the driver.

Then he shut the door.

Four

What was wrong with this woman?

That was the question Chadwick asked himself over and over as they rode toward the Cherry Creek Shopping Center, where the Neiman Marcus was located. He'd called ahead and made sure Mario would be there.

Women in his world loved presents. It didn't matter what you bought them, as long as it was expensive. He'd bought Helen clothing and jewelry all the time. She'd always loved it, showing off her newest necklace or dress to her friends with obvious pride.

Of course, that was in the past. In the present, she was suing him for everything he had, so maybe there were limits to the power of gifts.

Still, what woman didn't like a gift? Would flatly refuse to even entertain the notion of a present?

Serena Chase, that's who. Further proving that he didn't know another woman like her.

"This is ridiculous," she muttered.

They were sitting side by side in the backseat of the limo, instead of across from each other as they normally did. True, Serena had scooted over to the other side of the vehicle, but he could still reach over and touch her if he wanted to.

Did he want to?

What a stupid question. Yes, he wanted to. Wasn't that why they were here—he was doing something he wanted, consequences be damned?

"What's ridiculous?" he asked, knowing full well she might haul off and smack him at any moment. After all, he'd forced her into this car with him. He could say this was a work-related expense until he was blue in the face, but that didn't make it actually true.

"This. *You*. It's the middle of the afternoon. On a Wednesday, for God's sake. We have *things* to do. I should know—I keep your schedule."

"I hardly think…" He checked his watch. "I hardly think 4:15 on a Wednesday counts as the middle of the afternoon."

She turned the meanest look onto him that he'd ever seen contort her pretty face. "*You* have a meeting with Sue Colman this afternoon—your weekly HR meeting. *I* have to help Matthew with the gala."

Chadwick got his phone and tapped the screen. "Hello, Sue? Chadwick. We're going to have to reschedule our meeting this afternoon."

Serena gave him a look that was probably supposed to strike fear in his heart, but which only made him want to laugh. Canceling standing meetings on a whim—just because he felt like it?

If he didn't know better, he'd think he was having fun.

"Did the board meeting run long?" Sue asked.

"Yes, exactly." A perfect excuse. Except for the fact that someone might have seen them return to the brewery—and then leave immediately.

"It can wait. I'll see you next week."

"Thanks." He ended the call and tapped on the screen a few more times. "Matthew?"

"Everything okay?"

"Yes, but Serena and I got hung up at the board meeting. Can you do without her for the afternoon?"

There was silence on the other end—a silence that made him shift uncomfortably.

"I suppose I could make do without *Ms. Chase*," Matthew replied, his tone heavy with sarcasm. "Can you?"

If I thought you were anything like our father, Matthew had said the day before, *I'd assume you were working on wife number two.*

Well, he wasn't, okay? Chadwick was not Hardwick. If he were, he'd have Serena flat on her back, her prim suit gone as he feasted on her luscious body in the backseat of this car.

Was he doing that? No. Had he ever done that? *No.* He was a complete gentleman at all times. Hardwick would have made a new dress the reward for a quick screw. Not Chadwick. Just seeing her look glamorous was its own reward.

Or so he kept telling himself.

"I'll talk to you tomorrow." He hung up before Matthew could get in another barb. "There," he said, shoving his phone back into his pocket. "Schedule's clear. We have the rest of the afternoon, all forty-five minutes of it."

She glared at him, but didn't say anything.

It only took another fifteen minutes to make it to the shopping center. Mario was waiting by the curb for them. The car had barely come to a complete stop when he had the back door open. "Mr. Beaumont! What a joy to see you again. I was just telling your brother Phillip that it's been too long since I've had the pleasure of your company."

"Mario," Chadwick said, trying not to roll his eyes at the slight man. Mario had what some might call a *flamboyant* way about him, what with his cutting-edge suit, faux-hawk hair and—yes—eyeliner. But he also had an eagle eye for fashion—something Chadwick didn't have the time or inclination for. Much easier to let Mario put together outfits for him.

And now, for Serena. He turned and held a hand out to her. When she hesitated, he couldn't help himself. He notched an eyebrow in challenge.

That did it. She offered her hand, but she did not wrap her fingers around his.

Fine. Be like that, he thought. "Mario, may I introduce Ms. Serena Chase?"

"Such a delight!" Mario swept into a dramatic bow—but then, he didn't do anything that wasn't dramatic. "An honor to make your acquaintance, Ms. Chase. Please, come inside."

Mario held the doors for them. It was only when they'd passed the threshold that Serena's hand tightened around Chadwick's. He looked at her and was surprised to see something close to horror on her face. "Are you all right?"

"Fine," she answered, too quickly.

"But?"

"I've just…never been in this particular store before. It's…" She stared at the store. "It's different than where I normally shop."

"Ah," he said, mostly because he didn't know what else to say. What if she hadn't been refusing his offer due to stubborn pride? What if there was another reason?

Mario swept around them and clapped his hands in what could only be described as glee. "Please, tell me how I can assist you today." His gaze darted to where Chadwick still had a hold of Serena's hands, but he didn't say anything else. He was far too polite to be snide.

Chadwick turned to Serena. "We have an event on Saturday and Ms. Chase needs a gown."

Mario nodded. "The charity gala at the Art Museum, of course. A statement piece or one of refined elegance? She could easily pull off either with her shape."

Serena's fingers clamped down on Chadwick's, and then she pulled her hand away entirely. Perhaps Mario's extensive knowledge of the social circuit was a surprise to her. Or perhaps it was being referred to in the third person by two men standing right in front of her. Surely it wasn't the compliment.

"Elegant," she said.

"Fitting," Mario agreed. "This way, please."

He led them up the escalator, making small talk about the newest lines and how he had a spotted a suit that would be perfect for Chadwick just the other day. "Not today," Chadwick said. "We just need a gown."

"And accessories, of course," Mario said.

"Of course." When Chadwick agreed, Serena shot him a stunned look. He could almost hear her thinking that he'd said nothing about accessories. He hadn't, but that was part of the deal.

"This way, please." Mario guided them back to a private fitting area, with a dressing room off to the side, a seating area, and a dais surrounded by mirrors. "Champagne?" he offered.

"Yes."

"No." Serena's command was sudden and forceful. At first Chadwick thought she was being obstinate again, but then he saw the high blush that raced across her cheeks. She dropped her gaze and a hand fluttered over her stomach, as if she were nervous.

"Ah." Mario stepped back and cast his critical eye over her again. "My apologies, Ms. Chase. I did not realize you were expecting. I shall bring you a fruit spritzer—non-alcoholic, of course." He turned to Chadwick. "Congratulations, Mr. Beaumont."

Wait—what? *What*?

Chadwick opened his mouth to say something, but nothing came out.

Had Mario just said…*expecting*?

Chadwick looked at Serena, who suddenly seemed to waver, as if she were on the verge of passing out. She did not tell Mario that his critical eye was wrong, that she was absolutely *not* expecting. She mumbled out a pained "Thank you," and then sat heavily on the loveseat.

"My assistant will bring you drinks while I collect a few things for Ms. Chase to model," Mario said. If he caught the sudden change in the atmosphere of the room, he gave no indication of it. Instead, with a bow, he closed the door behind him.

Leaving Chadwick and Serena alone in the silence.

"Did he just say…."

"Yes." Her voice cracked, and then she dragged in a ragged breath.

"And you're…"

"Yes." She bent forward at the waist, as if she could make herself smaller. As if she wanted to disappear from the room.

Or maybe she was on the verge of vomiting and was merely putting her head between her knees.

"And you—you found out this weekend. That's why you were upset on Monday."

"Yes." That seemed to be the only word she was capable of squeezing out.

"And you didn't tell me?" The words burst out of him. She flinched, but he couldn't stop. "Why didn't you *tell* me?"

"Mr. Beaumont, we usually do not discuss our personal lives at the office." At least that was more than a syllable, but the rote way she said it did nothing to calm him down.

"Oh? Were we going to *not* discuss it when you started showing? Were we going to not discuss it when you needed to take maternity leave?" She didn't reply, which only made him madder. Why was he so mad? "Does Neil know?" He was terrified of what she might say. That Neil might not be the father. That she'd taken up with someone else.

He had no idea why that bothered him. Just that it did.

"I…" She took a breath, but it sounded painful. "I sent Neil an email. He hasn't responded yet. But I don't need him. I can provide for my child by myself. I won't be a burden to you or the company. I don't need help."

"Don't lie to me, Serena. Do you have any idea what's going to happen if I lose the brewery?"

Even though she was looking at her black pumps and not at him, he saw her squeeze her eyes shut tight. Of course she knew. He was being an idiot to assume that someone as smart and capable as Serena wouldn't already have a worst-case plan in place. "I'll be out of a job. But I can get another one. Assuming you'll give me a letter of reference."

"Of course I would. You're missing the point. Do you know how hard it'll be for a woman who's eight months pregnant to get a job—even if I sing your praises from the top of the Rocky Mountains?"

She turned an odd color. Had she been breathing, beyond those few breaths she'd taken a moment before?

Jesus, what an ass he was being. *She* was pregnant—so *he* was yelling at her.

Something his father would have done. Dammit.

"Breathe," he said, forcing himself to speak in a quiet tone. He wasn't sure he was nailing "sympathetic," but at least he wasn't yelling. "Breathe, Serena."

She gave her head a tiny shake, as if she'd forgotten how.

Oh, hell. The absolute last thing any of them needed was for his pregnant assistant to black out in the middle of the workweek in an upscale department store. Mario would call an ambulance, the press would get wind of it, and Helen—the woman he was still technically married to—would make him pay.

He crouched down next to Serena and started rubbing her back. "Breathe, Serena. Please. I'm sorry. I'm not mad at you."

She leaned into him then. Not much, but enough to rest her head against his shoulder. Hadn't he wanted this just a few days before? Something that resembled his holding her?

But not like this. Not because he'd lost his temper. Not because she was...

Pregnant.

Chadwick didn't have the first clue how to be a good father. He had a great idea of how to be a really crappy father, but not a good one. Helen had said she didn't want kids, so they didn't have kids. It had been easier that way.

But Serena? She was soft and gentle where Helen, just like his own mother, had been tough and brittle. Serena worked hard and wasn't afraid to learn new things—wasn't afraid to get her hands dirty down in the trenches.

Serena would be a good mother. A *great* mother.

The thought made him smile. Or it would have, if he hadn't been watching her asphyxiate before his very eyes.

"Breathe," he ordered her. Finally, she gasped and exhaled. "Good. Do it again."

They sat like that for several minutes, her breathing and him reminding her to do it again. The assistant knocked on the door and delivered their beverages, but Serena didn't pull away from him and he didn't pull away from her. He sat on his heels and rubbed her back while she breathed and leaned on him.

When they were alone again, he said, "I meant what I said on Monday, Serena. This doesn't change that."

"It changes *everything*." He'd never heard her sound sadder. "I'm sorry. I didn't want anything to change. But it did. *I* did."

They'd lived their lives in a state of stasis for so long—he'd been not-quite-happily married to Helen, and Serena had been living with Neil, not quite happily, either, it turned out. They could have continued on like that forever, maybe.

But everything had changed.

"I won't fail you," he reminded her. Failure had not been an option when he was growing up. Hardwick Beaumont had demanded perfection from an early age. And it was never smart to disappoint Hardwick. Even as a child, Chadwick had known that.

No, he wouldn't fail Serena.

She leaned back—not away from him, not enough to break their contact, but far enough that she could look at him. The color was slowly coming back into her face, which was good. Her hair was mussed up from where her head had been on his shoulder and her eyes were wide. She looked as if she'd just woken up from a long nightmare, like she wanted him to kiss her and make it all better.

His hand moved. It brushed a few strands of hair from her cheek. Then his fingers curved under her cheek, almost as if he couldn't pull away from her skin.

"I won't fail you," he repeated.

"I know you won't," she whispered, her voice shaking.

She reached up—she was going to touch him. Like he was touching her. She was going to put her fingers on his face and then pull him down and he would kiss her. God, how he would kiss her.

"Knock, knock!" Mario called out from the other side of the door. "Is everybody decent in there?"

"Damn."

But Serena smiled—a small, tense smile, but a smile all the same. In that moment, he knew he hadn't let her down yet.

Now he just had to keep it that way.

Five

"Breathe in," Mario instructed as he held up the first gown.

Serena did as she was told. Breathing was the only thing she was capable of doing right now, and even that was iffy.

She'd almost kissed Chadwick. She'd almost let herself lean forward in a moment of weakness and *kiss him*. It was bad enough that she'd been completely unprofessional and had a panic attack, worse that she'd let him comfort her. But to almost kiss him?

She didn't understand why that felt worse than letting him kiss her. But it did. Worse and better all at the same time.

"And breathe *all* the way out. All the way, Ms. Chase. There!" The zipper slid up the rest of the way and she felt him hook the latch. "Marvelous!"

Serena looked down at the black velvet that clung to

every single size-ten curve she had and a few new ones. "How did you know what size I'd need?"

"Darling," Mario replied as he made a slow circle around her, smoothing here and tugging up there, "it's Mario's job to know such things."

"Oh." She remembered to breathe again. "I've never done this before. But I guess you figured that out." He'd guessed everything else. Her dress size, her shoe size—even her bra size. The strapless bra fit a lot better than the one she owned.

"Which part—trying on gowns or being whisked out of the office in the middle of the day?"

Yeah, she wasn't fooling anyone. "Both." Mario set a pair of black heels before her and balanced her as she stepped into them. "I feel like an imposter."

"But that's the beauty of fashion," Mario said, stepping back to look her over yet again. "Every morning you can wake up and decide to be someone new!" Then his face changed. "Even Mario." His voice changed, too—it got deeper, with a thicker Hispanic accent. "I'm really Mario from the barrio, you know? But no one else does. That's the beauty of fashion. It doesn't matter what we were. The only thing that matters is who we are today. And today," he went on, his voice rising up again, "you shall be a queen amongst women!"

She looked at him, more than a little surprised at what he'd said. Was it possible that he really was Mario from the barrio—that he might understand how out of place she felt surrounded by this level of wealth? She decided it didn't matter. All that mattered was that he'd made her feel like she could do this. She felt herself breathe again—and this time it wasn't a strain. "You really are fabulous, you know."

"Oh," he said, batting her comment away with a

pleased grin, "I tell my husband that all the time. One of these days, he's going to believe me!" Then he clapped his hands and turned to the cart that had God only knew how many diamonds and gems on it. "Mr. Beaumont is quite the lucky man!"

But he wasn't. He wasn't the father of her baby and he wasn't even her boyfriend. He was her boss. The walls started to close in on her again.

She needed to distract herself and fast. "Does this happen a lot? Mr. Beaumont showing up with a fashion-challenged woman?" The moment she asked the question, she wished she could take it back. She didn't want to know that she was the latest in a string of afternoon makeovers.

"Heavens, no!" Mario managed to look truly shocked at the suggestion as he turned with a stunning diamond solitaire necklace the size of a pea. "His brother, Mr. Phillip Beaumont? Yes. But not Mr. Chadwick Beaumont. I don't believe he ever even joined his wife on such an afternoon. Certainly not here. I would recall *that*."

Serena breathed again. There wasn't a particularly good reason for that to make her so happy. She had no claim on Chadwick, none at all. And just because he hadn't brought a girl shopping didn't mean he hadn't been seeing anyone else.

But she didn't think he had. He worked too much. She knew. She managed his schedule.

"Now," Mario went on, draping the necklace around her neck and fastening it, "you may have woken up this morning a frugal..." He tilted his head to the side and looked at her suit, now neatly hanging by the door. "Account executive?"

"Close," she said. "Executive assistant."

He snapped his fingers in disappointment, but it didn't

last. "By the time Mario gets done with you, you will *be* royalty."

He held his arm out to her, for which she was grateful—those heels were at least two inches higher than her dress shoes. Then he opened the door and they walked out into the sitting room.

Chadwick was reclined in the loveseat, a glass of champagne in one hand. He'd loosened his tie, a small thing that made him look ten times more relaxed than normal.

Then he saw her. His eyes went wide as he sat up straight, nearly spilling his drink. "Serena...wow."

"And this is just the beginning!" Mario crowed as he led her not to Chadwick but over to the small dais in front of all the mirrors. He helped her up and then guided her in a small turn.

She saw herself in the mirrors. Mario had smoothed her hair out after he'd gotten her suit off her. Her face still looked a little ashen, but otherwise, she couldn't quite believe that was her.

Royalty, indeed. Chadwick had been right. This dress, just like her black dress at home, made her feel beautiful. And after the day she'd had, that was a gift in itself.

She got turned back around and saw the look Chadwick was giving her. His mouth had fallen open and he was now standing, like he wanted to walk right up to her and sweep her into his arms.

"Now," Mario said, although it didn't feel like he was talking to either Serena or Chadwick. "This dress would be perfect for Saturday, but half the crowd will be wearing black and we don't want Ms. Chase to blend, do we?"

"No," Chadwick agreed, looking at her like she hadn't announced half an hour ago that she was pregnant. If anything, he was looking at her like he'd never really seen her before. And he wanted to see a lot more. "No, we don't want that."

"Plus, this dress is not terribly forgiving. I think we want to try on something that has more flow, more grace. More…"

"Elegant," Chadwick said. He seemed to shake back to himself. He backed up to the loveseat and sat again, one leg crossed, appraising her figure again. "Show me what else you've got, Mario."

"With pleasure!"

The next dress was a pale peachy pink number with a huge ball gown skirt and a bow on the back that felt like it was swallowing Serena whole. "A classic style," Mario announced.

"Too much," Chadwick replied, with a shake of his hand. She might have been hurt by this casual dismissal, but then he caught her gaze and gave her a smile. "But still beautiful."

Then came a cornflower blue dress with an Empire waist, tiny pleats that flowed down the length of the gown, and one shoulder strap that was encrusted with jewels. "No necklace," Mario informed her as he handed her dangling earrings that looked like they were encrusted with real sapphires. "You don't want to compete with the dress."

When she came out this time, Chadwick sat up again. "You are…*stunning*." There was that look again—like he was hungry. Hungry for her.

She blushed. She wasn't used to being stunning. She was used to being professional. Her black dress at home was as stunning as she'd ever gotten. She wasn't sure how she was going to pull off stunning while pregnant. But it didn't seem to be bothering Chadwick.

"This one has a much more forgiving waistline. She'll

be able to wear it for several more months and it'll be easier to get back into it." Mario was talking to Chadwick, but Serena got the feeling that he was really addressing her—greater wearability meant better value.

Although she still wasn't looking at the price tags.

"I don't know where else I'd wear it," she said.

Chadwick didn't say anything, but he gave her a look that made her shiver in the best way possible.

They went through several dresses that no one particularly loved—Mario kept putting her in black and then announcing that black was too boring for her. She tried on a sunflower yellow that did horrible things to her skin tone. It was so bad, Mario wouldn't even let her go out to show Chadwick.

She liked the next, a satin dress that was so richly colored it was hard to tell if it was blue or purple. It had an intricate pattern in lace over the bodice that hid everything she didn't like about her body. That was followed by a dark pink strapless number that reminded her of a bridesmaid gown. Then a blue-and-white off-the-shoulder dress where the colors bled into each other in a way that she thought would be tacky but was actually quite pretty.

"Blue is your color," Mario told her. She could see he was right.

She didn't think it was possible, but she was having fun. Playing dress-up, such as it was. High-end dress-up, but still—this was something she'd had precious little of during her childhood. Chadwick was right—she *did* feel beautiful. She twirled on the dais for him, enjoying the compliments he heaped upon her.

It was almost like…a fairy tale, a rags-to-riches dream come true. How many times had she read some year-old fashion magazine that she'd scavenged from a recycling bin and dreamed about dressing up in the pretty things?

She'd thought she'd gotten that herself with her consign-ment store dress, but that was nothing compared to being styled by the fabulous Mario.

Time passed in a whirl of chiffons and satins. Soon, it was past seven. They'd spent almost four hours in that dressing room. Chadwick had drunk most of a bottle of champagne. At some point, a fruit-and-cheese tray had been brought in. Mario wouldn't let Serena touch a bite while she was wearing anything, so she wound up standing in the dressing room in her underthings, eat-ing apple slices.

She was tired and hungry. Chadwick's eyes had begun to glaze over, and even Mario's boundless energy was seeming to flag.

"Can we be done?" Serena asked, drooping like a wilted flower in a pale green dress.

"Yes," Chadwick said. "We'll take the blue, the pur-ple, the blue-and-white and...was there another one that you liked, Serena?"

She goggled at him. Had he just listed *three* dresses? "How many times do you expect me to change at this thing?"

"I want you to have all options available."

"One is plenty. The blue one with the single strap."

Mario looked at Chadwick, who repeated, "All three, please. With all necessary accessories. Have them sent to Serena's house."

"Of course, Mr. Beaumont." He gathered up the gowns in question and hurried from the room.

Still wearing the droopy green dress, Serena kicked out of her towering shoes and stalked over to Chadwick. She put her hands on her hips and gave him her very best glare. "*One*. One I shouldn't let you buy me in the first place. I do *not* need three."

He had the nerve to look down at her and smile his ruthless smile, the one that let everyone in the room know that negotiations were finished. Suddenly, she was aware that they were alone and she wasn't wearing her normal suit. "Most women would jump at the chance to have someone buy them nice things, Serena."

"Well," she snapped, unable to resist stamping her foot in protest, "I'm not most women."

"I know." Then—almost as if he were moving in slow motion, he stood and began taking long strides toward her, his gaze fastened on her lips.

She should do…something. Step back. Cross her arms and look away. Flee to the dressing room and lock the door until Mario came back.

Yes, those were all truly things she *should* do.

But she *wanted* him to kiss her.

He slipped one arm around her waist, and his free hand caught her under the chin again. "You're not like any woman I've ever known, Serena. I could tell the very first time I saw you."

"You don't actually remember that, do you?" Her voice had dropped down to a sultry whisper.

His grin deepened. "You were working for Sue Colman in HR. She sent you up to my office with a comparison of new health-care plans." As he spoke, he pulled her in tighter, until she could feel the hard planes of his chest through the thin fabric of the gown. "I asked you what you thought. You told me that Sue recommended the cheaper plan, but the other one was better. It would make the employees happier—would make them want to stay with the brewery. I made you nervous—you blushed—but—"

"You picked the plan I wanted." The plan she'd needed. She'd just been hired full-time. She'd never had health benefits before and she wanted the one with a lower copay and better prescription coverage. She couldn't believe he remembered—but he did.

Her arms went around his chest, her hands flat on his back. She wasn't pushing him away. She couldn't. She wanted this. She had since that day. When she'd knocked on the door, he'd looked up at her with those hazel eyes. Instead of making her feel like she was an interruption, he'd focused on her and asked for her opinion—something he did *not* have to do. She was the lowest woman on the totem pole, barely ranking above unpaid intern—but the future CEO had made her feel like the most important worker in the whole company.

He had looked at her then the same way he was looking at her right now...like she was far more than the most important worker in the company. More like she was the most important woman in the world. "You were honest with me. And what's more than that, you were *right*. It's hard to expect loyalty if you don't give people something to be loyal to."

She'd been devoted to him from that moment on. When he'd been named the new CEO a year later, she'd applied to be his assistant the same day. She hadn't been the most qualified person to apply, but he'd taken a chance on her.

She'd been so thankful then. The job had been a gift that allowed her to take care of herself—to not rely on Neil to pay the rent or buy the groceries. Because of Chadwick, she'd been able to do exactly what she'd set out to do—be financially independent.

She was still thankful now.

Still in slo-mo, he leaned down. His lips brushed against hers—not a fierce kiss of possession, but something that was closer to a request for permission.

Serena took a deep breath in satisfaction. Chadwick's scent surrounded her with the warmth of sandalwood on top of his own clean notes. She couldn't help it—she clutched him more tightly, tracing his lips with her tongue.

Chadwick let out a low growl that seemed to rumble right out of his chest. Then the kiss deepened. She opened her mouth for him and his tongue swept in.

Serena's knees gave in to the heat that suddenly flooded her system, but she didn't go anywhere—Chadwick held her up. Her head began to swim again but instead of the stark panic that had paralyzed her earlier, she felt nothing but sheer desire. She'd wanted that kiss since the very first time she'd seen Chadwick Beaumont. Why on God's green earth had she waited almost eight years to invite it?

Something hard and warm pressed against the front of her gown. A similar weight hung heavy between her legs, driving her body into his. This was what she'd been missing for months. Years. This raw passion hadn't just been gone since Neil had left—it'd been gone for much longer.

Chadwick wanted her. And oh, how she *wanted him*. Wanted to forget about bosses and employees and companies and boards of directors and pregnancies and everything that had gone wrong in her world. This—being in Chadwick's arms, his lips crushed against hers—this was right. So very *right*. Nothing else mattered except for this moment of heat in his arms. It burned everything else away.

She wanted to touch him, find out if the rest of him was as strong as his arms were—but before she could do anything of the sort, he broke the kiss and pulled her into an even tighter hug.

His lips moved against her neck, as if he were smiling

against her. She liked how it felt. "You've always been special, Serena," he whispered against her skin. "So let me show you how special you are. I *want* to buy you all three dresses. That way you can surprise me on Saturday. Are you going to refuse me that chance?"

The heat ebbed between them. She'd forgotten about the dresses—and how much they probably cost. For an insane moment, she'd forgotten everything—who she was. Who he was.

She *absolutely* should refuse the dress, the dinner, the way he had looked at her all afternoon like he couldn't wait to strip each and every dress right off her, and the way he was holding her to his broad chest right now. She had no business being here, doing this—no business letting her attraction to Chadwick Beaumont cloud her thinking. She was pregnant and her job was on the line, and at no point in the past, present or future did she require three gowns that probably cost more than her annual salary.

But then that man leaned backward and cupped her cheek in his palm and said, "I haven't had this much fun in…well, I can't remember when. It was good to get out of the office." His smile took a decade of worry off his face.

She was about to tell him that the champagne had gone to his head—although she was painfully aware that she had no such excuse as to why she'd kissed him back—when he added, "I'm glad I got to spend it with you. Thank you, Serena."

And she had nothing. No refusal, no telling him off, no power to insist that Mario only wrap up one dress and none of the jewelry, no defense that she did not need him to buy her anything because she was perfectly able to buy her own dresses.

He'd had fun. With her.

"The dresses are lovely, Chadwick. Thank you."

He leaned down, his five-o'clock shadow and his lips lightly brushing her cheek. "You're welcome." He pulled back and stuck out his arm just like Mario had done to escort her to the dais. "Let me take you to dinner."

"I…" She looked down at the droopy green dress, which was now creased in a few key areas. "I have to get back to work. I have to go back to being an executive assistant now." Funny how that sounded off all of a sudden. She'd been nothing but an executive assistant for over seven years. Why shouldn't putting the outfit back on feel more…natural?

A day of playing dress-up had gone right to her head. She must have forgotten who she was. She was really Serena Chase, frugal employee. She wasn't the kind of woman who had rich men lavish her with exorbitant gifts. She *wasn't* Chadwick's lover.

Oh God, she'd let him kiss her. She'd kissed him back. What had she *done*?

Chadwick's face grew more distant. He, too, seemed to be realizing that they'd crossed a line they couldn't uncross. It made her feel even more miserable. "Ah, yes. I probably have work to do as well."

"Probably." They might have been playing hooky for a few hours that afternoon, but the world had kept on turning. The fallout from the board meeting no doubt had investors, analysts and journalists burning up the bandwidth, all clamoring for a statement from Chadwick Beaumont.

But more than that, she needed to be away from him. This proximity wasn't helping her cause. She needed to clear her head and stop having fantasies about her boss. Fantasies that now had a very real feel to them—the feeling of his lips against hers, his body pressed to hers.

Fantasies that would probably play out in her dreams that night.

She couldn't accept dinner on top of the dresses. She had to draw the line somewhere.

But she'd already crossed that line.

How much farther would she go?

Six

Chadwick did not sleep well.

He told himself that it had everything to do with the disastrous board meeting and nothing to do with Serena Chase, but what the hell was the point in lying? It had *everything* to do with Serena.

He shouldn't have kissed her. Rationally, he knew that. He'd fired other executives for crossing that very same line—one strike and they were out. For way too long, Beaumont Brewery had been a business where men took all kinds of advantage of the women who worked for them. That was one of the first things he'd changed after his father died. He'd had Serena write a strict sexual harassment policy to prevent exactly this situation.

He'd always taken the higher road. Fairness, loyalty, equality.

He was not Hardwick Beaumont. He would not seduce his secretary. Or his executive assistant, for that matter.

Except that he'd already started. He'd told her he was taking her to the gala. He'd taken her shopping and bought tens of thousands of dollars worth of gowns, jewels and handbags for her.

He'd kissed her. He'd wanted to do so much more than just kiss her, too. He'd wanted to leave that gown in a puddle on the floor and sit back on the loveseat, Serena's body riding his. He wanted to feel the full weight of her breasts in his hands, her body taking his in.

He'd wanted to do something as base and crass as take her in a dressing room, for God's sake. And that was exactly what Hardwick would have done.

So he'd stopped. Thankfully, she'd stopped, too.

She hadn't wanted the dresses. She'd fought him tooth and nail about that.

But the kiss?

She'd kissed him back. Tracing his mouth with her tongue, pressing those amazing breasts against him— holding him just as tightly as he had been holding her.

He found himself in his office by five-thirty the next morning, running a seven-minute mile on his treadmill. He had the international market report up on the screen in front of him, but he wasn't paying a damn bit of attention to it.

Instead, he was wondering what the hell he was going to do about Serena.

She was pregnant. And when she'd come out in those gowns, she'd *glowed*. She'd always been beautiful—a bright, positive smile for any occasion with nary a manipulating demand in sight—but yesterday she'd taken his breath away over and over again.

He was totally, completely, one hundred percent confounded by Serena Chase. The women in Chadwick's world did not refuse expensive clothing and jewelry. They spent their days planning how to get more clothes, better jewels and a skinnier body. They whimpered and pleaded and seduced until they got what they wanted.

That's what his mother had always done. Chadwick doubted whether Eliza and Hardwick had ever really loved each other. She'd wanted his money, and he'd wanted her family prestige. Whenever Eliza had caught Hardwick *in flagrante delicto*—which was often—she'd threaten and cry until Hardwick plunked down a chunk of change on a new diamond. Then, when one diamond wasn't enough, he started buying them in bulk.

Helen had been like that, too. Oh, she didn't threaten, but she did pout until she got what she wanted—cars, clothes, plastic surgery. It had been so much easier to just give in to her demands than deal with the manipulation. In the last year before she filed for divorce, she'd only slept with him when he'd bought her something. Not that he'd enjoyed it much, even then.

Somehow, he'd convinced himself he was fine with that. He didn't need to feel passion because passion left a man wide open for the pain of betrayal. Because there was always another betrayal around the next corner.

But Serena? She didn't cry, didn't whine and didn't pout. She never treated him like he was a pawn to be moved until she got what she wanted, never treated him like he was an obstacle she had to negotiate around.

She didn't even want to let him buy her a dress that made her feel beautiful.

He punched the treadmill up another mile per hour, running until his lungs burned.

He could not be lusting after his assistant and that was final.

This was just the result of Helen moving out of their bedroom over twenty-two months before, that was all.

And they hadn't had sex for a couple of months before that. Yes, that was it. Two years without a woman in his arms—without a woman looking at him with a smile, without a woman who was glad to see him.

Two years was a hell of a long time.

That's all this was. Sexual frustration manifesting itself in the direction of his assistant. He hadn't wanted to break his marriage vows to Helen, even in the middle of their never-ending divorce. Part of that was a wise business decision—if Helen found out that he'd had an affair, even after their separation, she wouldn't sign off on the divorce until he had nothing left but his name.

But part of that was refusing to be like his father.

Except his father totally would have lavished gifts on his secretary and then kissed her.

Hell.

Finally his legs gave out, but instead of the normal clarity a hard run brought him, he just felt more muddled than ever. Despite the punishing exercise, he was no closer to knowing what he was supposed to do when Serena came in for their morning meeting.

Oh, he knew what he wanted to do. He wanted to lay her out on his desk and lavish her curves with all the attention he had. He wanted her to straddle him. He wanted to bring her to a shuddering, screaming climax, and he wanted to hold her afterwards and fall asleep in her arms.

He didn't just want to have sex.

He wanted to have Serena.

Double damn.

He threw himself into his shower without bothering to touch the hot water knob. The cold did little to shock him back to his senses, but at least it knocked his erection down to a somewhat manageable level.

This was beyond lust. He had a need to take care of

her—to *not* fail her. That was why he'd bought her nice things, right? Sure. He was just rewarding her loyalty.

She'd said that her ex hadn't responded to her email. There—that was something he could do. He could get that jerk to step up to the plate and at least acknowledge that he'd left Serena in a difficult situation. Yeah, he liked that idea—making Neil Moore toe the line was a perfectly acceptable way of looking out for his best employee, and it didn't involve kissing her. He doubted that Serena would hold Neil responsible for his legal obligations—but Chadwick had no problem putting that man's feet to the fire.

He shut the water off and grabbed his towel. He was pretty sure he had Neil's information in his phone. But where had he left it?

He rummaged in his pants pocket for a few minutes before he remembered he'd set it down on his desk when he came in.

He opened the door and walked into his office—and found himself face-to-face with Serena.

"Chadwick!" she gasped. "What are you—"

"Serena!" It was then that he remembered the only thing he had on was a towel. He hadn't even managed to dry off.

Her mouth was frozen in a totally kissable "oh," her eyes wide as her gaze traveled down his wet chest.

Desire pumped through him, hard. All he'd have to do would be to drop the towel and show her exactly what she did to him. Hell, at the rate he was going, he wouldn't even have to drop the towel. She wasn't blind and his body wasn't being subtle right now.

"I'm...I'm sorry," she sputtered. "I didn't realize...."

"Just checking my phone." *Just thinking about you.*

He glanced at his clock. She was at least an hour ahead of schedule. "You're early."

"I wanted...I mean, about last night..." She seemed to be trying to get herself back under control, but her gaze kept drifting down. "About the kiss..." A furious blush made her look innocent and naughty at the same time.

He took a step forward, all of his best intentions blown to hell by the look on her face. The same look she'd had the night before when he'd kissed her. She wanted him.

God, that made him feel good.

"What about the kiss?"

Finally, she dropped her gaze from his body to the floor. "It shouldn't have happened. I shouldn't have kissed you. That was unprofessional and I apologize." She rushed through the words in one breath, sounding like she'd spent at least half the night rehearsing that little speech. "It won't happen again."

Wait—what? Was she taking all the blame for that? No. It's not like she'd shoved him against the wall and groped him. He was the one who'd pulled her into his arms. He was the one who'd lifted her chin. "Correct me if I'm wrong, but I thought I was the one who kissed *you*."

"Yes, well, it was still unprofessional, and it shouldn't have happened while I was on the job."

For a second, Chadwick knew he'd screwed up. She was serious. He'd be lucky if she didn't file suit against him.

But then she lifted her head, her bottom lip tucked under her teeth as she peeked at his bare torso. There was no uncertainty in her eyes—just the same desire that was pumping through his veins.

Then he realized what she'd said—while she was on the job.

Would she be "on the job" on Saturday night? Or off the clock?

"Of course," he agreed. Because, even though she was looking at him like that and he was wearing nothing more than a towel, he was not his father. He could be a reasonable, rational man. Not one solely driven by his baser needs. He could rein in his desires.

Sort of.

"What time shall I pick you up for dinner on Saturday?"

Her lower lip still held captive by her teeth—God, what would it feel like if she bit his lip like that?—he thought he saw her smile. Just a little bit. "The gala starts at nine. We should arrive by nine-twenty. We don't want to be unfashionably late."

He'd take her to the Palace Arms. It would be the perfect accompaniment to the gala—a setting befitting Serena in a gown. "Ms. Chase," he said, trying to use his normal business voice. It was harder to do in a towel than he would have expected. "Please make dinner reservations for two at the Palace Arms for seven. I'll pick you up at six-thirty."

Her eyes went wide again—like they had the day before when he'd informed her he was sending her to Neiman's to get a dress. Like they had when he'd impulsively ordered all three dresses. Why was she so afraid of him spending his money as he saw fit? "But that's…"

"That's what I want," he replied.

And then, because he couldn't help himself, he let the towel slip. Just a little—not enough to flash her—but more than enough to make her notice.

And respond. No, she didn't like it when he flashed his wealth around—but his body? His body appeared to be a different matter entirely. Her mouth dropped open into that "oh" again and then—God help him—her tongue flicked out and traced over her lips. He had to bite down to keep the groan from escaping.

"I'll…I'll go make those reservations, Mr. Beaumont," she said breathlessly.

He couldn't have kept the grin off his face if he tried. "Please do."

Oh, yeah, he was going to take her out to dinner and she was going to wear one of those gowns and he would…

He would enjoy her company, he reminded himself. He did not expect anything other than that. This was not a quid pro quo situation where he bought her things and expected her to fall into bed out of obligation. Sex was not the same as a thank-you note.

Then she held up a small envelope. "A thank-you note. For the dresses."

He almost burst out laughing, but he didn't. He was too busy watching Serena. She took two steps toward the desk and laid the envelope on the top. She was close enough that, if he reached out, he could pull her back into his arms again, right where she'd been the night before.

Except he'd have to let go of the towel.

When had restraint gotten this hard? When had he suddenly had trouble controlling his urges? Hell, when was the last time he'd had an urge he had to control?

Years, really. Long, dry years in a loveless marriage while he ran a company. But Serena woke up something inside of him—and now that it was awake, Chadwick felt it making him wild and impulsive.

The tension in the room was so thick it was practically visible.

"Thank you, Ms. Chase." He was trying to hide behind last names, like he'd done for years, but it wasn't working. All his mouth could taste was her kiss.

"You have Larry coming in for his morning meeting." She didn't step back, but he saw the side-eye she was giving him. "Shall I reschedule him or do you think you can be dressed by then?"

This time, he didn't bother to hold back his chuckle. "I suppose I can be dressed by then. Send him in when he gets here."

She gave a curt nod with her head and, with one more glance at his bare chest, turned to leave.

He couldn't help himself. "Serena?"

She paused at the door, but she didn't look back. "Yes?"

"I…" He snapped off the part about how he wanted her. Even if it was the truth. "I'm looking forward to Saturday."

She glanced back over her shoulder and gave him the same kind of smile she'd had when she'd been twirling in the gowns for him—warm, nervous and excited all at once. "Me, too."

Then she left him alone in his office. Which was absolutely the correct thing to have done.

Saturday sure seemed like a hell of a long time off.

He hoped he could make it.

Serena made sure to knock for the rest of the week.

Not that she didn't want to see Chadwick's bare chest, the light hairs that covered his body glistening with water, his hair damp and tousled….

And certainly not because she'd been fantasizing about Chadwick walking in on her in the shower, leaning her back against the tiled wall, kissing her like he'd kissed her in the store, those kisses going lower and lower until she was blind with pleasure, then her returning the favor….

Right. She knocked extra hard on his door because it was the polite thing to do.

Thursday was busy. The fallout from the board meeting had to be dealt with, and the last-minute plans for the gala could not be ignored. Once Chadwick got his clothes on, she hardly had more than two minutes alone with him before the next meeting, the next phone call.

Friday was the same. They were in the office until almost seven, soothing the jittery nerves of employees worried about their jobs and investors worried about not getting a big enough payout.

She still hadn't heard from Neil. She did manage to get a doctor's appointment scheduled, but it wasn't for another two weeks. If she hadn't heard anything after that, she'd have to call him. That was all.

But she didn't want to think about that. Instead, she thought about Saturday night.

She was not going to fall into bed with Chadwick. Above and beyond the fact that he was still her boss for the foreseeable future, there were too many problems. She *was* pregnant, for starters. She was still getting over the end of a nine-year relationship with Neil—and Chadwick wasn't divorced quite yet. She didn't want whatever was going on with her and Chadwick to smack of a rebound for either of them.

That settled it. If, perhaps in the near future—a future in which Serena was not pregnant, Chadwick was successfully divorced and Serena no longer worked for him because the company had been sold—*then* she could be brazen and call him up to invite him over. *Then* she could seduce him. Maybe in the shower. Definitely near a bed.

But not until then. Really.

So this was just a business-related event. Sure, an extra fancy one, but nothing else had changed.

Except for that kiss. That towel.
Those fantasies.
She was in *so* much trouble.

Seven

Her hair fixed into a sleek twist, Serena stood in her bedroom in her bathrobe and stared at the gowns like they were menacing her. All three were hung on her closet door.

With the price tags still on them.

Somehow, she'd managed to avoid looking at the tags in the store. The fabulous Mario had probably been working overtime to keep them hidden from her.

She had tens of thousands of dollars worth of gowns. Hanging in her house. Not counting the "necessary accessories."

The one she wanted to wear—the one-shoulder, cornflower blue dress that paired well with the long, dangly earrings? That one, on sale, cost as much as a used car. *On sale*! And the earrings? Sapphires. Of course.

I can't do this, she decided. This was not her world and she did *not* belong. Why Chadwick insisted on dressing her up and parading her around was beyond her.

She'd return the dresses and go back to being frugal Serena Chase, loyal assistant. That was the only rational thing to do.

Then her phone buzzed. For a horrifying second, she was afraid it was Neil, afraid that he'd come to his senses and wanted to talk. Wanted to see her again. Wanted frugal, loyal Serena back.

Just because she was trying not to fall head over heels for Chadwick didn't mean she wanted Neil.

She picked up her phone—it was a text from Chadwick.

On my way. Can't wait to see you.

Her heart began to race. Would he wear a suit like he usually did? Would he look stiff and formal or…would he be relaxed? Would he look at her with that gleam in his eye—the one that made her think of things like towels and showers and hot, forbidden kisses?

She should return these things. *All* of them.

She slipped the blue dress off the hanger, letting the fabric slide between her fingers. On the other hand… what would one night hurt? Hadn't she always dreamed about living it up? Wasn't that why she'd always gone to the galas before? It was a glimpse into a world that she longed to be a part of—a world where no one went hungry or wore cast-off clothing or moved in the middle of the night because they couldn't make rent?

Wasn't Chadwick giving her exactly what she wanted? Why shouldn't she enjoy it? Just for the night?

Fine, she decided, slipping into the dress. One night. One single night where she wasn't Serena Chase, hardworking employee always running away from poverty. For one glorious evening, she would be Serena Chase, queen amongst women. She would be escorted by a man who wouldn't be able to take his eyes off her—a man who made her feel beautiful.

If she ever saw the fabulous Mario again, she was going to hug that man.

She dressed carefully. She felt like she was going too slowly, but she wasn't about to rush and accidentally pop a seam on such an expensive dress. She decided to go with a bolder eye, so she spent more time putting on eyeliner and mascara than she had in the last month.

She'd barely gotten her understated lipstick into the tiny purse that Mario had put with this dress—even though it was a golden yellow—when she heard the knock on the door. "One moment!" she yelled, as she grabbed the yellow heels that had arrived with everything else.

Then she took a moment to breathe. She looked good. She felt good. She was going to enjoy tonight or else. Tomorrow she could go back to being pregnant and frugal and all those other things.

Not tonight. Tonight was hers. Hers and Chadwick's.

She opened the door and felt her jaw drop.

He'd chosen a tux. And a dozen red roses.

"Oh," she managed to get out. The tux was exquisitely cut—probably custom-made.

He looked over the top of the roses. "I was hoping you'd pick that one. I brought these for you." He held the flowers out to her and she saw he had a matching rose boutonnière in his lapel.

She took the roses as he leaned forward. "You look amazing," he whispered in her ear.

Then he kissed her cheek. One hand slid behind her back, gripping her just above her hip. "Simply amazing," he repeated, and she felt the heat from his body warm hers from the inside out.

They didn't have to go anywhere. She could pull him

inside and they could spend the night wrapped around each other. It would be perfectly fine because they weren't at work. As long as they weren't in the office, they could do whatever they wanted.

And he was what she wanted to do.

No. No! She could not let him seduce her. She could not let herself *be* seduced. At least, not that easily. This was a business-related event. They were still on the clock.

Then he kissed her again, just below the dangly earring, and she knew she was in trouble. She had to do something. Anything.

"I'm pregnant," she blurted out. Immediately her face flushed hot. And not the good kind of hot, either. But that was exactly what she'd needed to do to slam on the brakes. Pregnant women were simply not amazing. Her body was crazy and her hormones were crazier and that had to be the *only* reason she was lusting after her boss this much.

Thank heavens, Chadwick pulled back. But he didn't pull away, damn him. He leaned his forehead against hers and said, "In all these years, Serena, I've never seen you more radiant. You've always been so pretty, but now... pregnant or not, you are the most beautiful woman in the world."

She wanted to tell him he was full of it—not only was she not the most beautiful woman in the world, but she didn't crack the top one hundred in Denver. She was plain and curvy and wore suits. Nothing beautiful about that.

But he slipped his hand over her hip and down her belly, his hand rubbing small circles just above the top of her panties. "This," he said, his voice low and serious and intent as his fingers spread out to cover her stomach, "just makes you better. I can't control myself around you anymore and I don't think I want to." As he said it, his hand circled lower. The tips of his fingers crossed over the demarcated line of her panties and dipped down.

The warmth from his touch focused heat in her belly—and lower. A weight—heavy and demanding and pulsing—pounded between her thighs. She didn't want him to stop. She wanted him to keep going until he was pressing against the part of her that was heaviest. To feel his touch explore her body. To make her *his*.

If she didn't know him, she'd say he was feeding her a line of bull a mile long. But Chadwick didn't BS people. He didn't tell them what they wanted to hear. He told them the truth.

He told *her* the truth.

Which only left one question.

Now that she knew the truth, what would she do with it?

The absolute last place Chadwick wanted to be was at this restaurant. The only possible exception to that statement was the gala later. He didn't want to be at either one. He wanted to go back to Serena's place—hell, this restaurant was in a hotel, he could have a room in less than twenty minutes—and get her out of that dress. He wanted to lay her down and show her *exactly* how little he could control himself around her.

Instead, he was sitting across from Serena in one of the best restaurants in all of Denver. Since they'd left her apartment, Serena had been…quiet. He'd expected her to push back against dinner like she'd pushed back against the gown that looked so good on her, but she hadn't. Which was not a bad thing—she'd been gracious and perfectly well-mannered, as he knew she would be—but he didn't know what to talk about. Discussing work was both boring and stressful. Even though this was supposed to be a business dinner, he didn't want to talk about losing the company.

Given how she'd reacted to him touching her stomach—soft and gently rounded beneath the flowing dress—he didn't think making small talk about her pregnancy was exactly the way to go, either. That wasn't making her feel beautiful. At least, he didn't think so. He was pretty sure if they talked about her pregnancy, they'd wind up talking about Neil, and he didn't want to think about that jerk. Not tonight.

Chadwick's divorce was out, too. Chadwick knew talking about exes and soon-to-be-exes at dinner simply wasn't done.

And there was the part where he'd basically professed how he felt about her. Kind of hard to do the chitchat thing after that. Because doing the chitchat thing seemed like it would minimize what he'd said.

He didn't want to do that.

But he didn't know what else to talk about. For one of the few times in his life, he wished his brother Phillip was there. Well, he *didn't*—Phillip would hit on Serena mercilessly, not because he had feelings for her but because she was female. He didn't want Phillip anywhere near Serena.

Still, Phillip was good at filling the silence. He had an endless supply of interesting stories about interesting celebrities he'd met at parties and clubs. If anyone could find *something* to talk about, it'd be his brother.

But that wasn't Chadwick's life. He didn't jet around making headlines. He worked. He went to the office, ran, showered, worked, worked some more and then went home. Even on the weekends, he usually logged in. Running a corporation took most of his time—he probably worked a hundred hours a week.

But that's what it took to run a major corporation. For so long, he'd done what was expected of him—what his father had expected of him. The only thing that mattered was the company.

Chadwick looked at Serena. She was sitting across from him, her hands in her lap, her eyes wide as she looked around the room. This level of luxury was normal for him—but it was fun seeing things through her eyes.

It was fun *being* with her. She made him want to think about something other than work—and given the situation, he was grateful for that alone. But what he felt went way beyond simple gratitude.

For the first time in his adult life—maybe longer—he was looking at someone who meant more to him than the brewery did.

That realization scared the hell out of him. Because, really—who *was* he if he wasn't Chadwick Beaumont, the fourth-generation Beaumont to run the brewery? That was who he'd been raised to be. Just like his father had wanted, Chadwick had always put the brewery first.

But now…things were changing. He didn't know how much longer he'd have the brewery. Even if they fended off this takeover, there might be another. The company's position had been weakened.

Funny, though—he felt stronger after this week with Serena.

Still, he had to say *something*. He hadn't asked her to dinner just to stare at her. "Are you doing all right?"

"Fine," she answered, breathlessly. She did look fine. Her eyes were bright and she had a small, slightly stunned smile on her face. "This place is just so…fancy! I'm afraid I'm going to use the wrong fork."

He felt himself relax a bit. Even though she looked like a million dollars, she was still the same Serena.

His.

No. He pushed that thought away as soon as it cropped up. She was not his—she was only his assistant. That was the extent of his claim to her. "Your parents never dressed you up and took you out to eat at a place like this just for fun?"

"Ah, no." A furious blush raced up her cheeks.

"Really? Not even for a special event?"

That happened a lot. He'd be eating some place nice—some place like this—and a family with kids who had no business being in a five-star restaurant would come in, the boys yanking on the necks of their ties and tipping over the drinks, the girls being extra fussy over the food. He'd sort of assumed that all middle-class people did something like that once or twice.

She looked up at him, defiance flashing in her eyes. The same defiance that had her refusing dresses. He liked it on her—liked that she didn't always bow and scrape to him just because he was Chadwick Beaumont.

"Did your parents ever put you in rags and take you to a food pantry just for fun?"

"What?"

"Because that's where we went 'out to eat.' The food pantry." As quickly as it had come, the defiance faded, leaving her looking embarrassed. She studied her silverware setting. "Sorry. I don't usually tell people that. Forget I said anything."

He stared at her, his mouth open. Had she really just said...*the food pantry?* She'd mentioned that her family had gone through a few financial troubles but—

"You picked the food bank for this year's charity."

"Yes." She continued to inspect the flatware, everything about her closed off.

This wasn't the smooth, flowing conversation he'd wanted. But this felt more important. "Tell me about it."

"Not much to tell." Her chin got even lower. "Poverty is not a bowl full of cherries."

"What happened to your parents?" Not that his parents had particularly loved him—or even liked him—but he'd never wanted for anything. He couldn't imagine how parents could let that happen to their child.

"Nothing. It's just that…Joe and Shelia Chase did everything to a fault. They still do. They're loyal to a fault, forgiving to a fault—generous to a fault. If you need twenty bucks, they'll give you the last twenty they have in the bank and then not have enough to buy dinner or get the bus home. My dad's a janitor."

At this, a flush of embarrassment crept over her. But it didn't stop her. "He'll give you the shirt off his back—not that you'd want it, but he would. He's the guy who always stops when he sees someone on the side of the road with a flat tire, and helps the person change it. But he gets taken by every stupid swindle, every scam. Mom's not much better. She's been a waitress for decades. Never tried to get a better job because she was so loyal to the diner owners. They hired her when she was fifteen. Whenever Dad got fired, we lived on her tips. Which turns out to not be enough for a family of three."

There was so much hurt in her voice that suddenly he was furious with her parents, no matter how kind or loyal they were. "They had jobs—but you still had to go to the food pantry?"

"Don't get me wrong. They love me. They love each other…but they acted as if money were this unknown force that they had no power over, like the rain. Sometimes, it would rain. And sometimes—most of the time—it wouldn't. Money flows into and out of our lives independent of anything we do. That's what they thought. Still think."

He'd never questioned having money, just because there had always been so much of it. Who had to worry about their next meal? Not the Beaumonts, that was for damn sure. But he still worked hard for his fortune.

Serena went on, "They had love, Mom always said. So who needed cars that ran or health insurance or a place to live not crawling with bugs? Not them." Then she looked up at him, her dark brown eyes blazing. "But I do. I want more than that."

He sat there, fully aware his mouth had dropped open in shock, but completely unable to get it shut. Finally, he got out, "I had no idea."

She held his gaze. He could see her wavering. "No one does. I don't talk about it. I wanted you to look at me for what I am, not what I was. I don't want *anyone* to look at me and see a welfare case."

He couldn't blame her for that. If she'd walked into the job interview acting as if he owed her the position because she'd been on food stamps, he wouldn't have hired her. But she hadn't. She'd never played the sympathy card, not once.

"Did Neil know?" Not that he wanted to bring Neil into this.

"Yes. I moved in with him partly because he offered to cover the rent until I could pay my share. I don't think… I don't think he ever really forgot what I'd been. But he was stable. So I stayed." Suddenly, she seemed tired. "I appreciate the dresses and the dinner, Chadwick—I really do. But there were years where my folks didn't clear half of what you paid. To just *buy* dresses for that much…"

Like a bolt out of the blue, he understood Serena in a way he wasn't sure he'd ever understood another person. She was kind and she was loyal—not to a fault, not at the sacrifice of her own well-being—but those were traits that he'd always admired in her. "Why did you pick the brewery?"

She didn't look away from him this time. Instead, she leaned forward, a new zeal in her eyes. "I had internship offers at a couple of other places, but I looked at the employee turnover, the benefits—how happy the workers were. I couldn't bear the thought of changing jobs every other year. What if I never got another one? What if I couldn't take care of myself? The brewery had all these workers that had been there for thirty, forty years—entire careers. It's been in your family for so long…it just seemed like a stable place. That's all I wanted."

And now that was in danger. He wasn't happy about possibly failing to keep the company in family hands, but he had a personal fortune to fall back on. He'd been worried about the workers, of course—but Serena brought it home for him in a new way.

Then she looked up at him through her dark lashes. "At least, that's all I *thought* I wanted."

Desire hit him low and hard, a precision sledgehammer that drove a spike of need up into his gut. Because, unlike Helen and unlike his mother, he knew that Serena wasn't talking about the gowns or the jewels or the fancy dinner.

She was talking about *him*.

He couldn't picture the glamorous, refined woman sitting across from him wearing rags and standing in line at a food pantry. And he didn't have to. That was one of the great things about being wealthy. "I promised you I wouldn't fail you, Serena. I keep my promises." Even if he lost the company—if he failed his father—

he wouldn't leave Serena in a position in which welfare was her only choice.

She leaned back, dropping her gaze again. Like she'd just realized she'd gone too far and was trying to backtrack. "I know. But I'm not your responsibility. I'm just an employee."

"The hell you are." The words were out a little faster than he wanted them to be, but what was the point of pretending anymore? He hadn't lied earlier. Something about her had moved him beyond his normal restraint. She was so much *more* than an employee.

Her cheeks took on that pale pink blush that only made her more beautiful. Her mouth opened and she looked like she was about to argue with him when the waiter came up. When the man left with their orders—filet mignon for him, lobster for her—Chadwick looked at her. "Tell me about you."

She eyed him with open suspicion.

He held up his hands in surrender. "I swear it won't have any bearing on how I treat you. I'll still want to buy you pretty things and take you to dinner and have you on my arm at a gala." *Because that's where you belong,* his mind finished for him.

On his arm, in his bed—in his life.

She didn't answer at first, so he leaned forward and dropped his voice. "Do you trust me when I say I'll never use it against you?"

She tucked her lower lip up under her teeth. It shouldn't look so sexy, but on her it did. Everything did.

"Prove it."

Oh, yeah, she was challenging him. But it didn't feel like a battle of wills.

He didn't hesitate. "My dad beat me. Once, with a belt." He kept his voice low, so no one could hear, but it didn't matter. The words ripped themselves out of a place deep inside of his chest.

Her eyes went wide with shock and she covered her open mouth with her hand. It hurt to look at her, so he closed his eyes.

But that was a mistake. He could see his father standing over him, that nice Italian leather belt in his hand, buckle out—screaming about how Chadwick had gotten a C on a math test. He heard the belt whistle through the air, felt the buckle cut into his back. Felt the blood start to run down his side as the belt swung again—all because Chadwick had messed up how to subtract fractions. Future CEOs knew how to do math, Hardwick had reminded him again and again.

That's all Chadwick had ever been—future CEO of Beaumont Brewery. He'd been eleven. It was the only time Hardwick Beaumont had ever left a mark on him, but it was a hell of a mark. He still had the scar.

It was all such a long time ago. Like it had been part of a different life. He thought he'd buried that memory with his father, but it was still there, and it still had the capacity to cause him pain. He'd spent his entire life trying to do what his father wanted, trying to avoid another beating, but what had that gotten him? A failed marriage and a company that was about to be sold out from under him.

Hardwick couldn't hurt him now.

He opened his eyes and looked at Serena. Her face was pale and there was a certain measure of horror in her eyes, but she wasn't looking at him like he feared she would—like she'd forgotten about the man he was now and only saw a bleeding little boy.

Just like he saw a woman he trusted completely, and not a little girl who ate at food pantries.

He kept going. "When I didn't measure up to expectations. As far as I know, he never hit any of his other kids. Just me. He broke my toys, sent my friends away and locked me in my room, all because I had to be the perfect Beaumont to run his company."

"How...how could he do that?"

"I was never his son. Just his employee." The words tasted bitter, but they were the unvarnished truth. "And, like you said, I don't tell people about it. Not even Helen. Because I don't want people to look at me with pity."

But he'd told her. Because he knew she wouldn't hold it against him. Helen would have. Every time they fought, she would have thrown that back in his face because she thought she could use his past to control him.

Serena wouldn't manipulate him like that. And he wouldn't do that to her.

"So," he said, leaning back in his chair, "tell me about it."

She nodded. Her face was still pale, but she understood what he was saying. She understood him. "Which part?"

"All of it."

So she did.

Eight

Serena clung to Chadwick's arm as they swept up the red-carpeted stairs, past the paparazzi and into the Denver Art Museum. Part of her clinginess was because of the heels. Chadwick took huge, masterful strides that she was struggling to keep up with.

But another part of it was how unsettled she was feeling. She'd told him about her childhood. About the one time she and her mom had lived in a women-only shelter for three days because her dad didn't want them to have to sleep on the streets in the winter—but her mom had missed him so much that she'd bundled Serena up and they'd gone looking for him. She'd told him about Missy Gurgin in fourth grade making fun of Serena for wearing her old clothes, about the midnight moves to stay ahead of the due rent, about eating dinner that her mom had scavenged from leftovers at the diner.

Things she'd never told anyone. Not even Neil knew about all of that.

In turn, he'd told her about the way his father had controlled his entire life, about punishments that went way beyond cruel. He'd talked in a dispassionate tone, like they were discussing the weather and not the abuse of a child too young to defend himself, but she could hear the pain beneath the surface. He could act like it was all water under the bridge, but she knew better. All the money in the world hadn't protected Chadwick.

She put her hand over her stomach. No one would ever treat her child like that. And she would do everything in her power to keep her baby from ever being cold and hungry—or wondering where her next meal was coming from.

They walked into the Art Museum. Serena tried to find the calm in her mind. God knew she needed it. She pushed aside the horror of what Chadwick had told her, the embarrassment of sharing her story with him.

This was more familiar territory. She'd come to the Art Museum for this gala for the previous seven years. She knew where the galleries were, where the food was. She'd helped arrange that. She knew how to hold her champagne glass—oh, wait. No champagne for her tonight.

Okay, no need to panic. She was still perfectly at ease. She was only wearing a wildly expensive dress, four-inch heels and a fortune in jewels. Not to mention she was pregnant, on a date with her boss and....

Yeah, champagne would be *great* right about now.

Chadwick leaned over and whispered, "Are you breathing?" in her ear.

She did as instructed, the grin on her face making it easier. "Yes."

He squeezed her hand against his arm, which she found exceptionally reassuring. "Good. Keep it that way."

It was almost ten o'clock. Once they'd started sharing stories at dinner, it had been hard to stop. Serena was both mortified that she'd told any of that to Chadwick and, somehow, relieved. She'd buried those secrets deep, but they hadn't been dead. They'd lived on, terrorizing her like a monster under the bed.

At some point during dinner, she'd relaxed. The meal had been fabulous—the food was a little out there, but good. She'd been able to just enjoy being with Chadwick.

Now they were arriving at the gala slightly later than was fashionable. People were noticing as Chadwick swept her into the main hall. She could see heads tilting as people craned their necks for a better view, could hear the whispers starting.

Oh, this was not a good idea.

She'd loved her black dress because it looked good— but it had also blended, something Mario had forbidden. Now that she was here and standing out in the crowd in a bold blue, she wished she'd gone with basic black. People were *staring*.

A woman wearing a fire engine red gown that matched her fire engine red hair separated from the crowd just as Serena and Chadwick hit the middle of the room. She fought the urge to excuse herself and bolt for the ladies room. Queens amongst women did not hide in the bathroom, and that was *that*.

"There you are," the woman said, leaning to kiss Chadwick on the cheek. "I thought maybe you weren't coming, and Matthew and I would have to deal with Phillip all by ourselves."

Serena exhaled in relief. She should have recognized Frances Beaumont, Chadwick's half sister. She was well liked at the Beaumont Brewery, a fact that had a great deal to do with Donut Friday. Once a month, she personally delivered a donut to every single employee. Apparently, she'd been doing it since she was a little girl. As a result, Serena had heard more than a few of the workers refer to her as "our Frannie."

Frances was the kind of woman people described as "droll" without really knowing what that meant. But her razor-sharp wit was balanced with a good nature and an easy laugh.

Unlike everyone else at the brewery, though, Chadwick didn't seem to relax around his half sister. He stood ramrod straight, as if he were hoping to pass inspection. "We were held up. How's Byron?"

Frances waved her hand dismissively as Serena wondered, *Byron?*

"Still licking his wounds in Europe. I believe he's in Spain." Frances sighed, as if this revelation pained her, but she said nothing else.

Chadwick nodded, apparently agreeing to drop the topic of Byron. "Frannie, you remember Serena Chase, my assistant?"

Frances looked her up and down. "Of course I remember Serena, Chadwick." She leaned over and carefully pulled Serena into a light hug. "Fabulous dress. Where did you get it?"

"Neiman's." Breathing in, breathing out.

Frances gave her a warm smile. "Mario, am I right?"

"You have a good eye."

"Of course, darling." She drawled out this last word until it was almost three whole syllables. "It's a job requirement when you're an antiquities dealer."

"Your dress is stunning." Serena couldn't help but wonder how much it cost. Was she looking at several thousand dollars of red velvet and rubies? The one good thing was that, standing next to Frances Beaumont in that dress, no one was noticing Serena Chase.

Chadwick cleared his throat. She glanced up to find him smiling down at her. Well, no one but him would notice her, anyway.

He turned his attention back to his sister. "You said Phillip is already drunk?"

Frances batted away this question with manicured nails that perfectly matched the color of her dress. "Oh, not yet. But I'm sure before the evening is through he'll have charmed the spirits right out of three or four bottles of the good stuff." She leaned forward, dropping her voice to a conspiratorial whisper. "He's just that charming, you know."

Chadwick rolled his eyes. "I know."

Serena giggled, feeling relieved. Frances wasn't treating her like a bastard at a family picnic. Maybe she could do this.

Then Frances got serious, her smile dropping away. "Chadwick, have you thought more about putting up some money for my auction site?"

Chadwick made a huffing noise of disapproval, which caused a shadow to fall over Frances's face. Serena heard herself ask, "What auction site?"

"Oh!" Frances turned the full power of her smile on Serena. "As an antiquities dealer, I work with a lot of people in this room who'd prefer not to pay the full commission to Christie's auction house in New York, but who would never stoop to the level of eBay."

Ouch. Serena had bought more than a few things off the online auction site.

"So," Frances went on, unaware of the impact of her words on Serena, "I'm funding a new venture called Beaumont Antiquities that blends the cachet of a traditional art auction house with the power of social media. I have some partners who are handling the more technical aspects of building our platform, while I'm bringing the family name and my *extensive* connections to the deal." She turned back to Chadwick. "It's going to be a success. This is your chance to get in on the ground floor. And we could use the Chadwick Beaumont Seal of Approval. It'd go a long way to help secure additional funding. Think of it. A Beaumont business that has nothing to do with beer!"

"I like beer," Chadwick said. His tone was probably supposed to be flat, but it actually came out sounding slightly wounded, as if Frances had just told him his life's work was worthless.

"Oh, you know what I mean."

"You always do this, Frannie—investing in the 'next big idea' without doing your homework. An exclusive art auction site? In this market? It's not a good idea. If I were you, I'd get out now before you lose everything. Again."

Frances stiffened. "I haven't lost *everything*, thank you very much."

Chadwick gave her a look that was surprisingly paternal. "And yet, I've had to bail you out how many times?" Frances glared at him. Serena braced for another cutting remark, but then Chadwick said, "I'm sorry. Maybe this one will be a success. I wish you the best of luck."

"Of course you do. You're a good brother." Instantly, her droll humor was back, but Serena could see a shadow of disappointment in her eyes. "We're Beaumonts. You're the only one of us who behaves—well, you and maybe Matthew." She waved her hand in his general direction. "All respectable, while the rest of us are desperately trying to be dissolute wastrels." Her gaze cut between Chadwick and Serena. "Speaking of, there's Phillip now."

Before Serena could turn, she felt a touch slide down her bare arm. Then Phillip Beaumont walked around her, his fingers never leaving her skin. He was quite the golden boy. Only an inch shorter than his brother, he wore a tux without a bow tie. It made him look disheveled and carefree—which, according to all reports, he was. Where Chadwick was more of a sandy blond, Phillip's coloring was brighter, as if he'd been born for people to look at him.

Phillip took her hand in his and bent low over it. "*Mademoiselle*," he said as he held the back of her hand against his lips.

An uncontrollable shiver raced through her body. She did not particularly like Phillip—he caused Chadwick no end of grief—but Frances was one-hundred-percent right. He was exceedingly charming.

He looked up at Serena, his lips curled into the kind of grin that pronounced him fully aware of the effect he was having on her. "*Where* did you come from, enchantress? And, perhaps more importantly, why are you on *his* arm?"

Enchantress? That was a new one. And also a testament to Mario's superpowers. Phillip stopped by the office on a semi-regular basis to have meetings with Chadwick and Matthew about his position as head of special promotions for the brewery. She'd talked to him face-to-face dozens, if not hundreds, of times.

Chadwick made a sound that was somewhere between clearing his throat and growling. "Phillip, you remember Serena Chase, my executive assistant."

If Phillip was embarrassed that he hadn't recognized her, he gave no sign of it. He didn't even break eye contact with her. Instead, he favored her with the kind of smile that probably made the average woman melt into his bed. As it was, she was feeling a little dazzled by his sheer animal magnetism.

"How could I forget Ms. Chase? You are," he went on, leaning into her, "*unforgettable*."

Desperate, she looked at Frances, who gave a small shrug.

"That's *enough*." No mistaking it this time—that was nothing but a growl from Chadwick.

If Chadwick had growled at anyone else like that, he would have sent them diving for cover. But not Phillip. Good heavens, he didn't even look ruffled. He did give her a sly little wink before he touched her hand to his lips again. Chadwick tensed next to her and she wondered if a brawl was about to break out.

But then he released his grip on her hand and turned his full attention to his brother. Serena heaved a sigh of relief. No wonder Phillip had such a reputation as a ladies' man.

"So, news," he said in a tone that was only slightly less sultry than the one he'd been using on her. "I bought a horse!"

"Another one?" Frances and Chadwick said at the same time. Clearly, this was something that happened often.

"You've got to be kidding me." Chadwick looked… murderous. There really was no other way to describe it. He looked like he was going to throttle his brother in the middle of the Art Museum. "I don't suppose this one was only a few thousand?"

"Chad—hear me out." At this use of his shortened name, Chadwick flinched. Serena had never heard anyone call him that but Phillip. "This is an Akhal-Teke horse."

"*Gesundheit*," Frances murmured.

"A *what*?" Chadwick was now clutching her fingers against his arm in an almost desperate way. "How much?"

"This breed is extremely rare," Phillip went on. "Only about five thousand in the world. From Turkmenistan!"

Serena felt like she was at a tennis match, her head was turning back and forth between the two brothers so quickly. "Isn't that in Asia, next to Afghanistan?"

Phillip shot her another white-hot look and matching smile. "Beautiful *and* smart? Chadwick, you lucky dog."

"I swear to God," Chadwick growled.

"People are staring," Frances added in a light, sing-song tone. Then, looking at Serena for assistance, she laughed as if this were a great joke.

Serena laughed as well. She'd heard Chadwick and Phillip argue before, but that was usually behind Chadwick's closed office door. Never in front of her. Or in front of anyone else, for that matter.

For once, Phillip seemed to register the threat. He took an easy step back and held out his hands in surrender. "Like I was saying—this Akhal-Teke. They're most likely the breed that sired the Arabians. Very rare. Only about five hundred in this country, and most of those come from Russian stock. Kandar's Golden Sun isn't a Russian Akhal-Teke."

"*Gesundheit*," Frances murmured again. She looked at Serena with a touch of desperation, so they both laughed again.

"He's from Turkmenistan. An incredible horse. One to truly found a stable on."

Chadwick pinched the bridge of his nose. "How much?"

"Only seven." Phillip stuck out his chest, as if he were proud of this number.

Chadwick cracked open one eye. "Thousand, or hundred thousand?"

Serena tried not to gape. Seven thousand for a horse wasn't too much, she guessed. But seven *hundred* thousand? That was a lot of money.

Phillip didn't say anything. He took a step back, though, and his smile seemed more...forced.

Chadwick took a step forward. "Seven *what*?"

"You know, one Akhal-Teke went for fifty million—and that was in 1986 dollars. The most expensive horse ever. Kandar's Golden Sun—"

That was as far as he got. Chadwick cut him off with a shout. "You spent seven *million* on a horse while I'm working my ass off to keep the company from being sold to the wolves?"

Everything about the party stopped—the music, the conversations, the movement of waiters carrying trays of champagne.

Someone hurried toward them. It was Matthew Beaumont. "Gentlemen," he hissed under his breath. "We are having a *charity* event here."

Serena put her hand on Chadwick's arm and gave it a gentle tug. "A very good joke, Phillip," she said in a slightly too-loud voice.

Frances caught Serena's eye and nodded in approval. "Chadwick, I'd like to introduce you to the director of the food bank, Miriam Young." She didn't know where, exactly, the director of the food bank was. But she was sure Ms. Young wanted to talk with Chadwick. Or, at least, had wanted to talk to him before he'd started yelling menacingly at his relatives.

"Phillip, did I introduce you to my friend Candy?" Frances added, taking her brother by the arm and pulling him in the opposite direction. "She's *dying* to meet you."

The two brothers held their poses for a moment longer, Chadwick glaring at Phillip, the look on Phillip's face almost daring Chadwick to hit him in full view of the assembled upper crust of Denver society.

Then the men parted. Matthew walked on the other side of Chadwick, ostensibly to lead the way to the director. Serena got the feeling it was more to keep Chadwick from spinning and tackling his brother.

"Serena," Matthew said simply. "Nicely done. *Thus far*," he added in a heavy tone, "the evening has been a success. Now if we can just get through it without a brawl breaking out—"

"I'm fine," Chadwick snapped, sounding anything but. "I'm just *fine*."

"Not fine," Matthew muttered, guiding them into a side gallery. "Why don't I get you a drink? Wait here," he said, parking Chadwick in front of a Remington statue. "Do *not* move." He looked at Serena. "Okay?"

She nodded. "I've got him."

She hoped.

Nine

Chadwick had never really believed the old cliché about being so mad one saw red. Turns out, he'd just never been mad enough, because right now, the world was drenched in red-hot anger.

"How could he?" he heard himself mutter. "How could he just buy a horse for that much money without even thinking about the consequences?"

"Because," a soft, feminine voice said next to him, "he's not you."

The voice calmed him down, and some of the color bled back into the world. He realized Serena was standing next to him. They were in a nearly empty side gallery, in front of one of the Remington sculptures that made the backbreaking work of herding cattle look glorious.

She was right. Hardwick had never expected anything from Phillip. Never even noticed him, unless he did something outrageous.

Like buy a horse no one had ever heard of for seven million damn dollars.

"Remind me again why I work myself to death so that he can blow the family fortune on horses and women? So Frances can sink money into another venture that's bound to fail before it gets off the ground? Is that all I'm good for? A never-ending supply of cash?"

Delicate fingers laced through his, holding him tightly. "Maybe," Serena said, her voice gentle, "you don't have to work yourself to death at all."

He turned to her. She was staring at the statue as if it were the most interesting thing in the world.

Phillip had done whatever the hell he wanted since he was a kid. It hadn't mattered what his grades were, who his friends were, how many sports cars he had wrecked. Hardwick just hadn't cared. He'd been too focused on Chadwick.

"I…" He swallowed. "I don't know how else to run this company." The admission was even harder than what he'd shared over dinner. "This is what I was raised to do."

She tilted her head to one side, really studying the bronze. "Your father died while working, didn't he?"

"Yes." Hardwick had keeled over at a board meeting, dead from the heart attack long before the ambulance had gotten there. Which was better, Chadwick had always figured, than him dying in the arms of a mistress.

She tilted her head in the other direction, not looking at him but still holding his hand. "I rather like you alive."

"Do you?"

"Yes," she answered slowly, like she really had to think about it. But then her thumb moved against the palm of his hand. "I do."

Any remaining anger faded out of his vision as the room—the woman in it—came into sharp focus.

"You told me a few days ago," she went on, her voice quiet in the gallery, "that you wanted to do something for yourself. Not for the family, not for the company. Then you spent God only knows how much on everything I'm wearing." He saw the corner of her mouth curve up into a sly smile. "Except for a few zeros, this isn't so different, is it?"

"I don't need to spend money to be happy like he does."

"Then why am I wearing a fortune's worth of finery?"

"Because." He hadn't done it because it made him happy. He'd done it to see her look like this, to see that genuine smile she always wore when she was dressed to the nines. To know he could still *make* a woman smile.

He'd done it to make her happy. *That* was what made him happy.

She shot him a sidelong glance that didn't convey annoyance so much as knowing—like that was exactly what she'd expected him to say. "You are an impossibly stubborn man when you want to be, Chadwick Beaumont."

"It has been noted."

"What do you want?"

Her.

He'd wanted her for years. But because he was not Hardwick Beaumont, he'd never once pursued her.

Except now he was. He was walking a fine line between acceptable actions and immoral, unethical behavior.

What he really wanted, more than anything, was to step over that line entirely.

She looked up at him through her thick lashes, waiting for an answer. When he didn't give her one, she sighed. "The Beaumonts are an intelligent lot, you know. They'll learn how to survive. You don't have to protect them.

Don't work for them. They won't ever appreciate it because they didn't earn it themselves. Work for you." She reached up and touched his cheek. "Do what makes *you* happy. Do what *you* want."

She did realize what she was telling him, didn't she? She had to—her fingers wrapped around his, her palm pressed against his cheek, her dark brown eyes looking into his with a kind of peace that he couldn't remember ever feeling.

What he wanted was to leave this event behind, drive her home, and make love to her all night long. She *had* to know that was all he wanted—however not-divorced he was, pregnant she was, or employed she was by him.

Was she giving him permission? He would not trap his assistant into any sexual relationship. That wasn't him.

God, he wanted her permission. *Needed* it. Always had.

"Serena—"

"Here we are." Matthew strode into the gallery leading Miriam Young, the director of the Rocky Mountain Food Bank, and a waiter with a tray of champagne glasses. He gave Serena a look that was impossible to miss. "How is everything?"

She withdrew her hand from his cheek. "Fine," she said, with one of those beautiful smiles.

Matthew made the introductions and Serena politely declined the champagne. Chadwick only half paid attention. Her words echoed around his head like a loose bowling ball in the trunk of a car.

Don't work for them. Work for you.

Do what makes you happy.

She was right. It was high time he did what he wanted—above and beyond one afternoon.

It was time to seduce his assistant.

* * *

Standing in four-inch heels for two hours turned out to be more difficult than Serena had anticipated. She resorted to shifting from foot to foot as she and Chadwick made small talk with the likes of old-money billionaires, new-money billionaires, governors, senators and foundation heads. Most of the men were in tuxes like Chadwick's, and most of the women were in gowns. So she blended in well enough.

Chadwick had recovered from the incident with Phillip nicely. She'd like to think that had something to do with their conversation in the gallery. With the way she'd told him to do what he wanted and the way he'd looked at her like the only thing he wanted to do was *her*.

She knew there was a list of reasons not to want him back. But she was tired of those reasons, tired of thinking she couldn't, she *shouldn't*.

So she didn't. She focused on how painful those beautiful, beautiful shoes were. It kept her in the here and now.

Shoes aside, the evening had been delightful. Chadwick had introduced her as his assistant, true, but all the while he'd let one of his hands rest lightly on her lower back. She'd gotten a few odd looks, but no one had said anything. That probably had more to do with Chadwick's reputation than anything else, but she wasn't about to question it. Even without champagne, she'd been able to fall into small talk without too much panic.

She'd had a much nicer time than when she used to come with Neil. Then, she'd stood on the edge of the crowd, judiciously sipping her champagne and watching the crowd instead of interacting with it. Neil had always talked to people—always looking for another sponsor for his golf game—but she'd never felt like she was a part of the party.

Chadwick had made her a part of it this time. She wasn't sure she'd ever truly feel like she fit in with the high roller crowd, but she hadn't felt like an interloper. That counted for a great deal.

The evening was winding down. The crowd was trailing out. She hadn't seen Phillip leave, but he was nowhere to be seen. Frances had bailed almost an hour before. Matthew was the only other Beaumont still there, and he was deep in discussion with the caterers.

Chadwick shook hands with the head of the Centura Hospital System and turned to her. "Your feet hurt."

She didn't want to seem ungrateful for the shoes, but she wasn't sure her toes would ever be the same. "Maybe just a little."

He gave her a smile that packed plenty of heat. But it wasn't indiscriminately flirtatious, like his brother's. All night long, that goodness had been directed at only one woman.

Her.

He slid a hand around her waist and began guiding her toward the door. "I'll drive you home."

She grinned at this statement. "Don't worry. I didn't snag a ride with anyone else."

"Good."

The valet brought up Chadwick's Porsche, but he insisted on holding the door for her. Then he was in the car and they were driving at a higher-than-average speed, zipping down the highway like he had someplace to be.

Or like he couldn't wait to get her home.

The ride was quick, but silent. What was going to happen next? More importantly, what did she want to happen next? And—most importantly of all—what would she *let* happen?

Because she wanted this perfect evening to end perfectly. She wanted to have one night with him, to touch the body she'd only gotten a glimpse of, to feel beautiful and desirable in his arms. She didn't want to think about pregnancies or exes or jobs. It was Saturday night and she was dressed to the nines. On Monday, maybe they could go back to normal. She'd put on her suit and follow the rules and try not to think about the way Chadwick's touch made her feel things she'd convinced herself she didn't need.

Soon enough, he'd pulled up outside her apartment. His Porsche stuck out like a sore thumb in the parking lot full of minivans and late-model sedans. She started to open her door, but he put a hand on her arm. "Let me."

Then he hopped out, opened her door and held his hand out for her. She let him help her out of the deep seats of his car.

Then they stood there.

His strong hand held tight to hers as he pulled her against his body. She looked up into his eyes, feeling lightheaded without a drop of champagne. All night long, he'd only had eyes for her—but they'd been surrounded by people.

Now they were alone in the dark.

He reached up and traced the tips of his fingers over her cheek. Serena's eyelids fluttered shut at his touch.

"I'll walk you to your door," he said, his voice thick with strain. He stroked her skin—a small movement, similar to the way he'd touched her on Monday.

But this was different. Everything was different now.

This was the moment. This was her decision. She didn't want sex with Chadwick to be one of those things that "just happened," like her pregnancy. She was in control of her own life. She made the choices.

She could thank him for the lovely evening and tell

him she'd see him bright and early Monday morning. She could even make a little joke about seeing him in a towel again. Then she could walk into her apartment, close the door and…

Maybe never have another moment—another chance—to be with Chadwick.

She made her choice. She would not regret it.

She opened her eyes. Chadwick's face was inches from hers, but he wasn't pressing her to anything. He was waiting for her.

She wouldn't make him wait any longer. "Would you like to come in?"

He tensed against her. "Only if I can stay."

She kissed him then. She leaned up in the painful, beautiful shoes and pressed her lips to his. There was no "kissing him back," no "waiting for him to make the first move."

This was going to happen because she wanted it to. She'd wanted it for years and she was darn tired of waiting. That was reason enough.

"I'd like that."

The next thing she knew, Chadwick had physically swept her off her feet and was carrying her up to her door. When she gave him a quizzical look, he grinned sheepishly and said, "I know your feet hurt."

"They do."

She draped her arms around his neck and held on as he took the stairs, carrying her as if she were one of the skinny women from the party instead of someone whose size-ten body was getting bigger every day. But then, she'd seen all his muscles a few days before. If anyone could carry her, it was him. His chest was warm and hard against her body.

Things began to tighten. Her nipples tensed underneath the gown, and that heavy weight between her legs seemed to be pulling her down into his body. Oh, yes. She wanted him. But the thing that was different from all her time with Neil was how intense it felt to want Chadwick.

Obviously, it'd only been a few months since the last time she'd had sex with Neil. Just about three months. That was how far along she was. But she hadn't felt the physical weight of desire for much, much longer than that. She couldn't remember the last time just thinking about sex with Neil had turned her on this much. Maybe it was her crazy hormones—or maybe Chadwick did this to her. Maybe he'd always done this to her and she'd forced herself to ignore the attraction because falling for her boss just wasn't convenient.

He set her down at the door so she could get her key out of the tiny purse. But he didn't let her go. He put his hands on her hips and pulled her back into his front. They didn't talk, but the huge bulge that pressed against her backside said *lots* of things, loud and clear.

She got the door open and they walked inside. She kicked off the pretty shoes, which made Chadwick loom an extra four inches over her. He hadn't let go of her. His hands were still on her hips. He was *grabbing* her in a way that was quickly going from gentle to possessive. The way he filled his palms with her hips didn't make her feel fat. It made her feel like he couldn't get enough of her—he couldn't help himself.

Yes. That was what she needed—to be wanted so much that he couldn't control himself.

He leaned down, his mouth against her ear. "I've been waiting for you for years." The strain of the wait made his voice shake. He pulled her hips back again, the ridge in his pants unmistakable. "*Years*, Serena."

"Me, too." Her voice came out breathy, barely above a

whisper. She reached behind her back and slid her hand up the bulge. "Is that for me?"

"Yes," he hissed, his breath hot against her skin. One hand released a hip and found her breast instead. Even through the strapless bra, he found her pointed nipple and began to tease it. "You deserve slow and sensual, but I need you too much right now."

As if to prove his point, he set his teeth against her neck and bit her skin. Not too hard, but the feeling of being consumed by desire—by him—crashed through her. Her knees began to shake.

"Slow later," she agreed, wiggling her bottom against him.

With a groan, he stepped away from her. She almost toppled over backward, but then his hands were unzipping her dress. The gown slid off her one shoulder and down to the ground with a soft rustle.

She was extra glad she hadn't gone with the Spanx. Bless Mario's heart for putting her in a dress that didn't require them. Instead, a matching lacy thong had arrived with the bra. Which meant Chadwick currently had one heck of a view. She didn't know if she should strut, or pivot so he couldn't see her bottom.

Once the gown was gone, she stepped free of it. Chadwick moaned. "Serena," he got out as he slid his hands over her bare backside. "You are...amazing." His fingers gripped her skin, and he pressed his mouth to the space between her neck and her shoulder.

Strut, she decided. Nothing ruined good sex like being stupidly self-conscious when he already thought she was amazing. She pulled away from him before he could take away her power to stand.

"This way," she said over her shoulder as she, yes, *strutted* toward the bedroom, her hips swaying.

Chadwick made a noise behind her that she took as a compliment, before following her.

She headed toward the bed, but he caught up with her. He grabbed her hips again. "You are better than I thought," he growled as his hands slipped underneath the lace of the thong. He pulled the panties down, his palms against her legs. "I've dreamed of having you like this."

"Like how?"

He nimbly undid her bra, tossing it aside. She was naked. He was not.

He directed her forward, but not toward the bed. Instead, he pushed her in the direction of her dresser.

The one with the big mirror over it.

Serena gasped at the sight they made. Her, nude. Him, still in his tux, towering over her.

"This. Like this." He bent his head until his lips were on her neck again, just below the dangling earrings. "Is this okay?" he murmured against her skin.

"Yes." She couldn't take her eyes off their reflections, the way her pale skin stood out against his dark tux. The way his arms wrapped around her body, his hands cradled her breasts. The way his mouth looked as he kissed her skin.

The driving weight of desire between her legs pounded with need. "Yes," she said again, reaching one arm over her head and tangling her fingers in his hair. "Just like this."

"Good. So good, Serena." Without the bra, she could feel the pads of his fingertips trace over her sensitive nipple, pulling until it went stiff with pleasure.

She moaned, letting her head fall back against his shoulder. "Just like that," she whispered.

Then his other hand traced lower. This time, he didn't pause to stroke her stomach. His fingers parted her neatly trimmed hair and pressed against her heaviest, hottest place.

"Oh, Chadwick," she gasped as he moved his fingers in small, knowing circles, his other hand stroking her nipple, his mouth finding the sensitive spot under her ear—his bulge rubbing against her.

Her knees gave, but she didn't go far. Her wet center rode heavy on his hand as his other arm caught her under both breasts.

"Put your hands on the dresser," he told her. His voice was shaking as badly as her knees were, which made her smile. He might be pushing her to the brink, but she was pulling him along right behind her. "Don't close your eyes."

"I won't." She leaned forward and braced herself on the dresser. "I want to see what you do to me."

"Yeah," he groaned, a look of pure desire on his face as he met her gaze in the mirror. A finger slipped inside. So much, but not enough. She needed more. "You're so ready for me." Then she felt him lean back and work his own zipper.

"Next time, I get to do that for you."

"Any time you want to strip me down, you just let me know. Hold on, okay?" Then he withdrew his fingers.

She watched as he removed a condom from his jacket pocket. It wasn't like she could get more pregnant than she already was, but she appreciated that he didn't question protecting her.

He rolled the condom on and leaned into her. She quivered as she waited for his touch. He bent forward, placing a kiss between her shoulder blades. Then he was against her. Sliding into her.

Serena sucked in air as he filled her. And filled her. And *filled* her. In the mirror, her eyes locked onto his as he entered her. She almost couldn't take it. "Oh, Chadwick," she panted as her body took him in. "Oh—oh—*oh*!"

The unexpected orgasm shook her so hard that she almost pulled off him—but he held her. "Yeah," he groaned. "You feel so beautiful, Serena. So beautiful."

He gripped her hips as he slid almost all the way out before he thrust in again. "Okay?" he asked.

"Better than okay," she managed to get out, wiggling against him. The boldness of her action shocked her. Was she really having sex with Chadwick Beaumont, standing up—in front of a mirror?

Oh, hell yes, she was. And it was the hottest thing she'd ever done.

"Naughty girl," he said with a grin.

Then he began in earnest. From her angle, she couldn't see where their bodies met. She could only see his hands when he cupped her breasts to tweak a nipple or slid his fingers between her legs to stroke her center. She could only see the need on his face when he leaned forward to nip at her neck and shoulder, the raw desire in his eyes when their gazes met.

She held on to that dresser as if her life depended on it while Chadwick thrust harder and harder. "I need you so much," he called out as he grabbed her by the waist and slammed his hips into hers. "I've always needed you *so* much."

"Yes—like that," she panted, rising up to meet him each time. His words pushed her past the first orgasm. She couldn't remember ever feeling this needed, this sexual. "I'm going to—I'm—" Her next orgasm cut off her words, and all she could do was moan in pleasure.

But she didn't close her eyes. She saw how she looked

when she came—her mouth open, her eyes glazed with desire. So hot, watching the two of them together.

A roar started low in Chadwick's chest as he pumped once, twice more—then froze, his face twisted in pleasure. Then he sort of fell forward onto her, both of them panting.

"My Serena," he said, sounding spent.

"My Chadwick," she replied, knowing it was the truth. She was his now. And he was hers.

But he wasn't. He couldn't be. He was still married. He was still her boss. One explosive sexual encounter didn't change those realities.

For tonight, he was hers.

Tomorrow, however, was going to be a problem.

Ten

Chadwick laid in Serena's bed, his eyes heavy and his body relaxed.

Serena. How long had he fantasized about bending her over the desk and taking her from behind? Years. But the mirror? Watching her watch him?

Amazing.

She came back in and shut the door behind her. Her hair was down now, hanging in long, loose waves around her shoulders. He couldn't remember ever seeing her hair down. She always wore it up. He could see her nude figure silhouetted by the faint light that trickled through her drapes. Her body did things to him—things he didn't realize he could still feel. It'd been so long.…

She paused. "You need anything?"

"You." He held out his hand to her. "Come here."

She slipped into bed and curled up against his chest. "That was…wow."

Grinning, he pulled her in for a kiss. A long kiss. A kiss that involved a little more than just kissing. He could *not* get enough of her. The feeling of her filling his hands, pressed against him—she was so much a woman. He'd brought three condoms, just in case. He had the remaining two within easy reach on her bedside table.

So he broke the kiss.

"Mmmm," she hummed. "Chadwick?"

"Yes?"

She paused, tracing a small circle on his chest. "I'm pregnant."

"A fact we've already established."

"But why doesn't that bother you? I mean, everything's changing and I feel so odd and I'm going to blow up like a whale soon. I just don't think…I don't feel beautiful."

He traced a hand down her back and grabbed a handful of her bountiful backside. "You are amazingly beautiful. I guess you being pregnant just reminds me how much of a woman you are."

She was quiet for a moment. "Then why didn't you ever have kids with Helen?"

He sighed. He didn't want Helen in this room. Not now. But Serena had a right to know. Last week, they might not have discussed their personal lives at the office—but this was a different week entirely. "Did you ever meet her? Of course you did."

"At the galas. She never came by the office."

"No, she never did. She didn't like beer, didn't like my job. She only liked the money I made." Part of that was his fault. If he'd put her before the job, well, things might have been different. But they might not have been. Things might have been exactly the same.

"She was very pretty. Very—"

"Very plastic." She'd been pretty once, but with every

new procedure, she'd changed. "She had a lot of work done. Lipo, enlargements, Botox—she didn't want to have a baby because she didn't want to be pregnant. She didn't want me."

That was the hard truth of the matter. He'd convinced himself that she did—convinced himself that he wanted to spend the rest of his life with her, that it would be different from his father's marriages. That's why he'd struck the alimony clause from the pre-nup. But he'd never been able to escape the simple fact that he was Hardwick's son. All he'd ever been able to do was temper that fact by honoring his marriage vows long after there was nothing left to honor.

"She moved out of our bedroom about two years ago. Then filed for divorce almost fourteen months ago."

"That's a *very* long time." The way she said it—air rushing out of her in shock—made him hold her tighter. "Did you want to have a kid? I mean, I get her reasons, but…"

Had he ever wanted kids? It was no stretch to say he didn't know. Not having kids wasn't so much his choice as it had been the path of least resistance. "You haven't met my mother, have you?"

"No."

He chuckled. "You don't want to know her. She's—well, in retrospect, she's a lot like Helen. But that's all I knew. Screaming fights and weeks of silent treatment. And since I was my father's chosen son, she treated me much the same way she treated Hardwick. I ruined her figure, even though she got a tummy tuck. I was a constant reminder that she'd married a man she detested."

"Is that what Helen did? Scream?"

"No, no—but the silent treatment, yes. It got worse over time. I didn't want to bring a child into that. I didn't want a kid to grow up with the life I did. I didn't…I didn't want to be my father."

He couldn't help it. He took her hand and guided it around to his side—to where the skin had never healed quite right.

Serena's fingertips traced the raised scar. It wasn't that bad, he told himself. He'd been telling himself that same thing for years. Just an inch of puckered skin.

Helen had seen it, of course, and asked about it. But he hadn't been able to tell her the truth. He'd come up with some lie about a skiing accident.

"Oh, Chadwick," Serena said, in a voice that sounded like she was choking back tears.

He didn't want pity. As far as the world was concerned, he had no reason to be pitied. He was rich, good-looking and soon to be available again. Only Serena saw something else—something much more real than his public image.

He still didn't want her to feel sorry for him. So he kept talking even as she rubbed his scar. "Do you know how many half siblings I have?"

"Um, Frances and Matthew, right?"

"Frances has a twin brother, Byron. And that's just with Jeannie. My father had a third wife and had two more kids with her, Lucy and David. Johnny, Toni and Mark with his fourth wife. We know of at least two other kids, one with a nanny and one with…" He swallowed, feeling uncertain.

"His secretary?"

He winced. "Yes. There are probably more. That was why I fought against *this*," he said, pressing his lips against her forehead, "for so long. I didn't want to be him. So when Helen said she wanted to wait before we had kids—and wait and wait—I said fine. Because that's different than what Hardwick did."

Serena pulled her hand away from his scar to trace small circles on his chest again. "Those are all really good reasons. Mine were more selfish. I didn't marry Neil because my parents were married and that piece of paper didn't save them or me. I always thought we'd have kids one day, but I wanted to wait until my finances could support us. I put almost every bonus you've ever given me into savings, building up my nest egg. I thought I'd like to take some time off, but the thought of not getting that paycheck every other week scared me so much. So I waited. Until I messed up." She took a ragged breath. "And here I am."

He chewed over what she'd said. "Here with me?"

"Well…yes. Unmarried, pregnant and sleeping with my boss in clear violation of company policy." She sighed. "I've spent my adult life trying to lead a stable life. I stayed with a man I didn't passionately love because it was the safe thing to do. I've stayed in this apartment—the same place I've lived since I moved in with Neil nine years ago—because it's rent-controlled. I drive the same car I bought six years ago because it hasn't broken down. And now? This is not the most secure place in the world. It…it scares me. To be here with you."

Her whole life had been spent running away from a hellish childhood. Was that any different from his? Trying so hard to not let the sins of the father revisit the son.

Yet here he was, sleeping with his secretary. And here she was, putting her entire livelihood at risk to fall into bed with him.

No. This would not be a repeat of the past. He would not let her fall through the cracks just because he wasn't strong enough to resist her. At the very least, he hadn't gotten her pregnant and abandoned her like his father would have—even if someone else had done just that.

"I want to be here with you, even if it complicates matters. You make me feel things I didn't know I was still capable of feeling. The way you look at me...I was never a son, never really a husband. Just an employee. A bank account. When I'm with you, I feel like...like the man I was always supposed to be, but never got the chance to."

She clutched him even tighter. "You never treated me like I was an afterthought, a welfare kid. You always treated me with respect and made me feel like I could be better than my folks were. That I *was* better."

He tilted her face back. "I will *not* fail you, Serena. This complicates things, but I made you a promise. I *will* keep it."

She blinked, her eyes shining. "I know you will, Chadwick. That means everything to me." She kissed him, a tender brush that was sweeter than any other touch he'd ever felt. "I won't fail you, either."

The next kiss wasn't nearly as tender. "Serena," he groaned as she slipped her legs over his thighs, heat from her center setting his blood on fire. "I need you."

"I need you, too," she whispered, rolling onto her back. "I don't want to look at you in a mirror, Chadwick. I want to see you."

He sat back on his knees and grabbed one of the condoms. Quickly, he rolled it on and lowered himself into her waiting arms. His erection found her center and he thrust in.

She moaned as he propped himself up on one arm and filled his other hand with her breast. "Yes, just like that."

He rolled his thumb over her nipple and was rewarded when it went stiff. Her breast was warm and full and *real*.

Everything about her was real—her body, her emotions, her honesty.

Serena ran her nails down his back as she looked him in the eye, spurring him on. Over and over he plunged into her welcoming body. Over and over, waves of emotion flooded his mind.

Now that he was with her, he felt more authentic than he had in years—maybe ever. The closest he'd ever come to feeling real was the year he'd spent making beer. The brewmasters hadn't treated him with distrust, as so many people in the other departments had. They'd treated him like a regular guy.

Serena worked hard for him, but she'd never done so with the simpering air of a sycophant. Had never treated him like he was a stepping stool to bigger and better things.

This was real, too. The way her body took his in, the way he made her moan—the way he wanted to take her in his arms and never let her go....

Without closing her eyes—without breaking the contact between them—she made a high-pitched noise in the back of her throat as she tightened on his body then collapsed back against her pillow.

He drove hard as his climax roared through his ears so loudly that it blotted out everything but Serena. Her eyes, her face, her body. *Her.*

He wanted her. He always had.

This didn't change anything.

"Serena..." He wanted to tell her he loved her, but then what did that mean? Was he actually in love with her? What he felt for her was far stronger than anything he'd ever felt for another woman, but did that mean it was love?

So he bit his tongue and pulled her into his arms, burying his face into her hair.

"Stay with me," she whispered. "Tonight. In my bed."

"Yes." That was all he needed right now. Her, in his arms.

What if this was love? With Serena tucked against his chest, Chadwick started to drift off to sleep on that warm, happy thought. He and Serena. In love.

But then a horrifying idea popped into his mind, jerking him back from peaceful sleep. What if this wasn't love? What if this was mere infatuation, something that would evaporate under the harsh light of reality—reality that they might have ignored tonight but that would be unavoidable come Monday morning?

He'd slept with his assistant. Before the divorce was final.

It was exactly what his father would have done.

Eleven

The smell of crisp bacon woke him.

Chadwick rolled over to find himself alone in an unfamiliar bed. He found a clock on the side table. Half past six. He hadn't slept that late in years.

He sat up. The first thing he saw was the mirror. The one he'd watched as he made love to his assistant.

Serena.

His blood began to roar in his ears as his mind replayed the previous night. Had he really crossed that line—the one he'd sworn he would never cross?

Waking up naked in her bed, his body already aching for her, seemed to say one hell of a *yes*.

He buried his head in his hands. What had he done?

Then he heard it—the soft sound of a woman humming. It was light and, if he didn't know better, filled with joy.

He got out of bed and put his pants on. Breakfast

first. He'd think better once he had a meal in him. As he walked down the short hallway toward the kitchen, he was surprised at how sore his body was. Apparently, not having sex for a few years and then suddenly having it twice had been harder on him than running a few extra miles would have been.

He looked around Serena's place. It was quite small. There was the bedroom he'd come out of. He made another stop at the bathroom, which stood between the bedroom and another small room that was completely empty. Then he was out into the living room, which had a shabby-looking couch against one wall and a space where a flat-screen television must have been on the other. A table stood between the living room space and the kitchen. The legs and the chairs looked a bit beat up, but the table was covered by a clean, bright blue cloth and held a small, chipped vase filled with the roses he'd brought her.

His wine cellar was bigger than this apartment. The place was clearly assembled from odds and ends, but he liked it. It looked almost exactly how he'd imagined a real home would look, one in which babies might color on the walls and spill juice on the rug. One filled with laughter and joy. A place that was a *home*, not just a piece of real estate.

He found Serena standing in front of the stove, a thin blue cotton robe wrapped around her shoulders, her hair hanging in long waves down her back. Something stirred deep in his chest. Did she have anything on under the robe? She was humming as she flipped the bacon. It smelled *wonderful*.

He had a cook, of course. Even though he didn't eat at home very often, George was in charge of feeding the household staff. If Chadwick gave him enough warning, George would have something that rivaled the best restaurants in Denver waiting for him. But if Chadwick didn't, he'd eat the same thing that the maids did. Which was the norm.

He leaned against the doorway, watching Serena cook for him. This felt different than knowing that, somewhere in his huge mansion, George was making him dinner. That was George's job.

Serena frying him bacon and, by the looks of it, eggs?

This must be what people meant by "comfort food." Because there was something deeply comforting about her taking care of him. As far as he could remember, no one but a staff cook had ever made him breakfast.

Was this what normal people did? Woke up on a Sunday morning and had breakfast together?

He came up behind her and slid his arms around her waist, reveling in the way her hair smelled—almost like vanilla, but with a hint of breakfast. He kissed her neck. "Good morning."

She startled but then leaned back, the curve of her backside pressing against him. "Hi." She looked up at him.

He kissed her. "Breakfast?"

"I'm normally up before six, but I made it until a little after," she said, sounding sheepish about it.

"That's pretty early." Those were basically the same hours he kept.

"I have this boss," she went on, her tone teasing as she flipped another strip of bacon, "who keeps insane hours. You know how it is."

He chuckled against her ear. "A real bastard, huh?"

She leaned back, doing her best to look him in the eye. "Nope. I think he's amazing."

He kissed her again. This time he let his hands roam away from her waist to other parts. She pulled away and playfully smacked the hand that had been cupping her breast. "You don't want your breakfast burned, do you? The coffee's ready."

She already had a cup sitting in front of the coffee-maker. Like everything else in her place, the coffeemaker looked like it was either nine years old or something she'd bought secondhand.

She hadn't been kidding. By the looks of her apartment, she really had put every bonus in savings.

It was odd. In his world, people spent money like it was always going out of style. No one had to save because there would always be more. Like Phillip, for example. He saw a horse he wanted, and he bought it. It didn't matter how much it was or how many other horses he had. Helen had been the same, except for her it was clothing and plastic surgery. She had a completely new wardrobe every season from top designers.

Hell, he wasn't all that different. He owned more cars than he drove and a bigger house than he'd ever need, and he had three maids. The only difference was that he'd been so busy working that he hadn't had time to start collecting horses like his brother. Or mistresses, like his father. For them, everything had been disposable. Even the horses. Even the people.

Serena wasn't like that. She didn't need a new coffee-pot just because the old one was *old*. It still worked. That seemed to be good enough for her.

He filled his mug—emblazoned with the logo of a local bank—and sat at the table, watching her. She moved comfortably around her kitchen. He wasn't entirely sure where the kitchen was in his family mansion. "You make breakfast often?"

She put some bread into a late-model toaster. "I've gotten very good at cooking. It's…"

"Stable?"

"*Reassuring*," she answered with a grin. "I bring home my own bacon *and* fry it up in the pan." She brought plates with bacon and eggs to the table, and then went back for the toast and some strawberry jam. "I clip coupons and shop the sales—that saves a lot of money. Cooking is much cheaper than eating out. I think last night was the first time I'd gone out to dinner in…maybe three months?" Her face darkened. "Yes. Just about three months ago."

He remembered. Three months ago, Neil and she had "mutually" decided to end their relationship.

"Thank you for making me breakfast. I've never had someone cook for me. I mean, not someone who wasn't on staff."

She blushed. "Thank you for dinner. And the dresses. I think it's pretty obvious that I've never had anyone spend that kind of money on me before."

"You handled yourself beautifully. I'm sorry if I made you uncomfortable."

That had been his mistake. It was just that she fit in so well at the office, never once seeming out of place among the high rollers and company heads Chadwick met with. He'd assumed that was part of her world—or at least something close to it.

But it wasn't. Now that he saw her place—small, neatly kept but more "shabby" than "shabby chic"—he realized how off the mark he'd been.

She gave him a smile that was part gentle and part hot. "It was fun. But I think I'll get different shoes for next time."

Next time. The best words he'd heard in a long, long time.

They ate quickly. Mostly because he was hungry and the food was good, but also because Serena shifted in her seat and started rubbing his calf with her toes. "When do you have to leave?"

He wanted to stay at least a little bit longer. But he had things to do, even though it was Sunday—for starters, he had an interview with *Nikkei Business*, a Japanese business magazine, at two. He couldn't imagine talking about the fate of the brewery from the comfort of Serena's cozy place. How could those two worlds ever cross?

The moment the thought crossed his mind, he felt like he'd been punched in the stomach. Really, how *could* their two worlds cross? His company was imploding and his divorce was draining him dry—and that wasn't even counting the fact that Serena was pregnant. And his assistant.

He'd waited so long for Serena. She'd done admirably the night before at dinner and then the gala, but how comfortable would she really be in his world?

They still had this morning. They finished breakfast and then he tried to help her load the dishwasher. Only he kept trying to put the cups on the bottom rack, which made her giggle as she rearranged his poor attempts. "Never loaded a dishwasher before, huh?"

"What gave me away?" He couldn't bring himself to be insulted. She was right.

"Thanks for trying." She closed the dishwasher door and turned to him. "Don't worry. You're better at other things."

She put her arms around his neck and kissed him. Yeah, he didn't have to leave yet.

He stripped the robe from her shoulders, leaving it in a

heap on the floor. No, nothing underneath. Just her wonderful body. With the morning light streaming through the sheers she had hung over her windows, he could finally, fully see what he'd touched the night before.

Her breasts were large and firm. He bent down and traced her nipple with his tongue. Serena gasped as the tip went hard in his mouth, her fingers tangling through his hair. *Sensitive*. Perfect.

"Bed," she said in a voice that walked the fine line between fluttery and commanding.

"Yes, ma'am," he replied, standing back to give her a mock salute before he swept her off her feet.

"Chadwick!" Serena clutched at him, but she giggled as he carried her back down the short hall.

He laid her down on the bed, pausing only long enough to get rid of his pants. Then he was filling his hands with her breasts, her hips—covering her body with his—loving the way she touched him without abandon.

This was what he wanted—not the company, not Helen, not galas and banquets and brothers and sisters who took and took and never seemed to give back.

He wanted Serena. He wanted the kind of life where he helped cook and do the dishes instead of having an unseen staff invisibly take care of everything. He wanted the kind of life where he ate breakfast with her and then went back to bed instead of rushing off for an interview or a meeting.

He wanted to have a life outside of Beaumont Brewery. He wanted it to be with Serena.

He had no idea how to make that happen.

As he rocked into Serena's body and she clung to him, all he could think about was the way she made him feel—how he hadn't felt like this in…well, maybe ever.

This was what he wanted.

There had to be a way.

Finally, after another hour of lying in her arms, he managed to tear himself away from Serena's bed. He put on his tuxedo pants and shirt and headed for the car after a series of long kisses goodbye. How amazing did Serena look, standing in the doorway in her little robe, a coffee cup in her hand as she waved him off? It almost felt like a wife kissing her husband goodbye as he went off to work.

He was over-romanticizing things. For starters, Serena wouldn't be happy as a stay-at-home wife. It would probably leave her feeling too much like she wasn't bringing home that bacon. He knew now how very important that was to her. But they couldn't carry on like this at work. The office gossips would notice something sooner or later—and once she began to show, things would go viral in a heartbeat. He didn't want to subject her to the rumor mill.

There had to be a way. The variables ran through his mind as he drove home. He was about to lose the company. She worked for him. A relationship was against company policy. But if he lost the company...

If he lost the company, he wouldn't be her boss anymore. She might be out of a job, too, but at least they wouldn't be violating any policy.

But then what? What was next? What did he *want* to do? That was what she'd asked him. Told him, in fact. Do what he wanted.

What was that?

Make beer, he realized. That was the best time he'd had at Beaumont Brewery—the year he'd spent making beer with the brewmasters. He *liked* beer. He knew a lot about it and had played a big role in selecting the seasonal drafts for the Percheron Drafts line of craft beers. What if…

What if he sold the brewery, but kept Percheron Drafts for himself, running it as a small private business? Beaumont would be dead, but the family history of brewing would live on in Percheron Drafts. He could be rid of his father's legacy and run this new company the way he wanted to. It wouldn't be Hardwick's. It would be Chadwick's.

He could hire Serena. She knew as much about what he did as anyone. And if they formed a new company, well, they could have a different company policy.

And if they got sixty-five dollars a share for the brewery…maybe he could walk into Helen's lawyer's office and make her that offer she couldn't refuse. Everyone had a price, Matthew had said, and he was right. He quickly did the math.

If he liquidated a few extraneous possessions—cars, the jet, property, *horses*—he could make Helen an offer of $100 million to sign the papers. Even she wouldn't be able to say no to a number like that. And he'd still have enough left over to re-incorporate Percheron Drafts.

As he thought about the horses, he realized this plan would only work if he did it on his own. He would get $50 million because he actually worked for the company. But his siblings would get about $15 to $20 million each. He couldn't keep working for them. Serena had been right about that, too. If he took Percheron Drafts private, he would have to sever all financial ties with his siblings. He couldn't keep footing the bill for extravagant purchases, and what's more, he didn't want to.

The more he thought about it, the more he liked this idea. He'd be done with Beaumont Brewery—free from his father's ideas of how to run a company. Free to do

things the way he wanted, to make the beer he wanted.
It would be a smaller company, sure—one that wouldn't
be able to pay for the big mansion or the staff or the garage full of cars he rarely drove.

He'd have to downsize his life for a while, but would
that really be such a horrible thing? Serena had lived
small her entire life and she seemed quite happy—except for the pregnancy thing.

He wanted to give her everything he could—but he
knew she wouldn't be comfortable with extravagance. If
he gave her a job in a new company, paid her a good wage,
made sure she had the kind of benefits she needed…

That was almost the same thing as giving her the
world. That was giving her stability.

This could work. He'd call his lawyers when he got
home and run the idea past them.

This *had* to work. He had to make this happen. Because it was what he wanted.

After Serena watched Chadwick's sports car drive
away, she tried not to think about what the neighbors
would say about the late arrival and very late departure
of such a vehicle.

But that didn't mean she didn't worry. What had she
done? Besides have one of the most romantic nights in
memory. A fancy dinner, glamorous gala, exquisite sex?
It'd been like something out of a fairy tale, the poor little
girl transformed into the belle of the ball.

How long had it been since she'd enjoyed sex that
much? Things with Neil had been rote for a while. A
long while, honestly. Something that they *tried* to do
once a week—something that didn't last very long or
feel very good.

But sex with Chadwick? Completely different. Completely *satisfying*. Even better than she'd dreamed it would be. Chadwick hadn't just done what he wanted and left it at that. He'd taken his time with her, making sure she came first—and often.

What would it be like to be with a man who always brought that level of excitement to their bed? Someone she couldn't keep her hands off—someone who thought she was sexy even though her body was getting bigger?

It would be *wonderful*.

But how was that fantasy—for that's what it was, a fantasy of epic proportions—going to become a reality? She couldn't imagine fitting into Chadwick's world, with expensive clothes and fancy dinners and galas all the time. And, as adorably hot as he'd looked standing in her kitchen in nothing but his tux trousers, she also couldn't imagine Chadwick being happy in her small apartment, clipping coupons and shopping consignment stores for a bargain.

God, how she wanted him. She'd been waiting for her chance for years, really. But she had no idea how she could bridge the gap between their lives.

In a fit of pique, Serena started cleaning. Which was saying something, as she'd already cleaned in anticipation of Chadwick possibly seeing the inside of her apartment—and her bedroom.

But there was laundry to be done, dishes to be washed, beds to be made—more than enough to keep her busy. But not enough to keep her mind off Chadwick.

She changed into her grubby sweat shorts and a stained T-shirt. What the heck was going to happen on Monday? It was going to be hard to keep her hands off him, especially behind the closed door of his office. But doing anything, even touching him, was a violation of company policy. It went against her morals to violate policies, especially ones she'd helped write.

How was she supposed to be in love with Chadwick while she worked for him?

She couldn't be. Not unless...

Unless she didn't work for him.

No. She couldn't just quit her job. Even if the whole company was about to be sold off, she couldn't walk away from a steady paycheck and benefits. The sale and changeover might take months, after all—months during which she could be covered for prenatal care, could be making plans. Or some miracle could occur and the whole sale could fall through. Then she'd be safe.

So what was she going to do about Chadwick? She didn't want to wait months before she could kiss him again, before she could hold him in her arms. She was tired of pretending she didn't have feelings for him. If things stayed the same...

Well, one thing she knew for certain was that things wouldn't stay the same. She'd slept with him—multiple times—and she was pregnant. Those two things completely changed *everything*.

She was transferring the bedsheets from the washer to the dryer when she heard something at the door. Her first thought was that maybe Chadwick had changed his mind and decided to spend the day with her.

But, as she raced for the door, it swung open. *Chadwick doesn't have a key*, she thought. And she always kept her door locked.

That was as far as she got in her thinking before Neil Moore, semi-pro golf player and ex-everything, walked in.

"Hey, babe."

"Neil?" The sight of him walking in like he'd never

walked out caused such a visceral reaction that she almost threw up. "What are you doing here?"

"Got your email," he said, putting his keys back on
his hook beside the door as he closed it. He looked at
her in her cleaning clothes. "You look…good. Have you
put on weight?"

The boldness of this insult—for that's what it was—
shook her back to herself. "For crying out loud, Neil. I
sent you an email. Not an invitation to walk in, unan-
nounced."

Another wave of nausea hit her. What if Neil had
shown up two hours before—when she was still tangled
up with Chadwick? Good lord. She fought the emotion
down and tried to sound pissed. Which wasn't that hard,
really.

"You don't live here anymore, remember? *You* moved
out."

Then he said, "I missed you."

Nothing about his posture or attitude suggested this
was the case. He slouched his way over to the couch—
her couch—and slid down into it, just like he always
had. What had she seen in this man, besides the stability he'd offered her?

"Is that so? I've been here for three months, Neil.
Three months without a single call or text from you.
Doesn't seem like you've missed me very much at all."

"Well, I did," he snapped. "I see that nothing's changed
here. Same old couch, same old…" He waved his hand
around in a gesture that was probably supposed to encom-
pass the whole apartment but mostly seemed directed at
her. "So what did you want to talk to me about?"

She glared at him. Maybe it would have been better if Chadwick *had* still been here. For starters, Neil
would have seen that nothing was the same anymore—

she wasn't, anyway. She wasn't the same frugal executive assistant she'd been when he'd left. She was a woman who went shopping in the finest stores and made small talk with the titans of industry and looked damn good doing it. She was a woman who invited her boss into her apartment and then into her bed. She was pregnant and changing and bringing home her own bacon and frying it up in her own pan, thank you very much.

Neil didn't notice her look of death. He was staring at the spot where the TV had been before he'd taken that with him. "You haven't even gotten a new television yet? Geez, Serena. I didn't realize you were going to take me leaving so hard."

"I don't need one. I don't watch TV." A fact she would have thought he'd figured out after nine years of cohabitating—or at least figured out after she told him to take the TV when he moved. "Did you come here just to criticize me? Because I can think of a lot better ways to spend a Sunday morning."

Neil rolled his eyes, but then he sat up straighter. "You know, I've been thinking. We had nine good years together. Why did we let that get away from us?"

She could not believe the words coming out of this man's mouth. "Correct me if I'm wrong, but I believe 'we' let that get away from 'us' when you started sleeping with groupies at the country club."

"That was a mistake." He agreed far more quickly than he had when Serena had found the incriminating text messages. They'd gone out to dinner that night to try and "work things out," but it'd all fallen apart instead. "I've changed, babe. I know what I did was wrong. Let me make it up to you."

This was Neil "making it up to her"—criticizing her appearance and her apartment?

"I'll do better. Be better for you." For a second, he managed to look sincere, but it didn't last. "I heard that the brewery might get sold. You own stock in the company, right? We could get a bigger place—much nicer than this dump—and start over. It could be really good, babe."

Oh, for the love of Pete. That's what this was. He'd gotten wind of the AllBev offer and was looking for a big payout.

"What happened? Your lover go back to her husband?"

The way Neil's face turned a ruddy red answered the question for her, even though he didn't. He just went back to staring at the space where the television used to be.

The more she talked to him, the less she could figure out what she had ever seen in him. The petty little criticisms—it wasn't that those were new, it was just that she'd gotten used to not having her appearance, her housekeeping and her cooking sniped at.

In three months, she'd realized how much she'd settled by staying with Neil. No wonder the passion had long since bled out of their relationship. Hard to be passionate when the man who supposedly loved you was constantly tearing you down.

Chadwick didn't do that to her. Even before this last week had turned everything upside down, he'd always let her know how much he appreciated her hard work. That had just carried over into her bed. Boy, had he appreciated her hard work.

Serena shook her head. This wasn't exactly an either/or situation. Just because she didn't want Neil didn't necessarily mean her only other option was Chadwick. Even if whatever was going on between her and Chadwick was nothing more than a really satisfying rebound—for both of them—well, that didn't mean she wanted to throw her-

self at Neil. She was no longer a scared college girl exist-
ing just above the poverty line. She was a grown woman
fully capable of taking care of herself.

It was a damn good thing to realize.

"I'm pregnant. You're the father." There. She'd gotten
it out. "That's what I needed to talk to you about. And
because *you* were sleeping around, *I* have to get tested."

For a moment, Neil was well and truly shocked. His
mouth flopped open and his eyes bugged out of his head.
"You're…"

"Pregnant. Have been for three months."

"Are you sure I'm the father?"

Her blood began to boil. "Of course you're the father,
you idiot. Just because you were sleeping around doesn't
mean I was. I was faithful to you—to *us*—until the very
end. But that wasn't enough for you. And now you're not
enough for me."

"I…I…" He seemed stuck.

Well, he could just stick. She was the one that was
pregnant. She'd spend the rest of her life raising his—
her—baby. But that didn't mean she had to spend the
rest of her life with him. "I thought you should know."

"I didn't want—I can't—" He wasn't making a lot of
progress. "Can't you just *end* it?"

"Get out." The words flew from her mouth. "Get out
now."

"But—"

"This is my child. I don't need anything from you, and
what's more is I don't *want* anything from you. I won't
sue you for child support. I never want to see you again."
She hadn't said that when he'd left the last time. Maybe
because she hadn't believed the words. But now she did.

Neil's eyes hadn't made a lot of progress back into

his skull. "You don't want money? Damn—how much is Beaumont paying you now?"

Was that all she was—a back-up source of funding? "If you're still here in one minute, I'm calling the police. Goodbye, Neil."

He got up, looking like she'd smacked him. "Leave your key," she called after him. She didn't want any more surprise visits.

He took the key off his key ring and hung it back on the hook.

Then he closed the door on his way out.

And that was that.

She looked around the apartment as if the blinders had suddenly been lifted from her eyes. This wasn't her place. It had never been hers. This had been *their* place—hers and Neil's. She'd wanted to stay here because it was safe.

But Neil would always feel like he was entitled to be there because it had been his apartment before she'd moved in.

She didn't want to raise her baby in a place that was haunted by unfaithfulness and snide put-downs.

She needed a fresh start.

The thought terrified her.

Twelve

"Ms. Chase, if you could join me in my office."

Serena tried not to grin as she gathered up her tablet. He was paging her a full forty minutes earlier than their normal meeting time. What a difference a week made. Seven days before, she'd been shell-shocked after realizing she was pregnant. This week? She was sort of her boss's secret lover.

No, best not to think of it in those terms. Company policy and all that.

She opened the door to Chadwick's office and shut it behind her. That was what she normally did, but today the action had an air of secrecy about it.

Chadwick was sitting behind his desk, looking as normal as she'd ever seen him. Well, maybe not *that* normal. He glanced up and his face broke into one huge grin. God, he was so handsome. It almost hurt to look at him, to know that he was so happy because of her.

He didn't say anything as she walked toward her regular seat. Instead, he got up and met her halfway with the kind of kiss that melted every single part of her body. He pulled her in tight, and his lips explored hers.

"I missed you," he breathed in her ear as he wrapped his arms around her.

She took in his clean scent, her body responding to his touch. How different was this from Neil telling her he missed her the day before? Chadwick wasn't all talk. He followed up everything he said with actions.

"Me, too." Now that she knew exactly what was underneath that suit jacket, she couldn't stop running her hands over the muscles of his back. "I've never wanted Monday to get here so fast."

"Hmmm" was all he replied as he took another kiss from her. "When can I see you again?"

She gave him a look that was supposed to be stern. It must not have come across the way she intended it to, because he cracked a goofy grin. "This doesn't count?"

"You know what I mean."

She did. When could they spend another night wrapped in each other's arms? She wanted to say tonight. Right now. They could leave work and not come back until much, much later.

That wasn't an option.

"What are we going to do? I hate breaking the rules."

"You wrote the rule."

"That makes it even worse."

Instead of looking disgruntled with her, his grin turned positively wicked. "Look, I know this is a problem. But I'm working on a solution."

"Oh?"

"It's in process." She must have given him a look because he squeezed her a little tighter. "Trust me."

She stared into his eyes, wanting nothing more than to go back to Saturday night. Or even Sunday morning.

But reality was impossible to ignore. "If you need any help solving things, you just let me know."

"Done. When's your doctor's appointment?"

She touched the cleanly shaven line of his chin. "Friday next week."

"You want me to come with you?"

Love. The word floated up to the top of her consciousness, unbidden. That's what this was—love. Even if she hadn't said the exact word, she felt it with all of her heart.

Her throat closed up as tears threatened. Oh, God, she was in love with Chadwick Beaumont. It was both the best thing that had ever happened to her and one hell of a big problem.

He ran his finger under her chin again—much like he had the week before—and smiled down at her. "You all right?"

"I am. You wouldn't mind coming with me?"

"I've recently discovered that it's good to get out of the office every so often. I'd love to accompany you."

She had to swallow past the lump in her throat.

"Are you sure you're all right?"

She leaned her head against his shoulder, loving the solid, strong way he felt against her. "I hope you get that solution figured out soon."

"I won't fail you, Serena." He sounded so serious about it that she had no choice but to believe him. To hope that whatever he was planning would work. "Now, I believe I have time tonight to have a business dinner with my assistant, don't I? We can discuss my schedule in a little more...detail."

How could she say no to that? It was a business-professional activity, after all. "I believe we can make that happen."

"So," Chadwick said, pulling back and leading her toward the couch. "Tell me about your weekend."

"Funny about that." Sitting on the couch, her head against his shoulder, she related what had happened with Neil.

"You want me to take care of it?"

The way he said it—sounding much like he had when he'd nearly started a fight with his brother at the gala— made her smile. It should have been him being something of a Neanderthal male. As it was, it made her feel…secure.

"No, I think he got the message. He's not getting anything out of me or this company."

She then told Chadwick how she was thinking of moving to a new place and making a clean break with the past.

He got an odd look on his face as she talked. She knew that look—he was thinking.

"Got a solution to this problem yet?"

He cupped her face in his hands and kissed her— not the heated kiss from earlier, but something that was softer, gentler. Then he touched his forehead to hers. "You'll be the first to know."

That lump moved up in her throat again. She knew he'd keep his promise.

But what would it cost him?

"Mr. Beaumont." Serena's voice over the intercom sounded…different. Like she was being strangled.

"Yes?" He looked at Bob Larsen sitting across the desk from him, who froze mid-pitch. It wasn't like Serena to interrupt a meeting without a damn good reason.

There was a tortured pause. "Mrs. Beaumont is here to see you."

Stark panic flooded Chadwick's system. There were only a few women who went by that name and all of the options were less than pleasant. Blindly, he chose the least offensive option. "My mother?"

"Mrs. *Helen* Beaumont is here to see you."

Oh, *hell*.

Chadwick locked eyes with Bob. Sure, he and Bob had worked together for a long time, and yes, Chadwick's never-ending divorce was probably watercooler fodder, but Chadwick had worked hard to keep his personal drama and business life separate.

Until now.

"One moment," he managed to get out before he shut the intercom off. "Bob…"

"Yeah, we can pick this up later." Bob was hastily gathering his things and heading for the door. "Um… good luck?"

"Thanks." Chadwick was going to need a lot more than luck.

What was Helen doing there? She'd never come to the office when they were semi happily married. He hadn't talked to her without lawyers present in over a year. He couldn't imagine she wanted to reconcile. But what else would bring her there?

He knew one thing—he had to play this right. He could not give her something to use against him. He took a second to straighten his tie before he opened his door.

Helen Beaumont was not sitting in the waiting chairs across from Serena's desk. Instead, she was standing at one of the side windows, staring out at the brewery campus. Or maybe at nothing at all.

She was so thin he could almost see through her, like

she was a shadow instead of an actual woman. She wore a high-waisted skirt that clung to her frame, and a silk blouse topped with a fur stole. Diamonds—ones he'd paid for—covered her fingers and ears. She wasn't the same woman he'd married eight years before.

He looked at Serena, who was as white as notebook paper. Serena gave him a panicked little shrug. So she didn't have any idea what Helen was doing there, either.

"Helen." In good faith, he couldn't say it was nice to see her. So he didn't. "Shall we talk in my office?"

She pivoted on her five-inch heels and tried to kill him with a glare. "Chadwick." Her eyes cut to Serena. "I don't concern myself with what servants might hear."

Chadwick tried his best not to show a reaction. "Fine. To what do I owe the honor of a visit?"

"Don't be snide, Chadwick. It doesn't suit you." She looked down her nose at him, which was quite a feat given that she was a good eight inches shorter than he was. "My lawyer said you were going to make a new offer—the kind of offer you've refused to make for the last year."

Damn it. His lawyers were going to find themselves short one influential client for jumping the gun. Floating a trial balloon was different than telling Helen he had an offer. He hadn't even had the time to contact AllBev's negotiating team yet, for crying out loud. There was no offer until the company was sold.

He couldn't take control of his life—get the company he wanted, live the *way* he wanted—until Beaumont Brewery and AllBev reached a legally binding agreement. And what's more, none of this was going to happen overnight or even that week. Even if things moved quickly, negotiations would take months.

Plus, he hadn't told Serena about the plan to sell Beaumont but keep Percheron. God, he'd wanted to keep this all quiet until he had everything set—no more ugly surprises like this one.

"There's a difference between 'refused' and 'been unable' to make."

"Is there? Are you trying to get rid of me, Chadwick?" She managed to say it with a pout, as if he were trying to hurt her feelings.

"I've been trying to end our relationship since the month after you filed for divorce. Remember? You refused to go to marriage counseling with me. You made your position clear. You didn't want me anymore. But here we are, closing in on fourteen months later, and you insist on dragging out the proceedings."

She tilted her head to the side as she fluttered her eyelashes. "I'm not dragging anything out. I'm just…trying to get you to notice me."

"*What*? If you want to be noticed, suing a man is a piss-poor way of going about it."

Something about her face changed. For a moment he almost saw the woman who'd stood beside him in a church, making vows about love and honor.

"You *never* noticed me. Our honeymoon was only six days long because you had to get back early for a meeting. I always woke up alone because you left for the office by six every morning and then you wouldn't come back until ten or eleven at night. I guess I could have lived with that if I'd gotten to see you on the weekends, but you worked every Saturday and always had calls and interviews on Sunday. It was like…it was like being married to a ghost."

For the first time in years, Chadwick felt sympathy for Helen. She was right—he'd left her all alone in that big house with nothing to do but spend money. "But you knew this was my job when you married me."

"I—" Her voice cracked.

Was she on the verge of crying? She'd cried some, back when they would actually fight about…well, about how much he worked and how much money she spent. But it'd always been a play on his sympathies then. Was this a real emotion—or an old-fashioned attempt at manipulation?

"I thought I might be able to make you love me more than you loved this company. But I was wrong. You had no intention of ever loving me. And now I can never have those years back. I lost them to this damn brewery." She brightened, anything honest about her suddenly gone. He was looking at the woman who glared at him from across the lawyers' conference room table. "Here we are. I'm just getting what I deserve."

"We were married for less than ten years, Helen. What is it you think you deserve?"

She gave him a simpering smile and he knew the answer. *Everything*. She was going to take the one thing that had always mattered to him—the company—and she wouldn't stop until it was gone.

Until he had nothing left.

The phone rang on Serena's desk, causing him to jump. She answered it in something that sounded like her normal voice. "I'm sorry, but Mr. Beaumont is in a…meeting. Yes, I can access that information. One moment, please."

"My office," he said under his breath. "*Now*. We don't need to continue this conversation in front of Ms. Chase."

Helen's eyes narrowed until she looked like a viper mid-strike. "Oh? Or is it that you don't want to have *Ms. Chase* in front of me?"

Oh, no. He'd finally done something he wanted—taken Serena out, spent a night in her arms—and he was going to pay for it. Damn it all, why hadn't he kept his hands off her?

Because he wanted Serena. Because she wanted him.

It'd all seemed so simple two days before. But now?

"I beg your pardon," Serena said in an offended tone as she hung up the phone.

Helen's mouth twisted into a smirk. "You should. Sleeping with other people's husbands is never a good career move for a secretary."

"You can't talk to me like that," Serena said, sounding more shocked than angry.

Helen continued to stare at her, fully aware she held the upper hand in this situation. "How could you, Chadwick? Dressing up this dumpy secretary and parading her about as if she was *worth* something? I heard it was a pitiable sight."

Damn it all. He'd forgotten about Therese Hunt, Helen's best friend. Serena's face went a blotchy shade of purplish red, and she actually seemed to sway in her seat, like she might faint.

If Helen wanted his attention, she had it now. He was possessed with a crazy urge to throw himself between Serena and Helen—to protect Serena from Helen's wrath. He didn't do that, but he did take a step toward Helen, trying to draw her attention back to him.

"You will watch your mouth or I will have security escort you out of this building and, if you ever set foot on brewery property again, I'll file a restraining order so fast your head will spin. And if you think I'm not making a big enough offer now, just wait until the cops get involved. You will get nothing."

"After what you put me through, you owe me," she screeched.

Keeping his cool was turning out to be a lot of work. "I already offered you terms that are in line with what I owe you. You're the one who won't let this end. I'd like to move on with my life, Helen. Usually, when someone files for divorce, they're indicating that they, too, would like to move on with their lives—separately."

"You've been *sleeping* with her, haven't you?" Her voice was too shrill to be shouting, but loud enough to carry down the halls. Office doors opened and heads cautiously peeked out. "For how long?"

This whole situation was spiraling out of control. "Helen—"

"How long? It's been years, right? Were you banging her before we got married? *Were you*?"

Once, Helen had seemed sweet and lovely. But it had all been so long ago. The vengeful harpy before him was not the woman he had married.

It took everything he had to keep his voice calm. "I *was* faithful to you, Helen. Even after you moved out of our bedroom. But you're not my wife anymore. I don't owe you an explanation for what I do or who I love."

"The hell I'm not your wife—I haven't signed off!"

Anger roared through his body. "You are *not* my wife. You can't cling to the refuge of that technicality anymore, Helen. I've moved on with my life. For the love of God, move on with yours. My lawyers will be in contact with yours."

"You lying bastard! You stand here and take it like a man!"

"I'm not doing this, Helen. Ms. Chase, if you could join me in my office."

Serena gathered her tablet and all but sprinted through his open office door.

"You can't ignore me. I'll take everything. *Everything*!"

He positioned himself between her and the doorway to his office. "Helen, I apologize that I wasn't the man you needed me to be. I'm sorry you weren't the woman I thought you were. We both made mistakes. But move on. Take my next offer. Start dating. Find the man who *will* notice you. Because it's not me. Goodbye, Helen."

Then, over the hysterical sound of her calling him every name in the book, he shut the door.

Serena hunched in her normal chair, her head near her knees.

Chadwick picked up his phone and dialed the security office. "Len? I have a situation outside my office—I need you to make sure my ex-wife makes it out of the building as quietly as possible without you laying a hand on her. Whatever you do, *don't* provoke her. Thanks."

Then he turned his attention to Serena. Her color was not improving. "Breathe, honey."

Nothing happened. He crouched down in front of her and raised her face until he could see that her eyes were glazed over.

"Breathe," he ordered her. Then, because he couldn't think of anything else to shock her back into herself, he kissed her. Hard.

When he pulled back, her chest heaved as she sucked in air. He leaned her head against his shoulder and rubbed her back. "Good, hon. Do it again."

Serena gulped down air as he held her. What a mess. This was all his fault.

Well, his and his lawyers'. *Former* lawyers.

Outside the office, the raging stopped. Neither he nor

Serena moved until his phone rang some minutes later. Chadwick answered it. "Yes?"

"She's sitting in her car, crying. What do you want me to do?"

"Keep an eye on her. If she gets back out of the car, call the police. Otherwise, just leave her alone."

"Chadwick," Serena whispered so quietly that he almost didn't hear her.

"Yes?"

"What she said…"

"Don't think about what she said. She's just bitter that I took you to the gala." The blow about Serena being a dumpy secretary had been a low one.

"No." Serena pushed herself off his shoulder and looked him in the eye. Her color was better, but her eyes were watery. "About her being alone all the time. Because you work *all the time*."

"I did."

But that wasn't the truth, and they both knew it. He still worked that much.

She touched her fingertips to his cheek. "You *do*. I know you. I know your schedule. You left my apartment on Sunday exactly for the reason she said—because you had an interview."

All of his plans—plans that had seemed so great twenty-four hours before—felt like whispers drifting into the void.

"Things are going to change," he promised her. She didn't look like she believed him. "I'm working on it. I won't work a hundred hours a week. Because Helen was right about something else, too—I didn't love her more than I loved the company. But that's…" His voice choked up. "But that's different now. I'm different now, because of you."

Her lip trembled as two matching tears raced down either cheek. "Don't you see the impossible situation we're in? I can't be with you while I work for you—but if I don't work for you, will I ever see you?"

"Yes," he said. She flinched. It must have come out more harshly than he'd meant it to, but he was feeling desperate. "You will. I'll make it happen."

Her mouth twisted into the saddest smile he'd ever seen. "I've made your life so much harder."

"Helen did—not you. You are making it better. You always have."

She stroked his face, tears still silently dripping down her cheeks. "Everything's changed. If it were just you and me…but it's not anymore. I'm going to have a baby and I have to put that baby first. I can't live with the fear of Helen or even Neil popping up whenever they want to wreak a little havoc."

The bottom of his stomach dropped out. "I'm going to sell the company, but it'll take months. You'll be able to keep your benefits, probably until the baby's born. It doesn't have to change right now, Serena. You can stay with me."

Tears streaming, she shook her head. "I can't. You understand, don't you? I can't be your dumpy secretary and your weekend lover at the same time. I can't live that way, and I won't raise my child torn between two worlds like that. I don't belong in your world, and you—you can't fit in mine. It just won't work."

"It will," he insisted.

"And this company," she went on. "It's what you were raised to do. I can't ask you to give that up."

"Don't do this," he begged. The taste of fear was so strong in the back of his mouth that it almost choked him. "I'll take care of you, I promise."

Helen had left him, of course. But underneath the drama, he'd been relieved she was gone. It meant no more fights, no more pain. He could get on with the business of running his company without having to gauge everything against what Helen would do.

This? This meant no more seeing Serena first thing every morning and last thing every night. No more Serena encouraging him to get out of the office, reminding him that he didn't have to run the world just so his siblings could spend even more money.

The loss of Helen had barely registered on his radar. But the loss of Serena?

It would be devastating.

"I can't function without you." Even as he said it, he knew it was truer than he'd realized. "Don't leave me."

She leaned forward, pressing her wet lips to his cheek. "You can. You will. I have to take care of myself. It's the only way." She stood, letting her fingers trail off his skin. "I hereby resign my position of executive assistant, effective immediately."

Then, after a final tear-stained look that took his heart and left it lying in the middle of his office, she turned and walked out the door.

He watched her go.

So this was a broken heart.

He didn't like it.

Thirteen

The door to Lou's Diner jangled as Serena pulled it open. Things had been so crazy that she hadn't even had time to tell her mom and dad that she was pregnant. Or that she had quit her great job because she was in love with her great boss.

Mom and Dad had an old landline phone number that didn't have voice mail or even an answering machine, if it worked at all. The likelihood of her getting a "this number is out of service" message when Serena called was about fifty percent. Catching her mom at work was pretty much the only guaranteed way to talk to her parents.

She'd put off going there for a few nights. Seeing her parents always made her feel uncomfortable. She'd tried to help them out through the years—got them into that apartment, helped make the payments on her dad's car— and there'd been the disastrous experiment with prepaid cell phones. It always ended with them not being able to keep up with payments, no matter how much Serena put toward them. She was sure it had something to do with sheer, stubborn pride—they would not rely on their daughter, thank you very much. It drove Serena nuts. Why wouldn't they work a little harder to improve their situation?

Why hadn't they worked harder for her? Sure, if they wanted to be stubborn and barely scrape by, she couldn't stop them. But what about her?

Yes, she loved her parents and yes, they were always glad to see her. But she wanted better than a minimum wage job for the rest of her life, pouring coffee until the day she died because retirement was something for rich people. And what's more, she wanted better for her baby, too.

Still, there was something that felt like a homecoming, walking into Lou's Diner. Shelia Chase had worked here for the better part of thirty years, pulling whatever shift she could get. Lou had died and the diner had changed hands a few times, but her mom had always stuck with it. Serena didn't think she knew how to do anything else.

Either that, or she was afraid to try.

It'd been nine days since Serena had walked out of Chadwick's office. Nine long, anxious days that she'd tried to fill by keeping busy planning her new life.

She'd given her notice to her landlord. In two weeks, she was going to be moving into a new place out in Aurora, a good forty minutes away from the brewery. It wasn't a radically different apartment—two bedrooms, because she was sure she would need the space once the baby started crawling—but it wasn't infused with reminders of Neil. Or of Chadwick, for that matter. The rent was almost double what she was paying now, but if she bought her baby things used and continued to clip coupons, she had enough to live on for a year, maybe more.

She'd applied for ten jobs—office manager at an insurance firm, administrative assistant at a hospital, that sort of thing. She'd even sent her resume to the food bank. She knew the director had been pleased with her work and that the bank was newly flush with Beaumont cash. They could afford to pay her a modest salary—but health insurance...well, she was covered by a federal insurance extension plan. It wasn't cheap, but it would do. She couldn't go without.

She hadn't had any calls for interviews yet, but it was still early. At least, that's what she kept telling herself. Now was not the time to panic.

Except that, as she slid into a booth that was older than she was, the plastic crackling under her growing weight, the old fear of being reduced to grocery shopping in food pantries gripped her.

Breathe, she heard Chadwick say in her head. Even though she knew he wasn't here, it still felt...comforting.

Flo, another old-timer waitress with a smoker's voice, came by. "'Rena, honey, you look good," she said in a voice so gravelly it was practically a baritone. She poured Serena a cup of coffee. "Shelia's waiting on that big table. She'll be over in a bit."

So just the thought of being back in this place that had barely kept her family above water was enough to make breathing hard. There was still something comforting about the familiar—Flo and her scratchy voice, Mom waiting tables. Serena's world might have been turned completely on its ear in the last few weeks, but some things never changed.

She smiled at Flo. "Thanks. How are the grandkids?"

"Oh, just adorable," Flo said, beaming. "My daughter got a good job at Super-Mart stocking shelves, so I watch the kids at night after I get off work. They sleep like angels for me."

As Flo went to make her coffee rounds, Serena pushed back a new wave of panic. A good job stocking shelves? Having her mom watch the kids while she worked the night shift?

Yes, a job was better than no job, but this?

She'd thought that she could never be a part of Chadwick's world and he could never be a part of hers—they were just too different. But now, sitting here and watching her mother carry a huge tray of food over to a party of ten, Serena realized how much her world had really and truly changed. Once upon a time, when she was in college, a night job stocking shelves *would* have been a good job. It would have paid the rent and the grocery bills, and that was all she would have needed.

But now?

She needed more. No, she didn't need the five-thousand-dollar dresses that she hadn't been able to bring herself to pack up and return to the store. But now that she'd had a different kind of life for so long—a life that didn't exist in the spaces between paychecks—she knew she couldn't go back to one of menial labor and night shifts.

A picture of Chadwick floated before her eyes. Not the Chadwick she saw every day sitting behind his desk, his eyes glued to his computer, but the Chadwick who had stood across from her in a deserted gallery. He had been trying just as hard as she was to make things work—even if those "things" were radically different for each of them. He had been a man hanging on to his sanity by the tips of his fingers, terrified of what would happen if he let go.

In that moment, Chadwick hadn't just been a handsome or thoughtful boss. He'd been a man she understood on a fundamental level.

A man who'd understood her.

But then Helen Beaumont had come in and reminded Serena exactly how far apart her world and Chadwick's really were.

Deep down, Serena had known she couldn't carry on with Chadwick while she worked for him. An affair with her boss—no matter how passionate or torrid—wasn't who she was. But hearing how Chadwick had neglected his wife in favor of his company?

It'd been like a knife in the back. Were she and Chadwick only involved because they'd spent more time together in the past seven years than he'd ever spent with his wife—because, as Chadwick's employee, she was the only woman he spent any time with at all?

What if he was only with her because she was available? Hadn't she stayed with Neil for far too long for the exact same reason—because that was the path of least resistance?

No. She would not be the default anymore. Stability wasn't the safest route. That's what had kept her mother chained to this diner for her entire life—it was a guaranteed job. Why risk a bird in the hand when two in the bush was no sure thing?

If whatever was going on between Chadwick and Serena was more than just an affair of convenience, it would withstand her not being his executive assistant. She was sure of it.

Except for one small thing. He hadn't called. Hadn't even texted.

She hadn't really expected him to, but part of her was still disappointed. Okay, *devastated*. He'd said all those lovely things about how he was going to change, how she made him a better person—words that she had longed to hear—but actions spoke so much louder. And he hadn't done anything but watch her go.

She might love Chadwick. The odds were actually really good. But she couldn't know for sure while she worked for him. More than anything else, she didn't want to feel like he held all the cards in their relationship. She didn't want to feel like she owed everything to him—that he controlled her financial well-being.

That was why, as painful as it had been, she'd walked away from his promise to take care of her. Even though she wanted nothing more than to know that the man she loved would be there for her and that she'd never have to worry about sliding back into poverty again, she couldn't bank on that.

She was in control of her life, her fate. She had to secure her future by herself.

Serena Chase depended on no one.

Which was a surprisingly lonely way to look at the rest of her life.

Her head swimming, Serena was blinking back tears when her mother came to her table. "Sweetie, look at you! What's wrong?"

Serena smiled as best she could. Her mother was not many things, but she'd always loved her *sweetie*. Serena couldn't hide her emotional state from her mom.

"Hi, Mom. I hadn't talked to you for a while. Thought I'd drop in."

"I'm kinda busy right now. Can you sit tight until the rush clears out? Oh, I know—I'll have Willy make you some fried chicken, mashed potatoes and a chocolate shake—your favorite!"

Mom didn't cook. But she could order comfort food like a boss. "That'd be great," Serena admitted. She was eating for two now, after all. "Dad coming to get you tonight?"

That was their normal routine. If he still had a car that worked, that was.

Mom patted her on the arm. "Sure is. He got a promotion at work—he's now the head janitor! He'll be by in a few hours if you can wait that long."

"Sure can." Serena settled into the booth, enjoying the rare feeling of her mother spoiling her. She pulled out her phone and checked her email.

There was a message from Miriam Young. "Ms. Chase," it read, "I'm sorry to hear that you're no longer with the Beaumont Brewery. I'd be delighted to set up an interview. The Rocky Mountain Food Bank would be lucky to have someone with your skills on board. Call me at your earliest convenience."

Serena felt her shoulders relax. She would get another job. She'd be able to continue being her own stability.

Mom brought her a plate heaped with potatoes and chicken. "Everything okay, sweetie?"

"I think so, Mom."

Serena ate slowly. There was no rush, after all. Yes, if she could get another job lined up, that would go a long way toward being *okay*.

Yes, she'd be fine. Her and the baby. Just the two of them. Tomorrow, at her first appointment, she might get to hear the heartbeat.

The appointment Chadwick had offered to attend with her.

She knew she'd be fine on her own. She'd hardly missed Neil after a couple of weeks. It'd been a relief not to have to listen to his subtle digs, not to clean up after his messes.

Even though she'd only had Chadwick in her bed for

a night, that night had changed everything. He had been passionate and caring. He'd made her feel things she'd forgotten she needed to feel. In his arms, she felt beautiful and desirable and wanted. Very much wanted. Things she hadn't felt in so long. Things she couldn't live without.

Now that she'd tasted that sort of heat, was she really going to just do without it?

As she ate, she tried to figure out the mess that was her life. If she got a job at the food bank, then she would be able to start a relationship with Chadwick on equal footing. Well, he'd still be one of the richest men in the state and she'd still be middle class. *More* equal footing, then.

Finally, the rush settled down just as Joe Chase came through the door. "Well, look who's here! My baby girl!" he said with obvious pride as he leaned down and kissed her forehead.

Mom got him some coffee and then slid into the booth next to him. "Hey, babe," her dad said, pulling her mom into the kind of kiss that bordered on not-family-friendly.

Serena studied the tabletop. Her parents had never had money, never had true security—but they'd always had each other, for better or worse. In a small way, she was jealous of that. Even more so now that she'd glimpsed it with Chadwick.

"So," Dad said as he cleared his throat. Serena looked back at them. Dad was wearing stained coveralls and Mom looked beat from a day on her feet, but his arm was around her shoulder and she was leaning into him as if everything about the world had finally gone right.

"How's the job?"

Serena swallowed. She'd had the same job, the same apartment, for so long that she didn't know how her parents would deal with this. "Well…"

She told them how she'd decided to change jobs and

apartments. "The company may be sold," she said as both of her parents looked at her with raised eyebrows. "I'm just getting out while I can."

Her mom and dad shared a look. "This doesn't have anything to do with that boss of yours, does it?" Dad asked in a gruff voice as he leaned forward. "He didn't do nothing he shouldn't have, did he?"

"No, Dad, he's fine." She wished she could have sounded a little more convincing when she said it, because her parents shared another look.

"I don't have to work weekends now," her dad said. "I can round up a few buddies and we can get you moved in no time."

"That'd be really great," she admitted. "I'll get some beer and some pizzas—dinner for everyone."

"Nah, I got a couple of bucks in my sock drawer. I'll bring the beer."

"*Dad…*" She knew he meant it. A couple of bucks was probably all he had saved away.

Mom wasn't distracted by this argument. "But sweetie, I don't understand. I thought you liked your job and your apartment. I know it was rough on you when you were young, always moving around. Why the big change now?"

It was hard to look at them and say this out loud, so she didn't. She looked at the table. "I'm three months pregnant."

Her mom gasped loudly while her dad said, "You're *what* now?"

"Who—" was as far as her mom got.

Her dad finished the thought for her. "Your boss? If he did this to you, 'Rena, he should pay. I got half a mind to—"

"No, no. Neil is the father. Chadwick wasn't a part of

this." Or, at least, he hadn't been two weeks ago. "I've already discussed it with Neil. He has no interest in being a father, so I'm going to raise the baby by myself."

They sat there, stunned. "You—you okay doing that?" her dad said.

"We'll help out," her mom added, clearly warming to the idea. "Just think, Joe—a baby. *Flo*!" she hollered across the restaurant. "I'm gonna be a grandma!"

After that, the situation sort of became a big party. Flo came over, followed by Willy the cook and then the busboys. Her dad insisted on buying ice cream for the whole restaurant and toasting Serena.

It almost made Serena feel better. They couldn't give her material things—although her proud dad was hell-bent on trying—but her parents had always given her love in abundance.

It was nine that night before she made it back to her cluttered apartment. Boxes were scattered all over the living room.

Serena stood in the middle of it all, trying not to cry. Yes, the talk with her parents had gone well. Her dad would have all of her stuff moved in an afternoon. Her mom was already talking about layettes. Serena wasn't even sure what a layette was, but by God, Shelia Chase was going to get one. The best Serena had been able to do was to get her mom to promise she wouldn't take out another payday loan to pay for it.

Honestly, she wasn't sure she'd ever seen her parents so excited. The change in jobs and apartment hadn't even fazed them.

But the day had left her drained. Unable to deal with the mess of the living room, she went into her bedroom. That was a mistake.

There, hanging on the closet door, were the dresses. Oh, the dresses. She could hardly bear to look at the traces of finery Chadwick had lavished on her without thinking of how he'd bent her over in front of the dresser, how he'd held her all night long. How he'd promised to go with her to the doctor tomorrow. How he'd promised that he wouldn't fail her.

He was going to break his promise.

It was going to break her heart.

Fourteen

Serena got up and shaved her legs in preparation for her doctor's appointment. It seemed like the thing to do. She twisted up her hair and put on a skirt and a blouse. The formality of the outfit was comforting, somehow. It didn't make sense. But then, nothing made a lot of sense anymore.

For example, she needed to leave for the doctor's office by ten-thirty. She was dressed by eight. Which left her several hours to fret.

She was staring into her coffee cup, trying to figure out the mess in her head, when someone knocked on the door.

Neil? Surely he wouldn't have come back. She'd done a pretty thorough job of kicking him out the last time.

Maybe it was her mom, stopping in early to continue celebrating the good news. But, after another round of knocks, she was pretty sure it wasn't her mom.

Serena hurried to the door and peeked through the peephole. There, on her stoop, stood Chadwick Beaumont.

"Serena? I need to talk to you," he called, staring at the peephole.

Damn. He'd seen her shadow. She couldn't pretend she wasn't home without being totally rude.

She was debating whether or not she wanted to be *totally* rude when he added, "I didn't miss your appointment, did I?"

He hadn't forgotten. Sagging with relief, she opened the door a crack.

Chadwick was wearing a button-up shirt and trousers, with no tie or jacket. The informality looked good on him, but that might have had something to do with the grin on his face. If she didn't know better, she'd say he looked…giddy?

"I didn't think you were going to come."

He stared at her in confusion. "I told you I would." Then he looked at what she was wearing. "You already have an interview?"

"Well, yes. I quit my job. I need another one." She cleared her throat, suddenly nervous about this conversation. "I was counting on a letter of recommendation from you."

The grin on Chadwick's face broadened. It was as if all his worry from the last few years had melted away. "I should have guessed that you wouldn't be able to take time off. But you can cancel your interview. I found a job for you."

"You *what*?"

"Can I come in?"

She studied him. He'd found her a job? He'd come for her appointment? What was going on? Other than him being everything she'd hoped he'd be for the last week and a half. "It's been ten days, you know. Ten days without so much as a text from you. I thought…"

He stepped into the doorway—not pushing her aside, but cupping her face with his hand and stroking her chin with his fingertips. She shuddered into his touch, stunned by how much it affected her. "I was busy."

"Of course. You have a business to run. I know that."

That's why Serena walked out. She needed to see if he would still have feelings for her if she wasn't sitting outside his office door every day.

"Serena," he said, his voice deep with amusement. "Please let me come in. I can explain."

"I understand, Chadwick. I really do." She took a deep breath, willing herself not to cry. "Thank you for remembering the appointment, but maybe it's best if I go by myself."

He notched up an eyebrow as if she'd thrown down the gauntlet. "Ten minutes. That's all I'm asking. If you still think we need some time apart after that, I'll go. But I'm not walking away from you—from what we have."

Then, just because he apparently could, he stroked his fingers against her chin again.

The need to kiss him, to fall back into his arms, was almost overpowering. But that emotion was in a full-out war with her sense of self-preservation.

"What did we have?"

The grin he aimed at her made her knees suddenly shake. He leaned in, his cheek rubbing against hers, and whispered in her ear, "*Everything*."

Then he slipped a hand around her waist and pulled her into his chest. His lips touched the space underneath her ear, sending heat rushing from her neck down her back and farther south.

God, how she wanted this. Why had she thought she could walk away from him? From the way he made her feel? "Ten minutes," she heard herself murmur as she managed to push him far enough back that she could step to the side and let him in.

So she could stop touching him.

Chadwick walked into her apartment and looked around. "You're already moving?"

"Yes. This was where I lived with Neil. I need a fresh start. All the way around," she added, trying to remember why. Oh, yes. Because she couldn't fall for Chadwick while she worked for him. And work was all he did.

She expected him to say something else, but instead he gave her a look she couldn't quite read. Was he... amused? She didn't remember making a joke.

As he stood in the middle of the living room, she saw for the first time that he was holding a tablet. "I had this plan." He began tapping the screen. "But Helen forced my hand. So instead of doing this over a couple of months, I had to work around the clock for the last ten days."

If this was him convincing her that he'd find a way to see her outside of work, he was doing a surprisingly poor job of it. "Is that so?"

He apparently found what he was looking for because he grinned up at her and handed her the tablet. "It won't be final until the board votes to accept it and the lawyers get done with it, but I sold the company."

"You *what*?" She snatched the tablet out of his hands and looked at the document.

Letter of intent, the header announced underneath the insignia of the brewery's law firm. *AllBev hereby agrees to pay $62 a share for The Beaumont Brewery and all related Beaumont Brewery brands, excluding Percheron Drafts. Chadwick Beaumont reserves the right to* *keep the Percheron Drafts brand name and all related recipes....*

The whole thing got bogged down in legalese after that. Serena kept rereading the first few lines. "Wait, what? You're keeping Percheron?"

"I had this crazy idea," he said, taking the tablet back from her and swiping some more. "After someone told me to do what I wanted—for me and no one else—I remembered how much I liked to actually make beer. I thought I might keep Percheron Drafts and go into business for myself, not for the Beaumont name. Here." He handed her back the tablet again.

She looked down at a different lawyer's letter—this one from a divorce attorney. *Pursuant to the case of Beaumont v. Beaumont, Mrs. Helen Beaumont (hereby known as Plaintiff) has agreed to the offer of Mr. Chadwick Beaumont (hereby known as Defendant) for alimony payments in the form of $100 million dollars. Defendant will produce such funds no later than six months after the date of this letter....*

Serena blinked at the tablet. The whole thing was shaking—because she was shaking. "I...I don't understand."

"Well, I sold the brewery and I'm using the money I got for it to make my ex-wife an offer she can't refuse. I'm keeping Percheron Drafts and going into business myself." He took the tablet from her and set it down on a nearby box. "Simple, really."

"*Simple?*"

He had the nerve to nod as if this were all no big deal—just the multi-billion dollar sale of an international company. Just paying his ex-wife $100 million.

"Serena, breathe," he said, stepping up and wrapping his arms around her. "Breathe, babe."

"What did you do?" she asked, unable to stop herself from leaning her head against his warm, broad chest. It was everything she wanted. He was everything she wanted.

"I did something I should have done years ago—I stopped working for Hardwick Beaumont." He leaned her back and pressed his lips against her forehead. She felt herself breathe in response to his tender touch. "I'm free of him, Serena. Well and truly free. I don't have to live my life according to what he wanted, or make choices solely because they're the opposite of what he would have done. I can do whatever I want. And what I want is to make beer during the day and come home to a woman who speaks her mind and pushes me to be a better man and is going to be a great mother. A woman who loves me not because I'm a Beaumont, but in spite of it."

She looked up at him, aware that tears were trickling down her cheeks but completely unable to do anything about it. "This is what you've been doing for the last ten days?"

He grinned and wiped a tear off her face. "If I could have finalized the sale, I would have. It'll still take a few months for all the dust to settle, but Harper should be happy he got his money *and* got even with Hardwick, so I don't think he'll hold up the process much."

"And Helen? The divorce?"

"My lawyers are working to get a court date next week. Week after at the latest." He gave her a look of pure wickedness. "I made it clear that I couldn't wait."

"But…but you said a job? For me?"

His arms tightened around her waist, pulling her into his chest like he wasn't ever going to let her go. "Well, I'm starting this new business, you see. I'm going to need someone working with me who can run the offices, hire the people—a partner, if you will, to keep things going while I make the beer. Someone who understands how I operate. Someone who's not afraid of hard work. Someone who can pick a good health care plan and organize a party and understand spreadsheets." He rubbed her back as he started rocking from side to side. "I happen to know the perfect woman. She comes very highly recommended. Great letter of reference."

"But I can't be with you while I work for you. It's against company policy!"

At that, he laughed. "First off—new company, new policies. Second off, I'm not hiring you to be my underling. I'm asking you to be my partner in the business." He paused then and cleared his throat. "I'm asking you to marry me."

"You *are*?"

"I am." He dropped to his knees so suddenly that she almost toppled forward. "Serena Chase, would you marry me?"

Her hand fluttered over her stomach. "The baby..."

He leaned forward and kissed the spot right over her belly button. "I want to adopt this baby, just as soon as your old boyfriend severs his parental rights."

"What if he won't?" She was aware the odds of that were small—Neil had shown no interest in being a father. But she wasn't going to just throw herself into Chadwick's arms and believe that love would solve all the problems in the world.

Even if it felt like that were true right now.

Chadwick looked up at her, his scary businessman face on. "Don't worry. I can be *very* persuasive. Be my wife, Serena. Be my family."

Could they do that? Could she work with him, not *for* him? Could they be partners *and* a family?

Could she trust that he'd love her more than he loved his company?

He must have sensed her worry. "You told me to do what makes me happy," he told her as he stood again, folding her back into his arms. "*You* make me happy, Serena."

"But…where will we live? I don't want to live in that big mansion." The Beaumont Estate was crawling with too many ghosts—both dead and living.

He smiled down at her. "Anywhere you want."

"I…I already signed a lease for an apartment in Aurora."

He notched an eyebrow at her. "We can live there if you really want. Or you can break the lease. I'll have enough left from my golden parachute that we won't have to worry about money for a long, long time. And I promise not to drop thousands on gowns or jewels for you anymore. Except for this one."

He reached into his pocket and pulled out a small dark blue box. It was just the right size for a ring.

As he opened it, he said, "Would you marry me, Serena? Would you make me a happy man for the rest of my life and give me the chance to do the same for you? I won't fail you, I promise. You are the most important person in my life and you will always come first."

Serena stared at the ring. The solitaire diamond was large without being ostentatious. It was perfect, really.

"Well," she replied, taking the box from him. "Maybe a gown every now and then…."

Chadwick laughed and swept her into his arms. "Is that a yes?"

He was everything she wanted—passion and love and stability. He wouldn't fail her.

"*Yes.*"

He kissed her then—a long, hard kiss that called to mind a certain evening in front of a mirror. "Good," he said.

It was.

*   *   *   *   *

AN EXCEPTION
TO HIS RULE

LINDSAY ARMSTRONG

For my family, Dave, Susie, Matt, Sally, Anabel and David for all their patience.

And my editor, Megan Haslam, for all her patience!

CHAPTER ONE

DAMIEN WYATT WAS lounging in an upstairs study.

He wore jeans, a khaki bush shirt and desert boots, all visible since his feet were up on the desk. His dark hair was ruffled and there were blue shadows on his jaw.

The windows were open and the roses in the garden below were in bloom. So was the star jasmine creeper clinging to the house. Beyond the garden wall a beach curved around a blue, inviting bay. You could hear the sound of the waves on the beach and there was a tang of salt in the air.

'Hang on,' he said with a sudden frown. 'Is it remotely possible that this Ms *Livingstone* we're talking about is actually *Harriet* Livingstone? Because, if so, forget it, Arthur.'

Arthur Tindall, art connoisseur and colourful dresser—he wore jeans and a yellow waistcoat patterned with black elephants over a maroon shirt—looked confused. 'You've met her?' he asked from the other side of the desk.

'I don't know. Unless there are two Harriet Livingstones, I may have,' Damien said dryly.

'There could well be. Two, I mean,' Arthur replied. 'After all, it's not the wilds of Africa where it was highly unlikely there'd be more than one *Doctor* Livingstone popping up out of nowhere.'

Damien grinned fleetingly. 'I take your point.' He sobered. 'What's your Harriet like? Tall, thin girl with wild hair and an unusual taste in clothing?' He raised an enquiring eyebrow.

Arthur looked blank for a moment. 'Tall, yes,' he said slowly. 'Otherwise, well, certainly not fat and her clothes are—I don't seem to remember much about her clothes.'

'Have you actually met her?' Damien enquired with some irony.

'Of course.' Arthur looked offended then brightened. 'I can tell you one thing: she has very long legs!'

'So does a stork,' Damien observed. 'I couldn't tell with my Ms Livingstone,' he added. 'I mean for someone that tall she obviously had long legs but whether they were—shapely—I couldn't say because they were all covered up in some kind of wraparound batik skirt.'

Arthur stared narrowly into the distance as if trying to conjure up a batik wraparound skirt then he blinked again and said triumphantly, 'Glasses! Large, round, red-rimmed glasses. Also...' he frowned and concentrated '...a rather vague air, although that may be due to being short-sighted, but as if her mind is on higher things.' He grimaced.

Damien Wyatt smiled unpleasantly. 'If it is the same girl, she ran into me about two months ago. At the same time she was wearing large, round, red-rimmed glasses,' he added significantly.

'Oh, dear! Not the Aston? Oh, *dear*,' Arthur repeated.

Damien looked at him ironically. 'That's putting it mildly. She had no insurance other than compulsory third party and the...*tank* she was driving survived virtually unscathed.'

'Tank?'

Damien shrugged. 'It might as well have been: a solid old four-wheel drive with bull bars.'

This time Arthur winced visibly. 'How did it happen?'

'She swerved to avoid a dog then froze and couldn't correct things until it was too late.' Damien Wyatt drummed his fingers on his desk.

'Was anyone hurt?'

Damien looked at him, his expression sardonic. 'The dog was retrieved by its owner *completely* unscathed. All she broke were her glasses.'

He paused as he recalled the melee after the accident and the curious fact—curious from the point of view that it should have stuck in his mind—that Harriet Livingstone had possessed a pair of rather stunning blue eyes.

'That's not *too* bad,' Arthur murmured.

'That's not all,' Damien remarked acidly. 'I broke my collarbone and the damage to my car was, well—' he shrugged '—the whole exercise cost me a small fortune.'

Arthur forbore to make the obvious comment that a

small fortune would hardly make the slightest dent in the very large fortune Damien Wyatt owned.

But Damien continued with palpable sarcasm, 'Therefore, dear Arthur, if there's any possibility it's one and the same girl, you do see there's no way I could let her loose here.' He removed his feet from the desk and sat up.

Arthur Tindall discovered he could certainly see something cool, determined and even quite grim in Damien's dark eyes but he also found he wasn't prepared to give up without a fight.

Whether it was the same girl or not, it did sound like it, he had to admit, but the thing was he'd promised Penny, his young and delicious yet surprisingly manipulative wife, that he would get the Wyatt job for her friend Harriet Livingstone.

He sat forward. 'Damien, even if she's the same girl—although we don't absolutely know that!—she's good,' he said intently. 'She's damn good. So's her provenance. Your mother's collection couldn't be in better hands, believe me! She's worked in one of the most prestigious art auction houses in the country.' Arthur emphasised this with rolling eyes and a wave of his hand. 'Her father was a noted conservator and restorer of paintings and her references are impeccable.'

'All the same, you've just told me she's vague and distracted,' Damien said impatiently. 'And *I've* had the woman literally run into me!'

Arthur said intensely, 'She may be vague over other things but not about her work. I've found her knowledgeable on not only paintings but porcelain, ceramics, carpets, miniatures—all sorts of things. And she's experienced in cataloguing.'

'She sounds like a one woman antiques roadshow,' Damien observed caustically.

'No, but she's the one person I could recommend who would have some familiarity with most of the odds and ends your mother collected. She's the one person who would have some idea of their value or who to get a valuation from, some idea of whether they need restoring, whether they *could* be restored, who could do it if it was possible, who—'

Damien held up his hand. 'Arthur, I get your point. But—'

'Of course,' Arthur interrupted, sitting back and looking magisterial, 'if it is the same girl, there's the distinct possibility nothing on earth would induce her to work for you.'

'Why the hell not?'

Arthur shrugged and folded his arms over his black and yellow waistcoat. 'I have no doubt you would have been quite scathing towards her at the time of the accident.'

Damien rubbed his jaw. 'I did ask her,' he said reminiscently, 'whether she'd got her driver's licence out of a cornflakes packet.'

Arthur whistled but said, 'I've heard worse. Was that all?'

Damien shrugged. 'I may have said a few other…less than complimentary things. In the heat of the moment, of course. My car *was* smashed. So was my collarbone.'

'Women don't necessarily see things like that in the

same way. About cars, I mean.' Arthur waved his hands again. 'Pure excellence, pure *fineness* in a motor vehicle and then to see it all smashed up may not affect them as deeply as a man.'

Damien chewed his lip then shrugged and picked up his phone as it buzzed discreetly.

Arthur got up and wandered over to the windows. It was a lovely view, he mused, but then Heathcote, home to the Wyatt dynasty, was a magnificent property. They ran cattle and grew macadamias with equal success in the Northern Rivers district of New South Wales but it was machinery—farm machinery, and lately mining machinery—that was the backbone of their fortune.

Damien's grandfather had started it all with a tractor he'd designed and manufactured but, so it was said, Damien had tripled it by investing in mining machinery. And all sorts of mining was happening all over Australia, Arthur thought rather ruefully.

His own connection with the Wyatts had started with Damien's father and his interest in art. Together they'd built up a collection to be proud of. Then, seven years ago, both his parents had been lost at sea when their yacht had capsized. Consequently Damien had inherited the collection.

It was the upheaval after this that had brought to light the full extent of his *mother's* collection of objets d'art—something the rest of the family had tended to overlook. In fact it wouldn't be unfair to say that Heathcote was stuffed to the rafters with them. But it had taken several more years for this decision to do something about them to be made, and hence to his advice being sought.

His first inclination had been to suggest that it should all be crated up and sent to an appropriate firm for assessing. Damien, however, supported by his aunt, had been disinclined to allow any of his mother's treasures to leave Heathcote and it had been their suggestion that he look for someone to do the job in situ.

No easy task since Lennox Head, Heathcote's nearest town, was a long way from Sydney and a fair way from Brisbane or the Gold Coast, the nearest large cities.

Therefore, when Penny had presented him with Harriet Livingstone he'd more or less looked upon it as a godsend...

Arthur turned from the view and studied Damien Wyatt, who'd swung his chair so he was partially facing the other way and was still talking on the phone. At thirty-one, Damien was loose-limbed, lean and deceptively powerful. He was well over six feet tall, broad-shouldered and he had the facility to look at ease in any milieu. Yet there was something about him that let you know that whilst he'd be good outdoors, good at battling the elements, good at managing vast properties, good with mechanical things, he'd also be good with women.

He certainly possessed a pair of fine dark eyes that often had a glint in them indicative of a mercurial personality and a lively intelligence.

Not to put too fine a point on it, Arthur ruminated, as his wife Penny had once remarked: you couldn't call Damien exactly handsome but he was devastatingly attractive and masculine.

He also had thick dark hair and he did possess a powerful intellect. Not only that, but he had an affection
for getting his own way and a *cutting,* irritable way it
was with him at times, as Harriet Livingstone had apparently encountered, poor girl.

So why, Arthur wondered suddenly, if she was the
same girl—and he was pretty sure she was—had she
been happy for him to go ahead and sound Damien
Wyatt out on this job? She must have recognised the
name. She must have some very unpleasant memories
of the incident.

She must, above all, find it extremely hard to believe he would ever offer her a job after smashing his
beloved Aston Martin with a vehicle not unlike a tank
and breaking his collarbone.

So what was behind it, this willingness even to meet
Damien Wyatt again? Did she have designs on him? Did
she, he swallowed at the mere thought, plan to, if she got
the job, fleece him of some of his mother's treasures?

'Hello!'

Arthur came back to the present with a start to see
that Damien had finished his call and was looking at
him enquiringly.

'Sorry,' he said hastily, and sat down again.

'How's Penny?'

Arthur hesitated. Despite the fact that Damien was
always unfailingly polite to Penny, it was hard to escape
the feeling that he didn't really approve of her.

Or, if not that, Arthur mused further, did Damien
view his belated tumble into matrimony after years of

bachelorhood with some cynicism? He was now approaching fifty and was twenty years older than Penny.

Probably, he conceded to himself. Not that Damien Wyatt had anything to be superior about on that score. He might not have been twenty years older than his wife but he did have a failed marriage behind him—a very failed marriage.

'Arthur, what's on your mind?'

Once again Arthur came back to the present with a start. 'Nothing!' he asserted.

'You seem to be miles away,' Damien commented. 'Is Penny all right or not?'

'She's fine. She's fine,' Arthur repeated, and came to another sudden decision, although with an inward grimace. 'Look, Damien, I've changed my mind about Harriet Livingstone. I don't think she's the right one after all. So give me a few days and I'll find someone else.'

It was a penetratingly narrowed dark gaze Damien bestowed on Arthur Tindall. 'That's a rather sudden change of heart,' he drawled.

'Yes, well, a blind man could see you two are unlikely to get along so…' Arthur left his sentence up in the air.

Damien settled more comfortably in his chair. 'Where are you going to find a paragon to equal Ms Livingstone? Or was that a slight exaggeration on your part?' he asked casually enough, although with a load of implied satire.

'No it was not!' Arthur denied. 'And I have no idea where I'm going to find one—be that as it may, I will.'

Damien Wyatt rubbed his jaw. 'I'll have a look at her.'

Arthur sat up indignantly. 'Now look here; you can't change your mind just like that!'

'Not many minutes ago you were hoping to goad me into doing *just* that.'

'*When*?'

'When you told me I'd be the last person on earth she'd work for. You were hoping that would annoy me or simply arouse my contrary streak to the extent I'd change my mind.' Damien's lips twisted. 'Well, I have.'

'Which streak prompted that, do you think? A rather large ego?' Arthur enquired heavily after a moment's thought.

Damien grinned. 'No idea. Bring her here for an interview tomorrow afternoon.'

'Damien—' Arthur rose '—I have to say I can't guarantee the girl.'

'You mean everything you told me about her provenance et cetera—' Damien raised his eyebrows sardonically '—was a lot of bull dust?'

'No,' Arthur denied. 'I followed up every reference she gave me and they all checked out, I've talked to her and sounded her out on a range of art work, as I mentioned, but—'

'Just bring her, Arthur,' Damien interrupted wearily. 'Just bring her.'

Despite this repeated command, Damien Wyatt stayed where he was for a few minutes after Arthur had gone, as he asked himself why he'd done what he'd just done.

No sensible answer presented itself other than that he *had* somehow felt goaded into it, although not because of anything Arthur had said.

So—curiosity, perhaps? Why would Harriet Livingstone want to have anything to do with him after, he had to admit, he'd been pretty unpleasant to her? Some quirky form of revenge?

More likely a quirky form of attaching herself to him, he thought cynically. All the more reason to have stuck to his guns and refused to see the girl.

What else could have been at work behind the scenes of his mental processes then? he asked himself rather dryly. Boredom?

Surely not. He had enough on his plate at the moment to keep six men busy. He had an overseas trip coming up in a couple of days, and yet...

He stared into the distance with a frown. Of course the possibility remained that it *wasn't* the same girl...

At three o'clock the next afternoon, Harriet Livingstone and Arthur Tindall were shown into the lounge at Heathcote by a tall angular woman with iron-grey hair cut in a short cap. Arthur addressed the woman as Isabel and kissed her on the cheek but didn't introduce her. Arthur was looking worried and distracted.

Damien Wyatt came in from outside through another door, accompanied by a large dog.

He threw his sunglasses onto a side table and said something to the dog, a young, highly bred and powerful Scottish wolfhound, that sat down obligingly although looking keenly alert.

'Ah,' Damien Wyatt said to Arthur after a brief but comprehensive study of Harriet, 'same girl.' He turned back to Harriet. 'We meet again, Miss Livingstone. I'd almost convinced myself you wouldn't be the same person or, if you were, that you wouldn't come.'

Harriet cleared her throat. 'Good afternoon, Mr Wyatt,' she said almost inaudibly.

Damien narrowed his eyes and cast Arthur an interrogative glance but Arthur only looked blank.

Damien returned his attention to Harriet Livingstone.

No batik wraparound skirt today, he noted: an unexceptional navy linen dress instead. Not too long, not too short, not too tight, although it did make her blue eyes even bluer. In fact her outfit was very discreetly elegant and so were her shoes, polished navy leather with little heels. This caused a faint fleeting smile to twist his lips as it crossed his mind that this girl probably rarely, if ever, wore higher heels. And he wondered what it must be like for a girl to be as tall, if not taller, than many of the men she met. Not that she was taller than he was...

Then there was her hair. Shoulder-length, fair and with a tendency to curl, it no longer looked as if she'd been pulled through a bush backwards. It was neatly tied up instead with a black ribbon. Her make-up was minimal. In fact it was all so...what? he asked himself. Well-bred, classic, timeless, discreet—he had no difficulty imagining her in the hallowed halls of some revered antique and art auction company or a museum.

But, and this caused him to frown rather than smile, the main difference between this Harriet Livingstone and the girl who'd run into him was that she was no longer thin. Very slender, perhaps, but no, not exactly skinny.

Despite being slender rather than skinny and despite her more composed outward presentation, it was, however, plain to see that she was strung as taut as a piano wire.

It was also plain to see—and his eyes widened slightly as his gaze travelled down her figure—that her legs were little short of sensational...

'Well,' he said, 'you were right, Arthur, but let's get down to brass tacks. We've organised a few of my mother's things in the dining room. Please come through and give me your opinion of them, Ms Livingstone.'

He moved forward and the dog rose and came with him but stopped to look at Harriet with almost human curiosity. And, as Harriet returned the dog's gaze, just a little of her tension seemed to leave her.

Damien noticed this with a slight narrowing of his eyes. And he said, somewhat to his surprise, 'I'm sorry, I forgot to introduce you—this is Tottie, Miss Livingstone. Her proper name is much more complicated. Something tells me you like dogs?'

Harriet put out a hand for Tottie to inspect. 'Yes. It's one of the reasons I ran into you,' she murmured. 'I thought I'd killed the dog and I—just froze.'

Arthur tut-tutted.

Damien Wyatt blinked, twice. 'Much worse in your estimation than killing me, I gather?'

Harriet Livingstone allowed Tottie to lick her hand then said quietly, 'Of course not. I didn't—I'm sorry but I didn't have time to think about you or anything else. It all happened so fast.'

'I'm suitably damned,' he replied. 'All right, let's get this show on the road.'

'If you're having second thoughts I'd quite understand,' Harriet said politely, with a less than polite glint in her eye, however.

She really doesn't like him, Arthur thought and rubbed his face distractedly. So why is she doing this?

But what Damien said took him even further by surprise. 'On the contrary, after what Arthur has told me about you I'm positively agog to see you in action. Shall I lead on?'

He didn't wait for her response but strode out with Tottie following regally.

Harriet put the exquisite little jade peach tree down on the table with a sigh of pleasure. And her gaze swept over the rest of the treasures spread out on the dining room table. 'They're all lovely—she had marvellous taste, your mother. And judgement.' She took off her red-rimmed glasses.

Damien was leaning his broad shoulders against the mantelpiece with his arms crossed. He did not respond to her admiration of his mother's collection but said, 'Is that a new pair or did you get them fixed?' He nodded towards her glasses resting on the table.

Harriet looked confused for a moment, then, 'Oh, it was only a lens that got broken so I was able to get a new one.'

'Red glasses.' He looked her up and down. 'Not quite

in keeping with the restrained elegance of the rest of you—today, that is.'

A fleeting smile twisted Harriet's lips. 'Ah, but it makes them a lot easier to find.' And, for a moment, she thought he was going to smile too but he continued to look unamused.

Harriet looked away.

'How would you catalogue them?' he asked after a moment. 'This is not even one tenth of them, by the way.'

'I'd photograph them in the sequence I came upon them and I'd write an initial summary of them. Then, when they were all itemised—' Harriet laced her fingers '—I'd probably sort them into categories, mainly to make it easier to locate them and I'd write a much more comprehensive description of them, their condition, any research I'd done on them, any work required on them et cetera. I'd also, if your mother kept any receipts or paperwork on them, try to marry it all up.'

'How long do you think that would take?'

Harriet shrugged. 'Hard to say without seeing the full extent of the collection.'

'Months,' Arthur supplied with gloomy conviction.

'Were you aware it was a live-in position, Miss Livingstone?' Damien queried. 'Because we're out in the country here, whoever does the job will spend an awful lot of time travelling otherwise.'

'Yes, Arthur did explain that. I believe there's an old stable block that's been converted to a studio and it has a flat above it. But—' Harriet paused '—weekends would be free, wouldn't they?'

Damien raised an eyebrow. 'Didn't Arthur tell you that?'

'He did,' Harriet agreed, 'but I needed to double- check.'

'A boyfriend you're eager to get back to?' Damien didn't wait for her response. 'If that's going to be a problem and you're forever wanting time off to be with him—'

'Not at all,' Harriet cut across him quite decisively.

'Not at all, you wouldn't be wanting time off all the time or not at all, there is no boyfriend?' Damien enquired.

Arthur coughed. 'Damien, I don't think—' he began but Harriet interrupted him this time.

'It's quite all right, Arthur.' She turned back to Damien. 'Allow me to set your mind at rest, Mr Wyatt. There is no fiancé, no husband, no lovers, in short, no one in my life to distract me in that direction.'

'Well, well,' Damien drawled, 'not only a paragon in your profession but also your private life.'

Harriet Livingstone merely allowed her deep blue gaze to rest on him thoughtfully for a moment or two before she turned away with the tiniest shrug, as if to say he was some kind of rare organism she didn't understand.

Bloody hell, Damien Wyatt found himself thinking as he straightened abruptly, who does she think she is? Not content with smashing my car and causing me considerable discomfort for weeks, she's—

He didn't get to finish this set of thoughts as the woman called Isabel popped her head around the door and offered them afternoon tea.

Arthur looked at his watch. 'Thank you so much, Isabel, but I'm afraid I won't have time. Penny wants me home by four.' He paused. 'What about you, Harriet? We did come in separate cars,' he explained to Damien.

Harriet hesitated and glanced at Damien. And because most of his mental sensors seemed to be honed in on this tall, slender girl, he saw the tension creep back as she picked up her purse and her knuckles whitened.

And he heard himself say something he hadn't expected to say. 'If you'd like a cup of tea, stay by all means, Miss Livingstone. We haven't finished the interview anyway.'

She hesitated again then thanked him quietly.

Isabel retreated and Arthur, looking visibly harassed, subjected them to an involved explanation of why he needed to be home. Plus he was obviously reluctant to miss any of the verbal duel he was witnessing. But he finally left. And the tea tray arrived but this time Damien introduced the bearer as his aunt Isabel, and invited her to join them.

'Sorry,' Isabel said as she put the tea tray down on the coffee table set in front of the settee in a corner of the dining room, 'but I'm popping into Lennox to pick up our dry-cleaning. Please excuse me, Miss Livingstone,' she added.

Harriet nodded somewhat dazedly and once again the door closed, this time on his aunt.

'I don't think there's anyone else who could interrupt us,' Damien Wyatt said with some irony. 'Do sit down and pour the tea.'

Harriet sank down onto the settee and her hand hovered over the tea tray. 'Uh—there's only one cup.'

'I never drink the stuff,' he said dismissively, 'so pour yours and let's get *on* with things.'

Harriet lifted the heavy silver teapot and spilt some tea on the pristine white tray cloth.

Damien swore beneath his breath, and came over to sit down beside her. 'Put it down and tell me something, Harriet Livingstone—why are you doing this? No, wait.'

He picked up the pot Harriet had relinquished and poured a cup of tea without spilling a drop. Then he indicated the milk and sugar but she shook her head. 'Th-that's fine, just as it comes, thank you.'

He moved the cup and saucer in front of her and offered her a biscuit that looked like homemade shortbread.

She shook her head.

'I can guarantee them. The cook makes them himself,' he said.

'Thank you but no. I—I don't have a sweet tooth.'

He pushed the porcelain biscuit barrel away. 'You look—you don't look as sk— as thin as you did that day,' he amended.

A flicker of amusement touched her mouth. 'Skinny you were going to say? I guess I did. I lost a bit of weight for a time. I've probably always been thin, though.'

'Sorry,' he murmured. 'But look, why *are* you doing this?'

Harriet hesitated and watched the steam rising gently from her tea.

'You obviously haven't forgiven me for the things

I said that day,' he continued. 'Most of the time since you've been here you've been a nervous wreck or, if not that, beaming pure hostility my way. The only thing that seems to relax you is contact with my dog or my mother's odds and ends.'

He broke off and looked rueful as Tottie rose, came over and arranged herself at Harriet's feet.

Harriet glanced at him briefly. In jeans, boots and a khaki bush shirt, with his thick hair ruffled and blue shadows on his jaw, he looked the epitome of a man of the land whereas, when she'd bumped into him, in a grey suit, he'd definitely been more of a high-flying businessman.

She shivered involuntarily. He'd been so angry in a quiet but deadly sort of way.

'Talk to me, Harriet,' he said firmly.

She took a sip of tea and then a deep breath. 'I need a job, quite urgently.'

'You—according to Arthur, anyway—are highly, if not to say über-qualified. Why would you want my job?' He frowned. 'It's stuck out in the country even if you don't have an army of lovers to worry about.'

'It…' Harriet paused '…suits me.'

'Why?'

A short silence developed between them and lengthened until he said impatiently, 'Oh, come on Harriet! I—'

'I just want to get this job,' she said with sudden intensity, 'on my merits.'

'Well, your merits are fine but I need to know more,' he said flatly.

'This kind of job doesn't grow on trees,' Harriet said

after a long moment. 'And it so happens it's the right district for me.'

'Why?'

Harriet sighed. 'My brother was badly injured in a surfing accident. He's now in a rehabilitation centre at—' she named a facility '—that's handy to Lennox Head and Heathcote. He has to learn to walk again. That's why—' she looked up at last and smiled with considerable irony '—when this job came up, it seemed like an answer to all my prayers. Until, that was—' She stopped abruptly.

'You found out whose job it was,' Damien supplied.

She didn't answer but looked away.

'You decided to proceed, however.' It was a statement, not a question.

'Yes.'

'And I suppose that's why you wanted to make sure the weekends were free? So you could see your brother. Talk about coals of fire,' he murmured wryly. He added impatiently, 'Why couldn't you have just told me all this in the first place?'

Harriet shrugged. 'Ever since I found out about the job, I've been…I have been a nervous wreck,' she conceded. She gestured. 'It would be so perfect but…' She shrugged again. 'To be perfectly honest, you're the last person I would want to accept a favour from.'

He grimaced. 'Needs must when the devil drives. You need the money?'

'I need the money,' she agreed rather dryly. 'This is a private hospital and it's not covered by my brother's medical insurance but it has a terrific reputation. And to be able to be close to Brett at the same time is an obvious bonus.'

'I see. Has it—' he paused and raised an eyebrow at her '—occurred to you that I was simply driving along minding my own business that day when all hell erupted, in a manner of speaking?'

She cast him a dark little look from beneath her lashes. 'Accidents happen.'

'Yes, but I thought you might be able to cut me a little slack—no, I see not,' he murmured as her lips set.

And, he continued, but to himself, you not only have amazingly long eyelashes, Harriet Livingstone, but a rather gorgeous mouth, severely sculptured yet somehow incredibly inviting. Plus—he allowed his dark gaze to roam over her—satiny-smooth skin, slender delicate wrists and lovely hands that I quite failed to notice the last time we met.

So that's it, Damien Wyatt, he castigated himself inwardly. Even with all the things you didn't notice then, this damn girl made an impression on you two months ago and that's why you felt goaded into seeing her again. What's more, she's making even more of an impression on you today, which is not going to lead *anywhere*, he told himself grimly.

But how to knock her back for the job?

In all decency you can't, he decided. So what to do if she keeps on making an impression on you?

A dry smile briefly twisted his lips—think of your poor car before it got fixed...

'Well, you've got the job if you want it,' he said

abruptly. 'Would you like to see the studio and flat before you make up your mind?'

Harriet clenched her hands in her lap. 'You don't have to feel sorry for me,' she said carefully. 'When one door closes another usually opens.'

'Harriet,' he warned, 'I don't appreciate being told what I should or should not feel but, if you want to get it right, I don't only feel sorry for you—most people would in the circumstances—but I feel as guilty as hell for the things I said over what was, you're right, an accident.'

'Oh…'

'Now, could we get *on* with it? You've barely had a drop of your tea,' he added with sudden frustration.

Harriet grabbed her purse. 'I'll leave it.'

She got up so precipitously, she tripped over Tottie and would have fallen to the floor if Damien hadn't lunged forward and caught her.

The next moments were confused as he untangled her from the dog, the coffee table and she ended up standing in the middle of the room in his arms.

'You wouldn't be accident-prone, would you?' he asked incredulously.

Harriet tried to free herself but, although he held her quite loosely, he made it plain he was not about to let her go. 'I…I suffer from a left-handed syndrome,' she said a little raggedly.

'What the hell's that?'

'My father's invention to explain the fact that I'm a bit uncoordinated at times.'

'So, yes—' he raised his eyebrows '—accident prone?'

She shrugged. 'Maybe. Would you mind letting me go?'

Damien Wyatt still had a spark of amusement in his eyes as he said wryly, 'Yes I would, heaven alone knows why. Well, for one thing I've never held a girl as tall as you but it feels good.'

'I…' Harriet opened her mouth to protest but he lowered his head and started to kiss her.

Shock seemed to take away all her powers of resistance and when he lifted his head she could only stare up at him with her eyes wide, her lips still parted and her heart beating heavily.

'Mmm…' He ran his hands up and down her back and hugged her. 'I must have been mad ever to think you were skinny, Ms Livingstone!'

Harriet gathered herself. 'This is…this is,' she started to say.

'Insane?' he supplied.

'*Yes*,' she agreed, almost biting her tongue in her frustration.

'You're not wrong. On the other hand, we've experienced quite a range of emotions—'

'That's—what's that got to do with it?' Harriet broke in desperately.

'We've been angry with each other,' he went on.

'You murderously,' she pointed out darkly.

'Well, not quite, but you've hated my guts,' he responded. 'I reckon we're destined to run through the whole spectrum—you know, your eyes are stunning.'

'I…they…'

'And there's your skin.' He transferred his hands to her arms and ran his palms down them. 'Smooth and satiny. As for your legs—by the way, I wouldn't ever wear that wraparound skirt again...' He paused as she moved convulsively and waited for her to quieten before he went on. 'Only because it's criminal to hide your legs.'

'Mr Wyatt,' Harriet said through her teeth, 'please don't go on and will you let me go!'

'In a minute. The other thing Arthur was right about; you have a slightly superior edge at times.'

Harriet, about to make a concerted effort to free herself, stopped dead and stared at him, completely mystified. 'What do you mean?'

'Well, for example, in the lounge earlier,' he elucidated, 'you looked at me as if I'd crawled out from under a rock.'

'I did not!' she denied.

'You probably don't realise you're doing it. Actually, what Arthur said was that you sometimes look as if your mind is on higher things.'

Harriet blinked. 'What does that mean?'

He dropped his arms and moved back half a pace but Harriet stayed where she was. 'That you think you're above this "mortal coil"?' he mused, and shrugged. 'Perhaps way above the sweaty realities of life and love, not to mention men? You did say there was no one. One has to wonder why.' He stopped and shrugged.

Harriet Livingstone very rarely lost her temper but when she did the consequences were often disastrous, mainly because she was tall enough to be effective about it. She advanced the half step towards Damien Wyatt and slapped his face. She did more.

'Oh, how I've wanted to do that,' she gasped but with great passion. 'Talk about being above the mortal coil—*you* obviously see yourself as the bee's knees!'

His lips twisted as he fingered his cheek. 'Bee's knees—haven't heard that one for a while. All the same, Stretch,' he responded, 'I—'

'*Don't* call me that,' she warned.

'Whatever.' He shrugged and took her in his arms and proceeded to kiss her again but this time there was a definite purpose to it. This time it was a battle, not a shocked passive response on her part and a more light-hearted exploration on his.

Until he lifted his head and said abruptly, 'No, no more anger and hate, Harriet.'

'What do you mean?'

'It's time to move on. No, don't do a thing, I'm not going to hurt you, it's just that fate seems to have intervened.' He shook his head. 'It certainly has for me.'

And this time, before he kissed her again, he drew her into his body and ran his hands over her in a way that made her go still and her eyes widen in a different kind of shock because it was as if he was imparting an electric current through her, a tide of sensuality she couldn't resist.

Then he released her and cupped her face in his hands and they looked into each other's eyes for a long, long moment. And as she breathed in the essence of Damien Wyatt it had a powerful effect on her. Not only did he bring the outdoors into the dining room—there were sweat stains on his shirt, his hair was ruffled—but a physical force and the aroma of pure man.

Then, as she searched his dark eyes and saw the way they were focused on her and felt the way his hands moved down to her hips and were gentle but skilful on her body, she got a different sense of him.

As if she was viewing the man behind the man. As if, underneath that prickly, easily prone to irritation exterior, there was a man who knew how to make love to a woman in a way that thrilled her and drove her to excesses she hadn't known she could reach...

And when he started to kiss her again, because of that sense of him, because of the rapturous tingling of all her senses, something she'd been denied for a long time, because of the feel of the hard planes of his body against her, because he was actually taller than she was and because there was something terribly, awe-inspiringly masculine about him unless you were a block of wood, she found herself kissing him back.

They drew apart briefly once. They were both breathing raggedly. He pulled the ribbon out of her hair and ran his fingers through it. She spread her fingers on his back and felt the sleek strength of it beneath his shirt.

Then he was kissing her again and her breasts were crushed against him as he held her hard.

It was the dining room door opening and a spontaneous whistle that brought Harriet Livingstone and Damien Wyatt back to earth.

Not that Damien betrayed any sign of discomfort, at first.

He released her in a leisurely way and tidied the collar of her dress before he said over her shoulder, 'Charlie, this is Harriet Livingstone. Harriet—' he put his hands on her shoulders '—it's OK. Meet my brother, Charles Walker Wyatt. He's renowned for rushing in where angels fear to tread.'

Harriet swallowed and put her hands up to try to tidy her hair before she forced herself to turn around.

Charles Walker Wyatt wasn't as tall as his brother Damien and he looked to be several years younger. He also bore an arrested expression on his face, as of one who had received a smack on the head when least expecting it.

'Holy...Mackerel, Damien!' he exclaimed then. 'The last thing I expected to find in the *dining room* of all places was you kissing a girl I've never laid eyes on! That's hardly *fools rushing in* material—wouldn't you agree, ma'am?' he appealed to Harriet as he advanced towards them.

'By the way, please forgive me,' he went on, 'for labelling you "a girl"—not that you're *not* but it sounds sort of generic and I don't mean to classify you like that. Not at all! But—'

'Charlie.' There was a definite warning note in Damien's voice.

'Damien?' Charlie replied, looking innocent. 'Just tell me what I'm allowed to say and do and I'll try not to put a foot wrong!'

'What anyone with a grain of courtesy or good sense would have done in the first place,' his brother replied evenly. 'Retreated and shut the flaming door!'

The last bit was said a little less than evenly and it

struck Harriet that Damien Wyatt was not completely unaffected by his brother's intrusion.

'Ah.' Charlie rubbed his chin. 'OK—but actually, I've had a better idea. What's wrong with me getting to know Miss Harriet Livingstone?' And he looked admiringly at Harriet.

'Everything,' Damien snapped. 'Just go away, Charlie!' he added, his irritation and rising impatience plain to be seen.

Something Charles Walker Wyatt obviously saw for himself because he sketched a salute, did a military about-turn and said, 'Just going, sir.' He marched out smartly.

Damien waited until the door closed before turning back to Harriet. 'Do you know something?' he said bitterly. 'Every time we get within cooee of each other, you and I, it turns out to be a shambles!'

Harriet swallowed. 'I think I should just go. It could never work.'

'*Go*?' he said through his teeth, 'How the hell can you kiss a guy like that and just go?'

CHAPTER TWO

'YOU STARTED IT,' Harriet said and immediately despised herself for sounding incredibly lame and childish. 'I mean...' But she found it impossible to sort out her thoughts let alone her emotions.

'If you hadn't tripped over the damn dog, I might not have started it,' he replied irritably. 'Anyway! How come Tottie is so taken with you?'

'I don't know.' Harriet shrugged helplessly. 'Dogs do just seem to take to me.'

'Look—' he studied her '—sit down and have another cup of tea—no, I'll pour it—hang on, I've got a better idea.' He guided her to a chair at the dining table and pulled it out for her. 'Sit down and study some of my mother's incomparable collection; it might calm you. While I pour us a drink.'

He turned away towards a cocktail cabinet.

Harriet drew a deep breath and combed her hair with her fingers but she couldn't find her ribbon so she had to leave it loose. She took a hanky out of her purse and patted her face. Then her attention was drawn to an exquisite cameo in an old-fashioned rose-gold and pin-point diamond setting and she forgot about the wreck she might look as she stared at it rapturously. And Damien Wyatt put a glass of brandy down beside her and pulled out a chair opposite to sit down with his own drink.

'Cheers,' he said.

Harriet hesitated.

'Don't think about it; just drink it,' he advised.

So she took a couple of sips and felt the brandy slip down and a warm glow of—what was it? Some confidence?—rise in its place.

But, before she could formulate anything sensible to say, he spoke. 'How well do you know Arthur?'

'Hardly at all. I know Penny better. We were at college together for a while, although she's a few years older. Then we lost track of each other until I came up to Ballina. It was quite an amazing coincidence. I literally bumped into her—no,' she said with her lips quirking suddenly as his eyebrows flew up, 'not the way I bumped into you. This was on the pavement as we were walking along.'

A gleam of amusement lit his eyes. 'I'm relieved to hear you say so. Go on.'

She looked rueful. 'So we had coffee and compared notes. She told me about Arthur and how they'd moved from Sydney to Ballina to get out of the rat race. She told me she'd started a picture-framing business and a small art gallery and how Arthur still dealt in art—he was born up here apparently.'

'Yes. He was a friend of my father's; more than that, he helped Dad establish his collection.'

'So I told her I'd also decided to get away from the rat

race and I was looking for a job. That's when she grew thoughtful and finally dragged me off to meet Arthur.'

'I see.' Damien swirled the liquid in his glass. 'So they didn't know—' he lifted his dark gaze to her '—about your brother?'

'No.' Harriet traced the rim of her glass with her forefinger then took another sip. 'I know it seems a bit deceitful, but I find it hard to deal with people feeling sorry for us.'

He was silent for a time, then, 'What were you doing up here two months ago, when you bumped into me?'

'I was checking out this rehabilitation centre. It was the first time I'd been to this area—another reason I was a bit dithery, I guess; I didn't know my way around.'

'It's not exactly a metropolis,' he said wryly then gestured as if to delete the comment. 'But you're living up here now? Your brother's in the rehab centre?'

Harriet nodded.

'Where are you living?'

She hesitated then took a sip of the brandy and shrugged. 'In a rented caravan in the caravan park. I do have a job—it's waitressing, so it keeps the wolf from the door, but—' She broke off.

'Only just?' he suggested.

She didn't respond but stared a bit blindly down at her glass.

'OK,' he said quietly, 'no more interrogations. The job is yours if you want it but what are we going to do?'

'Do?' she repeated.

He set his teeth. 'Yes, do! About the rest of it?'

Her deep blue eyes widened. 'The rest of it?'

He grimaced. 'You must have a short memory span as well as being accident-prone. Or do you often go around kissing guys like that?'

The confidence she'd got from a few sips of brandy ebbed a little at the same time as her eyes widened as the full memory of their passionate encounter hit her.

She took a larger mouthful of brandy.

'You had forgotten,' he marvelled.

'No. But we did get interrupted,' she responded tartly. 'I don't know about you, but I found it extremely embarrassing. Enough to make the rest of it, well...' She broke off as she searched for the right words.

'Pale into insignificance?' he suggested dryly.

'Not exactly,' Harriet denied and took another sip of her drink. 'But it did—move it back a bit if you know what I mean.' She paused and shrugged. 'It probably put it into its right perspective.'

'What would that be?'

She glinted him an assessing look from beneath her lashes, then thought—why should I try to spare his feelings? 'It was just something that happened in the heat of the moment, wasn't it?'

'Go on.'

Harriet hesitated, unable to read his expression but feeling a prickle of apprehension run through her. 'Well, you insulted me, I responded—'

'With a blow, allow me to remind you.' He looked sardonically amused.

Harriet compressed her lips. 'I'm sorry. I believe I had cause, however. Look—' she paused '—I wouldn't be surprised if you weren't still furious with me over your car.'

'Not to mention my collarbone. There are still some things I can't do. I'm not still furious, however.' Damien Wyatt crossed his arms and leant back with a frown growing in his dark eyes. 'Well, I may have been a bit annoyed but I have to say I'm mostly confused now. In fact I'm beginning to wonder if I'm hallucinating. Did you or did you not kiss me back almost like a woman starved for—that kind of thing?'

Harriet stared at the cameo for a long moment then looked at him squarely. 'Maybe. But it's best forgotten.'

'Why?'

Harriet pushed her glass away and stood up. 'Because I have no intention of getting involved with you, Mr Wyatt. Please don't take that personally. I'm…I'm… happy to be fancy-free, that's all.'

He stared at her and she was suddenly conscious that not only was she completely unable to read his thoughts but, more than that, it troubled her.

Why? Why should she care one way or another about what he thought of her? The sensual response he'd managed to draw from her had come about because he was experienced and worldly—she had little doubt of that— so why should she invest it with any special meaning or depth?

Well, she amended her thoughts, she had to take some responsibility for her reaction, surely? Starved? Perhaps—but she didn't even want to think about that…

'Would you mind if I went now? I'm sorry if I've

wasted your time but I honestly don't think it could work.'

Damien stayed absolutely still for a moment longer then he straightened and stood up, leaning his fists on the table. 'Yes, I would mind,' he said dryly, 'and I'll tell you why. I don't propose to have you on my conscience for a moment longer, whether I realise it or not, Harriet Livingstone.'

'You don't have to have me on your conscience!' she objected.

'Believe me, I'd rather not but—'

'What do you mean—whether you realise it or not?' Harriet broke in to ask with a frown.

He shrugged. 'I can't work out why else I agreed to see you again.'

Harriet linked her fingers together and told herself not to pursue this but some demon prompted her, rather than simply getting up and walking out, to say, 'If you think I could ever work for you, you must be mad, Mr Wyatt.'

Their gazes clashed.

'The job is yours, Miss Livingstone,' he replied deliberately. 'You can move in the day after tomorrow— I'll be gone then. I'm going overseas for some weeks, at least a month. Of course Isabel, who runs the house and the rest of it when I'm not here, will be in residence. So will Charlie, for a while anyway. Did Arthur get around to mentioning the remuneration package we thought was suitable?'

Harriet blinked. '…Yes.'

'You can add a twenty per cent commission on any items I decide to sell. Will that do?'

'I…I…' She hesitated.

'Don't go all dithery on me again, Harriet,' he warned. 'Finish your brandy,' he ordered.

She stared at him, deep hostility written into her expression. 'No. I've got to drive.'

'All right, but I need to know if you're going to take it or not.'

Harriet would have given the world to answer in the negative but if he was going to be away…and surely she could finish the job in a month if she worked day and night…?

'I'll take it,' she said barely audibly.

'Do you want to see the studio and the flat?'

'No.' She shook her head. 'I'm sure they'll be fine.'

He studied her narrowly with a glint of curiosity in his dark eyes. 'I can't work out if you're a superior, head-in-the-clouds although accident-prone academic type or a rather exotic bundle of nerves.'

Harriet took a breath and actually managed to smile. 'If it's any help, neither can I. Goodbye, Tottie,' she added and patted the dog's head.

Damien Wyatt looked heavenwards as Tottie came as close as such a regal-looking dog could to actually simpering.

At the same time, Harriet said, 'Oh! I wonder where I put my glasses?'

'Here,' he remarked flatly, picking them up from the dining table and handing them to her. 'I'll see you out.'

Harriet hesitated. 'I'm sure I could see myself out.'

'Not at all. After you.'

So it was that Harriet preceded him out of the dining room and out of the house to the driveway. There was only one vehicle parked there: hers.

Damien Wyatt took one look at it and swore. 'You're not still driving that damn tank, are you?' he asked with furious incredulity.

Harriet coloured slightly. 'It just refuses to lie down. Anyway, it's not mine, it's Brett's, my brother's. It's very good over rough and sandy terrain.'

'I believe you.' Damien favoured the vehicle with a lingering look of malice then transferred his gaze to Harriet.

'Well, enjoy your stay at Heathcote, Miss Livingstone.' A tinge of irony entered his dark eyes. 'Don't go about kissing too many men at the same time as you're happy to remain fancy-free. Oh, and watch out for Charlie. He is, not to put too fine a point on it, a womaniser.'

Harriet drew a deep breath. 'Perhaps he takes after you?' she said quietly, and climbed into her battered old vehicle.

He waited until she'd driven off before saying to Tottie, 'What the devil do you make of all that? OK, I know you're on *her* side, but I don't ever recall kissing a girl I've—virtually—just met like that.'

Predictably, Tottie didn't answer; she only yawned.

Damien Wyatt shrugged. In fact I haven't kissed anyone quite like that for a while, he added to himself. Been too busy, been somewhat cynical about the whole tribe of women, to be honest. What I need, if that's the case, is someone nice and uncomplicated who knows the rules of the game—doesn't expect wedding bells in other words—rather than importuning an accident-prone, scholarly type who drives a horrible vehicle and has the nerve to suborn my dog!

'That's you, Tottie,' he said severely but Tottie remained serenely unaffected.

'Of course you could always kind of…keep an eye on her while I'm away,' Damien added. 'Heaven knows what "a left-handed syndrome" could lead her into.'

'Permission to speak,' a voice said and Charlie strolled onto the drive.

'Don't start, Charlie,' Damien advised.

'She's gone, I see.' Charlie came to a stop beside Tottie and his brother. He shoved his hands into his pockets. 'Unusual vehicle. For a girl, I mean. Not to mention some kind of an antique dealer, according to Isabel.'

'It's her brother's, apparently. Listen, Charlie—' he explained Harriet's background and the agreement they'd reached '—so leave her alone, will you?'

Charlie looked offended. 'Acquit me! Would I try to steal your girl?'

'Yes,' Damien said flatly. 'Not that *she's* my girl—not that she's *my* girl—' He broke off and swore. 'But she's got a job to do here and the sooner it's done, the better.'

Charlie frowned. 'Why do I sense a mystery attached to Miss Harriet Livingstone? Smashing pair of legs, by the way.'

'I don't know,' Damien said shortly. 'How long are you here for?'

'Relax, Bro,' Charlie said cheerfully. 'I'm due back at

the base in a week. By the way, you are now talking to Flight Lieutenant Charles Walker Wyatt. Which is what I dashed into the dining room to tell you, incidentally.'

'Charlie!' Damien turned to his brother. 'Congratulations!' And he shook his brother's hand then enveloped him in a bear hug.

'I suspect I got it by the skin of my teeth but, yeah!'

'Come in and I'll shout you a drink.'

It was just before they were called into dinner that Charlie said thoughtfully, 'There's something about that girl, Damien. Easy to run onto the rocks there—take care.'

Damien Wyatt opened his mouth to deny that there was any possibility of his running onto any rocks with Harriet Livingstone but he closed it.

And he said musingly, 'I'm glad to hear you say so because for the last few hours I've been wondering what on earth got into me. So what do you think it is?'

Charlie shook his head. 'I don't know,' he said. 'But some women just have an aura of…reserve, maybe, with a dash of vulnerability, a tinge of heartbreak perhaps, and that—' he waved his tankard '—certain something you just can't put into words.'

'That *je ne sais quoi*,' Damien murmured. He frowned. 'And you sensed all this about Harriet Livingstone in—roughly two minutes?'

Charlie looked wise. 'I once decided to date a girl I saw riding past me on a bicycle. All I saw was the curve of her cheek and all this shiny brown hair floating out behind her but it was enough. I chased her in my car, persuaded her to pop the bike in the boot and have lunch with me. We dated for quite a few months.'

'What broke it up?' Damien enquired curiously.

'The Air Force. I didn't get to spend enough time with her. Anyway, getting back to you. After Veronica, well...' Charlie shrugged as if he didn't quite know how to go on.

'Veronica,' Damien repeated expressionlessly.

'Your ex-wife,' Charlie explained generously. 'Gorgeous girl, of course, but—tricky.'

Damien raised his eyebrows. 'Good at hiding it, though.'

'Met her match when she ran into you, *however*,' Charlie declaimed. 'I—'

'Charlie,' Damien said gently, 'the only reason I've let the discussion get this far is because I'm feeling rather mellow on account of your promotion but that's enough.'

'Right-ho! Just don't say I didn't warn you!'

'Isn't that the guy you ran into?'

Brett Livingstone sat in a wheelchair in his pleasant room in the rehabilitation centre but his expression was troubled.

Harriet sat in an armchair opposite. She'd come straight from Heathcote with the news of the job she'd got—she hadn't told her brother anything about it before in case it hadn't come off.

'Yes. But that's all in the past and it's not only what I love doing, it comes with accommodation.'

'Are you safe with him?'

'Safe?' Harriet stared at him. 'Of course.'

Brett looked angry. 'He sounded like a thug and a bully.'

Harriet bit her lip. 'It was a very beautiful car. But look; his aunt lives there. So does his brother from time to time, and there's staff. And he has this marvellous dog. Her name's Tottie and she's very highly bred.'

Brett smiled reluctantly as he studied his sister's bright expression. 'Any kind of a dog could get you in, Harry.'

She grimaced. 'I suppose so. But really, Brett, it's the kind of job most people who do what I do would dream about. And—' she hesitated, wishing fervently she'd never told her brother about running into Damien Wyatt '—I'm not a very good waitress,' she added humorously. 'Can I stay and have dinner with you?'

'Sure. Hey—' Brett sat forward '—how can I ever thank you?'

Harriet had never lived in a caravan before but several weeks of it now had convinced her she wasn't cut out to be a gypsy.

Despite the fact that the van was clean and modern, she felt claustrophobic and found it hard to sleep. Of course her state of mind for the last few months hadn't helped.

Lennox Head was situated in the Northern Rivers District of New South Wales. Not on a river itself, it lay between the Tweed and Richmond Rivers, and as well as a distinctive headland that attracted surfers from around the world and hang-gliders too, it had a marvellous seven-mile beach.

Inland, the country was green, fertile and undulating until it came up against the Border Ranges. Sugar was grown on the coastal flats; coffee and custard apples amongst others further inland but the biggest crop of the district was macadamia nuts. It was pleasant country, home to huge camphor laurel trees and many colourful shrubs.

When she got back to the van, Harriet changed and went for a brisk walk then came back and sat on a bench.

It was a quiet evening.

She could hear the surf, she could see stars, but she had no sense of freedom.

And she still had Brett on her mind...

At twenty, he was six years younger than she was and their mother had passed away when he was a baby. Looking after and worrying about her little brother had been a way of life for Harriet for as long as she could remember.

For that matter, looking after their father was something she'd done as she'd got older. Until his death a couple of years ago, he'd been a delightful person, humorous, always devising little surprises for his children, telling them marvellous stories but otherwise quite hopeless when it came to the mundane things of life like saving and planning for the future.

Therefore they'd lived from day to day to a certain extent—when work was plentiful it was a lobster month he'd used to say, when it wasn't plentiful, mince on toast. And they'd moved a lot between capital cities and major and minor art galleries.

However, it was thanks to her father that Harriet had acquired much of her knowledge of antiques and art. She'd shared his fascination for them and some of her earliest memories were of visits with him to art galleries and art auctions, memories of reading art history books with him.

Brett couldn't have been more different. Athletic and with a love of the sea, he'd decided on a career as a professional surfer. And he'd been slowly making a name for himself when he'd been struck down by a freak accident and for a while no one had expected him to walk again.

But he was—just, if you could even call the sweat-soaked, painful inch by inch progress that.

But at least, Harriet mused, he was getting the best treatment now, and she had enough resources to ensure this treatment was maintained.

Which led her thoughts onto the subject of Damien Wyatt and the incredible turn of events of the afternoon.

A tremor ran through her as she remembered being in his arms and the powerfully sensual effect he'd had on her.

How could she have been so affected? she wondered. Was it simply the human contact and warmth she'd responded to?

It had to be something like that because hadn't she sworn never to fall in love again?

She grimaced at how melodramatic it sounded and wondered suddenly if she did project a neurotic image.

And how about scholarly or academic as well as accident-prone? Superior?

Or how about just plain lonely?

She bit her lip and blinked away a sudden tear.

CHAPTER THREE

Two WEEKS LATER, memories of her time in the caravan had started to fade and she'd fitted into the Heathcote lifestyle easily.

The flat above the converted stable block was comfortable and self-contained. It had a galley-style kitchen with all mod cons that appealed to Harriet. She was a keen and innovative cook and it wasn't long before she had a variety of herbs growing in pots on the windowsills. There was a rather lovely old wooden refectory table with benches.

The lounge area had comfortable armchairs and a view of the sea. The one bedroom was home to a kingsized bed, the lightest, warmest quilts and was rather sumptuously decorated in shades of violet and thyme-green.

Isabel had confessed to being the decorator and also to having gone a bit overboard in the bedroom.

Isabel was becoming friendlier and friendlier. She was Damien and Charlie's father's sister; she'd never married and it was plain to see that she ran not only the house but the estate with a lot of care and affection.

She'd confided to Harriet once that she knew every inch of the estate and every nook of the house because she'd not only grown up at Heathcote but spent most of her life there.

She certainly handled the small army of staff required—gardeners, cleaners, stable hands and one highly temperamental cook—with ease. Well, she'd confessed to Harriet that she suspected the cook, a Queenslander, was not only temperamental but that he drank and she really should sack him but he claimed to have six children under ten. He also cooked like an angel...

It hadn't required much insight on Harriet's part to see that Isabel doted on her nephews.

And she very early on discovered that Isabel always carried out Damien's instructions.

This discovery came, in fact, on the day Harriet arrived to take up residence at Heathcote. Isabel came up to the flat that afternoon to see how Harriet had settled in and at the same time she handed over a set of car keys.

Harriet looked at the keys with a frown. 'What are these for?'

'There's a blue Holden in the garage. It's not new but it's in great condition. It's for you to use while you're here. In fact, if you give me your car keys, I'll get your vehicle parked elsewhere.'

'Do I...do I detect the hand of Damien Wyatt here?' Harriet said ominously.

Isabel grimaced. 'You do.'

'Well, if he thinks he can—'

'I've been told to let you go if you don't agree to the Holden,' Isabel interrupted, and patted Harriet's arm. 'Much easier to drive, I'm sure. Besides, there's something about your vehicle that—upsets Damien.'

'I can understand that, but Damien is not here,' Harriet pointed out to his aunt.

'Damien is always here,' Isabel remarked with some irony. 'He seems to have a sixth sense about the place even if he's a million miles away. Please?' she added.

Harriet breathed deeply. 'If you must know, I can't help thinking he's a bit of a control freak!'

'Oh, definitely!' Isabel agreed. 'More than a bit, in fact. But it was—' she put her head on one side '—rather a thoughtful thing to do, don't you think?'

Harriet pursed her lips. 'I suppose so,' she said at length, and flinched inwardly a little to hear herself repeating the bit about it being *rather a thoughtful thing to do* to Brett that evening when she drove over in the blue Holden to see him.

'Thoughtful?' Brett repeated as she wheeled him out to the car park to look at it. 'You sure the guy's not sweet on you, Harry?'

'Quite s…' Harriet paused then said hastily, 'I think *your* car keeps reminding him of what I did to his beloved Aston Martin with it.'

'But he's not here to see it,' Brett objected.

'He has eyes in the back of his head—or something like that,' Harriet said gloomily, then forced herself to brighten up. 'How's it going?'

'I've got a new physio,' Brett replied. 'She's really cool. I'm walking a wee bit further every day.'

Harriet narrowed her eyes as she picked up a jaunty note she hadn't heard in her brother's voice for a long time. And she found herself crossing her fingers metaphorically and sending up a little prayer at the same time that this 'she', this new physio, might just be the one to provide her brother with the spark he needed.

The other aspect of life at Heathcote, of course, was Charlie. He didn't spend a lot of time on the estate during his furlough but when he did he always popped in to see Harriet.

It was probably during the third such visit that Harriet confirmed what she'd first suspected—that Charles Walker Wyatt treated her in rather a strange manner.

And she couldn't help mentioning it at the same time as she couldn't keep a straight face. 'Charlie,' she said with a chuckle, 'do I look as if I've popped down from Mars?'

'Mars,' he repeated, looking startled. He was lounging at the refectory table eating an apple plucked from her bowl when he wasn't watching her in that curiously assessing way he had. 'What makes you say that?'

'You have a way of looking at me and sort of…testing everything I say as if it has a hidden meaning or *I* have something about me you just don't understand.'

'Ah.' Charlie took a large bite of his apple. 'Well…' He munched and thought. 'I've never met anyone quite like you, I guess.'

He paused and studied her thoughtfully. She wore tight black shorts and a sapphire-blue tank top. Her hair was bunched up on top of her head and she wore her red-rimmed glasses as she studied a recipe she was planning to make for her dinner. It was an unexceptional outfit by any standards and yet it emphasised how trim and slim her figure was, how long her legs were.

No wonder Damien had got a bit carried away, Charlie found himself thinking as Harriet reached up and took down a pottery casserole dish.

Even used as he is to the crème de la crème, there's certainly something, well, subtly, but all the same eye-catching about Ms Harriet Livingstone, Charlie thought. Why on earth did I promise to leave her alone...?

'Charlie?'

He came out of his thoughts to find Harriet staring at him. 'Uh—I've certainly never met anyone who works as hard as you do. You were still working at midnight when I got home last night!'

'That's because I'd like to finish this project before your brother gets—' She stopped abruptly.

'Before Damien gets home? Why?' he asked simply. Harriet shrugged.

'His bark is a lot worse than his bite, as I should know.'

'It may be but I...' She paused.

'And you certainly must have made quite an impression on him because, believe me,' Charlie said earnestly, 'he's usually intensely private about his affairs. I got put firmly in my place only a couple of weeks ago when all I did was mention Veronica's name. She's his ex-wife,' he added obligingly, and waited.

I will not rise to the bait, Harriet vowed.

'So am I—very private,' she said shortly then relented as Charlie's expression became wounded. 'Look, it was just one of those…things. He got furious with me over the accident. I got furious with him because I thought he was arrogant and high-handed and it all seemed to blow up again into—' She stopped and took a breath then said laconically, 'If I hadn't slapped his face I wouldn't have got myself so thoroughly kissed.'

'Slapped his face!' Charlie was wide-eyed and incredulously admiring.

'Yes,' Harriet replied shortly. 'Not that I'm proud of it, but he did call me Stretch, which is something I can't abide. And that is the last word I intend to say on the matter. So, off you go, Charlie, please. I need to concentrate on this recipe.'

The studio that had been converted from stables was a pleasure to work in. There was plenty of light, plenty of bench space, a lot of shelving, a sink, even a microscope as well as a computer.

But, of course, the other thing that made Harriet feel at home was Tottie's presence. The big dog became her constant companion. They went for walks together. They went down to the beach and they visited the stables together, where Harriet made special friends with one of the horses, a bubbly grey mare that went by the name of Sprite.

Stan, the stable foreman, offered to let her ride Sprite, if she rode, which she had as a child, but she declined and contented herself with taking the mare carrots every evening.

And there were other times when Harriet caught herself talking to Tottie as if she were human.

She'd wondered how Isabel would take this but it only amused her. 'She's always been Damien's dog,' she told Harriet, 'but of course he's away a lot so she doesn't get to see that much of him.'

So far as the business side of her stay at Heathcote went, one thing Harriet had insisted on was a system whereby all of Damien's mother's treasures were dual-catalogued. In other words, Isabel handled them first, kept her own record, then handed them over to Harriet.

'Did you think we'd not trust you?' Isabel had asked curiously when Harriet had suggested the scheme. 'You come so highly recommended.'

'It's always better to be safe rather than sorry,' Harriet had replied. 'This way we're both protected.'

And Arthur, who drove up from Ballina occasionally, agreed.

Three weeks after she'd arrived at Heathcote, it was a glorious summer's day and she and Tottie went down to the beach. No one else was home. Charlie had gone back to his base and Isabel, who sat on several committees, was in Lismore helping to co-ordinate a charity drive and was spending the night with a friend.

They were the only ones on the beach, she and Tottie, and they frolicked in the surf and played with a ball until finally Harriet called out that she had to get back to work.

But something else had engaged the dog's attention after she'd dropped the ball at Harriet's feet. She stiffened, growled low in her throat and then took off like a shaggy arrow in full flight.

Harriet turned and discovered there was a man standing beside her towel where she'd dropped it on the grass verge above the beach—a man Tottie obviously knew because she skidded to a halt in front of him, barked with obvious joy this time, and leapt up to lay her paws on his shoulders—Damien Wyatt.

Harriet froze. Then she swallowed nervously as their last encounter and the last thing she'd said to him, the insult she'd offered him, stood out clearly in her mind.

Plus, even from further down the beach she could see he was wearing a suit, just as he had the day of the accident when he'd been so angry.

She hesitated and looked down at herself. Her lemon and lime flowered bikini was reasonably modest but it was still a bikini and she would have much rather been wearing a boilersuit or a combat uniform with all its paraphernalia for this encounter.

There was nothing for it, however, than to stroll up the beach, to say hi as casually as she could and to pick up her towel and wrap it around her. Perhaps then she could say something along the lines of *You're home early!* or *Welcome home! I have enjoyed Heathcote*—Stop it! she commanded herself. Just do it…!

It was a nerve-racking trudge up the beach but, when she was halfway there, Tottie came prancing back to her with delight written into her movements and a smile on her doggy face.

In fact Harriet had to grin in spite of herself, so infectious was the dog's enthusiasm.

'Hello, Damien,' she said as she reached him, almost confident that Tottie had eased the situation for her. She certainly didn't trip or fall as she picked up her towel and wrapped it around her sarong-wise but then she glanced up at him and things changed.

He wore a grey suit with a white shirt and a dark blue tie but he'd loosened his tie and unbuttoned the top button of his shirt. His hands were shoved into his trouser pockets.

And it struck Harriet like a blow to her heart that she'd fooled herself over the past weeks. Fooled herself into believing she'd completely rationalised the effect Damien had had on her.

More than that; she'd buried herself in his mother's treasures and convinced herself she wasn't even thinking of him. Only to know now that he'd been there on the back roads of her mind all the time; he must have been because every intimate detail of the passionate encounter they'd shared came back to her.

Not only did they come back to her but they trapped her into immobility, with her breathing growing ragged and her senses stirring as she stared at him and thought of the feel of his tall body against hers, the delight his hands had wrought on her.

Trapped her staring at him as a sea breeze lifted his dark hair off his forehead and brought her out in goose bumps—was it the breeze or was it part of the effect he was having on her, so she couldn't speak, she couldn't tear her eyes away?

Then she noticed he was watching her just as intently

and there was a muscle flickering in his jaw that told a tale of its own as his gaze slid down to her legs, barely hidden under the towel.

Tottie came to the rescue. She bunted them both playfully, as if to say—*Come on, you two, don't just stand there!*

Harriet had to relax a little and smile. So did Damien.

He also said, 'I hope my dog has been taking good care of you?'

'She's been a very faithful friend these last couple of weeks.' Harriet squeezed out her hair. 'I didn't know you were coming home.'

'No.' His dark eyes lingered on her figure and her legs again below the towel. 'Something came up unexpectedly. You look…well.'

Harriet smoothed the towel. 'Thanks.' Her voice was husky and she cleared her throat. 'So do you.'

A smile appeared fleetingly in his eyes. 'We sound like a mutual admiration society, a stilted one at that. But anyway, how's your brother?'

He turned and indicated they walk up to the house.

'He's making good progress and I've enrolled him as an external student at the Southern Cross University in Lismore.'

'What subject?'

She grimaced. 'Sports Psychology. I was hoping to wean him away from that kind of thing but—no go.'

'Better than nothing—a lot better,' Damien commented.

'Yes—ouch.' Harriet stopped walking as she stepped on a stone in her bare feet.

He stopped immediately. 'All right?'

'Yes!' She stood on one leg and awkwardly tried to examine the sole of her other foot. 'Oh, it's nothing, I'll be fine.'

'Here.' And, before she knew what he was about, he'd picked her up and was carrying her towards the studio.

'You don't have to do this,' she protested after a silent, shocked couple of seconds.

'Too good an opportunity to allow to pass, on the other hand.'

'Mr Wyatt—'

'Ms Livingstone?' he parried. 'Surely we can go one step further—upstairs?' he asked as they arrived at the studio.

'Well, yes, but—'

'What I mean about one step further is surely we can use each other's given names now,' he said as he mounted the stairs and sat her down on the refectory table and examined the sole of her foot.

'Well, yes,' Harriet conceded and immediately felt like a broken record.

'Good. There's nothing wrong with your foot. You might have a bruise, that's all.'

'Thank you.' Harriet rested her palms on the table and could think of not another thing to say.

Damien Wyatt grimaced. 'OK,' he said. 'I seem to have rather bowled you over. Why don't we go our separate ways for the next couple of hours—I've got things to do anyway—then have dinner?'

Harriet licked her lips. 'I was planning to work.'

'Say that again.' Something rather chilly entered his eyes.

She blushed. 'I…' But she could only gesture helplessly.

'Still running away, Harriet?' he said softly.

'I…' She trailed off then gathered herself. 'There's nothing to run away from but—' she hesitated '—if you don't mind pasta you could come here for dinner.'

He looked surprised.

'What?' she queried.

'I guess I wasn't expecting that.'

'You may have some preconceived ideas about me that influence your judgement; you obviously do,' she retorted.

There was a challenging glint in her eyes as she continued. 'Uh, let's see.' And she started to tick off her fingers. 'Head-in-the-clouds, accident-prone, academic—oh, let's not forget superior and neurotic. No wonder you were surprised to be asked to dinner!'

His lips twisted and he looked about to reply, then as if he'd changed his mind. He did say, 'I'll look forward to it. Around six? I'll bring some wine. You can stay,' he added to Tottie, who was looking visibly torn as he walked to the door.

Harriet stared at the doorway for a long moment after he'd disappeared then she clicked her fingers and Tottie came to the refectory table and put her chin on Harriet's knee with a soulful sigh.

'You could have gone with him,' she said as she stroked the dog's nose. 'I'd quite understand. He may not appreciate divided loyalties. In fact I get the feeling he's a hard man with a lot of hang-ups.'

Tottie sat down and thumped her tail on the floor.

Harriet smiled then slid off the table and glanced at the kitchen clock and discovered she only had an hour to shower and change as well as produce dinner.

But when she reached the bathroom, she dropped the towel still wound round her and stared at herself in the mirror. Then she closed her eyes and breathed deeply as every sensation she'd experienced from the moment he'd picked her up in his arms and carried her upstairs to the moment he'd sat her down on the table—and beyond—came to her again.

The easy strength that had made her feel quite light despite her height. The movement of his muscles against her body, the feel of his heart beating against her as her own heartbeat had tripled. The hard wall of his chest that made her feel soft and so sensuous. The pure aroma of man she'd inhaled with delight...

She opened her eyes and stared at herself in something like shock as she thought—*this can't go on!*

It was a hurried shower she took. And she pulled on a pair of grey leggings patterned with white daisies and a white cotton shirt with puffed sleeves. She tied her hair back severely with a pink ribbon and didn't bother with any make-up, not that she needed any; walking in the sun and swimming in the sea the past few weeks had given her a golden glow.

'This is delicious but—correct me if I'm wrong—it's not pasta,' Damien said.

He'd changed into a denim shirt and jeans and they sat opposite each other at the refectory table that Harriet had set with blue woven mats, matching linen napkins and one of her herbs in a colourful pottery pot.

'Changed my mind,' she confessed. 'It's paella.'

'What's it got in it?'

Harriet rested her elbows on the table and dangled her fork in her fingers. 'Let's see, chicken and prawns, rice, saffron, of course, tomatoes, onions, garlic, baby peas—that's mainly it. I guess people have their own variations but that's mine.'

'If you'd told me I could have brought some Sangria.'

Harriet put her fork down and picked up her wine glass. 'It's a very nice Beaujolais.'

'Thanks. So,' he said thoughtfully, 'cooking is another of your accomplishments. You're a talented girl.'

'That's about the sum of it, though,' she said wryly. 'And I don't think I was born to cook. It came about through necessity.'

'How come?'

She explained about how she'd grown up.

'So that's why you're so protective of your brother,' he commented. 'I suppose in a way I'm the same with Charlie. Our father died when he was seventeen. I've been standing in loco parentis ever since.' He grimaced.

Harriet pushed her plate away and picked up her glass. 'Charlie's a honey,' she said warmly.

Damien narrowed his eyes. 'He hasn't been chatting you up, has he?'

'Not at all. He's been trying to pin me down, if anything. As in trying to work me out. He believes, he says, anyway, I'm not like anyone else he's met. Mainly, from what I can gather—' she shrugged ruefully '—because of my work ethic.'

'How's it going, work-wise?'

Harriet studied her wine. 'Another week should do it.'

'You would have finished before I came home, if things had run to schedule, in other words.'

Harriet took a sip of her wine, put the glass down and plucked a basil leaf from the herb pot and crushed it between her fingers. 'Yes.'

He shrugged. 'Still hell-bent on being fancy-free, in other words?'

'Ah.' Harriet got up and collected their plates. She took them to the sink then opened the fridge and withdrew a lemon meringue dessert. She put it on the table, together with a tub of ice cream.

'If that's meant to placate me,' he said with a sudden wicked gleam of amusement in his dark eyes, 'you've hit the right button, ma'am. I cannot resist lemon meringue. Just don't tell the cook. He believes he and only he can make a perfect meringue. Incidentally, I'm in his black books.'

Harriet looked a question at him.

'He wanted to cook dinner for me.'

She smiled absently and set a coffee pot on to percolate. 'You're popular.'

He didn't respond and she sat down and served his dessert in silence.

'What about you? Of course,' he said, 'you don't have a sweet tooth.'

She nodded and he ate in silence until he said, 'You know, you haven't tripped or spilled anything tonight, which means you must be feeling more at ease so—can I put a proposition to you?'

Harriet blinked several times. 'What?'

'That we at least agree we have a rather devastating effect on each other.' He paused as Harriet looked away at the same time as she coloured.

'Yes,' she said after a long moment, and started as the coffee began to perk.

'I'll get it.' He got up and, without much fuss, found mugs and milk and sugar. 'However,' he continued, 'for reasons best known only to us, we're not keen to—start anything.' He looked briefly amused. 'Sounds a bit juvenile, doesn't it, but you probably get my drift.'

Harriet nodded.

'Incidentally, why did you,' he said as he began to pour the coffee, 'ask me to dinner tonight?'

Harriet hesitated. 'I...I felt I owed you some explanation.'

He sat down. 'You don't "owe" me anything,' he said abruptly.

'Mr...Damien,' Harriet said sternly, 'you told me once you didn't appreciate being told what you should or should not feel, didn't you?'

He grimaced. 'Did I?'

'Yes! Well, I'm telling you I feel as if I owe you an explanation and that's that—damn!' she said with great feeling. 'Now you've got me all...' She trailed off frustratedly.

'Het up about nothing?' he suggested mildly.

She cast him a speaking look. 'Do you want to hear this or not?' she asked acerbically.

'Go ahead.'

'I fell in love. I...' She paused. 'I guess you could say I gave it my all. And we had...we did have some wonderful times. But then he noticed another woman and I could literally feel him slipping away from me. That's why...' She stopped.

'That's a fairly common thing to happen,' he said slowly. 'How long ago was this?'

'A year or so ago.' She shrugged.

'That's all?' he queried with a frown.

No, it's not all, Damien Wyatt, Harriet thought, but that's all you're getting, well...

'Well, I've wondered ever since whether I brought it on myself. I guess...' she twined her fingers together '...I may have been looking for someone to take over my life. No...' she frowned '...not that exactly, but someone I could depend on to make the right decisions for us. Rather than me having to, as I seemed to have grown up doing.

'But when it started to fall apart I couldn't help thinking I may have come across as too "needy" and it was probably a relief for him to get away,' she said with a wave of her hand. 'I still don't know the answer to that but, whatever, I'm not prepared to go through all that again. I thought…I should explain, though.' She hesitated because, of course, there was more but telling anyone was something she'd never been able to do yet…

Their gazes caught and held.

'But you don't seem to have that problem,' she said at last. 'I mean I get the feeling you'd be quite happy to "start something".' Her glance was very blue and tinged with irony.

He crossed his arms and studied her thoughtfully. 'Yes, but, to be perfectly honest, if there is such a thing as…' he paused as if searching for the right phrase '…*love ever after*, I don't think it's going to exist for me.'

Harriet's eyes widened. 'Your marriage…' She trailed off awkwardly.

He raised an eyebrow at her. 'Isabel?'

'No. Charlie.'

He looked heavenward. 'I might have known.' Then, 'Well, you probably don't need me to elaborate.'

'All he told me was her name—and that he'd got firmly put in his place for merely mentioning it a little while back.'

Damien grimaced. 'Sounds like Charlie.'

'Sounds like you, actually.' A faint smile twisted her lips. 'So, it left you disillusioned?'

'It did a lot more damage.' He looked across the room and his dark eyes were cold. 'But, yep, it certainly left me unwilling to repeat the experience—I know!' He raised his hand as Harriet opened her mouth. 'You're going to say with another woman it could be different. Perhaps. But not for me. I don't part easily from my grudges, be they personal or embracing an institution like marriage.'

Something like a shiver ran down Harriet's spine because she had a feeling his estimation of his character was correct...

'In a way, we're a bit alike,' he said then, drumming his fingers on the table. 'Too much responsibility at an early age, only it took us differently.' He paused, looking briefly humorous. 'You wanted someone to take over; I got too used to being in command to be able to bend at all.'

'How come?'

He shrugged. 'I was twenty-two when my father died. And we were about to be taken over so I had to stave that off and get us up and running again. That's when I made the dicey decision to expand into mining machinery when we'd always concentrated on agriculture and its machinery.

'Plus,' he said rather wryly, 'I think I was born with an "ornery" streak. Arthur agrees with me.'

'Talking of Arthur,' Harriet said with a smile, 'Penny is pregnant.'

Damien grimaced.

'You don't approve of her, do you?'

'I think she manipulates him shamelessly,' he said dryly, then grinned. 'He'll need plenty of support to get through this! He'll be a nervous wreck.'

Harriet laughed.

Damien put his coffee mug down and simply watched her. Her hair was tied back but becoming wayward as it escaped. Her skin was unbelievably smooth, her hands and wrists slender and elegant, and her eyes were like deep blue velvet and still sparkling with amusement.

He said slowly, with his dark gaze still resting on her, 'I don't know how the hell I didn't see it the first time we met but you're breathtaking when you laugh.'

'I had nothing to laugh about at the time,' she said, still smiling. But gradually it faded as she moved awkwardly and nearly knocked her coffee over.

'So nothing's changed?' he said barely audibly as his gaze tracked her awkward movements.

'N-no,' she stammered.

'It doesn't make it easier that we've both stated our cases and I think we've both indicated we're not talking love ever after?'

Harriet tilted her head as she studied him with a frown in her eyes. 'No,' she said slowly.

'Any special reason?' he enquired dryly.

'I'm—I don't think I'm like that. I seem to be an all or nothing kind of person. In that regard,' she said thoughtfully.

Damien Wyatt smiled in a way that brought to mind an unamused tiger. 'You shouldn't go around saying things like that, Harriet Livingstone.'

'Why not? I think it's true.'

'It's also an incendiary kind of statement,' he murmured dryly.

Harriet looked at him wide-eyed. 'I…I'm not sure what you mean…' She faltered into silence. Then a flood of colour poured into her cheeks as his meaning became plain and she jumped up so precipitously she took Tottie by surprise and she tripped over her.

This time Damien Wyatt was too far away to rescue her and she'd fallen to her knees when he got to her.

'It's all right, I can manage,' she panted and held a hand out as if to ward him off as she scrambled to her feet. 'I didn't mean to...to imply,' she went on, 'what you obviously thought I meant to imply.'

'What was that?' he enquired and looked as if he was having trouble keeping his face straight as he steadied her with his hands on her waist.

'That—oh! You know what I mean!' Her expression was seriously frustrated.

'That you're only great in bed when you believe you're in love?'

She nodded then shook her head, more frustrated than ever. 'I didn't say anything about being great in bed and—'

'I'd like to bet you are, though,' he broke in.

'There's no way you could possibly know that!' she said heatedly.

He gestured. 'You're talking to a guy who's kissed you, remember?'

Harriet subsided a little. 'Well,' she said uncertainly.

'And you did suggest you were an *all or nothing* kind of person in *that* regard, which suggests—which conjures up certain images,' he said gravely, but she just knew his dark eyes were laughing at her.

She took a distressed breath and formed her hands into fists. 'Don't laugh at me,' she warned.

'Or?' he queried, his hands still on her waist. 'You don't expect to slug it out with me, do you?' He eyed her clenched fists.

'I would like nothing better,' she confirmed with great feeling again.

'How about testing out the other side of the coin?' he suggested, and pulled her closer.

She stiffened and urged herself into battle mode. Resist this, she told herself fiercely. Don't fall under his spell as you did last time, don't get mesmerised again. Don't allow the somehow simply wonderful feeling of being in his arms to overcome you and make you dizzy with delight. Dizzy and delighted because he feels so strong, because he knows just how and where to touch you and arouse you… She started as he spoke again.

'How about—this?' And he slid his fingers beneath her top and cupped her breasts.

CHAPTER FOUR

HARRIET TREMBLED AND he felt it through his fingers.

'If it's nice for you, you only need to nod,' he said huskily. 'Believe me—' he moved his fingers across her nipples '—it's sensational for me.'

Harriet's lips parted and she unclenched her fists and grasped his wrists instead. She didn't nod but she did say, 'You have a way of doing that—that's breathtaking but—'

'You'd rather I didn't?' he suggested, narrowing his eyes suddenly.

Harriet closed her eyes briefly. 'I'd much rather fly to the moon with you, Damien Wyatt,' she said barely audibly, 'but I can't help knowing I'd regret it sooner or later.'

'Another incendiary statement.'

She bit her lip. 'I'm sorry, I'm really sorry.' And there were tears in her eyes.

He hesitated for a long moment then he withdrew his hands and smoothed her top down. 'You win,' he drawled.

Harriet flicked away the tears on her cheeks and

steeled herself for more mockery. It didn't come, not in the spoken form, anyway.

He turned away and sprawled out in one of the chairs at the table. 'Actually—' he ran a hand through his hair '—you're right, Ms Livingstone.'

But being right, Harriet discovered, didn't prevent him from subjecting her to a dark gaze full of dry amusement as he looked her up and down and mentally dispensed of all her clothes.

She bore that sardonic scrutiny and mental undressing for as long as she could, determined not to turn away and thereby give him the satisfaction of knowing he'd upset her, but was just about to protest when he spoke.

'Do you ride?'

Harriet blinked. 'Horses?'

'Well, I don't mean camels.'

'I have, as a kid,' she said cautiously.

He drummed his fingers on the table. 'Did you enjoy it?'

'Yes,' she replied but equally as cautiously as she wondered what was coming.

'Just tell me this, Harriet. Would it be purgatory for you if I suggested we get up at the crack of dawn tomorrow to take advantage of the low tide and go for a gallop down the beach? Tottie, I know, would love it.'

'If I could ride Sprite...' She paused and looked uncomfortable.

She saw him process this. 'So,' he murmured, 'you have a way with horses as well as dogs?'

Harriet spread her hands. 'Oh, I don't know.'

He raised an eyebrow. 'Sounds as if you've been chatting Sprite up already.'

'I suppose I have,' Harriet conceded ruefully.

'Then—are we on for tomorrow morning, about five?'

'I...' Harriet swallowed but nothing could stop the flow of images running through her mind of a dawn gallop followed by a swim then a huge breakfast. 'Yes,' she said.

'Good.' He stood up. 'Not—' he eyed her with a glint of pure devilry in his dark eyes '—that there'll be anything good about how to get to sleep tonight.'

It was no consolation to Harriet to reflect, as she tossed and turned in bed after Damien had gone, on one victory, one small victory perhaps, but all the same...

She'd successfully withstood the sensual onslaught Damien could inflict on her, although *inflict* wasn't the right word for it at all. But she had withstood the power of his masculine appeal, she'd tacitly told him to do his worst when he'd mentally undressed her—and then she'd gone and wrecked it all by agreeing to go riding with him.

'Damn!' She sat up in bed. 'I must be mad. Apart from anything else, I know he's only going to lead me to fresh heartache—I should be running for my life!'

At five o'clock the next morning she felt heavy-eyed and in an uneven frame of mind as she pulled on jeans, a jumper and sand shoes.

Twenty minutes later, trotting down the track from

the stables to the beach on the slightly fizzy Sprite, she was feeling marginally better, although only marginally, she assured herself.

By the time they reached the beach, the sun was turning the sky into a symphony of apricot as it hovered below the horizon and the placid waters reflected the colours back.

'Hang on,' Damien said as he took hold of Sprite's bridle and clipped on a leading rein so that she and Sprite were forced to adapt to his slower gait.

'What do you think you're doing?' Harriet asked.

'Taking precautions, that's all,' he replied.

'I can assure you, you don't need to!'

'You said you rode as a child. That could mean you haven't been on a horse for years.'

'I'm perfectly capable of riding this horse,' Harriet replied through her teeth.

'But you have to admit you're—well, if not exactly accident-prone, you do suffer from some weird syndrome that could cause all sorts of problems.'

'Mr Wyatt—' Harriet raised her riding crop '—don't say another word and let me go before I do something *you* might regret but *I* won't regret in the slightest!'

'Harriet,' he returned mildly, 'it's not very ladylike to keep attacking me.'

Harriet groaned. '*Let me go.*'

He hesitated briefly then unclipped the leading rein. Sprite, who'd been dancing around impatiently on the end of it, jostled his big brown horse, had the temerity to bestow a love bite on its neck, then, following Harriet's dictates, lengthened her stride and galloped away. Tottie raced after them joyously.

By the time they'd reached the end of the beach and galloped back, Harriet's mood had evened out—she was feeling far less grumpy and even of the opinion that this had been a good idea.

And, following Damien, she rode Sprite into the gentle low-tide surf. Both horses loved it and splashed energetically until finally they brought them out, led them to the edge of the beach and tied them loosely to trees.

'I'm soaked!' Harriet sank down onto the sand but she was glowing with enthusiasm as she sat cross-legged.

Damien cast himself down beside her and doodled in the sand with a twig. He hadn't shaved and he had a curious glint in his dark eyes as he looked across to study her.

'Tell me something,' he said. 'Are you not a morning person?'

Harriet opened her mouth, closed it, then she grinned. 'I am not. Well, not a very early morning person.' She was about to add—*and particularly not after a disturbed night*—but managed to hold that bit of information back. 'I take it you're the opposite?'

'Depends.'

'On what?'

'What's on offer in bed.'

Harriet looked heavenwards. 'Do men ever think of anything else?'

'Frequently.' He shot her an amused glance. 'Not,

generally, at five in the morning with a warm, compliant partner, however.'

Harriet frowned as the wheels of her mind worked through this. Then she turned to him incredulously. 'Did you get me up at that ungodly hour as a shot at me for not...for...not...for being...for not being in bed with you?' she said exasperatedly.

'If I did,' he said wryly, 'I had no idea the danger I was placing myself in. I'll probably think twice before I do it again.'

'Oh!' Harriet ground her teeth as she stared at him, so big, so relaxed, so attractive, even if he hadn't shaved and his hair was hanging in his eyes, not to mention the fact that he was teasing her mercilessly.

'But of course,' he went on before Harriet could speak, 'the real reason I got you up at the crack of dawn was because of the tide. You need a low tide and therefore firm wet sand to gallop on. By the way, where did you learn to ride like that?'

Harriet closed her mouth and subsided somewhat. Then she shrugged and smiled. 'My father decided it needed to be part of my education. He restored a couple of valuable paintings for a wealthy horse breeder who was once a jockey in exchange for riding lessons. He had a few other notions along those lines—I had tennis lessons under similar circumstances, not so successful; my—' she cast him a quirky glance '—weird syndrome interfered with me becoming a Wimbledon champion.'

He laughed and looked at her curiously again. 'You're full of surprises—docile and ladylike on one hand then quite a termagant.'

'Docile!' Harriet pulled a face. 'That sounds awful. So does termagant. I'm sure I'm not either of those.'

'You're also younger sometimes. The ladylike you could be ten years older.'

'That's ridiculous,' Harriet objected but found she had to laugh a little. 'You know, the art world takes itself very seriously sometimes, so one may get into the habit of *being* very serious-minded without quite realising it.'

He laughed then glanced at his watch. 'OK. I've got things to do.'

He got up and untied his horse but Harriet stayed where she was, quite unaware that she looked disappointed.

'Harriet?'

She looked up to see him frowning down at her.

'This is how you want it, isn't it?' he queried.

She froze then a heartbeat later she scrambled up. 'Sure! Let's go!'

But upstairs in the flat after she'd showered and was eating breakfast alone, it wasn't how she wanted it at all, she had to confess to herself.

She worked furiously for the next couple of days then Charlie came home for a long weekend and it was his birthday and he'd decided to have a party.

If she hadn't been so engrossed in her work, she'd have noticed the preparations going on in the big house, but she hadn't. Therefore it took her by surprise when Isabel asked her what she'd be wearing.

'Wearing?'

'To Charlie's birthday party.'

'When?'

Isabel clicked her tongue. 'Tomorrow. You're invited.'

'No I'm not.' Harriet put down the ivory figurine of a dolphin she was holding.

'But I put an invitation—' Isabel broke off, looked around and stepped over to the table beside the door where she picked up several items of mail, one of which she then brandished at Harriet, looking exasperated. 'Even if you didn't see this, surely you noticed that something was going on?'

Harriet coloured. 'No. I'm sorry. And thank you very much for inviting me—'

'Charlie did,' Isabel corrected.

'Charlie then, but I couldn't possibly come.'

'Why on earth not?' Isabel stared at her with the light of battle clearly lit in her dark Wyatt eyes.

Harriet heaved a sigh. 'I'm—I'm an employee, Isabel,' she said but tartly despite the sigh, 'and don't forget it! Look, I'm sorry if I sound snippy or rude but sometimes it's the only way to deal with you Wyatts.' To her horror, tears stood out in her eyes but she carried on relentlessly. 'I'm not coming and that's that.'

'Not coming where?'

Both Harriet and Isabel swung around to see Damien standing in the doorway.

'Charlie's party,' Isabel said bitterly.

Harriet turned away. There had been no more dawn rides on the beach; in fact she'd hardly seen Damien since that magical morning.

'That's OK,' Damien said easily. 'It's her choice.'

Isabel took a sharp angry breath. 'Men! You're all the

same; never there for you when you're needed. If anyone could have persuaded her, you could have. But, on top of being unreliable, most men are as thick as planks!' And she stormed past Damien and out into the night.

Harriet closed her mouth and blinked several times.

'Ditto,' Damien murmured. 'You wouldn't change your mind and come, would you, Harriet? If for no other reason than for me to regain some credibility in my aunt's eyes.'

Harriet hesitated then sighed. 'I might just put in an appearance. But that's all,' she warned.

'Far be it from me to urge you otherwise,' he said gravely. 'No, I wouldn't dream of persuading you to take part in what you might see as mindless revelry in some way beneath you—or whatever. So, good-night, Miss Livingstone,' he added reverently and he too stepped out into the night. He also closed the door.

Harriet discovered herself to be possessed of a burst of anger and she picked up an object to hurl it at the door, only to realise it was the ivory dolphin.

She lowered it to the table, breathing heavily, and she said to Tottie, 'That was a close call.'

Tottie wagged her tail and went back to sleep.

By eight o'clock the next evening, Charlie's party was starting to hum. The lounge had been cleared for dancing, a disco had been set up and the dining room hosted a magnificent buffet and a bar.

Guests from all over the Northern Rivers had descended on Heathcote, some from further afield like the Gold Coast.

Harriet got to know this because Charlie personally came to escort her to the party.

She looked down at herself just before Charlie climbed the stairs to the flat—not that she'd known he was coming. In fact she was grappling with nerves and the desire to find a hole to fall into. She was also hoping she wasn't over- or underdressed.

She wore a black dress with a loose skirt to just above her knees with white elbow-length sleeves and white panels in the bodice. It was a dress that emphasised the slenderness of her waist. With it she had on a ruby-red chunky necklace, her legs were golden and long and bare and she wore black suede high heels with ankle ties.

Her hair was pulled back into a knot but she'd coaxed some tendrils to frame her face. Her lips were painted a delicious shimmering pink and her eyes were made up with smoky shadow, her lashes just touched with mascara to emphasise their length.

'Holy Mackerel!'

Charlie stopped dead as he stepped into the flat and took in every detail about Harriet.

'Oh, boy!' he said then.

Harriet twisted her hands together. 'What's wrong?'

'It's not that, it's the opposite. Poor old Damien; is he in for…well. I hope you know what you're doing, Harriet.'

'Doing?'

Charlie blinked and frowned. 'You didn't set out to drive him wild?' He gestured to take her in from the tip of her head to her toes.

Harriet opened her mouth to deny this accusation but she closed it and coloured slightly. 'I haven't actually worn it before. Is it too…?' She didn't complete the sentence. 'I can change.'

'Don't you dare!' Charlie looked horrified. 'So you did set out to drive him wild?'

'I did not,' she denied.

'I wouldn't mind,' Charlie offered. 'I'm on your side.'

'I…' Harriet hesitated. 'He made a remark that cast me in the light of a docile priggish bore. So I thought I'd show him otherwise. But now, if you must know, Charlie, I'm sorry, but I really don't want to go to your party.'

'Made a remark, did he?' Charlie ignored the rest of her statement. 'He's done that to me. He has a way of doing it that makes you want to throw things—but what sweet revenge would this be. Come, my lady Harriet.' He held out his arm.

'Charlie…Charlie, this is not really me and I've changed my mind about…showing him anything.'

'No, you haven't,' Charlie disagreed as he led her to the top of the stairs. 'You've got a slight case of stage fright, that's all. But I'll be there!'

'So.'

Harriet stood on the terrace, sipping champagne and fanning herself.

There was a moon. There were also flaming braziers in the garden and the music flowing out was of a solid rock beat and loud enough to drown the sound of the surf beyond the garden wall.

'So,' she repeated without turning.

'You don't mind a dance, Miss Livingstone,' Damien observed, moving forward to stand beside her.

'I don't. At the right time and place,' she replied. She took another sip of champagne as she registered the fact that he was wearing a tweed jacket over a round-necked shirt, and jeans.

'I thought you were just going to put in an appearance.'

'I was. Your brother had other ideas.' She shrugged.

'You look—great. Quite unlike your alter ego.'

'Thank you. I suppose you mean my academic, neurotic—' she waved a hand '—and all the rest of it, side.'

'Well, certainly the you that looks as if you've stepped straight out of Christies or Sotheby's or a museum.' He paused then glanced across at her. 'What would happen if I asked you to dance?'

'Thank you so much, Damien, but—' she drained her champagne and put the glass down on the table beside her '—I think I've done enough partying,' she finished politely.

Their gazes locked. 'That's a pity.' He raised a dark eyebrow. 'Still scared and running, Harriet?'

Harriet put a hand to her throat. 'We've been through all this, Damien.'

He shrugged and studied his beer tankard. 'I don't think we made allowances for the effects of you looking so gorgeous and seriously sexy, you dancing, your legs on show; no sign of the eternal jeans or leggings you wear. It's almost as if you're issuing an invitation, Miss Livingstone.'

A tide of colour poured into Harriet's cheeks.

He studied it with interest. 'You are?'

'No. Oh! Look,' she said intensely, 'you persuaded me to come to this party. You then made—talk about an incendiary remark but in quite a different sense—you made my blood boil *in anger*,' she emphasised, 'with your comments about mindless revelry that I would find beneath me.'

'So you decided to show me a thing or two?' he hazarded.

'Yes,' she said through her teeth. 'Mind you—' she hesitated then decided she might as well go for broke '—I did intend only to put in an appearance, enjoy myself for a little while then retreat. The music got to me,' she added.

His lips twitched. 'I quite understand. The music is getting to me right now, as a matter of fact.'

Harriet narrowed her eyes and concentrated for a moment as she listened to the music, and grimaced.

'No good for you?' he queried as she barely restrained herself from moving to the beat.

'I couldn't exactly say that…'

'We could have a "no hands" agreement,' he suggested. 'We could just do our own thing,' he explained.

Harriet eyed him. 'What a good idea.' She smiled sweetly then laughed at his expression. 'It's OK. I'll take my chances.'

It was a phrase that was to haunt her during the rest of that night and the day that followed.

Because the fact of the matter was, she'd danced the rest of the night away with Damien.

She'd rocked and rolled, she'd been quiet and peaceful in his arms. She'd revelled in the feel of his hands on her, in the feel of his body against hers. She'd followed his lead and adapted her steps to his, once with a flourish that had flared her skirt out around her thighs so that she'd grimaced and pushed it down with a tinge of colour in her cheeks.

As she'd danced she'd recalled the last time she'd been in his arms and the intimacy of the way they'd kissed. And she'd wished they were alone as they'd been that day so she could run her fingers through the thick darkness of his hair and slide her hands beneath his jacket and shirt and feel those sleek muscles of his back...

And at the end she'd been wrapped in his arms, barely moving and loving it.

That was when the lights had come on. That was when people had started to leave. That was when she'd come to her senses, when she'd looked up into his eyes, when she'd seen the desire in them.

And when she'd freed herself urgently and fled from him, melting into the crowd of departing guests then running up the stairs to the flat, locking herself in and turning off all the lights.

She'd undressed shakily and thrown her dress onto the floor.

But as she'd climbed under the doona she'd known it was futile and ridiculous to blame a dress. She was the one to blame. She was the one who'd been unable to resist the feel of his arms around her, the one who'd got an incredible rush from matching her body to his as they'd danced. The one who had lost all her inhibitions at the hands of Damien Wyatt when she'd promised herself it was the last thing she would do...

There was no sign of Damien the next day.

In fact it was a curiously quiet day. Once the after-party clean-up had taken place, it was as if all the Wyatts and everyone else had melted away.

Isabel, at least, had explained that she was going to spend the night with a friend.

Charlie, Harriet assumed, had gone back to his base.

Not that she particularly wanted to face anyone after last night but it somehow added to her mood of doom and gloom to find herself feeling as if she were alone on the planet.

She'd just eaten her dinner when she heard footsteps on the outside stairway, and Damien arrived.

She half got up, sat down again and trembled inwardly at his expression.

Tottie was, of course, delighted to see him.

Harriet stood up again and collected her plate and knife and fork. 'I'm sorry,' she said. 'I don't know what got into me last night.'

'I didn't come to conduct a post-mortem into last night.' He looked at her sardonically. 'Any idea where Isabel is? She usually leaves a note.'

Harriet explained about the friend.

He looked even more irritated. 'Did she say which fr—?'

He stopped abruptly as Tottie growled suddenly and then, in a manner of speaking, all hell broke loose.

There was a whoosh of sound and the sky beyond the windows of the flat illuminated briefly in the direction of the house.

'What the devil...?' Damien shut his teeth hard then went on, 'It's the kitchen. Looks like the cook has finally decided to burn the place down.'

The cook hadn't—at least not consciously had he decided to burn the place down—but he had got drunk and he had allowed oil in a deep fryer to catch alight as he'd dozed with a bottle of bourbon in his fist.

He still had it—the bourbon bottle in his fist— when Harriet and Damien arrived on the scene as he stared, stupefied, from the relative safety of the vegetable garden, at the flames leaping out of the kitchen windows.

But within moments, or so it seemed, Damien had taken control. He'd rung for the fire brigade, he'd sent Harriet to waken Stan, the stable foreman, who was the only other person on the property, and he'd located several fire extinguishers, hoses and fire blankets. He also took a moment to attempt to send Harriet back upstairs to the flat.

'No,' she shouted over the crackling of the flames, 'I can hold a hose!'

'Yeah, but I don't want you tripping and falling over!'

'Listen to me, Damien Wyatt,' she yelled at him, 'it's only you who makes me do that—look out,' she screamed as a burning piece of wood fell from a window ledge right next to him.

He leapt away and she grabbed a hose and sprayed the sparks that had fallen on his boots and jeans.

'All right, listen,' he said. 'Be careful; be very careful.'

'I will, I will,' she promised fervently.

He stared down at her in the demonic firelight, then hugged her to him, and immediately turned away.

It was a frenetic scene as they tried to tame the leaping, crackling flames glowing orange against the background of a midnight-blue sky, a scene also of choking smoke pouring from the kitchen and a stifling charred smell.

And by the time the fire brigade arrived Harriet was blackened and soaked to the skin.

'Don't.' Damien loomed up in front of her and removed her hose from her hand. 'Don't do any more; you've done enough. It's under control now.'

'But...'

'Just do as I tell you, Harriet Livingstone,' he said and, without further ado, kissed her full on the lips. 'Be a good girl and go and get cleaned up.'

CHAPTER FIVE

HARRIET WENT, WITH the tips of her fingers pressed to her lips.

And she grimaced at the sight of herself as she went to take her third shower of the day. She dressed in jeans and a track top and concentrated on clearing away her dinner and putting a fresh pot of coffee on to perk.

Sounds of all the activity were starting to scale down as she worked, and finally she heard the fire engine drive away and an almost unnatural silence overtake Heathcote.

Not much later Damien and Tottie turned up, Damien also showered and in clean clothes, a grey track top and khaki cargo pants, and bearing a bottle of brandy.

Harriet reached for glasses. 'You must be a mind-reader.'

He grimaced. 'Nothing like a good fire to provoke the need for some Dutch courage.' He splashed two generous tots into the glasses.

'How bad is it?'

'The kitchen—cheers,' he said and touched his glass

to hers, 'the kitchen will have to be rebuilt. Thankfully, it didn't go any further.'

'How's the cook?'

Damien shook his head. 'A sodden wreck. Stan's looking after him. He's full of remorse and petrified he's going to lose his job.'

Harriet paused with her glass halfway to her mouth. 'He expects to keep it after nearly burning the place down?'

Damien shrugged and his lips twisted. 'According to Isabel, he's got six kids stashed away in Queensland so I'll get her to find him a position closer to home.'

Harriet looked surprised.

He looked wry. 'You didn't expect that?'

'Well, no,' she said. 'Sorry.'

'That's OK. I'm used to being in your bad books or, if not that, then suspected of some kind of dodginess or another.' He drained some of his brandy. 'Incidentally, we're going to have to use this kitchen until we get the house kitchen fixed.' He looked around.

'Oh. Of course.' She got up and poured the coffee and brought it back to the table. 'I don't suspect you of *dodginess*, whatever that means precisely.' She pushed his mug over to him and sat down with hers.

He drank some more brandy. 'You obviously suspect me of something, Miss Livingstone.'

Harriet grimaced. 'I did tell Isabel I thought you were a bit of a control freak.'

'What brought that on?'

Harriet looked at him askance. 'The car you insisted I drive.'

'Oh, that.' He lounged back and shoved his hands into his pockets.

Harriet studied him. His dark hair was still damp and there were blue shadows on his jaw. He looked perfectly relaxed and not as if he'd just fought a fire. For some reason, to have him so big and powerful and quite at ease in what she'd come to regard as her home annoyed her. 'Yes, that,' she said tartly.

He lifted his shoulders. 'I wouldn't be so far off the mark in believing you and your brother's vehicle were something of a menace on the roads but—' he sat up '—before you take umbrage, just the sight of it annoyed me enormously.'

Harriet stared at him.

'Does it make me a control freak to provide you with an alternative, though?' he mused gently. 'I don't believe so.'

Harriet continued to stare at him as several things ran through her mind. She'd experienced a maelstrom of emotions due solely to this man. She'd never stopped thinking about Damien Wyatt while he'd been away, even if she had been able to bury it in her subconscious. She'd been physically stirred by him. She'd told him some of her painful history. She'd cooked him dinner—she'd even made him a lemon meringue dessert.

She'd danced with him, ridden with him, been hugged and kissed by him—she could still feel the imprint of his mouth on hers, come to think of it—and her fingers went to her lips involuntarily at the mere thought of it.

Only to see that he was watching her intently.

She snatched her hand away as a tide of pink rose in her cheeks, then threw up her hands in serious frustration. 'Look,' she said levelly, 'because I'm not prepared to jump into bed with you doesn't mean to say I think you're dodgy, although it's just as bad but quite the opposite really.'

He frowned. 'What does that mean?'

Harriet bit her lip and could have shot herself—if ever she'd voiced an unwise utterance this was it…

'It doesn't matter,' she said stiffly.

'Oh, come on, Harriet,' he said impatiently, 'I can take it.' He looked briefly amused. 'Spit it out, Miss Livingstone.'

Harriet glared at him. 'If you must know, I suspect you of being far too good in bed, Mr Wyatt, for any girl's peace of mind.'

He sobered completely and stared at her narrowly. 'How, one has to ask,' he said slowly, 'did you work that out?'

Her eyes were full of irony. 'You're talking to a girl who's kissed you, remember?'

His lips twisted. 'So you did. Well—' he drained his glass and stood up '—on that note I think I'll leave you to your memories, Miss Livingstone, and I will take mine…somewhere else. Goodnight.' And he patted her on the head, told Tottie to stay put, and strolled out.

Harriet stared after him in a state of suspended animation. In other words, with her mouth open and her eyes huge and dark with disbelief.

Was this his retaliation for what she'd done last night?

Why did she feel disbelief, though? she found herself wondering. Because she'd been convinced he would react differently to what had been—talk about incendiary!—another incendiary statement she'd made.

All the same, a true statement, she reasoned with herself. She *was* deadly afraid that once she gave in to Damien Wyatt she'd be hooked. She'd be on a roundabout, in love with a man who didn't believe in love, who didn't believe in marriage…

As if she hadn't had enough trauma in that direction.

Damien Wyatt, after checking his property over thoroughly, and making sure the cook was in no position to do any more damage, climbed the stairs and walked into his bedroom but he didn't immediately go to bed. He didn't even turn the light on.

He stood instead at the open window and listened to the sea crashing onto the beach. From the sound of it, he judged it to be high tide or close to it. And he could see a tracing of phosphorous lying luminous on the beach as each wave receded.

But he was only registering the phosphorous absently. He was thinking of Harriet Livingstone. He could see her in his mind's eye, serving up her paella and her lemon meringue with that slim tall figure in daisy-patterned leggings and a white blouse.

Thinking of her last night as she'd looked lovely enough to stir any man's blood. And had danced in her own way, a way that was enough to tempt any man.

And tonight, soaked to the skin and her hands and

face blackened, then clean and neat again in jeans and a track top.

Hearing her saying the kind of things women who were not naïve couldn't say with a straight face—she was an all or nothing person in that direction. Sex and relationships, in other words. Accusing him of being too good in bed for her peace of mind...

He fingered the curtain then turned away and threw himself down in an armchair. The room was still in darkness but there was a lamp on the table beside the armchair. He pressed the button and soft light radiated from under the silk shade. And the bedroom came alive in its blue and gold trappings.

He'd inherited the master bedroom when his parents had passed away, although he hadn't moved into it until he'd married, and it still reflected his mother's taste. A four-poster bed, flocked wallpaper, tapestries—if it wasn't a superbly comfortable bed he'd have left the grandeur of this bedroom, which made him think it should belong in a French chateau, to darkness and silence after he and Veronica had separated.

Or, he mused, maybe it wasn't only the bed. Perhaps he continued to use the room as a warning to himself never to forget the trauma and betrayal Veronica had brought to him.

Maybe...

But where to place Harriet Livingstone in his scheme of things?

He moved restlessly. It was unfortunate but true, he had to admit, that he was extremely attracted to her, even if he couldn't quite analyse why.

What was more unfortunate about it was that he believed her when she said she wasn't built for affairs. Why he believed her, he couldn't say. Why he didn't see it as a ploy on her behalf to tell him she was an all or nothing girl, a ploy to set him on fire physically in a manner of speaking, he couldn't say either.

But what he'd considered the natural progression from a spontaneous attraction that had gripped them *both* was now fraught with all sorts of dangers...

It always had been from her point of view, he found himself conceding. She'd always known it was a road she couldn't, or shouldn't, travel.

He'd always thought, he conceded too with an inward grimace, that he could break her down or win her over to something that was fulfilling, pleasant but not too deep—no, not too deep.

'You're a fool, Damien Wyatt,' he told himself. 'Too blind to see that she is that kind of girl—a genuinely all or nothing girl. A girl who could be devastated if you had a relationship but didn't marry her—and now you've got to withdraw somehow.

'Why would it be so impossible to marry her?'

A pool of silence swallowed up his question.

Because he didn't believe he could trust any woman again? And therefore he didn't want to inflict the worst of his cynicism on Harriet Livingstone?

He stood up abruptly. The sooner he distanced himself from her the better.

Harriet, to her surprise, fell asleep as soon as her head touched the pillow and she slept deeply and dreamlessly the night of the fire.

As she studied herself in the bathroom mirror the next morning she couldn't help but notice that, despite that night of quality sleep, she looked tense. There seemed to be an undertone of worry to her expression.

'Damien,' she said softly to herself. 'Things between us are—a worry, aren't they? What am I going to do?'

She left the bathroom and suddenly remembered her kitchen would be on call and the least she could do was have some coffee ready.

It was Isabel who arrived first, looking shocked.

'Damien rang me earlier,' she told Harriet, puffing a bit after climbing the stairs. 'Thank heavens it didn't spread. I should have done something about Cook before now,' she added with a sigh. 'Thanks for helping to put it out.'

'I didn't do much, other than pointing a hose. Would you like some coffee?'

'Love some. I'm afraid you're stuck with me for meals and I'm not much of a cook,' Isabel confessed.

'That's OK. I enjoy it. In fact I was just going to cook some bacon and eggs for breakfast.'

'Yum! I'll stay put then.'

'What about Damien?' Harriet asked as she reached into the fridge for her breakfast ingredients.

'Oh, he's gone off again. Perth this time. Not sure when he'll be back. He's got some South African mining magnate he's dealing with.' Isabel waved a hand.

'Oh,' Harriet said.

'Didn't he mention it? I suppose he didn't have time,' Isabel continued without waiting for a response. 'He's

left me screeds of instructions to do with the kitchen—
you know, it did need renovating and modernising.'
Isabel chuckled.

Harriet smiled as well, but it wasn't really an amused
smile.

'So.'

It was late in the afternoon and she was sitting on a
bench with Tottie beside her on a small headland just
south of Heathcote homestead. It was an overcast day
with a cool breeze that was lifting Tottie's shaggy coat
and causing the seagulls to plane on the thermals.

They'd been for a long brisk walk and were on their
way home now.

'So,' Harriet said again. 'It's all off, Tottie. Your master has walked away without a word and I should be celebrating because I've always—almost—known I was
playing with fire just by being anywhere near him.'

'I'm not—' she put her arm around Tottie '—celebrating, though. I'm miserable. I feel abandoned. I feel
hard done by because he can come and go while I'm
stuck here because of his mother's collection, because
of Brett, not that I hold Brett responsible for anything...'

She stared out over the silvery sea. It was a choppy
seascape today with whitecaps that, if you knew anything about matters maritime, told you the breeze was
running at about twenty knots.

How did I know that? she wondered. Must have been
amongst quite a lot of the useless information I learnt
from Dad. Is any information useless, though?

She continued to stare out to sea and grimaced as

she saw a yacht sailing south and riding the waves a bit like a rocking horse. Then she felt Tottie stiffen and saw her nose quiver as she tested the wind. The final giveaway as the big dog bounded to her feet was the joyful bark she reserved for one person and one person only—Damien.

Harriet scrambled to her feet and there he was, climbing the headland towards them. Then she stood like a statue until he was right up to them and her eyes were wide and astonished because he wore a suit and a tie.

'I thought...I thought you were in Perth,' she stammered.

'I had planned to be,' he replied as he made a fuss of Tottie, 'but something wouldn't let me go.'

'What?' she asked huskily, her expression mystified.

'You.'

She blinked several times. 'I don't understand.'

'You once believed you owed me an explanation. I've come under the same compulsion.'

He paused and loosened his tie and once again the way the breeze lifted his dark hair gave her goose bumps.

'I thought it was best for us to—just cut this thing between us,' he said then, his dark eyes resting on the riot of curls in her hair the wind had whipped up. 'I thought that last night and right until I got to Sydney airport from Ballina this morning,' he said dryly. 'Then I changed my mind and flew back. Or, rather, it got changed for me by some arcane process I don't quite understand, but anyway—'

He stopped and looked around. 'Do you want to hear this here or back down—?'

'Here,' she broke in.

So they sat down on the bench and Tottie lay down at their feet with a look of pure contentment.

'It's about Veronica,' he said. 'She was, as Charlie insisted on putting it—' he looked heavenwards '—just gorgeous. Not only that; she was bright. She ran her own IT consultancy business. We had an affair, then we got married.

'I have to say,' he went on thoughtfully, 'that we fought as spectacularly as we did the opposite. But she wasn't cut out to stay at home and run things like Isabel does. That was something I often found irritating and often—' he shrugged '—held against her. Mind you, she had her own list of sins she held against me and, to be honest, the relationship was foundering. Then she discovered she was pregnant and, although she'd been rather secretive about it, I thought—it seemed to be a calming influence. I didn't realise she was simply subdued and—worried.'

Harriet looked down at her hands.

'And the baby came, a boy, no problems, until he was about six months old. Then he was diagnosed with a blood disorder and both Veronica and I were tested to establish our blood groups et cetera. That's when it emerged—' Damien stared out to sea for a long moment '—that I wasn't the baby's father.'

Harriet gasped.

'As you say,' he commented with some irony. 'At least that was my first reaction. Of course, after that, things got…much more animated. Accusations running thick and fast, along the lines of *Had she always been unfaithful?* Coming from me, that one,' he said. 'To be answered along the lines of *Who wouldn't be unfaithful to someone as cold and bloody-minded as me?* Hang on.'

He retrieved his mobile from his pocket, glanced at it and switched it off.

'So, as you can imagine, it was a shambles.'

'Yes,' Harriet breathed.

'It became even more so,' he said after a time.

'How?'

'It turned out she couldn't be sure *who* the father was but she'd reasoned I was the best bet, financially, anyway.'

Harriet put her hands to her face. 'She was…was she…?'

'She was promiscuous,' he said. 'That's probably a polite way of putting it. Of course I'd known I wasn't the first but it might be hard for you to imagine what it feels like to know you've been in a line of men even after the wedding, not to mention having some other man's child palmed off on you.'

'I'm surprised she kept the baby.'

'So was I,' he agreed, 'but I think she saw it as some kind of a hold over me if things got really tough between us. In the normal course of events, we may never have discovered he wasn't mine.'

'What happened to him?'

Damien stared out to sea. 'I made Veronica find out who the father was and these days, with DNA testing—' he shrugged '—you can do it and there's no way it can be denied. So I divorced her.' He stopped rather abruptly.

'Did you…did you have any kind of affection for the baby, when you thought he was yours?'

He frowned. 'I don't know if I had some premonition but no, not a lot. But I don't know if it was simply that I'm just not good with babies. Actually, I felt more for the poor kid when I found out he wasn't mine. And I've set up a trust for him and made sure that at least he'll know who his father is. I also paid for the procedures and treatment he needed and of course Veronica got a generous settlement. End of story.'

He got up and walked to the edge of the headland, staring out to sea with his hands pushed into his pockets and the breeze blowing his tie around.

'Of course not the end of the story,' he said over his shoulder and came back to sit down beside her.

'I didn't think it was,' Harriet said quietly, 'but—'

'Look,' he interrupted, 'if you're going to tell me it's highly unlikely it could ever happen for me like that again, you're right. The odds against it are enormous. I *know* that—intellectually. That doesn't mean to say I can make myself believe it in my heart. That doesn't mean to say I can bury all my cynicism, all my—' he broke off and shrugged '—disbelief that I could have been taken for such a flat.'

'Did you never suspect?' Harriet asked curiously.

'Sometimes. But she was good at diverting any doubts I may have had. And I'm not trying to say I was blameless myself. If anything was going to work for Veronica in a marriage, it was an anchorman. I could work that out, I could see,' he said intensely, 'that she was one of those high-powered people who often didn't know how to come down from the heights. But I couldn't… I—' he closed his eyes briefly '—just got more and more irritated and difficult to live with.'

Harriet looked across at him. His profile was rock-hard and she could see the tension in the set of his mouth and his shoulders. 'How can you be *sure* you're going to feel like this with another woman?'

'I've had a couple of—' he shrugged '—liaisons since then. They didn't last. I didn't want them to last because I felt stifled,' he said. 'I wanted to be free. I never, ever want to go through that kind of trauma again.'

He paused then he said sardonically, 'I would never have thought I was naïve going into marriage with Veronica; I certainly wasn't afterwards. I kept looking for signs, pointers, indicators that I was being taken for a fool again so that those liaisons became a nightmare of mistrust.'

He broke off and sighed. 'And I keep thinking of the consequences and how one innocent child got caught up in it all. That's why I'm better on my own. But I had to tell you this. Despite the fact that this attraction lies between us, it could never be more than that.'

He put his hand over hers. 'I'm sorry.'

Harriet blinked away a tear. 'That's OK.'

He paused then looked at her curiously. 'You really don't mind?'

Harriet smiled, just a gentle curve of her mouth.

'Yes, I do mind a bit but I always knew it couldn't work for me, so—'

'You're still in love with—whoever he was?'

Harriet considered and realised that until quite recently she might have believed that. Not any more, however. But it made no difference now. There was no future for her with Damien Wyatt…

She blinked several times as it hit her like a train all of a sudden that it mattered greatly to her to think there was no future for her with this man. He couldn't have spelled it out more clearly.

So, she thought, the tables have turned. I was the one who was eager to cut 'things' off between us; now I'm the one who…

'Harriet?'

'Uh—I don't know. But, for my own reasons, I really don't want to get involved like that again. You probably think I'm silly.' She stopped and shrugged.

There was a long silence. Then he said, 'Tottie will be devastated.'

Harriet smiled and blew her nose. 'Well, I ought to get back to work. Do you—' she hesitated '—do you want me to finish your mother's things?'

'Yes,' he replied promptly. 'I won't be here—no, I'm not going to try to go to Perth again today, but tomorrow I will.'

'Oh.' Harriet jumped up with a hand to her mouth. 'I'm cook tonight. I promised Isabel roast beef. Will you…?' She looked a question at him.

'Roast beef,' he repeated, his dark eyes full of amusement. 'Something else I can't resist.'

* * *

Harriet's roast beef was rare on the inside and dark brown on the outside. With it she served roast potatoes and pumpkin, green beans and a rich gravy.

'Mmm, that was delicious,' Isabel enthused as she put her knife and fork together. 'A girl of many talents!'

'She is,' Damien agreed and raised his glass to Harriet. 'If ever you need a job away from the job you do, you know where to come.'

'Apart from anything else, we know you won't burn down the kitchen,' Isabel said mischievously.

'On that subject, how is the gentleman—where is he?' Damien asked.

'I packed him off home to his wife and family today with three months' pay and a couple of contacts, both restaurants where he'd be too busy to get drunk and lonely. That wouldn't be sticky date pudding, by any chance?' Isabel asked of Harriet with equal proportions of trepidation and longing in her voice.

It was and it not only found favour with Isabel but also her nephew.

'Amazing.' he said, 'For someone who hasn't got a sweet tooth to produce such amazing desserts is quite—amazing.'

They all laughed.

'So you'll be in South Africa? For how long?' Isabel queried of Damien. 'Incidentally—' she frowned '—why did you come back today?'

'Something came up,' Damien replied. 'And I don't know how long I'll be in South Africa—a few weeks at least. As to why I'm going, there's a lot of mining in Africa.'

Isabel stood up and insisted on clearing the table and loading the dishwasher but she declined coffee and, with a yawn and her thanks for a perfect meal, she left them alone.

'You know—' Damien swirled the last of his Merlot in his glass '—I've been thinking. Why don't you stay on when all my mother's stuff is sorted? That's going to happen much sooner than your brother walking again by the sound of it. How is he doing?'

Harriet told him. 'He's got a new physio, a woman. I think he's fallen in love with her. Not too seriously, I hope.'

Damien grimaced. 'She's probably used to it and knows how to handle it. But if it's contributing towards his progress, it might be worth a few heartaches for him. Or...' he stretched his legs out '...who knows, it might become mutual. Anyway, to get back to this place, why don't you stay on? Isabel really enjoys your company. And I'm sure Charlie does too, when he's home.'

'I won't have anything to do, though,' Harriet objected.

Damien sat up. 'I've been thinking about that. Periodically, Arthur sends our paintings away to be cleaned. It's about that time now, so why don't *you* do it? Here.'

Harriet's eyes widened and her mouth fell open.

'Isn't that what your father did?'

Her jaw clicked as she closed her mouth. 'Yes. Well, he restored paintings too.' She stopped abruptly and bit her lip.

'Then?'

'I couldn't.' She clasped her hands on the table. 'I'd feel like a charitable institution.'

'Nonsense.' His tone was biting. 'It's a good business proposition. Arthur agrees.'

Harriet frowned. 'When have you had time to consult Arthur?'

'In this day and age of mobile phones it only took a few minutes. Did you think I had to rely on carrier pigeons or the bush telegraph?'

Harriet compressed her lips and looked at him mutinously.

'For crying out loud, just say yes, Harriet Livingstone.' He shoved his hand through his hair wearily. 'Thanks to you, I've been up since the crack of dawn, I've had to fly to Sydney and back again, not to mention loitering around Sydney Airport waiting for bloody flights.'

'I didn't ask you to do any of that!' she protested.

'Nevertheless, it was all due to you. Look, I won't be here, if that's what's worrying you. No coming home early this time.' He gazed at her ironically.

'But it could take me…a month!' She tried to visualise every painting in the house. 'It's very painstaking, careful work done properly.'

He pushed his wine glass away. 'I'll go on a safari,' he said flippantly. 'There's a lot of wildlife in Africa as well as mining.'

Harriet got up and put her hands on her hips. 'You're impossible.'

'That's what my wife used to tell me,' he drawled.

Harriet flinched then shrugged. 'She may have been right.'

'No doubt.' He watched her as she paced around the table. She'd changed into white pedal pushers and a loose apricot blouse with a distinctive pattern and a round neck. Her hair was tied back simply. 'Are you going to do it?'

'I don't know. I can't think straight!'

'Why don't you sit down and let me make you a cup of coffee? You could be more rational about things then.'

'I'm not being *irrational*,' Harriet said with extreme frustration. But she sat down and she didn't raise any obstacles when he got up to make the coffee.

And the wheels of her mind started to turn slowly rather than racing around uselessly.

It would be a solution.

It would provide not only the financial support she needed but, come to think of it, the moral support. She and Isabel had grown close. She also loved Heathcote. She was comfortable and secure here—and there were some marvellous paintings to work on when she finished her present job. Could she ask for more?

Despite her financial affairs being in much better repair thanks to Damien Wyatt's mother's treasures, once she wasn't earning, once she wasn't living rent free, living off her capital so to speak, she had a fair idea of how fast it would shrink.

But...

She looked across at his tall figure as he rounded up the coffee accoutrements, and had to marvel suddenly at how things had changed. How she'd hated him for his arrogance; how she'd hated the way he could kiss her without so much as a by-your-leave and leave her deeply moved. How she'd been so determined not to allow his effect on her to take root—only to discover that it had anyway.

But to discover at the same time why Damien Wyatt was so opposed to the concept of love ever after and the institution of marriage... A story that was painful even to think about.

She shivered suddenly and forced her mind away. And she asked herself if the wisest course of action for her peace of mind, if nothing else, was to go away from Heathcote as soon as she'd finished the first job.

But Brett! Brett—his name hammered in her mind. The more she could do for him, the more she could do to get him mobile again, the better and the sooner this nightmare would be over, for him as well as for her.

She held her peace for another couple of minutes until she had a steaming cup of Hawaiian coffee in front of her.

'I could do them,' she said slowly. 'The paintings. It would be one way to make sure Brett can stay on until his treatment is finished.'

'Good.' He said it briskly and in a way that gave her to understand it was a business deal between them and nothing more. And, before he could say any more, his phone rang.

'Excuse me, I'll take this downstairs; it's South Africa. Thank you for dinner, by the way.'

Harriet nodded and, moments later, she and Tottie were left alone.

'All sorted, Tottie.' Harriet dried sudden, ridiculous tears with her fingers. 'Dealt with, packed, labelled and filed away, that's me.'

She hugged Tottie then sat with her head in her hands for a while before she got up and resolutely put her kitchen to bed.

She was not to know that whilst Damien Wyatt might have sorted her out and locked her out of his life for the most part, his business life was about to become another matter. His PA, a man who'd worked closely with him for ten years, resigned out of the blue in order to train for his lifelong ambition—to climb Mount Everest.

If this wasn't trying enough, his South African trip was cancelled and the ramifications to his business empire as the lucrative business deal involved hung in the breeze were enough to make him extremely tense.

CHAPTER SIX

'TENSE, BLOODY-MINDED and all-round impossible,' Charlie said to Harriet one evening. 'That's Damien at the moment. It's like living under a thundercloud. I tell you what, I really feel for the poor sods he's interviewing for his PA position. I wonder if they have any idea what he might drive them to? I mean to say, it's got to be a pretty bizarre ambition, climbing Mount Everest.'

They were sharing what would have otherwise been a lonesome meal—Isabel was out and so was Damien.

Harriet had made hamburgers and chips, much to Charlie's approval.

Harriet had to laugh. 'I feel really guilty, though,' she said as she passed the ketchup to Charlie.

'You!' He looked surprised.

'I…' She hesitated. 'It was because of me that he didn't go to Perth and on to South Africa. I can't help wondering if that…if that—' she gestured widely and shrugged '—caused all this.'

Charlie frowned. 'Why "because of you" didn't he go?'

'Well, he missed his flight to Perth because he came

back to explain something.' Harriet bit her lip and berated herself for ever mentioning the matter but Charlie took issue with this.

'You can't open up a can of worms like that then play dumb,' he objected, 'but let me guess. You two had some sort of issue between you after my birthday party?'

Harriet sighed suddenly. 'Charlie, we've had issues between us since the day I smashed his car and his collarbone. Not to mention the day I slapped his face and he kissed me back. But his issues are…very complicated. And he wasn't supposed to be here while I finished the job,' she added, somewhat annoyed.

'Ah, well, so that explains—well, some of it! I didn't think some business deal hanging in the balance—I mean he's weathered a few of those before—was sufficient to cause this level of turmoil in my beloved brother.'

Harriet put her hands on her waist. 'That doesn't help me a lot, Charlie.'

'Or any of us! I think we'll just have to batten down the hatches and prepare for the worst. At least you can stay out of his way.'

This proved to be incorrect.

She was riding Sprite along Seven-mile Beach the next morning with Tottie at her stirrup. It was cool and crisp and the clarity of the air was amazing, dead flat calm water with hardly any surf, some pink clouds in a pale blue sky—and another horse riding towards her: Damien.

Her first thought was to gallop away in the opposite direction, and she started to do so but Sprite was no match for his horse and he caught her up.

By this time, some common sense had returned to Harriet and she slowed Sprite to a walk.

'Morning, Harriet.'

She glanced across at him as Sprite jostled his big brown horse and Tottie looked relieved. 'Hi, Damien.' Their breath steamed in the early morning cool.

'Running away again?'

'I guess that was my first intention,' she confessed and found herself curiously unsettled. He looked so big in a khaki rain jacket and jeans with his dark head bare. Not at all cuddly, she reflected, not at all affected by the post dawn chill, whereas she was bundled up in a scarlet anorak, navy track pants and a scarlet beanie.

'Why?'

'I think,' she said carefully and straightened the reins through her fingers, 'we're all a little nervous around you at the moment.'

He grimaced. 'That bad?'

She nodded.

'Of course things haven't exactly gone my way lately, business-wise,' he observed as they turned their horses onto the path from the beach.

'I'm sorry if I was—unwittingly—in any way the cause of that.'

He looked across at her. 'You weren't. Although, of course, you are part of the overall problem. After you.' He indicated that she should precede him through the archway that led to Heathcote and the stables.

But she simply stared at him with her lips parted, her eyes incredulous, so Tottie took the initiative and Sprite followed.

And it wasn't until they got to the stables that they took up the thread of the conversation.

They tied their steaming horses beside each other in the wash bay.

'What overall problem?' she asked at last as she hosed Sprite down.

'The one I have with going into the lounge, for example.'

Harriet turned her hose off and took a metal scraper off its hook. 'Why should that be a problem?' She scraped energetically down Sprite's flank then ducked under her neck to do her other side.

'Well, if I'd flown halfway around the world and was in another country I might have found it easier to think of other things than you at Charlie's party. At the moment, every time I walk into the damn lounge it strikes me again.'

Harriet dropped the scraper and it clattered onto the concrete at the same as Sprite moved uneasily and her metal shoes also clattered on the concrete.

Damien stopped hosing his horse and came round to see if Harriet was all right.

'Fine. Fine!' She retrieved the scraper and handed it to him. 'I think I've finished.'

'Thanks.' He hung up his hose and started to use the scraper on his horse.

They worked in silence for a few minutes. Harriet rubbed Sprite down with a coarse towel then she inspected her feet and finally threw a rug over her. But all the time her mind was buzzing. How to deal with this? How to deal with the fact that she still felt incredibly guilty about how she'd fled at the end of Charlie's party after…after…

Even days later, her cheeks reddened at the thought of how abandoned—that was about the only way she could describe it—she'd felt and how she'd run like a scared rabbit.

She clicked her tongue and backed Sprite out of the wash bay to lead her to her box, where there was a feed already made up for her thanks to Stan.

Perhaps it was that feed waiting for her that made Sprite a bundle of impatience to get to her stall, but she suddenly put on a rare exhibition that would have done a buck jumper proud, an exhibition that scattered Tottie and even caused Damien's horse, still tied in the wash bay, to try to rear and plunge.

'Sprite!' Harriet clung onto the lead with all her strength. 'Settle down, girl! What's got into you?'

'Tucker,' Damien said in her ear. 'I'll take her.'

And in a masterful display of horsemanship as well as strength, he calmed the mare down and got her into her box.

'Thank you! I was afraid I was going to lose her—another accident waiting to happen, to go down on my already tarnished record!' Harriet said breathlessly but whimsically.

Damien laughed as he came towards her out of the stable block and for an instant the world stood still for

Harriet. He looked so alive and wickedly amused, so tall and dark, so sexy...

And what he did didn't help.

He came right up to her, slid his hands around her waist under her anorak and hugged her. 'I wouldn't have held that against you,' he said, holding her a little away.

Without thinking much about it, she put her hands on his shoulders. 'No?' She looked at him with mock scepticism.

'No. I would have laid the blame squarely at the horse's feet. She's always been a bit of a handful. Hence her name. Typical female,' he added.

'Damn!' Harriet assumed a self-righteous expression.

He raised an eyebrow.

'I was full of approval for you but you went and spoilt it with your anti-feminist remark!'

'My apologies, Miss Livingstone. Uh—how can I make amends? Let's see, you did pretty damn good for a girl before I took over and—can I cook you breakfast?'

Harriet blinked. 'You cook?'

He shrugged. 'Some things. Bacon and eggs.'

'Only bacon and eggs?'

'More or less. Steak, I do steak as well.'

'I have both,' Harriet said slowly.

He laughed again, kissed her fleetingly on the lips, and removed his hands from her waist just as Stan came round the corner of the stables.

Fortunately Charlie turned up at the same time, wanting to know what all the hullabaloo was about and they repaired to the flat after Stan had offered to finish Damien's horse and put it in its box. And they had a jolly breakfast of steak, bacon and eggs.

Charlie even said, 'Notice how the sun's come out!'

Damien frowned. 'It's been up and out for a couple of hours.'

'I was speaking relatively,' Charlie said with dignity.

Damien narrowed his eyes as he studied his brother. 'I…think I get your drift,' he said slowly. 'My apologies.'

'That's all right. We'll forgive you, won't we, Harriet?'

She was clearing the table and about to pour the coffee but she couldn't help herself. She looked up and straight at Damien.

'Yes…' she said, but it sounded uncertain even to her own ears, nor could she mistake the ironic glint that came to his dark eyes as their gazes clashed.

So, she thought uneasily, he might laugh with me as he did this morning but I'm a long way from forgiven.

And although this lifting of the thundercloud, so to speak, over Heathcote, was much appreciated by Charlie and no doubt everyone else on the property, it brought Harriet mental anguish and confusion.

No longer was she able to keep Damien Wyatt on the back roads of her mind. Not that she'd been able to do that for a while but it seemed to have grown ten times worse day by day.

She was incredibly aware of him whenever he came within her orbit. He literally made her tremble inwardly and all her fine hairs rise. He made her tongue-tied now, never capable of thinking of anything to say.

He made the completion of the work on his mother's treasures and the paintings drag because she spent a lot of time day-dreaming.

Would she ever finish this job? she asked herself desperately once.

Then the kitchen was finished and Isabel organised a party to celebrate the fact.

'I don't think I've ever seen a renovation, especially not after a fire, be so swiftly and painlessly achieved,' Harriet murmured to Isabel as she was being given a tour of all the spectacular slimline stainless steel equipment and granite counters that now graced Heathcote's new bottle-green, white and black kitchen.

'Ever *seen* a renovation after a fire?' Isabel asked perkily.

'Well, no, but you know what I mean. By the way, you sounded just like your nephew—your older nephew,' she added.

Isabel laughed. 'Heaven forbid! Although he has been pretty good lately. But if you really want to know the reason for the speed and efficiency of this renovation, it's quite simple.'

'Your expert management of things?'

'Well, that too,' Isabel conceded. 'But it's money. It buys the best product, best workmen and in the long run it saves money.'

'Spoken like a true capitalist,' Harriet said but with affection.

'All right.' Isabel uncovered several platters on a long counter containing snacks. There were also plates and napkins plus bottles of champagne in ice buckets and gleaming glassware in amongst glorious vases of flowers.

'How many people have you asked?' Damien enquired as he pinched a smoked salmon savoury and had his hand slapped.

'Just the neighbours—don't,' Isabel replied.

'Just the neighbours!' Damien echoed. 'If you mean everyone we know around here that could be twenty to thirty.'

'Twenty-five. When has that ever been a problem?' Isabel enquired with her arms akimbo.

'Beloved, I was merely thinking that you must have done an awful lot of work. And I happen to know you don't like it.'

'Ah. I gave someone a trial run. She's applied for the cook's position. No, she's not here now,' she said as Damien looked around, 'but the proof will be in the pudding. There's plenty more to eat.'

One good thing about this party—people had been especially asked not to dress up since it was a kitchen party. So Harriet had been happy to attend in jeans and a lilac jumper. She'd been just as happy to leave after an hour although everyone else seemed to be content to stay on.

But it was a hollow feeling she encountered when she was upstairs in the flat. Hollow and lonely—hollow, ruffled and restless. And all due to watching Damien at his best.

Damien fascinating his neighbours with a blend of wit, seriousness, humour and setting not a few feminine pulses fluttering.

One of them was Penny Tindall, although she'd fought to hide it, Harriet thought with some scorn.

She almost immediately took herself to task for this uncharitable thought, not only uncharitable towards Penny but investing herself with a superiority she did not possess. If she did she wouldn't be feeling miserable, lonely, stirred up and generally like crying herself to sleep all on Damien Wyatt's account, would she?

But she knew herself well enough to know that sleep would not come, so she took herself downstairs, closed herself into the studio, drew the curtains and sat down on a high stool. She'd just finished notating a beautiful ivory chess set and she pushed it aside to study an object she wasn't all too sure about.

It resembled some giant curved tooth set on a brass base and embellished with scrimshaw of African wildlife—an elephant, a rhino, a lion, a cheetah and a buffalo.

She was handling it, turning it this way and that, when the door clicked open and Damien stood there.

They simply stared at each other for a long moment then he said, 'Can I come in?'

'Of course.' Harriet slipped off her stool and pushed her hair behind her ears. 'I…I…'

'Kitchen parties are not your cup of tea?' he suggested as he closed the door behind him.

'No. I mean…I haven't got anything against them really.' She grimaced. 'That sounds a bit weird.'

He didn't agree or disagree. He simply looked at her with patent amusement. Then he looked at the objects on the table and noticed the chess set.

'I was wondering where that had got to,' he commented. 'Charlie and Mum used to play a lot of chess. Charlie is a bit of a genius at it. Do you play?' He lifted a king, rotated it then set it down.

She nodded.

'Well?'

'Well enough.'

He studied her narrowly. 'Why do I get the feeling that's the guarded sort of response someone who is sensational at something gives you just before they set out to fleece you shamelessly?'

Harriet maintained a grave, innocent expression— for about half a minute, then she had to grin.

'You look like the proverbial Cheshire Cat,' he drawled. 'Did I hit the nail on the head?'

'I'm not bad at chess,' she confessed. 'I used to play with my father.'

'Don't think Charlie has had time to play for years.' He moved on and picked up the tooth-like object she'd been handling.

'Hello!' he said, as he picked it up. 'Haven't seen you for years!'

Harriet's eyes widened. 'You know it?'

'Sure,' he said easily. 'My mother showed it to me when she got it.'

Harriet's eyes widened further. 'So you know what it is?'

'Uh-huh. Don't you?'

'No. Well, a tooth of some kind from a whale maybe, but I can't find any paperwork that goes with it so I'm a little frustrated.'

He picked it up again. 'It's a tusk—a warthog tusk.'

Harriet's mouth fell open. 'Seriously?'

'Seriously. My mother was quite taken with African artefacts.'

Harriet frowned. 'Where are they?'

'Haven't you come across any more of them?'

'No. Apart from this, nothing.'

He sat down on the corner of the table. 'We'll have to consult Isabel.'

Harriet stared at the warthog tusk with its delicate scrimshaw. 'We'll have to get in an African expert,' she said.

'Couldn't you look it up?'

Harriet shrugged. 'Perhaps. How many do you think she had?'

'Hundreds,' he replied.

Harriet paled. 'But…that might mean I could be here for the next ten years!'

'Now that,' he agreed with a grin, 'could be a problem. Talk about growing old on the job.' But he sobered as she moved restlessly. 'Not to mention the other complications it would cause.' And the way his gaze roamed up and down her figure gave her no doubt that he meant complications in an extremely personal way.

'Uh—look, I'll think about it tomorrow,' she said hastily. 'Right now I should probably go to bed. I'll need—' she smiled shakily '—all my resources tomorrow if I'm to track down hundreds of things like wart-hog tusks.'

She laid the tusk back in its box, briefly tidied the table top, and came purposefully round the table towards the door.

Damien uncoiled his lean length from the stool and barred her way. 'Am I getting my marching orders, Miss Livingstone?' he said softly.

Her eyes flew to his. 'This was *your* idea—' She stopped abruptly and could have kicked herself.

'Mmm…' He scanned the way her breasts were heaving beneath the lilac wool. 'My idea for us to desist? So it was, but are you claiming you had another direction in mind for us?'

'No. I mean—' she bit her lip '—I don't know of any other way there could be and that's sad but probably a blessing in the long run.'

He put his arms around her. 'I didn't mean to make you sad. I could so easily…turn things around. Like this.'

His kiss, and although she'd known it was coming she did nothing about it, was like a balm to her soul.

She no longer felt hollow and lonely and restless. She felt quite different. Smooth and silken as his hands roamed beneath her jumper and his lips moved from hers to the hollows at the base of her throat to the soft spot where her shoulder curved into her neck.

Then he took her by surprise. He lifted her up and sat her on the table and she wound her legs around him—to have him grin wickedly down at her.

'If you only knew what your legs do to me,' he murmured, and his hands moved up to cup her breasts.

Harriet paused what she was doing, running her hands over the hard wall of his chest, and rested her hands on his shoulders. And she tensed.

'What?' he asked, his eyes suddenly narrowing.

'Someone coming,' she breathed and pushed him away so she could slide off the table and rearrange her clothes.

'Someone's always bloody coming,' he grated.

But whoever had been coming changed their mind and the footsteps receded.

Harriet let out a quivering breath.

'Would it matter if anyone saw us?' he asked abruptly.

She stirred. 'Surely it would complicate things even more?' She laced her fingers together. 'Damien…' She closed her eyes briefly. 'I'm sorry this happened. I'm sorry it keeps happening but if there's no future for us, if you're sure, I need—I need to go away from Heathcote.' Silent tears were suddenly coursing down her cheeks. She scrubbed at them impatiently. 'I have nearly finished your mother's things but if there are hundreds more…' She gestured helplessly. 'And the paintings. I don't see how I can stay. Surely you m-must—' her voice cracked '—agree?'

He took in her tear-streaked face and the anguish in her eyes. And for a moment a terrible temptation to say *Stay somehow we'll work it out, Harriet* rose in him. But another side of him refused to do it, a side that recalled all too clearly and bitterly how he'd been cheated and made a fool of…

'I'm sorry,' he said. 'This is my fault, what happened here tonight, not yours. It won't happen again, so please stay. Goodnight.'

He touched her wet cheek with his fingertips then he was gone.

Harriet took herself up to her flat and cried herself to sleep.

A week later their truce had held. Not that Damien had spent much time at Heathcote. But they were able to interact normally, or so she thought. As in the instance when she was explaining to him about his mother's artefacts.

'Isabel forgot to tell me,' she told him.

He lifted an eyebrow. 'What?'

'Oh, sorry, I should have started at the beginning. Your mother sold all her artefacts just before she…er… passed away. Somehow or other, the warthog tusk must have been overlooked.'

Damien grimaced and folded his arms across his chest. 'No doubt to your great relief.'

'Mostly,' Harriet said. 'I have to admit the thought of becoming an expert on apes and ivory et cetera was a little daunting.'

'Apes and ivory?'

'It comes from the Bible—Kings, First Book, chapter ten, verse twenty-two. *"…the navy of Tharshish bringing gold, and silver, ivory, and apes, and peacocks."* From Africa to King Solomon.'

'How did you come by that?' he queried.

'I did *some* research. It's fascinating.'

He studied her. She was now writing with her head bent and her expression absorbed. As usual, Tottie was lying at her feet. Her hair was loose and curly and she wore tartan trews and a cream cable stitch sweater. She looked at home on this cool autumn evening.

And if she wasn't close to becoming a part of Heathcote she wasn't far from it—or was she already? he wondered.

And was he mad not to make sure she stayed?

At the same moment his phone rang. He pulled it out of his pocket and studied it with a frown then he answered it tersely. 'Wyatt.'

Harriet looked up and she tensed as he said, '*What*?' and 'When and where?' in hard, clipped, disbelieving tones.

And she realised he'd gone pale and his knuckles around the phone were white, and a feeling of dread started to grip her although she had no idea what news he was getting.

Then he ended the call and threw his phone down.

'What?' she asked huskily. 'Something's happened.'

She saw his throat working and he closed his eyes briefly. 'Charlie,' he said hoarsely at last. 'His plane's gone down. Somewhere in the north of Western Australia. They either can't be more specific or it's classified information.'

He sat down and dropped his face into his hands then looked up. 'It's rugged terrain if it's the Kimberley. Rivers, gorges.' He drew a deep breath then crashed his fist on the table so that her coffee mug jumped and spilt. 'And there's nothing I can do.'

'I'm so sorry,' Harriet murmured and slid her hand across the table to cover his. 'I'm sure they'll be doing all they can.'

'There must be *something* I can do!' There was frustration written into the lines and angles of his face. He got up and looked around as if he had no idea where he was. He said, 'Excuse me, Harriet, but I can do more from my study and my computer.'

She rose hastily. 'Of course. I'll bring you a nightcap in a while if you like.' But she didn't think he'd even heard her as he loped down the stairs two at a time with Tottie hard on his heels.

Harriet marvelled at the dog's sensitivity; she obviously had no doubt where she was needed most tonight.

And to keep herself occupied and keep at bay images of a fiery crash and Charlie's broken body, she went downstairs to the studio to do some work of her own.

She was cleaning a delicate china figurine with a cotton bud dipped in a weak solution when Isabel, looking as if she'd aged ten years in the space of a few hours, came over from the big house.

'Any news?' Harriet asked.

Isabel shook her head and pulled out a stool. And she hugged her mohair stole around her.

'How's Damien?'

Isabel shook her head. 'He's…it'll kill him to lose Charlie. Me too, but more so Damien. They're really close, despite the way they josh each other. They got even closer after what happened with Veronica and Patrick.' Isabel stopped self-consciously.

'He's told me about her. So Patrick was the baby?'

'Uh-huh.' Isabel touched a finger to the figurine Harriet had finished cleaning and had dried. 'Hello, I remember you,' she said to it and again looked self-conscious. 'You must think I'm crazy,' she said to Harriet this time, 'but I do remember this figurine. It always sat on its own little circular table in the upstairs hall. That's where Damien's mother always kept it, but Veronica...' She trailed off.

Harriet said nothing.

Isabel shrugged. 'I don't know why I shouldn't tell you, seeing as you know some of it. It also helps to think of something else. If you've wondered why a lot of this stuff was more or less hidden, that was Veronica's doing. She didn't like antiques or objets d'art. A very modern girl was our Veronica, in more ways than one.' Isabel's tone was loaded with disapproval. 'Mind you,' she added, 'Damien said no to a lot of her plans for the modernisation of Heathcote.'

But then she sighed. 'One should never pass judgement on relationships because it's almost impossible to know the full story. And it's hard not to be biased, anyway.'

'How old is Patrick now?' Harriet asked.

'Let's see—nearly three.'

'I don't suppose Damien has any reason to have any contact with him?' She rinsed out a couple of cloths and suspended them from pegs from a dryer over the sink.

'No. Well, not directly.'

Harriet washed her hands and stood drying them

on a red and white checked towel as a frown grew in her eyes.

'He and Charlie worked out a plan. Because things are and always will be pretty tense between Veronica and Damien, I imagine—and because I can't quite hide my feelings—' Isabel grimaced '—Charlie sees Patrick fairly frequently. To make sure he's OK and to give him a constant man in his life, I guess you could say. Charlie somehow or other had a better understanding of Veronica than me or Damien. That sounds odd.' Isabel gestured a little helplessly.

'I don't think so. I think that's…Charlie,' Harriet said slowly. 'I wouldn't be surprised if Charlie keeps a sort of weather eye out for Damien.'

'Oh, I think he does.' Isabel rested her chin in her hands and studied Harriet. 'You're pretty perceptive yourself, my dear.'

Harriet grimaced. 'I don't know about that. So she— Veronica—didn't marry Patrick's father?'

Isabel shook her head. 'She hasn't remarried.'

'Is there any chance of them getting back together?'

'No.' Isabel said it quite definitely. 'It was one of those white-hot affairs that was too explosive to last, even apart from the drama over Patrick. Of course the double, triple even quadruple irony to it all is that Patrick was named after my father, Damien's grandfather.'

Harriet let the towel drop onto the counter. 'Oh, no!'

'Oh, yes.' Isabel shrugged. 'Not that there would be any point in changing his name and he'd been christened by the time they found out, anyway. But it does… it was such a mess.'

Harriet sat down. 'Do you think he'll ever marry again?'

Isabel stretched then she rocked Harriet to the core. 'Yes. If *you* would have him.'

CHAPTER SEVEN

'I...I BEG YOUR pardon?' Harriet stammered.

But Isabel simply looked at her wisely.

Harriet got up and did a turn around the studio with her arms crossed almost protectively. 'It couldn't work. The reason he came back from Perth—not that he ever got there—was to tell me why it couldn't work.'

'Why couldn't it?'

'He doesn't want to be married again. He's suspicious and cynical now and, even without any of that, he's a difficult, unbending kind of person and he admits that his habit of command was probably one of the reasons they fell out so badly.'

'Probably,' Isabel conceded. 'He's very much like my father, his grandfather, the first Patrick. The one who started it all. Dynamic, forceful—' Isabel nodded wryly '—difficult. Whereas my brother, Damien's father, was more interested in culture and the arts, passionate about sailing, that kind of thing. He was so nice—' Isabel looked fond '—but it's true to say we went backwards during his stewardship and it took all of Damien's grandfather's genes plus plenty of his own kind of steely determination to pull the business out of that slump.'

'The first thing that struck me about him,' Harriet said dryly, 'was how arrogant he was. I never felt more…more vindicated—that's not the right word, but it definitely was a release of some kind—when I slapped his face, although I got myself kissed for my pains.' She stopped and bit her lip.

'That first day you came to Heathcote?' Isabel queried and when Harriet nodded she laughed.

'Sorry,' she said, 'but I knew something had happened between you two. So did Charlie.'

'Charlie walked in on it,' Harriet said gloomily, 'that's how he knew.' Then she had to smile. 'If you could have seen his expression.'

But her smile faded and she put a hand to her mouth. 'Oh, God, please let him be OK!'

Isabel got up and came to put her arms around Harriet. 'I think we should go to bed. There's nothing we can do tonight. Goodnight, my dear.'

'Goodnight,' Harriet whispered back.

But, back up in the flat, Harriet had no desire to go to bed, she discovered, and not only on Charlie's account, although that feeling of dread was still running through her.

It was Isabel's bombshell that she also had on her mind. It was the fact that she'd been able to see it was no use denying to Isabel that she was helplessly, hopelessly in love with her nephew.

But how had she given herself away? She'd only admitted it to herself recently. Of course it had been bubbling away for longer than that; she just hadn't been aware of it.

'I must be incredibly transparent,' she murmured aloud. 'Maybe I do go around with my head in the clouds. Perhaps I was unaware of how I reacted when his name came up? Or perhaps Isabel and Charlie had been comparing notes? Did they see something in Damien, both of us, they hadn't expected to see?'

She shook her head and, with a heavy sigh, decided to take him a cup of cocoa.

What if he doesn't like cocoa? she immediately asked herself. He doesn't drink tea. They couldn't be less alike, tea and cocoa, however, but, if he needs some fortitude, what better than, say, an Irish coffee?

She found him in his study, staring out of the window.

The breeze had dropped and the sky had cleared so there was starlight on the water and a pale slice of moon.

He didn't move when she knocked softly; she didn't think he'd heard her.

She put the tray with two Irish coffees on his desk and walked over to him, making sure she approached from a wide angle so as not to startle him.

'Any news?' she asked.

He turned his head. 'No.'

'I brought us some—liquid fortitude.' She gestured to the tall glasses on the tray.

He glanced at them and sketched a smile—and held out his hand to her.

She hesitated for one brief moment then she took it,

knowing full well what was going to happen and knowing at the same time it was the least she could do for him because it all but broke her heart to see the suffering etched into his expression.

And she went into his arms with no hesitation at all. But he surprised her. He held her loosely and some of the lines left his face as he said, with a quirk of humour, 'There is something you could always put down on the plus side for me.'

'What?' she breathed, as his nearness started to overwhelm her.

'I'm taller.'

Her lips curved. 'Yes. You are.'

He raised a hand and traced the line of her jaw. 'Does it help? Or do you prefer your men shorter?'

'I do not,' she observed seriously. 'They make me feel like an Amazon. No, it's definitely a plus.'

'Good. I mean that makes me feel good. I was beginning to develop an inferiority complex. Not that I'll ever be able to even up the ledger.' He took a very deep breath. 'I'm talking nonsense but—what will I do without Charlie if it goes that way?'

Harriet slipped her arms around him and laid her head on his chest. 'Don't think like that. It hasn't happened yet, it may not happen.'

'It's so vast up there and if it's not dry and desolate, the shores and the creeks have crocodiles—I know, I've been fishing up there.' His arms tightened around her.

'But they must have very sophisticated tracking and search and rescue equipment. Don't give up hope.'

'You sound so sensible and sane. And you feel so good,' he added barely audibly.

'So...so do you,' she murmured back and raised her mouth for his kiss.

'This is getting out of hand,' he said some time later as they drew apart to take deep breaths and steady themselves. 'I hope you don't mind me doing this.'

Harriet regarded him gravely. 'It did annoy me, the last time.'

His eyebrows shot up? 'How come?'

She chuckled. 'You never asked me for my preferences in the matter. You just went ahead and did it.'

'Miss Livingstone,' he said formally, 'please tell me what your preferences are in the matter—*this* matter. So as not to be misunderstood.' He pulled her closer and cradled her hips to him.

Harriet took an unsteady breath. 'They appear to be very similar to yours in this instance.' And she linked her arms around his neck and stared into his eyes.

It was a long, compelling look they shared and Harriet strove to convey the sense that she understood his need and the starkness of his emotions and that she wanted to offer him some comfort.

He breathed urgently and said one word. 'Sure?'

'Sure,' she answered.

He looked around and gestured at the large comfortable settee. 'Here?'

'If you don't have a haystack or a loft?' she queried with laughter glinting in her eyes.

'I...' He hesitated then he saw that glint of laughter and for a moment his arms around her nearly crushed her.

'All right,' he said into her hair, and that was the last word spoken for a while.

But what followed didn't stop Harriet from thinking along the lines of, *I was right. I sensed that he'd know how to make love to a woman in a way that would thrill her and drive her to excesses she didn't know she could reach...*

Because that was exactly what happened to her. From a fairly timid lover—she suddenly realised this with a pang of embarrassment—she became a different creature.

She craved his hands on her body. She helped him to take her clothes off and she gloried in the way he touched and stroked her. She became impatient to help him shed his clothes.

She made no effort to hide her excitement as they lay together on the settee and he cupped her breasts and plucked her nipples, as he drew his fingers ever lower down her body.

And she clung to him as desire took her by storm and there was only one thing she craved—to be taken. So she moved provocatively against him and did her own fingertip exploration of him until he growled and turned her onto her back and made sure she was ready for him, then they were united in an urgent rhythm and finally an explosion of sensation.

'Oh!' she breathed, as she arched her body against him.

And he buried his head between her breasts as he shuddered to a final closure.

* * *

'Harriet?'

'Mmm…?'

'All right?'

'Oh yes.' Her eyes remained closed but she smiled a secret little smile.

He grinned and dropped the lightest kiss on her hair. 'Wait here.'

She moved in an urgent little protest. 'Don't go away.'

'I'll be right back.' But he checked his phone and glanced at his computer screen before he went out.

She looked a question at him but he shook his head.

And he was as good as his word; he was back in a couple of minutes with a sheet, a blanket and a couple of pillows. He'd also put on a pair of shorts.

He covered her and made sure she was comfortable.

Then he stopped. 'There are six bedrooms we could go to. I'm not sure why we didn't in the first place.'

'We weren't in the most practical frame of mind,' she suggested.

He sat down beside her and smoothed her hair. 'If I recall correctly, you were even talking about haystacks.'

'Silly talk.' She slipped her hand under her cheek. 'Love talk. Well—' she bit her lip '—you know what I mean—pillow talk, that's it!'

'Yes.'

Did he say it too soon? she immediately found herself wondering.

'Your Dutch courage drinks have gone cold,' he added.

Harriet grimaced.

'I'll get us something else.' He pushed his phone into his pocket.

'Don't.' Harriet sat up and pulled the sheet up. 'I mean, don't wake Isabel. She could be shocked even if she does think...' She broke off and hoped he didn't see the colour she felt rising in her cheeks.

But he appeared to notice nothing as he said, 'Isabel has her own apartment downstairs. It closes off and she doesn't hear a thing. I won't be long. Don't—' his lips twisted '—go anywhere.'

She didn't go anywhere but she did pull her knickers and her shirt on.

It wasn't brandy, as she'd been expecting, that he brought back—it was a bottle of champagne.

Harriet studied the dark green bottle with its gold foil and the two tall glasses on the tray that he deposited on his desk. 'Should we?' she asked tentatively. 'In the circumstances?'

His hair was hanging in his eyes. All he wore were shorts but he could hardly have been more magnificent as he picked up the champagne bottle, Harriet thought as she caught her breath. His shoulders were broad, his chest was sprinkled with dark hair, his diaphragm was flat, his legs long and strong. He was beautiful, she thought with a pang. How was she ever going to forget him...?

'In the circumstances,' he said as he unwound the wire around the cork, 'there is not only you and me to celebrate, there's Charles Walker Wyatt. Wherever you are, Charlie, may you be safe and sound!'

He popped the cork and poured the two glasses. He handed one to Harriet and clinked his against hers. 'Charlie,' he said.

'Charlie,' Harriet echoed. 'May you be safe and sound!'

His phone buzzed. He grabbed it and studied the screen, and breathed a huge sigh of relief as he read the message.

'They've found him. They've found the site where it came down and the crew are all alive. Charlie has a broken arm and leg and a few gashes but otherwise he's mostly OK.'

Harriet flew off the settee into his arms. 'Oh, thank heavens! Do you think they heard us, whoever is in charge of these things up there? I mean in heaven as well as North Western Australia? I think they must have!'

He laughed down at her. 'You could be right.'

'Where is he?'

'They're taking him to Darwin Hospital. They'll keep him there for a few weeks. Where's your glass?'

'Here.' She went to retrieve it from the end table beside the settee and he held it steady in her hand while he refilled it.

Then he looked down at her and raised an eyebrow. 'So—I'm over and done with, am I?'

Harriet looked down at herself. 'Not at all,' she denied. 'I just felt a little—undressed.' She grimaced. 'Not that I'm particularly—overdressed at the moment.'

'Stay like that,' he advised. 'Because I'll be right back. I'll just pass on the news to Isabel.'

* * *

She was sitting on the settee with the sheet covering her legs when he came back. He brought his glass over and sat down beside her. He dropped his arm over her shoulders.

'Cheers!'

'Cheers!' She sipped her champagne then laid her head on his shoulder. 'Any particular person in mind this time?'

'Yes.' He drew his hand through her hair. 'Us.'

'Well, we've both got brothers on the mend, so yes— to us!'

'True,' he agreed, 'but I meant a toast to what just happened here on this settee between us and the hope that it may continue to happen for us, not necessarily in a study or a haystack—a bed would do,' he said with a glint of humour. 'In other words, when will you marry me, Harriet Livingstone?'

Harriet, in the echoing silence that followed his words, asked herself why she should not have expected this. Because he'd *told* her he could never overcome the cynicism he'd been left with after the debacle of his first marriage?

'Harriet?' He removed his arm and put his fingers beneath her chin to turn her face to his. 'What?'

Her eyes were wide but dark and very blue. 'You said…' she began quietly.

'Forget what I said earlier,' he ordered. 'Have you never said or done something and almost immediately started to wonder why you did it?' He didn't wait for an answer. 'Well, I have and that was one of them. Anyway, things have changed.'

'Nothing's changed,' she denied.

'There you go again,' he drawled. 'You kissed me once and were all set to walk away from me. Don't tell me that modus operandi extends to making love to me as if—' he paused, and looked deep into her eyes '—your soul depended on it, then walking away?'

Harriet breathed heavily with great frustration. 'I don't have a "modus operandi" I employ like that,' she said through her teeth.

'So why did you make love to me like that?'

She opened her mouth then gestured, annoyed. 'I felt sorry for you—I felt sorry for *me*. It was so lonely and scary not knowing what had happened to Charlie; it was awful. That's—' she lifted her chin '—why I did it.'

'There had to be more than that.'

Harriet moved restlessly then she sighed. 'Yes. Of course. We obviously—' she shrugged '—are attracted.'

'Thank you,' he said with considerable irony. 'So why's it such a bad idea? We both appeared,' he said dryly, 'to have forgotten our inhibitions and our hang-ups as well.'

Harriet acknowledged this with a tinge of colour mounting in her cheeks but she said, 'Temporarily, yes, but you can't spend your life in bed. And I get the feeling marriage can create a pressure cooker environment for those hang-ups if they're still lingering.'

'Don't,' he advised, 'come the philosopher with me, Harriet Livingstone.'

She bristled. 'Don't be ridiculous! It's only common sense.'

He grinned fleetingly. 'OK. How about this, then? If you won't marry me, would you consider a relationship? That should give our hang-ups the freedom to rattle in the breeze rather than build up all sorts of pressure.'

Harriet sat up. 'No, I will not! And I'll tell you why. You've got me on your conscience again, haven't you? You couldn't change so suddenly otherwise. Well, you don't need to. I'll be fine.'

He sat up, all trace of amusement gone. 'Listen,' he said harshly, 'if I have got you on my conscience, I've got good reason. You came here to Heathcote obviously traumatised—I wouldn't be surprised if you were traumatised the day you ran into me. You were as skinny as a rake—and all because some guy had passed you over for another girl—'

'Not just another girl,' Harriet threw in. 'My best friend.'

Damien paused.

'Someone I loved and trusted,' she went on. 'We met in our last year at school. I hadn't made any close friends up until then because we moved around so much. That's why I think she meant so much to me. Then Carol and I went to the same college and we did everything together. We backpacked around Europe. We did a working holiday on a cattle station; we did so much together.

'And all the while we dated guys, but not terribly seriously until I met Simon and she met Peter. And for a few months we double-dated. But then we drifted apart. Simon and I were talking marriage. Carol and Pete weren't so serious.' She stopped and shrugged.

'And then Simon wasn't so serious,' Damien contributed.

Harriet nodded. 'I think Carol tried to avoid it but it didn't work. And *they* got married. So you see, it was a double betrayal. That's what made it so painful. And in the midst of it all my father died and my brother had this accident…and…I was alone. Everything that meant the most to me was gone or, if not gone, terribly injured. I don't know how I got myself together but, once I did, I decided I was the only one I could rely on.'

'I see—I do see,' he said gently.

'And it's not something I want to go through again, any kind of a betrayal. And that's why—' she turned to Damien '—I'm not prepared to marry you or be your mistress because you've got me on your conscience.'

'I—'

'No.' She put her hand over his. 'I'm certainly not prepared to fall in love with you, only to find you don't trust me, to find you don't and never will believe in love ever after.'

'What you need,' he said after a long, painful pause, 'is someone like Charlie.'

Harriet jumped in astonishment.

'I don't mean Charlie per se,' he continued, looking annoyed with himself. 'I mean someone uncomplicated, with no hang-ups and no habit of command. No back story.'

He pushed the sheet aside and stood up.

Harriet stared up at him, her lips parted, her eyes

questioning. 'What…what's going to happen now?' she queried unevenly.

Damien Wyatt looked down at her and his lips twisted. 'Nothing.'

'Nothing,' she echoed.

'What did you expect?'

'I…I don't know,' she stammered.

'That I'd kick you out?'

'Well, no. I mean—not precisely.' Harriet reached for her pedal pushers and stepped into them.

'I'll be off to Darwin first thing tomorrow and I'll stay with Charlie for as long as he needs me. Then—' he grimaced '—I'll rearrange my Africa trip. Whilst you can finish my mother's things and start on the paintings.'

'I'm not sure if I can do that.'

'You should. I'm sure it'll do your brother good to have you around.'

Harriet bit her lip.

He watched her intently.

She became conscious of his scrutiny. And it seemed to bring back the whole incredible sequence of events as they'd unfolded in this very room, not the least her passionate response to his lovemaking. It did more than that. It awoke tremors of sensation down her body and a sense of longing in her heart—a longing to be in his arms, a longing to be safe with him, a longing to be beloved…

She closed her eyes briefly because, of course, that wasn't going to happen. All the same, how to leave him?

'I don't know what to say,' she murmured.

'Not easy.' A smile appeared fleetingly in his eyes. 'Thanks but no thanks?' he suggested.

Harriet flinched.

'Or maybe just, from me, anyway—take care?' he mused. 'Yes, in your case, Harriet Livingstone, I think that's particularly appropriate. Don't drive into any more Aston Martins, or anything, for that matter; you take care now. By the way, if there are any consequences you wouldn't be so head-in-the-clouds as not to let me know?'

Harriet took a sobbing little breath, grabbed her shoes and ran past him out of the door.

CHAPTER EIGHT

'HARRIET, YOU'RE WORKING your fingers to the bone!' Isabel Wyatt accused as she stood in the studio doorway, shaking raindrops off her umbrella a couple of weeks later. 'It's Sunday,' she continued. 'Even if you're not religious, you need a rest. What is the matter?'

'Nothing! Come in. I'll make you a cuppa. I'm just working on the Venetian masks. It's a pity they got so dusty. Look at this lovely Columbina!'

Harriet held up a white porcelain half-mask studded with glittering stones and dyed feathers.

'Where does the name come from?'

'A Columbina is a stock character in Italian comedy, usually a maid who's—' Harriet shrugged '—a gossip, flirty, a bit of a wag and in English known as a soubrette.'

'Obviously not above disguising herself with a mask for the purpose of delicious secret liaisons,' Isabel said.

Harriet paused her dusting operation as the word *liaison* struck a chord with her, and for a moment she wanted to run away to the end of the earth as she thought of Damien Wyatt.

But she forced herself to take hold.

'Something like that,' she murmured. 'There are examples in this collection of all the different materials used to make masks, did you know? Leather, for example.' She held up a mask. 'Porcelain, as in the Columbina, and of course glass. Did you know the Venice Carnival goes back to 1162, when the Serenissima, as she was known then, defeated the Patriarch of Aquileila?'

'I did know that bit, as a matter of fact.' Isabel took the leather mask from Harriet. 'I've been to the Venice Carnival. It was also outlawed by the King of Austria in 1797 but no one knows exactly what prompted the population of Venice to be so exceedingly taken up with disguising themselves. Come along.'

'Where?'

'Upstairs to your kitchen, where *I* will make you a cuppa. Now don't argue with me, Harriet Livingstone!'

'What happened?' Isabel asked about twenty minutes later when they both had steaming mugs of tea in front of them on the refectory table as well as a plate of rich, bursting with cherries fruitcake.

'You mean…?' Harriet looked a question at Isabel.

'I mean with you and Damien—I'm not a fool, Harriet,' Isabel warned. 'Look, I wasn't going to say anything but you're so obviously…upset.'

Harriet frowned. 'We wouldn't suit, that's all.'

'And that's why you've been working all hours of the day and night and looking all haunted and pale?' Isabel looked at her sardonically.

'I need to get this job finished,' Harriet said sharply. 'It's really started to drag—I just couldn't seem to get on top of it! Even the kitchen's been rebuilt whilst I didn't seem to be getting much further forward! But I need to put Heathcote behind me and I wish I'd never laid eyes on Damien Wyatt.'

'I'm glad you didn't say all the Wyatts.' Isabel stared at her.

Harriet looked away. 'I'm sorry. No, of course not you, Isabel. Or Charlie. But, ideally, I'd like to be gone before Damien and Charlie get home from Darwin. Look—' she turned back to Damien's aunt '—it's impossible for us to be in the same place now. Believe me.'

Isabel opened her mouth, hesitated, then said, 'So you're not going to do the paintings?'

'I…I…no.'

'How about your brother?'

Harriet licked her lips. 'He's making…progress.' But of course Brett was at the back of her mind, and how much easier it would be to make ends meet if she did stay on and do the paintings. But all the guilt in the world associated with Brett couldn't make her stay, not now, not after…

She sighed inwardly and pushed the plate of fruitcake towards Isabel. 'I made it to welcome Charlie home,' she said desolately and stood up abruptly to cross over to the window and stare out at the dismal, rainswept landscape. 'He loves fruitcake.'

'They'll be home shortly.'

'Autumn has come with a vengeance,' Brett said.

Harriet huddled inside her coat and agreed with him.

They were outside, despite the chill—Brett loved being outdoors whenever he could so she'd pushed him in his wheelchair to a sheltered arbour in the grounds. The breeze, however, had found its way around the arbour and it wasn't as sheltered as she'd thought it would be.

'I want to show you something,' he said.

Harriet looked enquiring and hoped he didn't notice that she was preoccupied but she couldn't seem to help herself. She was not only preoccupied but she was trying to dredge up the courage to tell him she was going back to Sydney...

'Here.' He took the rug she'd insisted on draping over his legs and handed it to her.

'Oh, I'm all right,' she protested.

'Actually, you look half-frozen,' he responded with a grin, 'but all I want you to do is hold it for a couple of minutes.'

And, so saying, he levered himself out of the wheelchair and, with a stiff, slightly jerky gait but, all the same, walked around the arbour completely unaided and came to stand in front of her.

Harriet's mouth had fallen open and her eyes were huge.

'What do you think of that?' he asked with obvious pride.

Harriet jumped up and flung her arms around him. 'Oh, Brett,' she cried joyfully. 'That's such an improvement! When? How? Why? I mean...' She stopped. 'You've been holding out on me!' she told him.

'Yes. I wanted it to be a big surprise.' He hugged

her back then rocked slightly. 'There's still a way to go, though.'

'Sit down, sit down,' she insisted immediately, 'and tell me all about it. I think I can guess a bit of it, though. Your new physiotherapist?'

Brett sat down in his chair and nodded. 'Yes. Ellen has made a huge difference, but not only as a physio. She—' he paused '—she got me talking. See, I seemed to reach a plateau that I couldn't get beyond and she asked me one day if there was anything I was worried about, other than the obvious. And I found that there was and it was something that made me feel helpless and hopeless.'

'What?' Harriet asked fearfully.

He smiled at her and put his hand over hers. 'You,' he said simply.

Harriet gasped.

'Because of all the things you gave up for me,' he said. 'Because I didn't know how I could ever repay you. Because I didn't much like the sound of this guy you went to work for but there was not a damn thing I could do about it.'

'Oh, Brett!'

'And somehow I found myself telling Ellen all this— she said the best thing I could do for you was to walk again. It just seemed—' he shook his head '—to put the fire back into me,' he marvelled. 'But there's still a way to go.'

'And will Ellen be with you down that road?' Harriet asked.

'I think so. I hope so. She...we—' he managed to

look embarrassed and uplifted at the same time '—really get along.'

Harriet hugged him again. 'I'm so glad. So glad,' she repeated, 'because I'm going back to Sydney tomorrow. I know, I know,' she said to his look of surprise, 'it's a bit out of the blue but I've finished the job at last! And I'd like to look around for another one. Also, I told you about his brother?' Brett nodded. 'Well, they're due home from Darwin in a couple of days and it'll be a family time, I'm sure.'

Brett stared at her. 'What's he done to you?'

'Done?' She blinked.

'Yep,' Brett said grimly. 'Damien Wyatt.'

'Nothing! He's been quite—he's been quite kind, all things considered—'

'Don't give me that, Harry,' Brett said concernedly. 'I can see with my own eyes that you look all haunted.'

Harriet put a hand to her mouth. 'Do I really—? I mean, am I really that easy to read—? I mean—'

'Yes, you are. For someone who goes into her own little world quite frequently, you're amazingly easy to read,' he said somewhat dryly.

Harriet bit her lip then took a deep breath. 'If there's any trauma, he didn't cause it,' she said. 'I did. And I want you to believe that and—' she stood up '—I want you to put it out of your mind and continue this…this marvellous recovery. Ellen is right, you see; it's the *very* best thing you could do for me.'

'I can't let you go like this,' Isabel said the next morning as she watched Harriet pack her stuff into Brett's battered old four-wheel drive. 'Damien will never forgive me!'

It was another blustery autumn day.

'Stop worrying about it,' Harriet advised her. 'Between the two of you, you'll have enough on your minds helping Charlie to get better without worrying about me. Besides which, I'm not that bad a driver,' she added with some asperity.

'There could be differing views on the matter.' Isabel looked mutinous. 'Look, take the Holden!'

'I couldn't possibly take the Holden,' Harriet argued. 'It doesn't belong to me!'

'Ah!' Isabel pounced on an idea. 'It could be said to belong to *me*, however!'

Harriet didn't stop packing up her vehicle.

'What I mean is,' Isabel continued, 'I have a share in Heathcote, which includes all the equipment and machinery, so I am able, equally, to dispose of—things. Therefore I can gift you the blue Holden!' she finished triumphantly. 'Isn't that how they phrase it these days?'

Harriet put the last of her bags into the four-wheel drive and closed the back door.

She walked over to Isabel and put her arms around her. 'I'll never forget you,' she said softly. 'Thank you for being a friend and—I have to go. I can't explain but don't blame Damien.'

Isabel hugged her then took out her hanky.

But a parting just as hard was still to come.

Tottie was sitting disconsolately beside the open driver's door.

'Oh,' Harriet said softly as a knot of emotion she'd

been hoping to keep under a tight rein unravelled and her tears started to fall. 'I don't know what to say, Tottie, but I will miss you so much.' She knelt down and put her arms around the big dog. 'I'm sorry but I have to go.'

A few minutes later she was driving down the long, winding drive.

In her rear-view mirror she watched Isabel hold on to Tottie's collar so she couldn't chase after Harriet, then the house was out of sight and the double gateposts were approaching and the tears she'd held on to so tightly started to fall.

There was a sign on the road to be aware of a concealed driveway entrance to Heathcote.

There was no sign inside Heathcote to the effect that the portion of the road that went past the gates was hidden from view due to some big trees and a slight bend in it.

Still, Harriet had negotiated this many times so perhaps it was because that she was crying and had misted up her glasses that accounted for the fact that an ambulance driving into the property took her completely by surprise and caused her to swing the wheel and drive into one of the gateposts.

Damien put Harriet carefully into a chair and said in a weary, totally exasperated way, 'What the hell am I going to do with you?'

'Nothing,' Harriet responded tautly and eyed him with considerable annoyance.

They were in the flat above the studio, where all

Harriet's belongings had been unloaded from Brett's vehicle and where she now sat in an armchair with one foot swathed in bandages and resting on a footstool.

The ambulance had picked Charlie and Damien up from Ballina airport because, due to his casts and stitches, fitting into a normal vehicle would have been difficult for Charlie.

The ambulance had escaped unscathed from the incident at the gate. So, yet again, had Brett's four-wheel drive. The gatepost was another matter. It had collapsed into a pile of rubble. And Harriet had somehow sprained her ankle.

The male nurse accompanying Charlie had attended to it.

'Nothing,' Harriet repeated, 'and I would appreciate it if you didn't tower over me like that or treat me like an idiot!'

'My apologies,' Damien said dryly and sat down opposite her. 'It's not the first time this has happened, however.'

'And it might not have happened if…if people hadn't made…hadn't cast aspersions on my driving or if I hadn't been…' She shook her head and closed her eyes. 'It doesn't matter.'

'Been crying?' he suggested.

Her lashes lifted. 'How did you know that?'

He grimaced. 'You looked as if you'd been crying— red eyes, you still had tears in your eyes, as a matter of fact, and tearstains on your cheeks.'

There was a longish pause, then she said, 'It was

only Tottie I was crying over.' She paused. 'And perhaps Isabel.'

'Despite her aspersions on your driving?'

'How did you know *that*?'

'She told me. She feels very guilty and has asked me to apologise.'

Harriet shrugged. 'She meant well,' she said gruffly.

'So there's no possibility there was a skerrick of regret in you about leaving me?'

An uneasy silence developed until Harriet said carefully, 'You know it could never have worked, Damien.'

'I know I made a tactical error in asking you to marry me there and then. My intentions were the best, though.'

'Yes.' Harriet looked across at him. 'You thought I'd go into a decline if you didn't. You thought it could all be worked out on a pragmatic basis. Above all, you had me on your conscience again.'

'Maybe,' he said. 'But look, we're both stuck here for a while so we need to come to an arrangement.'

Harriet raised an eyebrow. 'You're staying?'

He nodded. 'I've postponed Africa while Charlie recovers.'

'I should be fine within a week at the most. It's only a sprain.'

'It's quite a severe sprain. The nurse told you to take it easy for at least a fortnight.'

'I could go crazy in a fortnight,' Harriet said gloomily.

'Not if you start on the paintings.'

She turned her head to look out of the window at the

scudding clouds. 'Back to the paintings again. They're starting to haunt me.'

'Of course we could spend a few days in Hawaii or Tahiti.' His glance was ironic. 'Together,' he added and favoured her with a loaded glance.

Harriet took a sharp breath but what she was about to say went unuttered as Tottie was at last allowed into the flat, with Isabel close behind.

And Damien Wyatt observed the reunion between his aunt, his dog and—the thorn in his side?—not a bad description, he decided, and found himself feeling so annoyed on all fronts, he took himself off to, as he told them, go and see how Charlie was.

But Charlie still had the nurse with him, checking him out.

So Damien continued on to his study, but that wasn't a good idea either. That brought back memories of a girl who'd loved him in a way that could only be described as 'all or nothing'.

It also reminded him that he still fancied Harriet Livingstone, although he was undoubtedly angry with her. Angry with her for turning him down again? Angry with her for driving into the gatepost?

'Just plain angry with her,' he mused and, coming to a sudden decision, reached for the phone as he swung his feet up onto the desk.

Fortunately Arthur answered. Exchanging inanities with Penny would have been too much for him, Damien decided.

'Arthur,' he said, 'Damien. Can you spare a bit of time up here at Heathcote?'

Arthur rubbed the bridge of his nose. 'Well, Penny is pregnant so I don't like to leave her, not for too long anyway.'

'How pregnant *is* Penny?'

'About five months.'

For crying out loud, Arthur, Damien thought but did not say, she's going to keep you dancing attendance for the next four months!

He cleared his throat. 'Uh…of course. It's just that Harriet could do with some help.'

'Harriet?' Arthur repeated. 'I thought she was fine and almost finished.'

'She was. She is finished but I've suggested she cleans the paintings for us rather than sending them away.'

'Wonderful idea,' Arthur responded heartily. 'I'm sure she'd do a great job!'

'Yes, well, she doesn't quite see it that way and that's probably because she's a bit incapacitated at the moment. But I thought if you could come up and go through them with her—you know, if she had someone to discuss them with, someone who really knows what they're talking about, it could help.'

There was a short silence then Arthur said on a curious note, 'Incapacitated?'

'She's sprained her ankle.'

'How?'

Damien grimaced. 'She…ran into the gatepost. In that…tank.'

A sudden silence came down the line, then, 'I don't believe it! The girl's a menace behind the wheel.'

'Uh, there may have been extenuating circumstances.'

'What?' Arthur enquired. 'A dog or two that escaped completely unscathed?'

Damien's lips twisted. 'No. But anyway, she's a bit down in the dumps and I didn't—' he paused and was struck by a brainwave '—I didn't believe Penny would like to think of Harriet like that.'

'Of course not,' Arthur agreed. 'I'll come up tomorrow morning. How's Charlie?'

Damien put the phone down a few minutes later. Then he lifted the receiver again and proceeded to order not one but two wheelchairs, and two pairs of crutches.

CHAPTER NINE

'HOW'S PENNY?'

Harriet and Arthur were in the dining room and Arthur was pushing her around in a wheelchair from painting to painting. Harriet was taking notes.

'Well, we were expecting morning sickness, of course, and *some* form of—I don't know—maybe emotional highs and lows, some weird cravings like pickles on jam, but she doesn't seem to have *ever* been better.'

Harriet hid a smile. Arthur sounded quite worried.

'That's *good* news,' she said. 'Sounds as if she's having an uncomplicated pregnancy. Oh!' Harriet stared at a picture on the wall. 'I can't believe I never noticed that before.'

'Tom Roberts. Heidelberg School. One of my favourites. I was lucky to get that,' Arthur said complacently

'I love his beach scenes,' Harriet said dreamily. 'Where did you find it?'

Arthur pushed her a bit further on and into the hall as he told her the story of how he'd acquired the Tom Roberts for Damien's father. Harriet listened, genuinely fascinated, and they spent a pleasurable couple of hours going through the Wyatt collection.

In fact, when they'd finished and he'd wheeled her back to the studio, Harriet said energetically, 'Arthur, I'll need—'

'I'll get all the stuff you need, Harriet. It's quite some time since they were last done—I've been urging Damien to do it for a while so I'm really pleased he's asked you. You seem to—' he eyed Tottie, who was lying next to the wheelchair '—fit in here really well, too.'

Harriet opened her mouth to dispute this but that could only sound churlish, so she simply nodded.

He went shortly thereafter but sought Damien out before driving off.

He was up in his study, which gave Arthur a sense of déjà vu.

'Come in,' Damien responded to his triple knock.

'Mission accomplished,' Arthur said. 'She's going to do them. She even sounds quite enthusiastic about it now.'

'Thanks, mate.'

Arthur fingered his blue waistcoat with purple airships on it as he pulled up a chair. 'Unusual girl that, you know.'

Damien couldn't help a swift glance at the settee across the room, and made the sudden unspoken decision to have it moved elsewhere. 'Yes, I do, as a matter of fact,' he replied dryly.

'Penny reckons it's a case of still waters running

deep with Harriet Livingstone and she doubts she'll ever get over Simon Dexter.'

Damien frowned. 'I thought they hadn't seen each other since college when they bumped into each other, Penny and Harriet?'

'They hadn't, but word gets around and Penny has quite a network of old friends, so when Harriet bobbed up—she did some research, you might say. And—'

'Simon *Dexter*,' Damien interrupted. 'Elite golfer who's earned himself a million dollars recently, play-boy, heart-throb—that Simon Dexter?'

Arthur nodded. 'Can't imagine what brought them together in the first place. I mean, she's not a groupie type, she's not a sporting type. The way she keeps run-ning into things suggests she may even be a bit unco-ordinated, not to mention short-sighted.'

'Suffers from a left-handed syndrome, in fact,' Damien supplied.

'Never heard of it.'

'That makes two of us. Uh…hasn't Simon Dexter been on the news lately—for other reasons?'

'Could well have been; I haven't been much tuned into the news lately. And I should be getting home.' Ar-thur stood up. 'You'll have your hands full, what with Charlie and Harriet, but at least her—er—incarceration, if you could call it that, is only for a couple of weeks.

'Yes.'

And, to Arthur's surprise, after that single yes, Damien seemed to fall into some kind of reverie and didn't appear to notice his departure.

By the time Arthur had gone, Harriet was also deep in thought for a time.

Along the lines of wondering whether she'd been conned into staying on and doing the paintings.

Surely not. She could hardly be in Damien Wyatt's good books at the moment, after knocking back both his proposals as well as knocking down his gatepost.

But he had rung Arthur and Arthur had tapped into her love of art and managed to imbue her with a feeling of enthusiasm, even eagerness for the project.

Why, though? Why would he want her to stay on?

She shook her head and her thoughts returned to Arthur and how, despite his waistcoats, she enjoyed talking to him about art.

Arthur, she thought with a fond little smile. How on earth was he going to get through the rest of Penny's pregnancy, let alone the birth?

The next morning her ankle was more swollen than it had been, and more painful, so Charlie's nurse conceded that there might be something broken and she should have an X-ray. Isabel drove her in to Lismore, where an X-ray revealed a hairline fracture and a cast was applied to her ankle. She was warned to keep her weight off it while it healed.

Easier said than done, as she discovered. She was exhausted after hopping up the stairs to the flat on one foot, even with Isabel's help.

'We'll have to do something about this,' Isabel said worriedly. 'You can't go through this every time you want to get out or home. Damien should have thought of that. I'll speak to him.'

'Don't worry about it,' Harriet told her. 'Just please say hello to Charlie. And tell him in a few days I'll actually get to see him.'

Isabel went away, still looking worried.

And, an hour or so later, Isabel, Stan and Damien mounted the steps to the flat and moved Harriet and her belongings down to the ground floor of the house.

She didn't protest. She didn't have the energy.

Her new quarters were a guest suite, with a sitting room and separate bedroom, pretty and floral and comfortable, with a view over the garden.

Isabel unpacked for her and brought her a cup of tea but she was alone when Damien came in with a knock and closed the door behind him. He didn't beat about the bush.

'What's wrong?'

Harriet stared up at him, and licked her lips. 'What do you mean?' she asked huskily. 'I…I've broken a bone in my ankle.'

He sat down opposite her wheelchair. 'I know that but I was wondering—' he paused '—whether you'd heard that Simon Dexter and his wife Carol have split up.'

Harriet gasped and her eyes widened.

'It's been on the news. He's a newsworthy figure nowadays. More so perhaps than when you knew him?'

'Yes.' She stared at him. 'I…I...no, I hadn't heard.'

'Do you play golf?' he asked.

'Oh, no!'

'I thought you might have had golf lessons in similar circumstances to your riding lessons.'

'No.' She shook her head.

'So how did you and Simon Dexter get together?'

Harriet looked away and clasped her hands in her lap.

'Don't tell me,' Damien said softly as a tide of pink entered her cheeks, 'that you ran into him?'

She said stiffly, 'Not with a car. Well, not exactly a car.'

'I hesitate to wonder what "not exactly a car" could be,' he marvelled.

Harriet tossed him an irate look. 'A golf buggy, of course.'

'Of course! How dumb can I get? How did it happen?'

'My father did play golf. I was going around with him one morning when he asked me to drive the buggy up to the green while he made a shot from the rough and then took a shortcut not suitable for buggies, to the green. I'd never driven one before but it seemed pretty simple.' She raised her eyebrows. 'Famous last thoughts.'

'You obviously didn't kill Simon or maim him.'

'No.' Harriet paused and a frown grew in her eyes. 'How did you know it was Simon Dexter? I didn't think I mentioned his surname.'

Damien studied his hands for a moment then grimaced. 'Arthur.'

'Arthur doesn't know him.'

'Penny, then.'

'Penny doesn't know him either,' Harriet objected.

'Ah, but Penny runs this spy ring, MI55. She's actually M in disguise, or—' he raised an eyebrow '—is she Miss Moneypenny?'

Harriet went from bristling to calming down to smiling involuntarily. 'I still don't understand how it came up,' she said, though.

'We were worried that you seemed to be down in the dumps.'

She took a breath and sat back. 'I don't know how I feel. I—it's terribly sad actually, isn't it?'

He didn't agree or disagree. He posed a question instead. 'So what is it?'

'What is what?'

'If it's not Simon Dexter, what's making you look as if your heart's breaking?'

Harriet swallowed. 'I didn't know I was. Look, it's probably just my ankle, bound up with feeling like a fool and...' She tailed off.

He raised his eyebrows. 'In what way?'

Harriet sighed. 'Surely I don't have to spell it out for you?'

He rubbed his jaw. 'You're regretting knocking back my offers of marriage?' Sheer irony glinted in his dark eyes.

'I'd be a fool to want to be married to you after...after what happened with your first wife—and how it affected you,' she said slowly. 'No. I feel stupid, that's all.'

Damien studied her thoughtfully. Her hair was clipped back to within an inch of its life—no wavy tendrils today, as there'd been on the night of Charlie's birthday party, no discreet make-up to emphasise her

stunning eyes, no shimmering lipstick rendering those
severe lips doubly inviting.

No gorgeous dress that showed off those amazing
legs—not only tracksuit trousers today but a cast on her
ankle… So what was it about her that made how she
looked a matter of indifference to him?

It struck him suddenly that she was the most unaware
girl he'd ever known. She certainly didn't flash her legs.
She didn't bat those long eyelashes except when she was
thinking seriously and tended to blink.

Was that why it didn't matter whether she was
dressed up or down—he still fancied her? Then he was
struck by a thought.

'You're not,' he said at last, with his eyes suddenly
widening, 'pregnant, are you?'

Harriet opened and closed her mouth. 'No.'

'I'm sorry,' he said dryly. 'That wasn't a very good
way of phrasing things, but if you are—'

'I'm not,' she broke in.

'Sure?'

Harriet eyed him. 'Yes.'

They stared at each other for a long moment, she
with a spark of anger in her eyes, he suddenly completely inscrutable.

'Harriet,' he said, 'there's no point in hiding it from
me.'

'I'm not hiding anything from you!' she protested.
'It was—unlikely, anyway.'

'That has been a trap for the unwary since time im-
memorial,' he said dryly. 'We both stand convicted of

thoughtlessness there, however.' He shrugged and a glint of humour lit his eyes. 'Could we blame Charlie?'

'Blame Charlie for what? Thanks, mate,' Charlie said to his male nurse as he was pushed into the guest suite. 'Harriet! I can't believe we're both in wheelchairs!'

'Charlie!' Harriet had to laugh because, from the neck up, it was the same old Charlie and his infectious smile and mischievous expression hadn't changed. Otherwise, he had his right arm in a cast and a sling and his left leg stretched out in a cast.

'Oh, Charlie!' She hoisted herself out of her wheelchair and hopped across to him on one foot to kiss him warmly. 'I'm so glad to see you, even if you did render us thoughtless! Oh, nothing,' she said to Charlie's puzzled look. 'Nothing!'

They had dinner together that night.

The new cook produced barbecued swordfish on skewers with a salad, followed by a brandy pudding.

'Mmm,' Charlie said, 'if he doesn't burn down the kitchen, he may be as good as old cookie.'

'She,' Isabel contributed. 'I decided there'd be less chance of that with a woman.'

I can't believe I'm doing this, Harriet thought. I can't believe I'm sitting here like one of the family after actually driving away from Heathcote and planning to stay away for ever. I can't believe Damien is doing the same!

She glanced across at him but found his expression difficult to read, except to think that he looked withdrawn.

* * *

After dinner, however, everyone seemed to go their separate ways.

Charlie's nurse insisted he go to bed. Isabel went out to a meeting after wheeling Harriet into the guest suite and Damien went up to his study.

Harriet sat for several minutes in the wheelchair then decided she was exhausted. She used the crutches Damien had hired to get herself changed and finally into bed.

She was sitting up in bed arranging a pillow under her foot when she remembered she hadn't locked the door and she was just about to remedy this when the outer door clicked opened and Damien walked in.

Harriet went to say something but her voice refused to work and she had to clear her throat.

He must have heard because, with a light tap on the open door, he came through to the bedroom.

'OK?' He stood at the end of the bed and studied her in her ruffled grey nightgown.

Harriet nodded. 'Fine, thanks. Have you come to...?' Her eyes were wide and questioning.

'I haven't come to take up residence,' he said rather dryly. 'I've come to talk.'

'Oh.'

His lips twisted. 'What would you have said if I'd indicated otherwise?'

Harriet swallowed. 'I'm not sure.'

He studied her comprehensively then turned away and pulled a chair up. 'If you're worried about staying on to do the paintings, can I make a couple of points?'

He didn't wait for her approval. 'You really seem to enjoy this place, you love art and I guess—' he grimaced '—it's not a bad place to convalesce.' He paused and listened for a moment, then grinned and got up to let Tottie in.

She came up to the bed and rested her muzzle next to Harriet.

Harriet's eyes softened as she stroked the dog's nose. 'I've left you once, with disastrous consequences,' she murmured. 'Could I do it again?'

'You don't have to,' Damien said. 'There's something else you could do. I told you Charlie plays chess?'

She nodded after a moment.

'He's going to need some help to get through this period. Obviously he can't spend the whole time playing chess, but you two might be able to come up with ways to keep each other occupied—you're going to have the same problem for a while. You can't spend your life cleaning paintings.'

Harriet looked up at him. 'What about you?'

'What about me?'

She sat up and plaited her fingers. 'Will you be here?'

'Yes. But I'll be busy. Africa is coming to me, you see.'

Harriet blinked several times. 'Come again?'

He grimaced. 'I've reversed things. Instead of taking my machinery there, I've invited this company I'm dealing with to come here. I may not—' he paused then continued gravely '—be able to offer them wildlife safaris with lions, leopards, buffalo, elephants and hippos, to name a few, but there's the Great Barrier Reef, the

Kimberley, Cape York, Arnheim Land and some wonderful fishing. If they feel like a bit of danger there are
plenty of crocodiles to dodge.'

Harriet blinked again then had to laugh. 'Is that what
big business is all about?'

'That's better… It has a part.'

'What's better?' Harriet asked curiously.

He shrugged after a moment. 'It's the first time I've
seen you laugh since you demolished the gatepost.

'But look, I'll obviously be here at times. If you're
worried I'm liable to harass you on the subject of…on
any subject, don't be.'

Harriet turned her attention to Tottie, still sitting pa-
tiently beside the bed, and wondered at the reaction his
statement brought to her. It had a familiar feeling to it…

But Damien didn't elaborate. He felt in his pocket for
his phone, and glanced at the screen. 'Sorry,' he murmured. 'I need to take this. Sleep well.' And he walked
out, switching off the overhead lights so that she only
had her bedside lamp to deal with. Tottie pattered after
him at a click of his fingers. He closed the door.

She lay back after a moment and turned the bedside lamp off. And she pulled the spare pillow into her
arms and hugged it as she examined that familiar feeling she'd experienced only minutes ago on hearing he
didn't intend to harass her.

Why should that make her feel hollow and lonely at
the same time as she felt ruffled and restless? It didn't
make sense. She should be relieved if anything. The last
thing she should feel like was crying herself to sleep.

It could never work—any other arrangement with

Damien could never work; she knew that in her heart and soul, didn't she? It would hurt her dreadfully if she came to be mistrusted because he couldn't help it now; if she could never get right though to him, if she lost him...

But how to cope with *this* hurt. Living in the same house with him, even if he wasn't home a lot, wanting him, wanting to be special to him, loving him...

CHAPTER TEN

THREE MONTHS LATER there were no more wheelchairs or crutches at Heathcote.

Both Charlie and Harriet were recovered, Harriet completely, Charlie almost there; and Damien Wyatt had been as good as his word. Then again, he'd hardly spent any time at Heathcote at all.

But he came home one evening, three months on, with the news that he'd swung his South African deal at last, which was exceedingly good news, he told them, but he needed a break.

'So I'll be home for a while,' he said, laying his napkin down on the table. He still wore a grey suit with a blue shirt but he'd discarded his tie. 'By the way, that dessert was almost up to your standards, Harriet,' he added.

'It was up to her standard—it was hers,' Isabel said.

Damien looked down the table at Harriet. 'How come?'

'Uh…' Harriet hesitated.

'The new cook proved to have light fingers in more ways than one,' Charlie said. 'She was a good cook, made marvellous pastry, actually, but when we began to discover we were missing minor amounts of money— you know what it's like, at first you think maybe you were mistaken and you didn't have it or you'd spent it or whatever, but then not only did it happen more often but she got bolder and took larger amounts.'

'So you fired her,' Damien said to Isabel.

'I didn't exactly fire her; she has an elderly mother to support. I…I let her go. I haven't found anyone to replace her yet, so Harriet very kindly stepped into her shoes.'

'What would we do without Harriet?' Damien murmured. 'But what is it about Heathcote that attracts either arsonists or petty thieves?'

'Cookie wasn't really an arsonist,' Isabel argued. 'Just…careless.'

Damien grimaced then pushed back his chair. 'OK, well, thanks, Harriet. And could you spare me a few moments of your time? I'll be upstairs in my study.'

Isabel said she would deal with the dishes and Harriet closed herself into the flat above the studio. She'd insisted on moving out of the house once she was mobile again.

Her emotions now, three months on and having received what had almost amounted to an order to beard Damien in his den, were hard to define.

He'd almost made it sound, she marvelled with clenched fists, as if she'd gone out of her way to make herself indispensable to the Wyatt family; as if she had a secret agenda to her own advantage.

When, if she was honest, the last three months *had* had a secret agenda, they'd been mostly sheer torture for her.

When he'd been home she'd had to use all her will-power to be normal and unaffected in his presence. When he'd been gone, it had taken all her willpower not to pack her bags and run for cover. But that would have meant deserting not only Brett but Charlie.

The other sticking point had been the Heathcote paintings. Her estimation of a month to clean them had proved to be optimistic. Even if she'd worked as tirelessly as she had for the most part over his mother's treasures, she'd have taken longer than a month.

But trying to keep Charlie occupied at the same time—until she'd had a brainwave—had slowed her down a lot. The brainwave had been to introduce Charlie to Brett. They'd hit it off immediately.

Her other sticking point with the paintings had been the generous amount she'd already been paid—Damien had simply paid the money into her account without consulting her.

The result was she felt honour-bound to either finish the job or pay the money back. But Brett still had some treatment to go through…

All this, though, she reasoned as she pulled on a blue cardigan over her shirt and jeans, was minor compared to the other inner havoc she'd experienced. The lonely nights when he was only a few steps away from her—that knowledge had kept her tossing and turning.

The lonely nights when she had no idea where he was—or who he was with.

The frisson that ran though her every time she walked through the dining room and recalled their first meeting and that passionate embrace. Recalled the feel of him, the taste of him, his wandering touch that had lit a fuse of sensation within her—if he had a problem with the lounge, her nemesis was the dining room, the memory had never gone away...

And now this, she thought.

A hard, bright, difficult Damien who'd ordered her up to his study as if she were a schoolgirl. A room she hadn't been in since the night Charlie...don't even think about it, she warned herself.

Despite the stern warning to herself, she stood outside the study for a couple of moments, trying to compose herself. Then she knocked and went in. Tottie followed her.

He was lounging behind his desk. There was a silver tray with a coffee pot and two cups on the desk. The windows were open on an unusually warm spring night and there was the sound and the salty air of the sea wafting in.

'Ah,' Damien said. 'I see you've brought your reinforcement.'

Harriet pushed her hair behind her ears. 'If you don't want her here—'

'Of course I don't mind her being here,' he said irritably. 'She *is* my dog. Sit down.'

Harriet looked around and froze. There was no longer the settee where they had... She stopped that thought in its tracks. Instead there were two elegant chairs covered in navy leather.

'You... I...' She turned back to Damien. 'I mean...
nothing.' She swallowed and pulled one of the chairs
up but was unable to stop herself from blushing a bright
pink as she sat down. Tottie arranged herself at her feet.

Damien steepled his fingers beneath his chin and
studied her meditatively. 'You think I should have kept
it, the settee? As a memorial of some kind?'

Harriet's blush deepened but she said, 'No. I mean—'
she gestured '—it was entirely up to you. What did you
want to see me about?'

He stared at her then said abruptly, 'What are we
going to do?'

'Do?' Harriet blinked.

'I hesitate to remind you, Harriet Livingstone, but
that's exactly what you said to me once before in highly
similar circumstances. The day we first met here.'

Her eyes widened.

'I asked you what we were going to do and you repeated "do" as if—as if nothing had ever happened between us or, if it had, it meant nothing,' he said savagely.

'Y-you—' her voice quivered and, to her amazement,
she heard herself go on '—got rid of the settee. As if it
meant nothing.'

'I didn't get rid of it,' he denied. 'I had it moved to
my bedroom, just in case I should be plagued by any
erotic images of you during a business meeting.'

Harriet blinked and this time her cheeks grew so
hot she had to put her hands up to cover them. 'I can't
believe I...said that.'

He looked darkly amused for a moment. 'Maybe your

innermost sentiments got the upper hand. Harriet, we can't go on like this. I can't anyway.'

He sat back and Harriet was suddenly shocked to see how tired he looked.

She opened her mouth but he waved a hand to forestall her. 'Don't say it. I know what you'll say anyway. You'll offer to go, just like you did the last time. Well, it's been a couple of times now but I can't guarantee a gatepost for you to drive into this time.'

'Wh…what do you suggest?' she asked. 'You say we can't go on like this but you don't want me to go.'

'Marry me,' he said after a long tense pause. 'I've given you three months to recover from Simon Dexter and your best friend Carol.'

Harriet gasped. 'You didn't have to—' She stopped abruptly. 'I mean…I mean there's still Veronica, there's still the way you feel—'

His dark eyes were mocking. 'You have no idea how I feel. I had no idea what it was all about so there was no way you could have known,' he said.

'I don't understand.' Harriet blinked almost frenziedly.

'Then I'll tell you.' He sat forward. 'I can't cope any more.'

'I still don't understand.'

'Harriet—' he fiddled with a pen for a long moment then looked into her eyes '—can I tell you a story?'

She nodded.

'I couldn't…right from the beginning I couldn't get you out of my mind. I told you that was why I agreed to see you again?'

'Two months later, though. I mean—I don't mean to nit-pick but it was that.'

He grimaced. 'You're entitled to nit-pick. But from then on I couldn't get you out of my mind. I couldn't believe you were still driving that ghastly old tank and I had to do something about it. I couldn't believe how much I worried about you. I couldn't believe how I kept coming up with jobs for you. I couldn't believe,' he said dryly, 'how the thought of your legs kept interfering with my sex life.'

Her lips parted. 'You mean…?' She looked incredulous.

'It's true. After I kissed you the first time,' he said wryly, 'I decided I'd either gone a bit mad or I needed some nice girl who understood the rules—no wedding bells, in other words—and I found a couple. But the trouble was, they had ordinary legs.'

Harriet put a hand to her mouth. 'I don't believe this,' she said indistinctly.

'You should,' he replied. 'Of course, it wasn't only their legs. I simply didn't seem to be attracted to anyone any more—anyone who wasn't you, that is.'

'Are you serious?'

He studied her wide eyes and the look of shock in them. 'I've never been more serious, I've never been as confused, as I was for a while, in my whole life. I've never felt as rejected as I did the night of Charlie's accident when you…'

'Don't.' Harriet closed her eyes briefly. 'I felt terrible then, and the night of his birthday party.'

'Good,' he said gravely but his eyes were wicked.

She bit her lip. 'I did seriously not want to be on your conscience, though, I still do,' she said then with more spirit. 'I mean I still don't want to be—there,' she elucidated.

'I know what you mean and you're not. It's something else altogether and it only started to come home to me when you ran into the gatepost.'

'Don't,' she pleaded. 'Don't bring up those things. They meant nothing.'

'Maybe not to you but they did to me. They were all part of the picture, you see.'

'What picture?' She frowned at him.

'The picture I loved. I *loved* you, Harriet Livingstone. That's why I cared so much about you. The thing I'd thought could *never* happen for me, had snuck up and hit me on the head, and I realised I was going to spend the rest of my *life* worrying about you.'

They gazed at each other and she thought he suddenly looked pale.

'And loving you because I just can't help myself. All the rest of it, all my grudges and heaven knows what else, they suddenly counted for nothing.'

'Damien,' she whispered.

'Nothing had the power to change that or flaw it or make the slightest difference to how I felt about you. Remember the night you told me you weren't pregnant?'

She nodded.

'I couldn't believe how disappointed I was.'

Harriet stared at him with her lips parted. 'But...but you went away. You told me you wouldn't be harassing me on—on any subject.'

He grimaced. 'And I even managed to stick to that. But don't forget you told me that same day that you'd be a fool to want to be married to me after Veronica and how it had left me. You also hadn't had time to absorb the news about Simon Dexter and your best friend. And I thought—' He stopped abruptly.

'What?' she asked.

'That I could never get you to believe me.' He looked suddenly irritated to death. 'Especially after I'd told you *why* it was no good us contemplating any future together.' He gestured. 'I was also afraid that you could never love me.'

'Never love you?'

He froze as she repeated the phrase as if it had never occurred to her.

'Harriet,' he said ominously, 'you told me at the beginning that you were quite happy to remain fancy-free and you never, even after you slept with me, changed your position other than to a slight tinge of regret when I told you about Veronica!'

'Damien,' she said, 'can I tell you my story? It's not as long as yours but that slight tinge of regret you sensed when you told me about Veronica was in fact a torrent of sudden understanding. I *was* determined to stay "fancy free", I'd fooled myself into thinking I had but it suddenly hit me—that I'd fallen head over heels in love with you and it was the saddest moment of my life.'

He got up and came cautiously round the desk, almost as if he was feeling his way in the dark. 'You said you were sad about Simon.'

'No.' She shook her head. 'I was sad for Carol.' She shrugged.

'So.' He sat down on the corner of the desk. 'Have I been living in hell for these long months because I was a blind fool?' He pulled her upright and into his arms.

'I wouldn't say that. I guess we both had our demons.' She put her hands on his upper arms and all restraint suddenly vanished as they were consumed by an overwhelming hunger.

Harriet felt the blood surging through her veins as if she were on fire at his lightest touch. She felt incredibly aware of her body and of his. But it was more than that for Harriet, more than a sensual arousal that rocked them both; it was a feeling of safety, as if she'd come home, as if a part of her that had been wrenched away had been restored to her.

And when they drew apart she was crying as well as laughing, she was in a state of shock that told Damien more than words could how deep her feelings were.

'Harriet. Harriet,' he said into her hair as he cradled her in his arms, 'it's OK. We've made it. Don't cry.'

'I can't help it. I'm so happy.'

'Come.' He picked her up.

'Where?' she queried.

'You'll see.'

He took her to his bedroom, not the one his parents had used, not the one he'd shared with Veronica—a different room but with a familiar settee along one wall.

'See?' He put her down on it and sat down beside her.

Her tears changed to laughter. 'I couldn't believe how that upset me, the thought that you'd got rid of it!'

His lips twisted. 'You've no idea how good that is to hear.'

'Why?' she queried innocently

'Well, this old settee has brought back some memories.' He allowed his dark gaze to roam over her figure.

'I thought it might be something like that.' Her eyes glinted with humour but only for a moment, then desire replaced the humour and she put her hands on his shoulders, and hesitated.

He frowned. 'What is it?'

'Some other memories. The first time you kissed me it crossed my mind that you knew how to make love to a woman in a way that thrilled her and drove her to excesses she didn't know she could reach... I was right. That night and this settee proved it to me. It had never happened to me like that before. I didn't—' she smiled wryly '—quite recognise myself, even if I had believed I was an all or nothing person.'

Damien stared into her eyes for a long, long moment.

'Harriet,' he said finally, in a husky voice unlike his own, 'if you continue to make incendiary statements like that—we may never get off this settee.'

She laughed then they sobered and their need for each other was so great it wasn't only the settee that became involved but the floor then the bed.

'So you will marry me?' he said when they were lying in each other's arms, sated and in the dreamy aftermath of their passion.

'Yes.' She ran her fingers through his hair.

'Tomorrow?'

Harriet laughed softly. 'I don't think you can do it that fast but if you could I would.'

'On the other hand, coming back to reality, if we're going to do this,' he reflected, 'we might as well do it with style. Not big but with style.'

'Do you think I look all right?' Harriet said to Isabel two weeks later.

She was dressed and ready for her wedding.

She wore a white dress with lacy sleeves and a bouffant skirt that skimmed her knees. Her hair was fair, glossy and coaxed into ringlets. But she stared at herself in the bedroom mirror and sighed.

'You look beautiful,' Isabel replied. She'd been in a state of constant excitement ever since the wedding had been announced.

Harriet sighed again, however, as she continued to gaze at her reflection in the mirror.

'What?' Isabel queried as she produced a pair of new shoes out of a box for Harriet.

'It's just that when I first met Damien I looked a mess. Then, the next time we met, I looked like an attendant out of a museum. I'm just wondering if he doesn't prefer me looking—unusual.' She sat down on the bed to put her new shoes on.

'Honey,' Isabel said, 'believe me, he will love this you as much as all the others.'

'*You* look lovely,' Harriet said, taking in Isabel's camellia-pink linen suit. 'And I can't thank you enough for...for everything. You've been marvellous.'

Isabel sat down on the bed next to Harriet and picked up her hand. 'I knew someone once,' she said. 'I thought he was my north and my south but I wasn't prepared to play second fiddle to his career. And it would have meant a lot of time on my own. It would have meant bringing up our kids virtually on my own, it would have meant being the other woman to a career that was almost like a mistress to him. So I said no when he mentioned marriage.'

Isabel paused and looked into the distance. 'I sent him away and I've regretted it ever since.'

Harriet caught her breath. 'Can't—surely you could have—wasn't there some way you could have got together again?'

Isabel shook her head. 'By the time I'd realised what I'd done, and it took a few years to *really* realise it, he'd married someone else. So—' Isabel patted Harriet's hand again '—to see you and Damien so much in love and getting married when I was afraid it wasn't going to happen, when I thought it all was going to fail, means a lot to me.'

'Now you've made me cry!'

'Here, just fix your make-up and you'll be fine. But first, let me do this.' And she hugged Harriet warmly.

It was a beautiful day and the garden was looking its finest.

There was a table set up for the marriage celebrant with a cloth of gold and a marvellous bouquet of flowers fresh picked from the garden that morning. There were chairs set out for the guests on the lawn and there was a sumptuous buffet laid out on the veranda.

The guests, more than Harriet had expected, comprised close family friends and, of course, family. Charlie was there—apart from the slightest limp, he was quite recovered from his accident and he'd brought along a stunning brunette. He was also the best man.

Brett Livingstone was there, also almost fully mobile now and engaged to his physiotherapist. It was he who was to give Harriet away.

Arthur and Penny Tindall were there. Arthur wore a morning suit.

Harriet drew a very deep breath as she stepped out from her guest suite and paused for a moment.

Brett was waiting for her. And Damien who, thanks to Isabel's sense of tradition, she had not seen since yesterday, was waiting at the table in the garden with Charlie by his side.

'Ready?' Brett mouthed, his eyes full of affection as he held out his arm.

She nodded and something brushed against her legs—Tottie. Tottie, with a ribbon in her collar and a wide smile, as if to say, *It's OK. I'm here.*

Then she was beside Damien, who was looking quite breathtakingly handsome in a dark suit. And Brett stepped back, leaving her to her fate…

They exchanged a long glance that sent tremors through Harriet because that was the effect Damien had on her and always would, she suspected. Then his lips twisted and a wicked little glint lit his eyes. 'I like your dress. I was afraid you'd wear something long.'

'I was afraid you mightn't marry me if I did,' she whispered back.

'For crying out loud, who mightn't marry whom? Don't tell me you two are having second thoughts!' Charlie intervened, although sotto voce. 'I'm a nervous wreck already.'

'Why?' Damien and Harriet asked simultaneously.

'In case I lost the ring or dropped it or did something otherwise stupid.' He ran his finger round his neck inside his collar. 'Damn nerve-racking business this getting married bit. I might have second thoughts about it myself!'

Both Harriet and Damien laughed and the marriage celebrant cleared her throat and asked if she could proceed.

All three participants in front of her replied in the affirmative in a rather heartfelt manner, so she did.

Not many minutes later, Damien Richard Wyatt and Harriet Margaret Livingstone were pronounced man and wife and the bridegroom was told he might kiss the bride.

Damien put his arms around her. 'I *love* you,' he said and bent his head to kiss her lips.

But, at that moment, Penny Tindall, who had a rather penetrating voice, said, 'Arthur…Arthur, the baby's coming!'

And before the bemused gaze of the whole congregation plus the bridal party, Arthur Tindall sprang to his feet, and fainted.

'Things are running true to form,' Damien said to

Harriet. 'There's something about us getting within a cooee of each other that just invites chaos!'

They laughed together and went to rescue Arthur.

'It was always my deepest fear,' Arthur said that evening as he clutched a glass of brandy, 'that I would have to deliver the baby. That's what did it. That's what made me faint.'

In fact Penny's baby had been delivered in a maternity ward, as planned, admittedly after a rather fast trip in an ambulance, but both mother and daughter were fine.

* * * * *

LET'S TALK
Romance

For exclusive extracts, competitions
and special offers, find us online:

MILLS & BOON

THE HEART OF ROMANCE

A ROMANCE FOR EVERY READER

ODERN

Prepare to be swept off your feet by sophisticated, sexy and seductive heroes, in some of the world's most glamourous and romantic locations, where power and passion collide.

STORICAL

Escape with historical heroes from time gone by. Whether your passion is for wicked Regency Rakes, muscled Vikings or rugged Highlanders, awaken the romance of the past.

EDICAL

Set your pulse racing with dedicated, delectable doctors in the high-pressure world of medicine, where emotions run high and passion, comfort and love are the best medicine.

ue Love

Celebrate true love with tender stories of heartfelt romance, from the rush of falling in love to the joy a new baby can bring, and a focus on the emotional heart of a relationship.

Desire

Indulge in secrets and scandal, intense drama and plenty of sizzling hot action with powerful and passionate heroes who have it all: wealth, status, good looks…everything but the right woman.

EROES

Experience all the excitement of a gripping thriller, with an intense romance at its heart. Resourceful, true-to-life women and strong, fearless men face danger and desire - a killer combination!

To see which titles are coming soon, please visit

millsandboon.co.uk/nextmonth

JOIN US ON SOCIAL MEDIA!

Stay up to date with our latest releases, author
news and gossip, special offers and discounts, and
all the behind-the-scenes action
from Mills & Boon...

 millsandboon

 millsandboonuk

 millsandboon

It might just be true love...

MILLS & BOON

MODERN

Power and Passion

Prepare to be swept off your feet by sophisticated, sexy and seductive heroes, in some of the world's most glamourous and romantic locations, where power and passion collide.

MILLS & BOON
MEDICAL
Pulse-Racing Passion

Set your pulse racing with dedicated, delectable doctors in the high-pressure world of medicine, where emotions run high and passion, comfort and love are the best medicine.

MILLS & BOON
True Love
Romance from the Heart

Celebrate true love with tender stories of heartfelt romance, from the rush of falling in love to the joy a new baby can bring, and a focus on the emotional heart of a relationship.